to Robert Reynolds

A Kendall O'Dell Mystery

SEEDS OF VENGEANCE

Enjoy the adventure in #4!

9/16/6

OTHER BOOKS IN
SYLVIA NOBEL'S AWARD-WINNNG
<u>KENDALL O'DELL MYSTERY SERIES</u>

Deadly Sanctuary
The Devil's Cradle
Dark Moon Crossing

Also

Chasing Rayna
A Romantic Suspense Novel

Published by
Nite Owl Books
Phoenix, Arizona

VISIT OUR WEBSITE:
<u>WWW.NITEOWLBOOKS.COM</u>
TO READ THE FIRST CHAPTER
OF EACH BOOK AND FOR UPDATES
ON BOOK SIGNING APPEARANCES
OR NEW RELEASES BY THIS AUTHOR

A Kendall O'Dell Mystery

SEEDS OF VENGEANCE

SYLVIA NOBEL

Nite Owl
Books

Phoenix,
Arizona

Phoenix,
Arizona

For information, contact Nite Owl Books
4040 E. Camelback Road, #101
Phoenix, Arizona 85018-2736
PHONE 602.840.0132
1.888.927.9600
FAX 602.957.1671
E-mail: Niteowlbooks@cox.net
www.niteowlbooks.com

ISBN 978-0-9661105-6-2

Cover Design by
ATG Productions
Christy A. Moeller – Phoenix, Arizona

Library of Congress Control Number: 2006925272

ACKNOWLEDGMENTS
*****

The author wishes to acknowledge the
invaluable assistance of the following people:

Laura C. Fulginiti, PhD., D-ABFA,
Forensic Anthropologist, Phoenix, AZ
The Honorable Daniel G. Martin,
Administrative Law Judge, Phoenix, AZ
Raymond Roe, Detective,
Homicide Unit, Phoenix, AZ
Mark Linder, Police Officer, Phoenix, AZ
Roil Armstrong, Deputy Sheriff,
Yavapai County Search & Rescue Coordinator,
Forest Patrol Division
Brian Dando, Attorney at Law
Tina Williams, Editorial Services
Donna Jandro, Editorial Services
Rose Hockenberger, Editorial Services
Brandon Williams, Computer Consulting
Chris Lovelace, Systems Engineer
Matt Lovelace, Criminalist, Phoenix, AZ
Bill Toma, Art Bronze Inc., Scottsdale, AZ
The *Wickenburg Sun* Staff
Joel J. Thomas, *The Yellow Sheet*, Yarnell, AZ
Harold Perlman, Pharmacist, Prescott, AZ
Chauvin Emmons, Prescott, AZ
Leo Scott, Prescott, AZ
Prescott Fine Arts Association
Dave Coulter, Humboldt, AZ
A.L. "Lucky" Jackson, Phoenix, AZ
Calumet & Arizona Guest House,
Bisbee, Arizona
Henrietta Scott, Blythe, CA
Kelly Scott-Olson and Christy A. Moeller,
ATG Productions, Phoenix, AZ

Extra special thanks to:
**Dr. Laura Fulginiti for her friendship, expertise, and allowing
me a rare glimpse into her fascinating profession.**
and
**My husband, Jerry, for his encouragement and
driving endless miles on lonesome Arizona
back roads to assist in my research.**

To My Loving Family,
Wonderful Friends
And
Devoted Fans

Thank you for your continuing
Encouragement
And support

1

I should have been paying attention. But, I wasn't. Instead of tuning into the animated chatter of our informal editorial meeting, staying focused on story assignments and considering proposed feature possibilities from my co-editor, Morton Tuggs, and staff reporters, Jim and Walter, my thoughts rolled away like a tumbleweed in a stiff wind.

If I angled the ring finger of my left hand just right, the two-carat diamond caught the luminous rays of November sunlight slanting through the blinds behind me. The mesmerizing collage of radiant colors temporarily resurrected the giddy elation that had consumed me when Tally slipped it on my finger that glorious Saturday evening twelve days ago. A mere forty-eight hours later, my sky-high euphoria had crashed and burned. The very day we'd planned to announce our engagement to his mother, Ruth, came word that Tally's uncle, Superior Court Judge Riley C. Gibbons, had been reported missing, having failed to return from a weekend elk-hunting trip in the Coconino National Forest near Flagstaff. Despite a rigorous ground and air search conducted by the Yavapai County Sheriff's

Office and Posse, of which Tally was an active member, hopes dimmed that the judge would be found alive in the rugged wilderness after a fierce winter storm slammed into the area. It sent temperatures plunging and blanketed the northern part of the state with more than two feet of snow, while lower elevations endured three days of snow flurries interspersed with icy rain.

Much to my dismay, Tally had suggested that, in light of his mother's fragile emotional state and her deepening despair concerning the fate of her former brother-in-law and lifelong friend of Tally's late father, Joseph Talverson, it would be advisable to delay our announcement until there was some news of the judge's whereabouts. It was hardly a secret that I resided at the very top of Ruth Talverson's least favorite persons list and even though Tally hadn't stated it aloud, I knew he feared that the knowledge that I would soon be her daughter-in-law might push his mother to the brink of a mental meltdown, where in my mind the disagreeable woman had never been all that far from in the first place.

I swiveled the chair a few inches to my left and glanced out the window, amazed at the surreal transformation of the normally bone-dry desert now covered with two inches of fresh snow dumped during the second storm in slightly over a week. An anomaly to be sure. A mound of creampuff clouds obscured the craggy mountain peaks while the surrounding foothills looked as if they'd been sprinkled with powdered sugar. Across the street in the vacant lot, the stately saguaro cactus had assumed a rather whimsical appearance, sporting a cap of frosty silver while the tips of its six upturned arms reminded me of white mittens. Snow. I hadn't thought I'd ever see it again since leaving Pennsylvania last April.

After sweating my brains out for the past eight months, the longest, hottest summer of my entire life had mercifully ended. I'd have to check to be sure, but I think autumn consisted of approximately five hours followed by this sudden winter. Bam. No subtlety to the weather here in the desert, no sir. Back East, the first week of November usually ushered in endless months of leaden gray skies. Not here. Today, brilliant sunlight prevailed, promising to bump the temperature up into the 50's, which to me seemed totally comfortable at last, but had my co-workers scurrying to don winter coats and whine vociferously about the freezing cold. Apparently I still had not yet undergone the magical blood-thinning phenomenon that supposedly affects people who relocate from colder regions to Arizona. Because of the expected warm-up, Tally had informed me that he would not be coming into the office so that he could participate in the search party once again. After spending a blissful night together snuggled in each other's arms, he'd grimly advised me at breakfast this morning that if the judge wasn't found by the end of the day, it was likely the search would be called off. Permanently. It was obvious by his anxious glance that he feared such a decision would magnify his mother's ongoing emotional crisis.

"Which means what?" I'd demanded, eyeing him with suspicion, my tone edging towards petulant. "Are you saying that we postpone telling her indefinitely?"

"Well...um...."

The ensuing hesitation transmitted volumes. "Tally! Our engagement party is less than six weeks away." His noncommittal shrug combined with his taciturn expression ignited my ultra-short fuse. I inhaled to the bottom of my lungs before responding in a voice that sounded perfectly reasonable to me. "How long do you think it's going to be until someone tells her that we've rented the entire ballroom at the Whispering Winds?"

Appearing pained, he began, "Look, I understand how you feel—"

"Do you? In case you've forgotten, you invited half this town, and my whole family is coming, including some cousins from Ireland I haven't seen since I was in high school!" I smacked my hand on the table for emphasis, causing my new kitten, Marmalade, to leap about three feet in the air. Orange fur spiked on her back and claws scrabbled on the tile for traction as she streaked from the kitchen.

Observing the kitten's reaction to my outburst, Tally leveled me a perceptive frown and pushed away from the table. "Well, I wondered how long it would take," he groused, crossing to snatch his fleece-lined Levi's jacket and black Stetson from the coat rack. "Apparently your promise to practice the fine art of patience is now history. And in less than two weeks."

"Tally—"

"Look, it's not going to be a big deal if we wait a few more days. You're being overly dramatic as usual and just a tad unreasonable."

I thought my chest would burst. "Come on, Tally, give me a break. I think…I believe I've been super patient so far and I know how much you're dreading this encounter—trust me I am too—but we *have* to tell her tonight. Delaying is not going to make it any easier. She's going to hate the idea of us being married whether she finds out tonight, a month from now, or—and please don't take this the wrong way—whether your uncle is found today or not. So…can't we just get it over with?"

He jammed his hat on. "Also typical. It's your way or no way."

Remembering the look of wounded agitation darkening his ruggedly handsome features before he'd stomped out the door made my heart shrink with regret. I wished now that I could take back my ultimatum. Maybe it wouldn't hurt to wait until the weekend. When, oh when, would I ever learn to keep my mouth shut?

As if sensing my unhappy thoughts, Walter Zipp piped up, "Hey, Kendall, any more news about Judge Gibbons since they found his pickup on that forest service road?"

I turned back to the group. "Nope."

Lips pursed solemnly, he murmured, "That's too bad."

"Yeah," I concurred, hoping against hope that a miracle would occur and they'd find the man today alive and well. But, what were the chances of surviving a second storm with sub-zero temperatures?

"Kind of a strange coincidence that he disappeared at this particular time, if you ask me," Jim Sykes remarked, flicking a lock of bleached blond hair away from his forehead while he eyed us with his usual bratty know-it-all smirk.

All eyes turned to him, so I asked, "What makes you say that?"

He tipped his chair back, laced his fingers behind his neck, and said with an air of self-importance, "Oh, nothing much." He paused for effect before continuing with, "It's probably just a fluke, but ah…guess who I heard was back in town?"

"Who?" we all chimed in simultaneously.

"Randy Moorehouse."

Tugg nodded sagely. "Je-zuss. I wondered if he'd come back here."

Walter Zipp, who'd hired on less than two months earlier, echoed my own puzzlement. "Who's Randy Moorehouse?"

Jim threw in, "A real bad-ass dude better known to his old biker buddies as Pig Pen."

Tugg chuckled. "I'm not sure why he's called that, but you can ask Tally when you see him. I remember him mentioning one time that he went to high school with Moorehouse and his sister."

I frowned at Jim and Tugg. "So, what's the guy's connection with the judge?"

"Ready for a gruesome story?"

I perked up. "Always."

"Hmmm. Let's see, I guess it's been about ten years ago," Tugg began, looking introspective. "I was still working at the *Arizona Republic* in Phoenix at the time, but from what I recall Moorehouse was sentenced to Death Row for murdering his old lady."

"Really? He killed his mother?"

A wry smile. "No. Old lady is biker lingo for girl-friend, right, Jim?"

"Correctomunde," he replied, a speculative gleam lighting his eyes. "Of course, Randy swore up and down that he'd been framed, but he couldn't explain why the ax that had been used to chop the poor lady up like a cube steak was found hidden underneath his mobile home two days later."

"Interesting," I murmured, repulsed, but oddly intrigued as well.

"Moorehouse had been in trouble a couple of times before. He was a member of an outlaw biker gang called the Desert Devils." Tugg continued, "Three weeks ago he was released from prison."

"Why?"

He shook his head in disgust. "You know the drill. One of these zealous anti-death-penalty lawyers got hold of his case and after eight years of appeals finally got him a new trial. The prosecution's main witness, a woman who claimed she'd seen him and another man standing alongside his motorcycle close to where the body was found that night, could not be located. The blood evidence against him had been misplaced and they could not conduct any DNA tests so..." he palmed his hands upward, "the judge overturned his conviction."

Jim leaned forward expectantly. "Who do you think put Randy Moorehouse on Death Row in the first place?"

Uh-oh. An uneasy mixture of excitement and cold dread wrestled around in my stomach. "I'm guessing the honorable Judge Riley C. Gibbons."

Jim clicked his tongue and nodded. "Bingo."

I sat back in my chair. Well, well. That added a disturbing element to the equation. Thus far, none of our inquiries to the sheriff's office had netted any hint of foul play. If Tally was aware of the man's return, he hadn't mentioned it to me. And now with this evening's showdown looming, did I dare broach the subject to him beforehand? No. Probably best to wait and tell him afterwards. "Walter, why don't you see what you can find out about Mr. Moorehouse's activities since he's come back to town," I suggested, jotting it on the assignment sheet. "And it might also be noteworthy to check out some of the judge's other cases and determine if anyone else may have had a score to settle with him."

His face fell. "How much time do you want me to spend on this? There are probably hundreds of cases and I'm betting the cops are checking them out right now."

"I'm sure they are, but they've got a lot of fish to fry and we've got time."

"Okay. How far back do you want me to go? It could take months."

I pondered his question. He had a point. Since the U.S. Supreme Court changed the law, Arizona juries now imposed the death penalty instead of judges. "Concentrate on cases prior to 2002, but I'm also interested in unexpected rulings like hung juries or mistrials, questionable plea deals, anything where either the accused or members of the victim's families may have felt the judge rendered an incorrect decision. Who knows how many people are out there holding a grudge."

He saluted. "I'm all over it."

We nailed down assignments for the next day and then moved on to the following week. "Jim, can you do a piece on the antique car show opening next weekend?"

"Can't. I'm gonna be out of town."

I had forgotten and made note of it.

"I'll take it," Tugg offered, scribbling on his notepad. "A pal of mine's entering a car he just restored."

I studied the list of upcoming events. "Okay, well, Walter, if you can cover the bowling tournament and square dance competition, I'll handle the dedication of the old Hansen House and do a piece on the arts and crafts festival. I have to be out at the fairgrounds anyway since I promised Ginger I'd help her and Nona in their booth for a couple of hours Saturday afternoon."

Walter scratched his sizeable belly and yawned. "Will do."

8

The four of us exchanged story ideas for another fifteen minutes or so and then chairs scraped as everyone rose. I chatted a few minutes longer with Tugg and he'd no sooner ambled out than Ginger appeared in the doorway, her honey-colored eyes sparkling. She tapped the thick pile of folders cradled in one arm and announced with an eager smile, "Sugar, put on your thinkin' cap. We got a boatload o' decisions to make about this here shindig. You want to mosey on over to the Iron Skillet and yak over lunch or ya want me to snag us a couple of sandwiches off the roach coach and eat at your desk?"

I made a face at her. "Is it just me, or do the words roach and sandwich not sound terribly appetizing in the same sentence?"

Giggling, she swiped a hand in my direction. "Oh, flapdoodle, the food ain't that bad. But, any hoot, I'd just as soon scoot over yonder to the café. A little bird told me today's special is their signature homemade chicken potpie."

I grinned. "Say no more."

"Gimme five and I'll meet ya out front." She scurried down the hallway and I smiled to myself and thought as I had many times these past eight months how lucky I was to have found a loyal friend like Ginger King. It had been her idea to have an engagement party in the first place, and she was so pumped that she'd insisted on assuming responsibility for the lion's share of details involved in the planning—extra details that I couldn't seem to wedge into my tight schedule.

Chicken potpie. My usually robust appetite, dulled by the tense exchange with Tally earlier, returned with a vengeance that sent my belly into a series of squeaky spasms. Best eat a hearty meal now because I had a feeling

I'd be too stressed out to eat again before driving out to the Starfire Ranch for my five o'clock rendezvous with Tally. I shrugged into my windbreaker and hauled my purse from the bottom desk drawer. By the time I got to the reception area Tugg's daughter, Louise, was positioning the headset over her short, dark curls. She issued me a full-toothed grin while chirping, "Good morning, *Castle Valley Sun*." I smiled back. Luckily for us she'd agreed to help out in a pinch by assisting Ginger at the reception desk and temporarily holding down the fort in classifieds until we had news of our absent—and much missed employee— Lupe Alvarez. She'd been deported back to Mexico where she awaited word on her application for legal immigration. I still suffered a measure of guilt knowing that my involvement in the mind-boggling story I'd broken only weeks ago had made me partially responsible for her deportation. We'd all been heartened when our new publisher, Thena Rodenborn, had agreed to hire an immigration attorney to help expedite her case.

My mouth dropped open at the sight of Ginger bundled into a bulky coat, hat, scarf and fur-lined boots. "Good grief, Ginger, it's not *that* cold outside. This isn't Alaska."

"Speak for yourself, darlin'," she sniffed, pulling on a pair of bubblegum pink gloves. "Wait 'til you been here a while longer. Pretty soon when it drops below seventy degrees you'll be huntin' for a sweater like the rest of us."

Once outside, I had to admit it was chillier than I'd expected. When a strong gust of icy wind grabbed a handful of my hair and slapped it across my face, I zipped the windbreaker a little higher and stuffed my hands into the pockets. Watching the parade of fluffy white clouds sail across the sky, I couldn't suppress a pang of sadness when I thought about the plight of Judge Gibbons. Even though Tally had told me he was in excellent physical shape for age sixty-two, what were the odds that he could still be alive after almost two weeks in the elements? I chastised myself again for appearing to be unsympathetic in Tally's eyes. I'd make it up to him later.

I found the cold weather bracing, but Ginger's teeth were chattering like a pair of maracas after we'd walked the three blocks to the Iron Skillet. Pushing inside the double glass doors, a wall of warm air saturated with animated conversation and clanking dishes met us as we threaded our way through the crowded restaurant answering the friendly waves and greetings of local townspeople. The appetizing aroma of oil-drenched French fries lifted my spirits as we slid into a booth. "Aren't you going to take off your coat?" I asked, peeling mine away and setting it beside me on the red vinyl seat.

"N…n..nnnnot y…yyyyet," she replied, still shivering as she plopped the files onto the table while eyeing the laminated menu with appreciation. "Besides the potpie, I might just order me a bowl of hot vegetable soup to soak my feet in."

For the first time that day I laughed out loud. "Ginger, you're priceless."

"Of course I am." She glanced around the room and then turned back to me, her freckled face suddenly alight with mischief. "Here comes Lucy. Quick now, wave your hand around so she don't miss seeing that big ol' rock on your finger."

Crap. I'd forgotten to take my ring off again. Outside of staff members, only a handful of people in town were aware of our engagement. Looking back, if I'd known our announcement was going to be put on hold, I'd

11

have never told my loveable but gossipy pal. True to her character, she was unable to resist the idea of tormenting the sultry-eyed woman who'd spent the past twenty-five years pursuing Tally's affections. I shot her a warning look. "I know it's killing you, but you only have to keep this secret one more day," I whispered, dipping my hand into my lap. "Tomorrow you can hire a skywriter for all I care."

She gawked at me. "Y'all telling Ruth today?"

"Shhhhh."

She clamped her mouth shut as Lucinda Johns sidled up to the table, her enormous boobs straining against the buttons of her stained pink uniform as she set silverware and two glasses of water on the table. As usual, she made me feel self-consciously flat, as if I were still wearing my first training bra. "What can I get you girls?" she asked, unsmiling, her voice a sullen monotone. She scribbled our order on the pad, studiously avoiding eye contact with me before turning on heel to slink away. She might as well have worn a sign announcing *I'm jealous as hell and I hate your guts.*

In the process of extricating herself from coat, scarf and hat, Ginger fluffed her recently dyed strawberry blonde curls and shot me an impish grin. "Man, you ain't never going to win any popularity contests with her."

"Ask me if I care what Miss Boobalicious thinks."

That sent her into another round of giggles. "Okay, out with it," she demanded, leaning forward, her face alight with anticipation. "I thought you and Tally wasn't about to spill the beans to his ma about you bein' betrothed until y'all found out what happened to the judge."

I hesitated. "We had a bit of a disagreement about that and I kind of insisted we get it over with tonight."

She rolled her eyes. "Disagreement my size eight foot! For pity's sake, are you two squabbling again?"

"Not really. I feel like I've set a world record for patience, but he thinks I'm being unsympathetic because I don't think it's wise to wait any longer."

"I'm with ya on this one, honey. Time's a wastin'."

"I hate to even say this aloud, but...what if the poor guy is never found? He wouldn't be the first person to disappear into the hinterlands of Arizona. It seems like people vanishing into thin air constitute half the stories I've filed since I moved here."

Curiosity danced in her eyes. "Have you two rehearsed how you're goin' to break it to her?" she asked, chewing on a soda cracker, obviously relishing the drama of the impending confrontation. "How do you think she's goin' to take it?"

I grimaced. "Badly. That's why I think our announcement should be short and sweet and soon."

Ginger nodded agreement. "You got my vote. That way Tally won't have time to change his mind and you can get a runnin' start out the door before she's got time to throw somethin' at ya."

"That and I think it would be a total disaster if she hears it from someone else first. That'll really cook my proverbial goose."

The faint frown lines on her forehead deepened. "At least you're lucky she don't drive."

"That's true. She doesn't get into town that often but remember, Jake knows and so does Ronda." I felt fairly confident that Tally's longtime ranch foreman would keep his mouth shut, but I wasn't so sure about Tally's younger sister, whose best friend just happened to be Lucinda. Ronda was always cordial, but also didn't seem overly excited about having me for her sister-in-law. Perhaps she was wishing it would be Lucinda instead. "It's just a matter of time before something slips out. I want to get this squared away tonight, so if his mother decides to go mental on us, hopefully she'll have time to recover before my family arrives."

Ginger reached for the pile of folders. "Dumplin', I'm with you a hundred and fifty percent. Alrighty then. You got a passel of decisions to make so let's get started." She pushed the salt, pepper and napkins against the wall and set a book of sample invitations in front of me. "You can take this home and talk with Tally about design, color, paper texture, fonts and how y'all want 'em worded. Here's a bunch of menu suggestions. Also, we got to think about what kind of flowers to get, oh, and you need to decide whether to hire a band and if not, here's the names of a couple of DJs—"

The multitude of details gave me an instant headache. "Ginger, wait. I just can't make— "

Ignoring me, she continued, "...and here are some spiffy ideas for cake decorations," she said spreading a sheaf of papers before me. "Ain't they purty? And then there's table centerpieces...Oh! And guess what else? Last night, Doug was talkin' to me about this lady artist named Myra..." she mumbled, running her finger down one sheet. "Yep, here we go. Colton. Myra Colton. I've seen her work and it's real good! She lives up yonder in Yarnell and—"

"An artist?" I interrupted, unable to quell my rising irritation. "Why are we talking about an artist?"

"Because Doug told me that she also carves knock 'em-dead ice sculptures! So, I was a thinkin' maybe we oughta—"

"Ginger, stop!"

She froze, gaping in surprise. "What's the matter?"

"I...listen, I just can't make any big decisions right at this moment. There's...well, I've got a lot of things on my mind. I'm sorry. I know you've gone to a lot of trouble, but..." I pushed my hair back and shifted uncomfortably in my seat. "To be truthful, a big part of me would rather not even bother with this engagement party."

Ginger's face went stark white. "Well, geez Louise," she cried. "What are you sayin', girl? Have you gone and changed your mind about marrying Tally?"

2

My heart jumped when a couple of nearby diners turned curious faces towards us. "Ginger!" I whispered fiercely. "Keep it down."

She pinched her lips shut. "Sorry."

I leaned in closer. "Don't misinterpret me. I'm not saying I don't want to get married. I asked him to marry *me*, remember? The problem is Ruth. She's a cantankerous old woman and I hate the idea of groveling for her permission. We're not underage teens, for Christ's sake. Tally just turned thirty-four and I can't even believe that I'm going to be thirty next year."

"I hear ya," Ginger remarked, appearing thoughtful. "But, sugar pie, you'd best remember what Nona always says, 'a man who treats his ma like a queen will most likely treat you like one too.'"

I couldn't help smiling at her grandmother's homespun wisdom. "I know he'll be a lot happier if we have her blessing, but don't you think it would be simpler for everyone involved if we…well, eloped to Las Vegas or something?"

Ginger's mouth fell open. "But...but what about your folks and the rest of your kin? You're goin' to disappoint a whole bunch of people who are all looking forward to this party."

"Admit it, Ginger, you're far more enthusiastic about the whole wedding scene than I am."

"Well, what of it? Listen to me, girl, I'd be down on my knees thanking the good Lord right now if Doug would pop the question. I was kinda hoping that maybe if he sees how happy you and Tally are a little bit of the magic might rub off on him." She narrowed her eyes. "I think the question of the day is why ain't *you* more excited? Is it because you was married before?"

"No, I don't think that's it."

"Okay then, it's gotta have something to do with you getting your butt kicked by that no good rat, Grant what's-his-face."

"Jamerson," I filled in morosely, staring off into the distance. Heartache and utter mortification returned full force as memories of his sordid, behind-my-back affair with one of my co-workers at the *Philadelphia Inquirer* came flooding back. Following on the heels of my divorce and the move from my dad's small hometown newspaper to the big time in Philly, I'd fallen hard for my mentor, Grant Jamerson. Not only did I admire his abilities as a top rate investigative journalist, his blonde good looks and vibrant sense of humor had captivated me from the moment our eyes had locked. I'd been truly nuts about the guy. It was hard to believe that this time last year we'd been engaged. "Look, I can't think of anything I want more than to be Tally's wife, but...I still don't think his mother is ever, I mean *ever* going to get over the fact that I look so much like you know who."

She nodded solemnly. "I know it ain't nice to speak ill of the dead, but Stephanie was a no-good, conniving, two-timin' little bitch. You ain't nothing like her at all."

Her reference to Tally's late wife mirrored that of most people in town who had ever crossed paths with her. But Tally's mother harbored a very special, very bitter grudge, believing that Stephanie's despicable behavior and volatile temper tantrums had been the cause of her husband's fatal heart attack. "Tally is sticking to his theory that she'll eventually accept me for who I am, but frankly I think it's going to be disastrous having *two* Mrs. Talversons living under the same roof."

Her brows hiked up in surprise. "So, you finally made up your mind."

"About what?"

"Changing your name."

I grimaced, remembering how much I'd disliked my former married name. Prigge. A large percentage of people I'd met referred to me as Kendall Piggy. And some of the misspellings on mail I'd received had been downright hilarious. "It remains a major source of friction. Tally insists that I be Mrs. Bradley James Talverson. Period. No keeping O'Dell for professional reasons or even O'Dell hyphen Talverson. To be honest, I'm not sure I'm ready to do that."

"Why not?"

"I guess it's an independence issue."

Ginger's nostrils flared. "Well, get over it, darlin'. It ain't like we got a lot of time to plan this party and you sure don't want to be scrappin' with your intended the whole time over something as petty as that."

"Really? Do you think I'm being petty?"

"Just a mite. Here you've gone and landed yourself one of the nicest, richest, finest-looking and certainly most eligible men in the whole dang county and you're busy havin' a hissy fit over whether or not to change your last name. Well, excuse me, we should all be so fortunate." Her stern look of censure served to remind me of the promise I'd made to myself to cherish this man's love and to address my numerous shortcomings.

"You're right. From now on I'm going to...oh shit, here comes Lucinda." Ginger tossed me an anxious look before she swept the incriminating evidence of our impending nuptials onto her lap. I had to suppress a chuckle at her attempt to appear nonchalant as Lucinda set the steaming bowls of chicken potpie onto the table. "Can I get you gals anything else?" she asked, hands on ample hips, her suspicious glance bouncing between the two of us.

"I think we're just hunky dory," Ginger responded with a happy lilt in her voice. "This smells mighty fine."

It was more than fine. In was in fact, the best chicken potpie I'd ever tasted. After scooping out the last savory bite of tender crust, it was an effort not to lick the last drops of gravy from the bottom of the bowl. We ran out of time to reach any decisions concerning the engagement party, so I paid the bill, and after stopping to chat with a few of the locals, we pushed outside into the invigorating wind. On the way back to the office, I thanked Ginger for all the work she'd done to date and she seemed mollified when I promised her that we'd get together soon to finalize the details.

The remainder of the afternoon flew by at a record pace, probably because it was so busy but mostly because my heart grew increasingly heavy as the sun dipped towards the horizon. The dreaded face-off with Tally's mother loomed large. I gave myself a needed pep talk. Stay focused, stay upbeat, and don't be intimidated by the woman's hair-trigger temper and erratic mood swings.

Tugg was still at his desk when I waved good-bye and headed home driving the green pickup truck Tally had loaned me. My precious blue Volvo, a casualty of my last assignment, had been stolen, stripped and abandoned in the southern Arizona desert. The incident still pained me. Damn, I'd loved that little car. Babied and pampered, it had served me well throughout four snowy Pennsylvania winters, during the long cross-country drive last spring and since then, the thousands of miles spent traversing Arizona. The scheduled trip to Phoenix last weekend in search of a new car had also been postponed while Tally joined the search for the judge.

Much of the snow had melted during the daylight hours, and now as dusk descended, the remaining patches scattered in the vast desert landscape flanking Lost Canyon Road appeared lavender in the afterglow of the setting sun. I stole a glance at my watch, feeling the crunch of time. If I hurried, I'd have just enough time to shower, change clothes and feed Marmalade. Thoughts of my new kitten cheered me. I had never really fancied myself a cat person until she'd come into my life two weeks prior. Growing up in Pennsylvania, we'd always owned dogs due to my mother's severe allergy to cats. I'd worried a bit that exposure to cat fur would aggravate my asthma, but probably because of the new medication, it hadn't. Now, I couldn't imagine life without my little peach-colored companion and I wondered how she'd fare at the rambling ranch house at the Starfire in the company of two barking Labs, a new puppy and most recently, Attila, the shiny, black Doberman Tally had adopted following the death of the dog's owner, another victim of the diabolical story I'd scooped during my stay at the Beaumont ranch in southern Arizona weeks earlier. It was but one more hurdle on my growing list. But right now I had to concentrate on the stressful showdown ahead. And on that subject my mind veered to an incongruous thought. What to wear? Exactly what criteria does one apply when choosing the appropriate outfit in which to appear before a person who totally despises you? What color does one wear while bearing the unwelcome news that you'll soon be moving into that person's home?

When I pulled into the driveway, an immediate sense of peace washed over me. I cut the engine, lowered the windows and just sat there allowing myself a moment of solace, listening to the solitary whisper of the wind while taking in the shimmering halo of mauve and crimson illuminating the western skyline. Wow. When I turned to the east, the serrated spires of Castle Rock blazed in vibrant shades of copper and coral before slowly fading to pale salmon in the last remnants of light. Double wow. Another award-winning sunset. I had the urge to applaud as I stepped out into the bracing desert air. As I walked towards the house, I was gripped by an odd sense of melancholy. As elated as I was to become Tally's wife I knew I would forever miss this cozy ranch house. Funny. Even though I was renting, a strong sense of ownership burned inside me.

Marmalade was waiting near the front door as usual, her welcoming cries and rattling purr filling the silence of the house. I knelt to pet her. "Hey, there, pretty girl, glad to see me?" She clawed her way into my arms and I carried her to the kitchen. "How about a treat?" I said, opening the cupboard and grasping a can of tuna.

"It's a special night, so why shouldn't you be part of the celebration?" She apparently agreed, practically turning the bowl over to get to the contents.

Smiling at her antics, I reached for the phone to check for messages. Oh boy, Mom had called again. No time to respond now. I'd have more news later anyway. And it would be good, I hoped. Scrolling back, I noted that there were three calls from a number I didn't recognize. I punched in the code while rushing to my bedroom to survey my wardrobe. I saved the first message from my mother asking that I call her as soon as possible. Oh man. More than likely, she was still bent on trying to change my mind. Dad and I always got along famously, but my mother and I rarely saw eye to eye on anything. She apparently had a different vision for my future and never passed up an opportunity to voice her opinion on what a mistake I was making marrying an Arizona rancher. It was troubling that both mothers objected to our union. I deleted two more hang-ups before hearing Tally's voice, sounding far away and indistinct. After the hissing and clicking stopped I made out "...be a little late...wait for me before...something... something...news...tell her...located the...something...of..." some background noise I couldn't identify, a buzz and then dead air. I replayed it, but still couldn't make out what he'd said. I tossed the phone on the bed, shed my clothes and climbed into the shower. Cell phones. I viewed them much the same as I did computers—wonderful when they worked, terrible when they didn't. Tally refused to own a cell phone, so he must have borrowed one from another posse member. It was a relief to know that he was going to be late, so the pressure was off to be there at exactly five p.m. But then, maybe not. Ruth was expecting us, so it might behoove me to arrive on time. No use handing her additional ammunition to add to her list of my apparent inadequacies.

I was ready in record time, dressed conservatively in a plaid western shirt, black jeans and boots. Once again, I slipped off the ring and stuffed it into my pocket, rejoicing in the knowledge that, after tonight, I would no longer have to hide it. I scrutinized my reflection in the full-length mirror, calculating that the heels probably added three inches to my five-foot eight-inch frame. Good. Height is always an advantage in a confrontation. Since my unruly red hair was the most striking similarity to the late, and much despised, Stephanie Talverson, I took care to tamp it down as much as possible, wetting and winding it into a thick braid that hung half way down my back. A little blush and light lipstick finished the job. There. The perfect ranch wife. I grabbed my jacket and headed to the door, stopping to pet Marmalade on the way out. "Be back soon, baby. Slay lots of nasty old spiders while I'm gone."

In full darkness with only a few lights twinkling from distant ranches, I drove towards the Starfire with dread tightening around my belly like a cold belt, unable to avoid the memories I'd been pushing to the back of my mind all week. Ginger's innocent remark at lunch had launched them to the forefront. Talk about the irony of ironies. It wasn't lost on me that had I married Grant last spring as originally planned, I would now be enjoying the company of the most wonderful mother-in-law on the face of the planet. Phyllis Jamerson and I had hit it off from the beginning. Beautiful, refined, and highly educated, she was everything one could wish for. It wasn't surprising that she and my mother, who taught language arts at the local community college in Spring Hill, had become fast friends while they'd excitedly planned for my wedding. And even after the heartache of returning Grant's ring, then tearfully disclosing the news to her, Phyllis had remained supportive of my decision. In an odd twist of fate, she and my mother had remained on good terms and I guess that's why I'd felt compelled to write the note informing her of my engagement to Tally. It seemed only right.

When the lights of the Starfire Ranch came into view, I steeled myself as I pulled in and parked next to Ronda's blue pickup. I stepped out and stood in the cold night air soaking in the beauty of the ebony sky glimmering with starlight. I lingered there another ten minutes hoping Tally would show up but the road behind me remained cloaked in silence. Casting a last apprehensive glance at the sprawling two-story ranch house, I murmured a little prayer, climbed the wooden stairs leading to the porch, and then paused another moment to gather my thoughts before rapping on the front door. My knock set off a barrage of barking and, as I expected, the door was not answered immediately. It was Ruth's usual routine—pretending she didn't know I was there. Wistfully, I looked beyond the pipe fencing towards the long horse barn several hundred yards to my right. Lights blazed from every window, no doubt signifying that Ronda was inside enjoying the company of her horses as usual. Who could blame her? I was going to need all the patience I could muster, knowing full well that the ornery side of me would love nothing better than to smack the crap out of this spiteful woman.

I knocked louder and finally the porch light popped on and the door swung inward to reveal Ruth Talverson in all her glory, or lack thereof. While I'd taken great pains to dress for dinner and the special announcement she was not yet privy to, she appeared disheveled, as if she'd been doing yard work for a week and forgot to bathe. Clad in soiled jeans and a ratty-looking shirt, her iron-gray hair hung limply around her deeply grooved cheeks. Not unexpectedly, she wore an expression of barely concealed irritation. Nice. I'd done quite a few pieces on manic depression, now popularly referred to as bi-polar illness, while working at the *Philadelphia Inquirer*. This troubled lady certainly fit the bill as far as I was concerned. Tally had warned me about her bouts of clinical depression and Ginger had confided to me that she'd been hospitalized several times in the past, and had suffered a complete nervous breakdown following the death of Tally's father. I'd expressed my reservations about her reaction to our news, but Tally seemed confident she would soften her stance against me. "Hello, Ruth," I said, forcing a synthetic smile. "How are you tonight?"

Still standing behind the screen door flanked by the dogs, her deep-set eyes glittered with reproach. Okay. Obviously, she was not happy to see me. "Where's Tally?" she snapped, her gaze flitting past me to search the darkness.

A naughty thrill of elation flashed through me with the sudden realization that he'd called me and not her. I couldn't help myself. "Oh? He didn't call you? He left me a message saying he would be a little late."

"Why?"

"I'm not sure. The message was garbled."

Her scowl intensified. "I see," she grumbled, adding with a complete lack of enthusiasm, "I guess you'll want to wait inside."

As opposed to what? Standing outside in the cold? I swallowed my annoyance and brushed past her into the kitchen. My entrance sparked a renewed barrage of barking from the two older dogs and anxious whining from the rambunctious puppy. They rushed at me with happy doggy faces, jumped, pawed, and slobbered all over me. "Okay, fellas, settle down," I finally ordered with a laugh, trying to pet each of them while shedding my jacket. At least they seemed glad to see me.

Wordlessly, Ruth moved to the stove, removed the lid from one of two saucepans and stood with her back to me while she stirred the contents. I wrinkled my nose. Whatever it was didn't smell terribly appetizing. I already knew that their regular cook, Gloria, who consistently served savory melt-in-your-mouth meals, was in Mexico visiting her sister for a few weeks. That left us to suffer the consequences of Ruth's culinary endeavors that usually consisted of transforming perfectly fine food into a series of mystery stews, or her signature dish, a casserole containing questionable ingredients and topped with a mound of crushed, burned potato chips. No matter. The tight knots of anxiety squeezing my stomach squelched my normally hearty appetite anyway.

"So...ah...what's cooking?" I asked in an expectant tone, taking the first plunge into what was usually a conversational abyss.

She turned her head slightly. "You like fried okra?"

Did I? I knew it was green and in the vegetable family, but I wasn't positive I'd ever actually tasted it before. Nevertheless, I responded with forced enthusiasm, heartened to be engaging in what was as close to a real conversation as we'd ever had before. "Yeah, sure. It sounds...delicious."

"Good." She turned back to the stove and lifted the lid on a second saucepan.

I cleared my throat. "Anything I can do to help?"

Keeping her back to me, she answered, "No."

"I haven't seen you for awhile. Anything new or interesting going on?" I asked in a bubbly tone, hoping to keep a dialogue going.

"No."

A heavy curtain of silence dropped between us. I interpreted the rigid set of her shoulders as a return to her usual pattern of non-communication. Stifling a sigh of aggravation, I sat down at the kitchen table and played with the dogs, trying to ignore the fact that she was ignoring me. My impatience level escalated with each passing minute until it was sheer torture to sit and endure her unspoken censure of me, apparently for deeds committed by a woman I'd never met. More than anything, I wanted to break down the stoic façade of this terminally morose woman and initiate a frank discussion. But I had no idea how to begin. As of that moment, things weren't looking good. I had a sinking feeling her reaction to our engagement, no matter how diplomatically we presented it, would be nothing short of volcanic. I stared at the kitchen clock. Where was Tally?

Struggling for patience, my pulse rate climbed steadily. As I sat there digging deep inside, searching for a character trait I sorely lacked, I had to grudgingly admit that my likeness to the late Stephanie Talverson probably wasn't the only reason Ruth disliked me. And if I were to be totally honest with myself, she would be right.

Because my all-consuming passion to be the best investigative reporter on earth continually led me to seek out stimulating story possibilities—or, as Tally often described it, my need for a constant adrenaline fix—I'd been involved in a couple of close calls since my arrival at the *Sun*. Inadvertently, I had dragged Tally into several dicey situations with me. I don't think he had elaborated to

Ruth how close we'd come to disaster this last time around, but she'd obviously read the accounts in the newspaper or learned of it through Ronda or other acquaintances. Even though she'd never verbalized her fears, I sensed that she very much resented me involving her only son in my risky escapades. Serving as the newspaper's sports reporter these past two years, Tally had most likely never encountered anything more dangerous than the occasional foul ball until he'd gotten involved with me. Even though it was disappointing to me, no doubt Ruth was pleased about his recent decision to resign his present position as of the first of the year to focus his attention on the ranch.

The uncomfortable silence between us lengthened, and my agitation heightened with each tick of the second hand. Apparently even the dogs were bored because one by one they exited through the pet door. I wished I could escape through the pet door with them. Should I excuse myself and wait in the living room? I arched my neck towards the dimly lit room beyond the dining area. It occurred to me that during the few times I'd been in the house, I'd rarely left the kitchen. In fact, I'd had only one quick tour of the entire place. From what I remembered, Ruth and Ronda had adjoining bedrooms and separate baths on the first floor, and Tally occupied a suite of rooms upstairs. Once again the thought of living here with this crabby old woman gave me a royal case of the shivers.

What the hell was taking Tally so long to get here? Damn him for leaving me stranded in this uncomfortable situation. Maybe he wasn't going to make it at all. I wished I'd been able to understand his truncated message. What was the point of waiting any longer? No sooner had I decided I was out of there than I heard the welcome rumble of his truck accompanied by Attila's high-pitched yelps that prompted answering barks from the other dogs. Thank heavens! My immediate relief was tempered by a swell of anxiety. With the moment of truth now upon us, it was a struggle to remember our carefully rehearsed words.

I jumped to my feet, raced to the door and jerked it open. Attila yapped joyously. "Hey, big guy, how are you?" I patted his silky fur and grinned with relief when Tally stepped inside behind him. "Boy, am I glad to see you!" Under ordinary circumstances, I would have thrown my arms around his neck and kissed him until I ran out of breath but with Ruth glowering at us, I restrained myself. I sensed something was wrong when I caught his hand. It was icy cold. His smudged clothes looked damp and his complexion had a peculiar grayish hue.

He squeezed my hand, saying to his mother, "Sorry I'm late."

"Dinner's ready," was her bland response. "Did you stop at the Post Office box and pick up the mail?"

"No."

"Damn it," she fumed, slamming a spoon onto the counter, "It's been four days. I want my magazines."

I was poised to suggest that if she'd learn to drive a car she could quit bitching and get the mail herself, but Tally laid a hand on my arm and said under his breath, "You did get my message, I hope?" He appeared to be signaling me with his wide-eyed stare. "Well, sort of," I answered, attempting to interpret an underlying meaning in his statement. "I mean, not much of it, but hey, you're here now and that's all that matters." The odd intensity of his steady gaze disturbed me, but I attributed it to the fact that he was probably feeling as anxious as I was. Since I'd long since breached my tolerance threshold, all I could think of was making our announcement as quickly as possible.

Why wait until after dinner? I dug into the pocket of my jeans to retrieve the ring before swinging around to face her dour expression. "Ruth, Tally and I have some exciting news to share and we hope you'll be as happy as we are—"

"Kendall, not now," Tally cut in harshly, yanking me to his side and almost off my feet.

I gawked at him in amazement. "What?"

"Come outside. We have to talk first."

I couldn't believe it. He'd made me wait in agony for over an hour and now it appeared that he was backing out at the last minute. I set my jaw. "No. We're going to do this now."

"No, we're not." He leaned in whispering fiercely in my ear. "Trust me, this isn't the right time."

I glared back at him. Not the right time? There would never be a right time to tell her. "Tally, you promised me—"

Before I could finish my sentence, he barked, "Ma, we'll be back in a minute." Then, amid my storm of protests, he unceremoniously dragged me outside onto the porch, slamming the door behind us.

Angrily, I wrenched my arm from his grasp. "Just what the hell do you think you're doing? First, you leave me twisting in the wind with—"

"Kendall, will you shut up for a minute! Please."

Stunned by his outburst, I suddenly realized the stern light in his eyes conveyed not anger, but distress. My inner radar clicked on. "What's going on?"

He hesitated before placing a hand on each of my shoulders and looking deep into my eyes. "Kendall, do you remember the promise you made me two weeks ago?"

"Which one?" I'd had a fairly extensive list.

"The one where you promised to chain yourself to your desk instead of jumping head first into another…possibly dangerous assignment."

My interest level shot skyward. "What assignment would that be?"

His grip tightened. "I mean it." He drew in a deep breath. "Look, I can't ask you not to do your job…but I'd prefer you didn't go anywhere near…what I'm about to tell you."

It's questionable as to which was more powerful, my exasperation with his cryptic behavior or my mushrooming curiosity. "Come on, Tally. How can I promise you something when I don't know what you're talking about?"

He paused a few more maddening seconds before saying in a somber tone, "We found the judge's body a couple of hours ago."

"Oh no. That's what you were trying to tell me. I'm really sorry."

"Damn cell phones." He pulled me into his embrace. "It's not your fault," he said, gently stroking my back. "But, I'm sure you understand now why this is not the most opportune moment to tell my mother about our plans."

I drew back and searched his eyes. "Tally, I'm making a titanic effort to be more sympathetic when it comes to your mother's fragile temperament and all, but this isn't entirely unexpected. After all, the poor man had been exposed to the elements for almost two weeks. Listen, why don't we just tell her like we rehearsed and then you can gently break this…this other news to her in the morning."

He removed his hat and raked a hand through his thick hair. "It's not going to be that simple."

"Why not?"

"Because he didn't die from exposure."

"What do you mean?"

"He had a bullet wound in his chest."

"Uh-oh. A hunting accident?"

"Doubtful."

An acute sense of apprehension gripped me. "What are you getting at?"

"Kendall, we didn't find him near Flagstaff where the truck was located last week."

It felt like cold fingertips tickling the back of my neck. "Where *did* you find him?"

"The handyman discovered his body floating in one of the natural springs on his own property this afternoon."

"Oh, my God!" My mind did a quick back flip. I vaguely recalled Tally mentioning that the judge and his present wife had, within the past year, purchased the old Hidden Springs Guest Ranch, which in its heyday had served as an exclusive hideaway for celebrities, royalty, politicians and the affluent. "So...what are you saying? He died from a gunshot wound or he drowned?"

"We don't know for sure."

I eyed him with growing suspicion. "Tally, quit beating around the bush."

He slumped onto the bench beneath the amber porch light and twirled his hat in a furious circle, always an indication of distress. When he finally looked up at me, the ominous expression on his face chilled my gut. "We weren't even sure it *was* him until I recognized the watch I'd given him for Christmas about ten years ago. Whatever the cause, there is no doubt that he was murdered."

My mouth went dry. "Wait a minute. Didn't you say he was just found a few hours ago?"

"Yep."

"Then, how can you make a definitive statement like that before forensic tests have been performed?"

"Easy. His head is missing."

3

News of the grotesque decapitation shook Castle Valley to the core of its foundations. The site where the judge's body had been discovered was cordoned off while a swarm of local law enforcement personnel and a forensic specialist, called in from the Maricopa County Medical Examiner's office in Phoenix, pored over every inch of soil within a half mile of the crime scene. Divers combed the waters of the pools. By the time a full week elapsed, no definitive clues had been discovered. The pall hanging over the town was as thick as the unusual cloud cover that had blanketed the state for several days. The result of everyone's efforts produced only one serious investigative lead or person of interest—ex-convict Randy Moorehouse. If the authorities did have any significant information, they were sitting on it. Who and why anyone would have committed such an atrocity dominated every conversation and had everyone wandering around in a profound state of shock. For me, the judge's death held far more personal significance due to my relationship with Tally. While shaken up as much as anyone by the hideous nature of the crime, I was doubly disturbed that yet another tragedy had befallen the Talverson family. Ruth had been so traumatized her shrink had sedated her for three days and Tally seemed withdrawn and deeply troubled. He'd been insistent that I not be alone at my isolated house in the desert. When he'd been unable to stay for several nights because of his mother's delicate emotional state, I'd acquiesced and stayed two nights with Ginger. After that, if he couldn't stay overnight, he'd arrange to have a couple of his ranch hands patrol the grounds of my place until dawn. While I appreciated his concern, I felt no hint of impending danger. To me, the circumstances did not suggest a crime of passion or the attack of a madman. By its very nature it appeared that this had been a carefully premeditated crime aimed directly at Riley Gibbons. Of course, I wondered along with everyone else what kind of a sick mind had been at work, but secretly had to admit that it had ignited my sense of morbid fascination.

Everywhere I went it seemed as if people were looking over their shoulders. Time after time, I encountered townspeople clustered together, whispering in hushed tones, their eyes dark with apprehension. A byproduct of the blood-curdling murder was the land office sales of deadbolt locks and home security systems—both concepts at odds with this peaceful desert town where nothing of consequence usually happened.

By the time we gathered in my office for our usual Friday morning editorial meeting, additional details about the judge's life and mystifying death had begun to emerge. With Tugg taking a vacation day and Tally gone to drive his mother to her shrink's appointment in Phoenix, there were only three of us present. Whereas I would normally be right in the thick of things, I was instead relegated to the sidelines. And it was killing me. But in deference to Tally's wishes that I not be professionally involved, I concealed my frustration and agreed to assign the story to Walter Zipp. It took every smidgen of willpower I possessed to go along with Tally's request.

Needless to say, I was now *persona non grata* in the eyes of Tally's mother. Hadn't my cheerful, well-intentioned words promised to deliver happy news? Instead, after I'd left the ranch last week, Tally had the sorry task of informing her of Judge Gibbons's horrific fate. Glumly, I wondered how I'd ever be able to make things right with her. As it now stood, she still didn't know about our engagement. The new plan was to tell her this coming weekend. But only if Tally felt she was psychologically ready to handle it, and only after I'd agreed to apologize for causing her such extreme distress, even though it had been unintentional on my part.

As every law officer knows, if significant evidence at a crime scene is not discovered within the first critical twenty-four hours the case begins to turn cold. That sobering fact served to jumpstart the level of community anxiety. Understandably, the primary concerns were who had killed the prominent judge and what was the motive? Staring down at the file photo of the attractive, gray-haired man, I imagined that the next question on everyone's mind was probably the same as mine. Why had someone gone to the extra trouble of cutting his head off? To me, the last and most disconcerting question was, where was it?

"Okay," I said, addressing Walter after he and Jim had pulled their chairs close to my desk. "What have you got so far?"

His lips puckered in a grimace. "Well, I hate to say it, but I haven't made a hell of a lot of *head*way."

Eyes twinkling with mischief, Jim piped up, "How much *does* a head weigh?"

"Jimbo, you are one sick puppy." They both roared with laughter while I rolled my eyes. "Okay, guys, whenever you're ready," I finally said after they'd given each other a high five.

"Sorry." Walter cleared his throat and told us he had repeatedly pressed for details from Sheriff Marshall Turnbull and also Deputy Duane Potts, who'd been assigned as the case agent in charge of the scene. At this point in the investigation, they had very little to go on in the way of physical evidence. "At least that's the official word," Walter pointed out, appearing skeptical. "More than likely they've got something, but they're keeping it under their hats."

"Any other leads besides Randy Moorehouse?" I asked.

Walter glanced at his notepad. "Nope. They've had him in for questioning twice, but apparently they've got nothing to tie him to the murder. I drove out to interview him day before yesterday and let's just say he wasn't exactly overjoyed to see me. All he'd tell me was that he had nothing to do with it and that he's sticking to his story. He claims he was out delivering flowers for his sister that day and—"

I stared at him blankly, interjecting, "Delivering flowers for his sister? Who's his sister?"

"Rulinda Platt."

I shrugged and Jim filled in, "She and her mom run the Posey Patch Florist over on Kokopelli."

Suddenly the name clicked. That was the name of the florist on Ginger's contact list for the engagement party. "Okay, I know who you're talking about."

"Right now, Randy is living in a camper out back of her place while he's building an addition over her garage. When he got out of prison a couple of weeks ago, Rulinda gave him a job driving a delivery van since nobody else in town seemed interested in hiring him." Walter scrunched his nose in distaste. "I can't say as I'd blame people. He's one scary-looking dude. He's twice my size and has spent more than a few hours inhabiting tattoo parlors. I stopped by her shop yesterday and asked if she had any thoughts on the judge's death and I can attest to the fact that she's not mourning his demise. Here's her direct quote," he said, holding up his notes. "'As far as I'm concerned I hope Judge Gibbons is rotting his nuts off somewhere in the deepest, darkest, hottest corner of Hell. Him sending my brother to prison for a crime he never committed ruined his life, my life, and damn near tore the whole family apart.'"

"If we paraphrase the nuts part, I think we can go with that entire quote," I commented dryly.

Jim threw in, "I remember reading that Rulinda raised holy hell after Randy's conviction. She got herself some face time on TV calling Judge Gibbons every name in the book. Then she got involved with a couple of these protest groups who organize candlelight vigils every time one of these guys is executed and she's responsible for getting the case reopened."

"Interesting. So, let's go back to her brother. You say he was delivering flowers the day the body was discovered? Can he account for his time?"

"Apparently. But, get this. One of his regularly scheduled deliveries was to Hidden Springs."

I gave Walter an appraising look. "Even more interesting."

"He told the sheriff that he was there just long enough to drop off their weekly delivery. After that, he stopped to have lunch and a beer with a couple of his biker brothers over at the Hitching Post Saloon. He claims he was there for several hours. But, who knows? You know the code among these people. They take care of their own and you can bet your sweet ass that even if he wasn't there as long as he says he was, to a man, none of them would say anything to the contrary."

"Hmmm. Okay. So what's the story with the judge's widow?" Tally had just mentioned to me in passing a couple of weeks ago that they'd been separated for several months.

Walter tapped his notepad with a pencil. "On that subject, I've barely scratched the surface. You probably already know he was married to Ruth Talverson's older sister, Ginny, for many years."

"Of course."

"After her death Riley remained single for a good long time. Apparently he earned quite a reputation as a ladies' man until he finally got hitched again about three years ago to a woman by the name of..." he paused and flipped a page, his eyes searching. "Damn, I had it here a minute ago."

I filled in, "I remember Tally mentioning her name once or twice. Is it La Donna?"

"Righto," Walter replied, nodding. "La Donna Hendricks. She's been a flight attendant for twenty-five years, married previously. During the past year she was diagnosed with fibromyalgia. The disease has progressed to the point that she went on medical leave about four months ago, just about the time she and the judge separated. She moved into one of the guest cottages next door to the main residence. Apparently because of her physical limitations she couldn't handle the stairs any longer and was having trouble keeping up with the everyday operations of the place in addition to overseeing the ongoing renovations to the original structure."

"Where has the judge been living all this time?"

"During the week he stayed at his condo in Scottsdale, but he usually drove up here every weekend and…well, you're gonna love this," he crowed, shooting me a wily grin. "Apparently the old guy wasn't one to let grass grow under his feet. A couple of weeks before his um…untimely departure, he moved his new girlfriend into the old hotel."

That was a surprise. If Tally had known this fact, he'd never shared it with me. But then I had only a vague knowledge of the man's existence, having overheard Tally mention his name once or twice in passing. "So, the judge's girlfriend and his widow are both living at Hidden Springs? How does that work?"

Walter's wide grin was decidedly sardonic as he exchanged a meaningful look with Jim. "Sounds pretty kinky, huh?"

"Just a little."

"Looks like the judge had a little trouble keeping his pants zipped," Jim remarked with a ribald snicker.

Walter joined in with a hearty chorus of laughter before continuing with, "Apparently. Now, unfortunately, I haven't been able to snag an interview with either of these ladies yet to confirm all these rumors, but I was able to corner the housekeeper the other day outside the grocery store."

"What's her name?" I asked, absently drumming my pen on the desk.

"Bernita Morales. Nice lady, probably late fifties, early sixties. Anyway, according to her, when..." he paused to glance at his notes again, "Miss Marissa Van Steenholm moved into the largest suite of rooms on the first floor of the hotel, La Donna gave the judge what for. I guess she was screaming at him so loudly some of the guests thought she'd gone off the deep end and checked out early. Anyway, Bernita told me that La Donna refused to leave the premises even though the divorce papers had been filed. She immediately counter-sued and their attorneys were still trying to hash out the property settlement when well...you know." In a macabre gesture, he swiped his forefinger across his throat in a slicing motion that sent a shiver up my spine.

I shook my head thoughtfully. "This whole scenario sounds like a plot for a really bad soap opera, or maybe a good one."

Walter's good-natured grin turned devilish. "Hang onto your head...I mean hat. It gets a whole lot better." Assuming a self-satisfied expression, he shifted his bulk and flipped the page over. "The grieving widow, La Donna, is claiming that the lovely Marissa, who'd worked as a clerk in Riley's Phoenix office, and by the way is a good thirty years younger than him, was banging the handyman while the judge was in Phoenix."

"Whoa, whoa, whoa. The handyman? Back up. You're talking about the guy who discovered the body?"

"One and the same. Duane gave me the stats on this guy. His name is Winston Rudy Pendahl. He's a forty-two-year-old ex-con with a mile-long rap sheet ranging from vandalism starting at age twelve to petty theft as a teenager and on to burglary and aggravated assault. The highlight of his distinguished criminal career was a six-year

41

gig in Florence for taking out a guy with a claw hammer. Of course he claims it was self-defense and that he's been living a squeaky clean life since he got out of prison ten years ago. He fessed up the minute they brought him in for questioning. Said he knew they'd find out about his past, so he laid it out for them." Walter leaned forward, his expression provocative. "Something else noteworthy. Guess who the presiding judge was during the trial for Pendahl's last conviction?" He cupped a hand to one ear, smiling expectantly while Jim and I chimed in, "Judge Riley C. Gibbons."

"You got it."

I sat back in my chair. "Doesn't it seem odd to you that Judge Gibbons would employ a person with such a questionable background? Especially someone he'd sentenced to prison?"

Walter lifted his massive shoulders. "I had the same thought. Apparently Winston had been hired by the previous owner of Hidden Springs and since the conviction was so many years ago and his appearance had changed, the judge probably didn't realize who the guy was. I'm sure he couldn't keep track of all the ex-cons running around who'd appeared in his courtroom."

"Do the authorities consider him a person of interest?"

"Not at this time. Duane told me that he was questioned and released. In fact, the really disturbing thing about this case is after a week of the authorities scouring the area practically twenty-four-seven, they still haven't found enough evidence to point the finger at anyone else for that matter. But like I said, that's the official word."

We all sat there for a few seconds mulling over his statement in silent speculation before I said, "Um...getting back to the judge, Tally told me that the medical examiner's office hasn't released the body for burial yet. Any word on when that will happen?"

"From what they tell me, they're really short-staffed and running way behind on their caseload. But, since this one's high profile they bumped it to the front and gave it to the top dog. Have you heard of Dr. Nora Bartoli?"

"I think I've read about her. Isn't she a forensic anthropologist?"

"Right."

Walter peeked at his notes again. "Anyway, she finished her examination yesterday and the...remains should be released today for burial preparation at the Heritage Memory Mortuary in Prescott." He glanced at his notes again. "According to the funeral director the visitation will be next Monday night starting at six o'clock at the Prescott United Methodist Church on Gurley Street in Prescott and then the judge will be laid to rest in the family plot at the Arizona Pioneers Home Cemetery at 2 p.m. on Tuesday."

Jim piped up, "So...I'm guessing it won't be an open casket?"

Walter grinned. "Getting *ahead* of me today, Jimbo?"

"No, but I think we may be in over our *heads* on this one."

I rolled my eyes. "You two are just awful."

"Let me add another element of intrigue to this equation," Walter continued, his hazel eyes glimmering with excitement. "Riley Gibbons had a new will drawn up two weeks prior to his disappearance."

I raised a brow. "Now *that* is noteworthy."

"Oh, it's more than that. Get this. He deeded the hotel over to the very fortunate Marissa Van Steenholm."

I gawked at him. "Really? I'm assuming La Donna Gibbons plans to contest it."

"I would if I were her."

"Good job, Walter." As pleased as I was with his efforts I could hardly stand it. Every fiber of my being screamed out to be front and center in the ongoing investigation but all I could do was sit by and listen. "How'd you find out about this?"

He grinned broadly. "Deputy Potts."

"Duane? How would he know?"

"He got called in during the reading of the will."

"Why?"

"To restore order." Walter looked extremely pleased with himself. "According to the judge's attorney, Richard Mills, La Donna Gibbons was already in a high state of agitation when she arrived. When he got to the part about the deceased leaving the Van Steenholm woman the hotel, which is smack dab in the middle of the Hidden Springs property, La Donna went ape shit. Mills reported that she lunged at Marissa like an enraged lion, or lioness. I guess it was quite a brawl. When Duane finally arrived and got her calmed down, she demanded that he arrest Marissa."

The whole affair sounded as unbelievable as a B-movie script and I wished to hell I'd been there to witness it. "Arrest her? Why?"

"La Donna told him she'd just returned from her bank in Phoenix and claimed the safe deposit box, which supposedly held in the neighborhood of a quarter of a million dollars in gold coins was empty as a dry lake bed. Nothing left but a rubber band and a paper clip."

"Whaa hoo!" Jim hooted. "So she thinks the girlfriend got there before she did?"

"Right as rain," Walter concurred, nodding smugly. "It's her contention that Marissa and the handyman had been in cahoots the whole time and says the missing coins provides a clear motive for the two to have murdered her husband. But Marissa denies it and claims she overheard La Donna and the judge having a whopping argument the night before he left for his hunting trip. She says La Donna threatened to kill him. He was scheduled to meet some friends at a designated spot outside Flagstaff but, of course, he never showed up. Another fascinating sidebar...his hunting rifle is nowhere to be found."

I stared at him. "So...do the authorities suspect he was shot with his own gun?"

"Same caliber, but ballistics can't say for certain without the weapon."

As I processed all the data, I had to remind myself once again that I must remain on the sidelines. There was no way on earth that Tally was going to release me from my promise. I sighed inwardly, glad for once that he was absent from our staff meeting. Less than six months had elapsed since I'd uncovered the startling events surrounding his wife's murder two years prior. And now with this new information rising to the surface like pond scum, Tally would hate the idea of his family being in the glare of the media spotlight once again.

"Okay, Walter, stay on top of it. Oh, and while you're researching the judge's cases, it might be interesting to pinpoint anything unusual that jumps out at you."

"Whoa, Nelly. How many years back do you want me to check? Ten? Fifteen? Which cases? If I concentrate on that I won't get much else done."

"Good point." I thought for a few seconds. "I'll call Ginger's brother, Brian, and see if we can enlist his help. He's a whiz on the Internet and can probably compile a list for us in a couple of days. You can coordinate which years each of you will cover so you don't overlap."

Walter's grateful smile reflected relief. "Thanks."

I went over the assignment sheet and Jim reminded me again that he would be on vacation the following week. "While you guys are all here freezing your buns off, I'll be on the beach in Cabo working on my tan," he joked on the way out the door.

"Lucky bastard," Walter griped, rising to his feet, rubbing his lower back. "I heard there's more crappy weather heading this way. They're predicting an additional foot of snow for the high country and we might get a couple of inches of rain here."

The rest of the day was a blur of details and by four o'clock I was whipped. I leaned back in my chair and stretched, thinking that Tally had probably returned to the ranch by now with Ruth. If she were in what Tally described as the "right frame of mind" then we would break the news to her this evening.

As if on cue, the phone rang and it was Tally. "Hey there, I was just thinking about you."

"I was thinking about you, too," came his warm response.

"How did things go with your mother today?"

"A little better. She didn't say much on the way back from Phoenix."

"What's different about that?" He didn't respond to my little dig so I continued. "So, do you think she's ready to hear our news without having a major cow or a minor stroke?" I asked tentatively.

Dead air for a few seconds. "She's been on a new medication for about a week now and has been pretty mellow the past couple of days. Hard to tell, but I guess we'll give it another shot."

"Try not to sound too enthusiastic."

He chuckled. "Believe me, I want to get it over with as much as you do. I'm just concerned that it might send her over the edge again."

The edge was right. "I'm assuming that she'll be expecting me to grovel before her with mega apologies for my unfortunate choice of words last week."

"It's your call, but I have a feeling it will earn you some Brownie points."

I set my pride on the back burner. "What time shall I put in my appearance?"

"Why don't you come right now?"

I glanced up at the wall clock. "Now? It's a little early for dinner, isn't it?"

"I have something to show you before it gets dark."

"Oh? Are you going to give me a hint?"

"Nope. You'll find out when you get here."

Now I was thoroughly intrigued. I glanced at my cluttered desk, piled with work, and made an instant decision. There wasn't anything that couldn't wait until Monday. "Okay. I'm out of here."

"Don't come to the house. Meet me in the barn."

"The barn? Why?"

"No more questions. See ya."

Before I could say another word, he hung up.

4

Accustomed as I was to Tally being a man of few words, nonetheless the cryptic nature of his invitation was puzzling. That aside, my spirits perked up considerably. I cleared off my desk and when I stepped into the lobby to tell Ginger I was leaving early, she eyed me with curious appraisal. "You think Tally is goin' to get off the dime tonight so we can get this ball rollin'?"

"That's the plan. Oh, and that reminds me." I dug in my purse and pulled out my engagement ring, polished the diamond on my sleeve and slipped it on my finger. "I'm not hiding this anymore. My hope is that when Ruth sees this, she'll know we're serious and it will force her to accept the reality of the situation."

There was a twinkle of mocking challenge in her eyes. "You tell him for me, that if he don't get with the program, I'm gonna kick his fine-looking hiney all the way to Prescott and back."

I could not keep from laughing. "I'll be sure to give him that message."

She favored me with her endearing grin. "You do that. And good luck tonight. I got all necessary toes and fingers crossed."

I gave her a thumbs-up as I headed towards the front door.

"You'd best bundle up. It's supposed to get mighty cold tonight."

"Will do. See you tomorrow at the fairgrounds."

She called after me, "Let's pray that big ol' storm they're predicting holds off 'til Monday or we'll be up the creek."

"Gotcha." If a weather change was impending there was no evidence of it. The steady wind had done its job and there wasn't a cloud in sight as I pulled out of the parking lot and drove towards the Starfire with the fervent hope that this evening would be more fruitful than my previous visit. By the time I turned the truck onto Quail Crossing the cobalt blue sky was fading to a dainty turquoise. The western horizon, blushed an eye-catching shade of watermelon red, tinted the desert foliage and surrounding mountains to a rich rosy gold. There was less than half an hour of daylight left, and having become accustomed to fifteen or sixteen hours of daylight during the endless, white-hot days of summer, I still hadn't gotten used to dusk falling by five o'clock. I parked in front of the house and strolled towards the barn. I had just reached the side door when Tally's longtime foreman swung it open and touched the brim of his dog-eared Stetson. "Evenin', Miz O'Dell."

"Hey, Jake, how are you?"

"Just dandy." The sunny smile on his leathered face emphasized the deep laugh lines around his ever-squinting blue eyes. "In fact, I couldn't be dandier." Normally low-key, he seemed uncharacteristically animated.

"Well, that's good."

"Tally's out in the back corral waiting for you."

"Okay, thanks." Why did I get the strange feeling he'd been on the lookout for me?

"You have a nice evenin'." Still grinning, he tapped the brim of his hat again and strode past me.

"You too." I watched him amble towards the bunkhouse with that slight limp of his before I turned to enter the large horse barn. As always, it was ripe with the overpowering smell of hay and straw mixed with manure. Several of Tally's prize-winning Appaloosa mares stretched their necks over the stall doors and I stopped to pet each of them, pausing a little longer to stroke the silky muzzle of Tally's favorite stallion located at the far end, away from the mares. "Hey there Geronimo, what's cookin' with you today?" I murmured, before continuing towards the back door.

I walked outside into the rosy twilight, inhaling the crisp evening air, and spotted Tally standing with his back to me beside a gate that opened into one of the smaller corrals. "Hey, cowboy!" I shouted, hurrying across the clearing towards him. He glanced over his shoulder and greeted me with a grin and friendly wave. When I reached his side he said in a husky tone, "Come here, I missed seeing you today," before enfolding me in a warm embrace and kissing me deeply. Savoring the sensation of his muscular body, I returned his ardent kiss with enthusiasm. As far as I was concerned, time could have stopped right there forever and I wouldn't have cared. But, suddenly, he pulled his mouth from mine and whispered in my ear. "I have something to show you."

A bit breathless, I purred seductively, "I'll bet you do. So…you want to go into the barn and…relax in the loft for awhile before dinner?"

"That's a difficult invitation to decline," he replied, the twinkle in his eyes matching his teasing smile. "But, I'm afraid I can't…for the moment anyway. Come into the corral with me for a minute," he said, taking my hand and leading me towards the gate.

I stared up at him, feeling deflated and mystified by his odd behavior. "Tally, what's going on?"

He put two fingers to his lips and blew out a sharp whistle. A ripple of surprise swept over me when one of the double barn doors flew open and Jake reappeared leading a stunning black Appaloosa with a perfect speckled white blanket on the hindquarters. Stepping with a lively gait, holding its tail aloft, the horse whinnied loudly. Jake grinned and exchanged a conspiratorial look with Tally who then turned to me. "So, what do you think of her?" he asked with a speculative glint in his eyes.

I watched the horse prance around the corral and marveled, "I think she's the most gorgeous creature I've ever laid eyes on."

He nodded in agreement and said softly, "Good. She's yours."

I stared at him, dumbfounded. "What?"

"My engagement gift to you. Say hello to Starlight Sky. Since you're going to be living here soon, I thought it was high time you had a horse of your own. I picked her especially for you."

Our eyes connected and even in the pale remnants of daylight I couldn't miss the deep affection reflected in his intense gaze. I was so overcome with emotion, my heart so filled with joy I was speechless for long seconds.

"Tally, you continue to amaze me. She is magnificent. I'm…I'm completely blown away," I finally managed to articulate with a mild tremor in my voice. If Jake hadn't been present, I would have thrown myself into his arms again, but instead I whispered in his ear, "If things go well this evening with your mother, perhaps you can get away after dinner and stay over at my place for a change." I brushed my lips along his cheek. "I'll see that you're properly rewarded for your generosity."

He drew back, his lips stretching into his crooked smile. "Now that is definitely too good of an offer to pass up."

He held my gaze until I heard Jake approaching us with Starlight Sky at his side. "Well, you two are quite a pair," I said turning to acknowledge the older man. "I had a feeling something was up by the way you were acting earlier. But I never expected anything like this."

"I think you're gonna like this little lady's canter," Jake replied with a cagey grin. "Smooth as melted butter."

"Hey there, pretty girl," I murmured, stroking the horse's velvety muzzle and then running my hand along her smooth neck and withers. Apparently pleased, she snuffled softly and bumped her nose against my arm. I still couldn't believe that she was mine. Prior to my move to Arizona, I'd only ridden a couple of times, but since meeting Tally, it was a foregone conclusion that I was going to have to learn to handle a horse. He'd worked with me endless hours, teaching me the finer points of western horsemanship. Now, there were few things I found more exhilarating than a flat-out gallop across the open desert, rejoicing in the sense of total freedom, relishing the rush of the wind in my face.

A full butterscotch moon was peeking over the top of Castle Rock by the time Jake lead the spirited mare back towards the barn. Aware of the sudden drop in temperature, I zipped my jacket higher and drew in a contented breath. Given a choice, I would have preferred to stay right there and smooch with Tally, but we couldn't put off the inevitable any longer. "I guess we'd best get this over with," I said with a sigh, once again experiencing the familiar knot of apprehension tighten my stomach.

We traded a long searching look before Tally announced, "Let's do it."

We marched towards the house hand in hand and I was more than cognizant that the outcome of the evening pretty much depended on how I handled myself in the next few minutes. The dogs met us at the kitchen door with their usual joyous yelps and as we stepped inside the warm room, I braced myself for a glimpse of Ruth's usual dour expression. Instead, delighted relief tingled through me at the sight of Tally's sister Ronda standing at the stove. My disposition improved appreciably along with my appetite. At least I wouldn't have to endure Ruth's censure *and* her wretched cooking. Congratulating myself on being granted a short reprieve, I called out with enthusiasm, "Whatever you're cooking smells heavenly. I'm starving."

Ronda turned and pinned me with a look of wry amusement. "When aren't you starving?" She tucked a strand of dark auburn hair behind one ear and motioned with her chin towards the table. "Help yourself to chips and salsa. The enchilada casserole will be ready in about twenty minutes." To Tally she said, "That rancher named Gabe Horton, you know the one from Colorado you talked to last week?"

"Yeah?"

"He phoned earlier. He's going to drive four of his mares down."

"Great."

"Oh, and Ted wants to bring his mare over tomorrow morning around eight. You going to be around that early?"

"I can be."

"He wants you to call him back tonight about another matter too, but he won't be home until around nine." She arched a triumphant brow. "I think he's finally made the decision to go ahead and buy Saint."

Tally's eyes lit with interest. "All right."

I knew Tally had a big weekend planned. He was expecting to entertain several other horse ranchers who were interested in purchasing some of his prize-winning Appaloosa stallions. I scooped a generous portion of thick salsa onto a tortilla chip and popped it in my mouth. Just right, tangy tomato sauce spiced with fresh scallions and cilantro. "Yum!"

Tally draped our jackets on the wall hook. "Where's Ma? Don't tell me she's gone to bed already?"

"Nope. But she did say she wasn't hungry and won't be eating dinner with us."

Instantly suspicious, I stopped in mid-chew. "Did she know I was coming?"

"She saw you drive up."

A wave of irritation closed my throat. I put the chips down and dusted the crumbs from my hands. It was obvious she was planning to give me the cold shoulder once again. I leveled a challenging look at Tally. "There you have it. She's up to her old tricks."

Scowling, Tally slapped his hat against his thigh before jamming it onto the hook. "Damn it." He appeared lost in thought for a moment, obviously agonizing about what to do next before his expression hardened to grim resolve. "Where is she?" he growled to Ronda.

She thumbed over her shoulder. "As far as I know she's still in Dad's study. She's been in there for hours moping over the old photograph albums again." She shook her head sadly. "Like that's going to bring him back."

Tally's sigh of exasperation accompanied an eye roll.

His sister cocked her head to one side, eyeing him shrewdly. "What's going on? Why are you two so ticked off?"

He lifted my left hand and pointed to the ring, whispering, "Because, we planned to tell her about this."

Ronda's gaze turned sympathetic. "I see."

"What happened? She seemed fine a couple of hours ago. What set her off?"

An elongated shrug. "You know her, up one minute, down the next."

"Great." Tally looked as glum as I felt, but I pushed away my frustration and steeled myself for battle. I'd had it with Ruth and her obstinate mood fluctuations. I was on a mission and the word retreat wasn't in my game plan.

"You know what? I don't give a crap if she is in a snit," I announced firmly. "Let's just do it."

Tally and Ronda exchanged an anxious glance. "Kendall," he began cautiously, "maybe we shouldn't—"

My cheeks flamed. "Shouldn't what? Shouldn't tell her? Are you suggesting we put it off again? Let her continue to run the show? No way. Not this time. I'm done tiptoeing around her. Maybe you guys are intimidated because she's *your* mother, but she sure as hell isn't mine.

So, Tally, you can relax. You're off the hook." I stomped towards the closed door of Joe Talverson's former study. "I'll tell her myself."

"Kendall! Damn it, wait..." he caught up with me and grabbed my arm. "Simmer down. I'm coming with you. We'll tell her together just as we planned."

Heartened, I beamed him a grateful smile and gave him a quick kiss. "Okay."

We approached the door and after only a moment's hesitation, Tally pushed it open. Prepared to face her wrath, the words I'd waited so long to say remained locked in my throat at the sight of Ruth sitting in a chair weeping softly, an array of photo albums spread out around her feet. "Oh, my darling," she sobbed, her eyes closed as she clutched one of the photos to her breast. "My love, my only love, why did you have to leave me?"

5

It was too late to withdraw. Ruth looked up at us with a startled gasp, shoved the photo and a folded piece of white paper into the album on her lap and slammed it shut. "Why didn't you knock?" she groused, dabbing the end of her nose with a tissue, her dark eyes misted with misery. She presented a rather pathetic picture sitting there alone with only the memories of her deceased husband as company. Even though I knew she detested me, the sight of another human being suffering from such acute grief tugged at my sensibilities and my heart softened towards her.

Knowing Tally, I half expected him to back down, but before I could utter one word of the carefully rehearsed speech I'd gone over in my mind a thousand times, he announced without fanfare, "Ma, Kendall and I are getting married." Instead of the heated response I expected, Ruth remained silent, appearing slightly shell-shocked as he continued with, "We'd like to have your blessing, but if you can't give us that, you may as well know that we're getting married with or without it." He met my eyes squarely and when he reached for my hand, I thought my heart would burst with pride. It was time. I inhaled a deep breath and turned to face his mother.

"Ruth, I know you and I got off to a rocky start last spring, but considering the fact that I'm going to be living here soon it will be a lot easier for all of us if you and I could be friends. For starters, you're going to have to let go of the fact that I bear a resemblance to Stephanie. Yes, I have red hair, but that's where the similarities end. I'm nothing at all like her. I'm very sorry about your husband's death but since I played no part in it, I'd appreciate it if you'd quit blaming me for something I didn't do." Even though my pulse was beating like an out of control metronome, it was a relief to finally verbalize what had been on my mind.

Her frosty expression moderated to some degree, but she said nothing for another long minute before stating in a neutral tone, "I'm not really that surprised to hear your news." While I wouldn't describe her response as a rousing endorsement, she did not seem as irate as I'd expected. But when she focused on me, her usual expression of disapproval had an added element—intense and calculated speculation. A current of unease flowed through me when she said to Tally in an ultra-calm voice, "Tally, would you please leave us alone for a few minutes?"

He slid me an uncertain glance, his eyes seeking my permission before answering her. I nodded abruptly, then he asked, "You sure you're okay, Ma?"

"Yes. Close the door so we can have some privacy."

After he left the room, Ruth motioned for me to take a seat opposite her. I perched stiffly on the brown leather recliner, feeling more and more puzzled by her curious behavior. As the silence stretched on, I fidgeted under her critical scrutiny, finally blurting out, "I know if you were choosing a wife for Tally it probably wouldn't be me, but what you see is what you get." I managed to smile but it faded quickly when she remained stone-faced. I was at a loss as to how to approach her. Nothing seemed to work. I cleared my throat. "Tell you what. I'm willing to come to the center if you are. If you'll make just the teensiest effort to get to know me you'll find I'm not the terrible person you imagine me to be." I thought it was a pretty good speech but again she did not respond, just continued staring at me. I shifted restlessly, my stomach hollow with hunger, my short temper warming up on the launch pad. What was wrong with her? Did she want to talk or not? How did Tally and Ronda stand living with this creepy old woman? And how the hell was I going to?

"All right," I ventured, trying another tack. "I'm guessing that you're still pissed at me because of last weekend. I apologize if I upset you. I was anxious to tell you about our plans and...well, I just...look, I had no knowledge of Judge Gibbons's death at that moment. It was an honest mistake and...and if there's anything I can do to make it up to you...well, ask away."

Still she said nothing; just sat there rubbing her forefinger back and forth across her lips, her eyes cool and shrewd. I sprang to my feet. "Okay, that's it. I'm not going to play this silly game with you. You said you wanted to talk but apparently you don't."

I made it as far as the door when she cried out, "Please come back!" I hesitated, debating as to whether to keep walking or give this cantankerous, neurotic nutcase another chance. Tight-jawed, I turned back to her.

"Yes?"

"Sit down. I do want to talk," she said motioning toward the recliner. Ahhhhh! She was making me crazy. With a pang of foreboding locked in my stomach, I retraced my steps and sat down again.

"Did you mean that about making it up to me?"

Uh-oh. I hadn't expected her to latch onto my offer so soon. "Yes," I answered cautiously.

"Perhaps there is something you can do for me." The spark of cunning in her dark eyes eclipsed her usual look of blank preoccupation. "You're an investigative reporter, right?"

Her unexpected question made me hesitate. "Yes."

"And Tally says you're very, very good at it."

"Well...ah...I'm glad to hear that." Where was she going with this?

"Tell me something. How is what you do different from being a regular reporter?"

Bemused by the sudden change of subject I had to hide my surprise. "Well, I...um...kind of go beyond just fulfilling assignments. If I find a story that really interests me I dig a little deeper than a staff reporter might otherwise do and that's been known to get me into trouble on occasion." I grinned at her. "I always tell people that investigative reporters are pretty much like private detectives without the big payoff."

She didn't blink. She didn't return my smile. "I see." Appearing thoughtful, her gaze roamed the oak paneled room, skimmed past the mounted elk head, the floor to ceiling bookshelves, the colorful Navajo rug hanging above an enormous roll-top desk, and finally came to rest on a black and white photograph of two young cowboys on horseback.

"Why do you ask?"

Her eyes still fixed on the photograph, she said, "I have something I want you to do for me. If you'll agree to it, I promise that I will set aside my objections and give you and Tally my blessing."

Unreal. Tally would no doubt be thrilled to hear this news, but my instinctive reaction to her offer was guarded. "What is it that you want?" Her way-out-there demeanor disturbed me greatly but perhaps this would present the opportunity to get in her good graces.

She leaned forward, her eyes burning with a strange light. "I want you to find out who killed Riley Gibbons."

"What?"

"You heard me."

My mind swam with confusion. "Why me?"

She lifted one thin brow. "Why not you? You didn't seem to have any trouble getting in the middle of all those other stories I've read about in your newspaper. I thought you said investigative reporting is what you do?"

"It *is* what I do." Her unexpected request spiked my curiosity, but at the same instant Tally's plea that I steer clear of the Gibbons case echoed in my head. "Believe me, I'd like nothing better than to follow up on this story...but I can't."

Her eyes flashed. "Why not?"

I could have easily told her, but I wasn't anxious to share details of my private conversation with Tally. "I just...can't, that's all. Look, the sheriff's office is working on it and I'm sure in due time—"

With a sharp grunt of agitation, she rose to her feet and began to pace the room. "In time," she muttered, twisting her hands. "In time, my ass." She swung around to face me again. "I know that Duane Potts is heading up the investigation and in my opinion, the man is a moron. A week has gone by and what do they have to show for it? Nothing! Absolutely nothing." More pacing. "I've watched those TV crime shows where they talk about cold case files. If they don't find something soon that's where this one is going to end up." Her usually colorless complexion was growing flushed.

In a soothing tone, I suggested, "Okay, Ruth, calm down—"

"Don't you see? At this rate, it's unlikely they'll ever find out what happened!" Her blood pressure must have been skyrocketing because her cheeks were now ruddy and her breathing erratic. "Finding out who did this is very important to me. Riley and my Joe were closer than most brothers. He was a much loved member of our family for many years, a dear friend as well as my brother-in-law." Her voice rose to a wail. "I haven't been able to think straight since this…nightmare began. My doctor tells me I need to sleep, but I can't get it out of my mind. I can't eat, I can't concentrate on anything."

Not only did her obvious distress intrigue me, so did the fact that she seemed completely lucid for a change. She'd always given me the impression that she wasn't quite with it, that she existed in her own personal fog of misery, unaware of events that went on beyond the boundaries of the Starfire. Apparently, I was wrong.

Her eyes were pinpoints of accusation. "I don't understand why you won't help me. Apparently you didn't mean what you said about making things right."

Feeling trapped, I hedged, "I…I did mean it, but, well…unfortunately, this is the *one* thing I can't do for you."

"Well, so much for your word." Like a petulant child, she turned her back on me. "You can go now," she said with a dismissive wave of one hand.

I didn't miss the quaver in her voice. An overwhelming sense of frustration gripped me. Rats! For Tally's sake, for the sake of our future together, it was imperative that Ruth and I somehow transcend our animosity for one another and at least attempt to establish a semi-cordial relationship. Talk about dumb luck! She was handing me the opportunity to pursue the Gibbons story but how could I tackle her request without pissing off Tally? "Ruth, try to understand, it's not a matter of my not wanting to do it, far from it." I sighed with exasperation. "If you must know, Tally asked me to stay out of it."

Her head whipped around and she looked like I'd slapped her. "Listen to me," she said through gritted teeth. "It's *because* of Tally that it's imperative you find Riley's killer."

Was she serious or was this more nonsensical rambling? Whatever, the uneasy chill pooling in my belly increased markedly. "What are you talking about?"

She pulled at the loose skin on her neck. "I know this will probably sound a little crazy but what the hell? Everyone in town knows old Ruth Talverson is nuttier than a Christmas fruit cake." She hesitated another couple of seconds before adding, "I believe Riley is dead because of me."

Nuttier than a Christmas fruitcake was probably right on the money. "Why would you think that?" I asked warily, wishing I could escape from this sticky situation.

"Because God has put a curse on me."

I wanted to bolt from the room. She'd sounded perfectly rational a few minutes ago. Not now.

"Did Tally ever tell you that my mother died giving birth to me?"

"No."

A look of intense anguish shone in her eyes. "She was beautiful. And only twenty-nine years old." Her features hardened. "My father blamed me for her death. He thought I was bad luck. He wouldn't touch me, wouldn't even look at me most of the time." She swallowed hard. "When I was four years old he hung himself from the barn rafters."

I stared at her in horrified disbelief. "That's…awful. I'm sorry."

Her lips were pressed together so hard the skin around her mouth looked white. When she spoke again her voice was soft, wistful. "Maybe he was right. My grandparents took us in and within a year, my grandfather had died of pneumonia and then my brother Dan was thrown from a horse and broke his neck. Ten years ago I lost my precious sister Ginny to cancer…" She stared at the photograph again. "Lord knows I've done some things in my life I'm not proud of but I've tried my best to make things right with God." Her lips twisted with contempt. "For all my efforts God still sent that devil-bitch Stephanie to take my Joe away from me." She turned back to me and when our eyes met I felt a zing of shock run through me at the expression of panic reflected in her impassioned gaze. "And now Riley is gone. Don't you see the pattern? Everyone close to me dies." She approached me and stood so close I could smell the stench of stale cigarette smoke on her breath, in her hair. "We don't have time for the authorities to muddle through this," she cried, grabbing my wrist hard. "I'm not worried about myself but you *must* find out what happened to Riley before something terrible happens to Tally or Ronda."

"Ruth, you can't be serious."

"I've never been more serious about anything in my life. I'll drop all of my objections to this wedding if you'll do this one thing for me."

Convinced the woman was not operating on all cylinders, I maintained my cool with difficulty. It would be easy enough to verify the family history with Tally, but I found her quicksilver mood swings disconcerting. Aware that she was accustomed to manipulating people, I chose my words with care as I disengaged my arm from her talon-like grip. "I'll tell you what. I'll check around, make a few inquiries and see what I come up with. Will that make you happy?" The moment the words left my lips I wished I could have retrieved them.

Her eyes brightened perceptibly. "It will make me very happy."

"Okay then." I crossed to the door and pulled it open. "I'm going to dinner now. Are you coming?"

"No." She reached for her cigarettes, fired one up and blew out a column of acrid smoke. "I'm going to bed."

How odd. It was only a hair after six o'clock. She brushed past me to the doorway and I watched her shuffle away from me along the hallway, blue smoke trailing behind her. She opened her bedroom door and paused to glance over her shoulder. "I'll be expecting to hear from you soon." Having gotten her way, a look of supreme satisfaction replaced her look of despair. But there was something else behind her eyes that I couldn't quite put my finger on. As she closed the door to her room, I could not suppress the innate feeling that she wasn't being entirely truthful with me.

6

Standing there in the hallway, it took another couple of seconds to fully realize what I'd done. Would I never learn? What was I thinking? It had been less than two weeks since my grandiose pledge to Tally that I would hunker down at the office and steer clear of another dicey assignment. And I'd meant it...at the time. I marveled at the rapid-fire turn of events. No matter how many promises I made to myself, no matter how I tried to avoid it, trouble always seemed to find me. Even though I was stunned by the unexpected outcome, I couldn't deny the tingle of excitement I felt at the idea of jumping into this investigation. Ruth had handed me an incredible prize. If I handled things right, I rationalized, I could help restore peace and harmony to this sorrowful household. His mother's acceptance of me would no doubt come as a huge relief to Tally, but my heart shrank when I pictured his reaction to the news that there were strings attached to her sudden turnabout. Undoubtedly there would be major fireworks. I hated to have it spoil the evening, but what would be the harm in asking a few of the people involved in this case a couple of questions? After all, it *was* my job. Because of my propensity for landing myself in hot water, I feared his knee-jerk reaction might be volcanic, but hey, the circumstances were different this time, weren't they? I would be doing his mother a favor. Simple as that. It wasn't *my* idea. I agonized whether to tell him straight out or wait until later when we were alone at my house. Maybe later would be better. And to set the mood, perhaps tonight was the night to model the sexy black lace teddy I'd purchased online a couple of weeks ago. Throw in the fishnet stockings and my new pair of high heels and that just might mollify him. I started in surprise when Tally suddenly stuck his head around the doorway.

"I was wondering how long you were going to be in there." He pinned me with an expectant look. "Well...what happened?"

I beamed him a megawatt smile. "The short version is I apologized to her and she's given us her blessing."

The expression of admiration spreading across his face made me want to cry. Frap! Who was I kidding? Black teddy or not, he was going to be royally ticked off.

"I'm impressed," he said with a slow nod of approval. "You were in there so long I was beginning to wonder if you'd done each other in."

I walked towards him, deadpanning, "I had to promise her our firstborn child."

He chuckled. "What did you say that made her change her mind?"

"I'm not sure. I think I won her over with my charming personality."

He cocked a skeptical brow. "Really?" He glanced behind me. "Where is she?"

"Gone to bed." In an effort to deter further questions, I hooked my arm through his elbow and led him into the den. "Hey, before we eat I want to ask you something."

"What?"

I pointed to the photo on the wall. "I know the man on the left is your father. Who's the other guy?"

He frowned at me as if I should know. "Riley. I think they were both in their mid-twenties when that particular picture was taken."

I pulled away and stood under the photograph, studying the shadowed faces of the two dark-haired young men squinting into bright sunlight. Joe Talverson had been a nice-looking man but Riley Gibbons could have passed for a movie star. "Tell me about Riley."

"Why do you want to know?" he asked from behind, a note of caution entering his voice.

I swung around. "Just curious. Your mother is pretty depressed about his death."

There was no mistaking the gleam of suspicion forming in his brown eyes. "You going to tell me what she said to you?"

I sweetened my tone and slipped my elbow through his. "Can we talk about it after dinner? I'm starving."

His expression remained quizzical, but he did not press me further. Elated yet edgy about Tally's possibly explosive reaction to my decision, I still managed to put away three helpings of Ronda's spicy chicken enchilada casserole topped with guacamole and garnished with a mound of chopped lettuce and tomatoes. While we ate, through a series of judiciously worded questions, I was able to verify Ruth's version of the family history.

"Unfortunate, but true," Ronda remarked with a slight sniff, piling a dome of sour cream on her wedge of casserole. "Bad luck does seem to follow her around. She's always had a real 'woe is me' attitude with a capital W." She arched a guarded glance into the hallway and lowered her voice to just above a whisper. "Tally and I have lived with her moodiness our whole lives and we've decided that she's not really happy unless she has something to complain about."

Grimacing, Tally chimed in, "Seems like she lives under this little black cloud. Instead of enjoying life she spends all her time waiting for the next shoe to fall. In her case it seems to be a self-fulfilling prophecy."

"Yeah," Ronda concurred with an emphatic nod. "Riley's death is just another piece in her personal puzzle of doom."

It was the opening I'd been waiting for. "I notice neither of you refer to him as Uncle Riley. Why is that?"

"Well, technically speaking he hasn't been our uncle for over ten years," Ronda stated. "He and Dad always stayed in touch, but he didn't come around as often after Aunt Ginny died."

"So...what kind of a person was he?"

They exchanged a protracted stare before Ronda spoke. "We were just talking earlier about how bizarre it is that he of all people would die in such a mysterious manner. If it had been someone else he'd have been fascinated with the situation."

"What do you mean?"

"He was a huge mystery buff. Just devoured whodunits and a lot of times he'd pass them along to us."

I grinned. "I can relate to that. Mysteries are my first choice of reading material too."

Ronda gave me a knowing look. "I'd be surprised if you'd said otherwise. Anyway," she continued, "he got a big kick out of attending these murder mystery weekends that are sometimes held at old hotels, especially the ones that are rumored to be haunted. You know, where all the guests get a list of clues to follow and the one who solves the mystery wins something."

Tapping a forefinger to his lips, Tally added thoughtfully, "I think one of the major reasons he bought Hidden Springs was his fascination with the old hotel's history."

Ronda's gaze turned inward. "Yeah, that and the fact that he loved the outdoors. Aunt Ginny wasn't much for camping, but he'd go off for days at a time. He mentioned that the Hidden Springs property is adjacent to a wilderness area so I'm sure that played a part in his decision to buy it too. It's such a shame. I always liked Riley. He was…a unique guy."

"How so?"

"Well…how should I phrase this," she mused, munching on a tortilla chip. "I guess you'd call him a Renaissance man. Besides all the outdoor activities, he loved classical music, he was a gourmet cook and in addition to mystery novels he loved history and philosophy. He was always repeating lines of poetry and he was well-known for quoting some of the great philosophers when he handed down sentences in court." She giggled. "Some newspaper reporter at the *Arizona Republic* dubbed him the 'proverb judge.' I'm sure him citing Ralph Waldo Emerson was lost on most of the people who stood before his bench."

Tally interjected, "What puzzled me was why he and Dad were such good friends."

"Why do you say that?" I asked, wondering if I dared eat a fourth helping of the casserole. Better not.

He hitched one shoulder slightly. "Because it didn't seem like they had much in common besides their mutual interest in ranching, hunting and books. Our dad wasn't the easiest guy in the world to get along with." His sheepish grin was revealing. Ginger had regaled me with stories of Joe Talverson's gruff personality and fiery temper. Except for an occasional outburst Tally seemed fairly even-tempered, but there were times I could see glimpses of Ruth's brooding behavior.

"Did you interact much with him?"

"Sure," Ronda put in, popping another chip into her mouth. "We saw Aunt Ginny a lot more than him, but when he did visit he was always really nice to us. He'd bring books and toys. Oh, and he loved pulling practical jokes on us."

"How did he and your dad meet?" I asked her.

"In elementary school. After his family moved here from Prescott, Riley's dad bought the old Circle B Ranch and he also worked at the feed store. Ma was in the same grade as his sister, Charlotte, only a year behind Dad and Riley."

I raised a brow. "Oh? I didn't realize they'd all been acquainted for that long."

Tally grinned and pushed away from the table. "Not a difficult task back then. Ranching families all knew each other. Castle Valley was just a wide spot in the road and there was only one school. Aunt Ginny was three years his senior so it was kind of a surprise to everyone when Riley married her."

Ronda eyes grew wistful. "Not to me. She was really pretty...and fun. She loved kids. Always had a ready

71

smile. Gosh, some of my best memories are of us playing cards and board games together. We'll have to show you pictures. She's the spitting image of our maternal grandmother."

"You might find this interesting," Tally interposed. "When Riley decided to study law after high school he and Aunt Ginny moved out East. Guess where?"

I shrugged.

"Philadelphia."

"No kidding?"

"Yep. Apparently he gained quite a reputation in the prosecutor's office for having an unusually high conviction rate."

Ronda said, "Aunt Ginny bragged that he was the darling of the local media and very popular in Philadelphia social circles. I guess the women liked him a lot too."

Remembering Riley's dark good looks I didn't doubt that. "How long ago did he live there?"

Humor shimmered in Tally's brown eyes. "Long before your time at the *Inquirer*. Let's see…you were probably all of eight years old."

"Things were sailing along great for them when Aunt Ginny developed breast cancer," Ronda inserted, rising to clear the dishes from the table. "She wanted to be closer to Ma so they moved to Phoenix. She was in remission for five or six years before the cancer came back. When that happened Ma insisted Aunt Ginny come and live here at the ranch so she could take care of her. It was a pretty awful time. After she died Ma was so depressed she didn't leave her room for months. Riley stayed in Phoenix after that and we only heard from him a couple of times a year until he bought Hidden Springs. I think we saw more of him during this past year than in the previous ten."

"So, you've met his new wife?"

Ronda said, "We stopped and talked with Riley and La Donna at the Iron Skillet a few times, we saw them together with Charlotte at the rodeo last spring and then again at the Gold Dust Days parade."

"What do you think about their separation and him moving his girlfriend into the hotel?" I watched them both carefully for their reactions.

"I didn't even know about that until a couple of days ago," Ronda murmured, looking uncomfortable.

Tally shook his head slowly, his expression introspective. "Riley never hid the fact that he enjoyed the company of women, but...even for him that kind of behavior was surprising."

"Did you also hear about the gold coins missing from his safe deposit box?"

Tally's gaze narrowed with suspicion. "Why are you asking so many questions about Riley?"

Might as well ease him into it. "Well, partly because I'm just curious and partly because your mother seems...exceptionally upset by what happened to him."

"We're all upset about it," Ronda remarked while stacking plates in the dishwasher. She paused and turned somber eyes to me. "It's not every day that a person you've known all your life dies in such an awful manner. It bugs me that nobody seems to have any idea who may have done it or why."

"No, not every day. But that reminds me," I said, returning my attention to Tally. "Did you know a guy named Randy Moorehouse was back in town?"

Dead silence for a few seconds before he answered gravely, "Yeah, I heard."

"Why didn't you mention it to me?"

"I didn't think it would matter one way or the other."

"Well, it didn't until Tugg filled me in on his background. Does it bother you knowing he's living here in Castle Valley again?"

He hesitated slightly. "I don't know."

"You think he may have had something to do with the judge's death?"

"Don't know. He certainly had sufficient reason to hate him."

"Especially if he was innocent of the charges against him."

A little shrug. "We'll probably never know."

"Tugg said you two have known each other quite awhile."

"Yeah," Tally said, his eyes reconnecting with Ronda's. "We went to school with him and his sister Rulinda. Their mom, Jolene, ran the flower shop up until last year when she had a mild stroke. They had a pretty tough life."

"How so?"

Ronda jumped in. "They all got regular beatings from their old man before he drank himself into an early grave. Rulinda was a little rough around the edges, but Randy, he always had an in-your-face attitude."

Even though it was a serious subject, I couldn't help asking, "I have to know. Why was he called Pig Pen?"

Tally's irreverent smile lightened the somber mood. "Probably because he smelled like one."

Ronda wrinkled her nose in agreement. "He's not kidding. I don't know why, but the guy always smelled to high heaven, like he mainlined raw garlic and onions."

"It was so bad nobody wanted to sit next to him in class," Tally concurred, passing me a wry grin. "Either he never bathed, never heard of deodorant, or both. Whatever, it earned him that distinction."

"Did people call him that to his face?"

"Nobody was that stupid. The guy was built like a sumo wrestler and he always carried a knife in one boot. People gave him a wide berth. After he joined that outlaw biker gang most folks weren't too surprised when he was arrested for hacking up his girlfriend." He paused, looking reflective. "Throughout the trial and afterwards he maintained that one of the other members was responsible for the crime."

"Have you seen him since his release?"

The frown lines between his brows deepened. "No, and why do you want to know? Kendall, what's going on?"

Oops! I'd crossed the line with one too many questions. Fortunately, he was distracted when the phone rang. Ronda rose to answer it. "Yeah, that would be great," I heard her say. "We just finished with dinner so come any time." She cradled the receiver and turned towards us. "Lucy's on her way over with a movie if you guys are interested in watching it with us."

Oh yeah, that's what I wanted to do. Spend my evening in the company of a woman who hated my guts. I wondered what her reaction would be when she got a load of my engagement ring. It troubled me that not only was she Ronda's best friend, she regularly visited the Starfire Ranch to ride her horse that she boarded. From what I could tell she still had her sights set on Tally and after the wedding we were bound to run into each other on the property. Not a happy thought.

I pushed away from the table and stood. "Thanks, but I've got a ton of laundry to do and a full day ahead of me tomorrow."

Ronda gave a careless shrug. "Just thought I'd ask. What about you, Tally?"

"Nope. I've got to call Ted back and finish some paperwork before I head over to Kendall's place." He smiled at me, a wicked glimmer in his eyes. "We haven't had much quality time together these past couple of weeks and we've got some heavy duty celebrating to do."

Ronda grinned knowingly. "Gotcha." To me she asked, "So, how'd you like your engagement present?"

I clapped my hands together. "She's fabulous! I can't *wait* to ride her." It dawned on me then that the pressure was on to find an equally unique gift for Tally. How the heck was I going to top a horse? At the kitchen door he helped me into my jacket then grabbed the collar and pulled me close to him. We exchanged a smoldering look and I whispered, "I'll see you later, big guy. And I'm serious about making sure this will be a night you won't soon forget."

"You'll get no argument from me." His fervent kiss sent a fiery tingle all the way down to the tips of my toes. He drew back and said in a low husky tone, "I'll get this work done as fast as I can and be on your doorstep no later than ten."

Good. That would give me a couple of hours to tidy up the place, chill a bottle of wine and relax in a leisurely bubble bath. I gave him a coy wink. "I'll be waiting."

I pushed outside into the icy night air and literally skipped down the porch steps, my spirits soaring. I felt more optimistic than I had in weeks. Things were finally going my way. As I drove away from the Starfire, I twirled the diamond ring on my finger as I weighed my options. I could approach Tally tonight regarding Ruth's plea for help and fire up a whopping argument or I could keep quiet and enjoy an evening of blissful romance. The decision was not difficult. My news could darn well keep until tomorrow. I couldn't wait to get back into the game again. After weeks of idling in neutral my imagination kicked into overdrive as the list of story possibilities spread out before me like a stretch of wide open road. First on the agenda would be to visit the crime scene at Hidden Springs. After that, there was certainly no shortage of potential suspects awaiting my cross examination—from Randy Moorehouse to Winston Pendahl to La Donna Gibbons and Marissa Van Steenholm—plus all the enticing unknowns which would include painstaking research into Judge Gibbons's past court cases, chiefly those involving homicides.

As soon as I reached my place I parked the truck and hurried inside, even though it would have been nice to linger outdoors and savor the desert panorama illuminated under the silvery light of the winter moon. I had slightly less than two hours to get everything prepared.

Marmalade greeted me by throwing herself down at my feet. She rolled onto her back demanding to be noticed. I stooped to rub her cream-colored tummy. "Hey, baby girl, I'm back." Like a puppy, she followed me from room to room as I scurried about setting the stage for what I hoped would be an unforgettable romantic interlude.

The blinking light on my phone caught my attention and I quickly scrolled through the list of numbers. Oh boy. Mom had called again. We'd been playing phone tag for over a week now. And there was another number I didn't recognize with a Pennsylvania area code. I set the phone in the base. I'd deal with the calls tomorrow. After starting a load of laundry, I lit a fire in the fireplace. Then, I strategically positioned jars of scented candles in the living room and bedroom, tidied up the kitchen, slid a bottle of wine into the refrigerator and finally immersed myself in a steaming tub filled with peach scented bubble bath where I allowed myself a full half hour to unwind from the day's events.

My skin pink from soaking, I dabbed on perfume, freshened my makeup, applied red lipstick and slipped into the lacy teddy, thigh high stockings and four inch heels. The results were spectacular if I do say so myself.

Wrapping myself in the sheer black negligee, I could not refrain from smiling as I imagined the look on Tally's face. I arranged my long curly hair in an alluring style and appraised the final results in the full-length mirror. Yep. Pretty hot stuff. I looked like an ad right out of Victoria's Secret. It was going to be so great.

My heels clicking on the tile floor, I rushed around lighting the candles. Then I stood back and surveyed my handiwork. Perfect. Everything was perfect. I'd no sooner turned on soft music and switched off the lamp than I saw headlights lighting the driveway. Nine-fifty. Right on time.

My heart pounding in anticipation, I draped myself in a suggestive position on the couch and waited. And then I waited some more. He was sure taking his sweet time getting to the door.

When I finally heard his light knock I called out, "Come and get it, cowboy!" After several seconds of silence, I wondered if he'd heard me. "I said come in," I repeated in a lilting tone.

Over the music, I heard a muffled, "Kendall?" and noticed the knob turning. Why didn't he just use his key?

Assuming that he'd forgotten it, I rose from the couch, struck a sexy pose and whipped the door open.

"Hey, cowboy, what do you think of thi...?" The words died on my lips. Great shockwaves of mortification rolled over me as I stared in disbelief into the stunned blue eyes of my ex-fiancé Grant Jamerson.

7

"What do I think?" Grant answered, slowly breaking into a mischievously lecherous grin, his wide-eyed gaze skimming over my slightly clad body. "That I've died and gone straight to heaven. Talk about an unexpected welcome. Zowee!"

Dumbfounded, I was unable to formulate a proper response, or any response at all for that matter. I clutched the see-through gown tightly around my middle as if that would do any good.

"You sure weren't easy to find. What are you doing out here in the middle of friggin' nowhere?" A hint of petulance underscored his words.

I finally located my absent voice. "I think a better question is what the hell are *you* doing here?"

An odd look marched across his clean-cut features. "Two reasons. Officially, I'm here to do a piece on Judge Riley Gibbons's funeral next week."

"Why?"

"Because he used to live in Philadelphia."

"So? That was twenty years ago."

"True. But apparently he was kind of a legend in the DA's office, ran with the muckety muck of high society and was on the fast track for governor." He shot me a disarming grin. "But probably more importantly, he and my new editor were still close personal friends."

"Okaaaay. But, why didn't you let me know you were coming?"

"I tried."

That shut me up for a minute. Damn. That must have been the number on my caller ID I hadn't recognized, and I didn't check the messages. Eying him suspiciously, I pressed, "And the second reason you're here?"

He hesitated, his intense gaze boring into mine. "To see you."

Immediately on guard, I stiffened. "Why?"

"To find out what it'll take to get you to forgive me."

My emotions seesawed wildly as snippets of our white-hot love affair danced in my head, only to be tempered by the crushing humiliation caused by his infidelity. "Forgive you? After what you did to me? Why should I?" Unable to suppress the sarcasm in my tone, I tacked on, "And how is the lovely Elise these days?"

Appearing chastened, he ruffled his pale blonde hair. "If it makes you feel better, we're not seeing each other anymore."

"What a pity."

"Look, I don't blame you one bit for being pissed at me. I'll be the first to admit that I acted like a complete, and I mean complete, shitheel—no assembly or parts required."

"You got my vote on that."

His eyes softened into that irresistible, little boy look that I'd known so well. "If you'll let me, I'd like to try to make it up to you."

"I don't believe this."

His expression became truly angelic. "I mean it. Losing you was the stupidest mistake of my life. I'm sorry as hell that I hurt you."

Unable to muster a reply, I just stood there blinking at him in amazement.

Again, he flashed his award-winning smile, the one that used to make me melt. "My mother sends her best wishes."

I nodded in silence.

"You did know she had hip replacement surgery last week, didn't you?"

"No, I didn't. Is she all right?" I wondered if that was why my mother had been trying to reach me.

"She's doing okay." He jammed his hands into his jacket pocket. "Aren't you going to invite me in?"

"Absolutely not! In fact, you have to leave. Now. Go!"

He looked crushed. "Oh, come on, Kendall. I've just come three thousand miles to see you. I've been driving in circles for over an hour in this godforsaken empty desert hunting for your place…" he paused, adding dryly, "No surprise it's called Lost Canyon Road."

"Grant—"

"Have a heart. I'm starving, I'm tired…and it's pretty nippy out here." With naughty observation he arched one perfect blonde brow. "Don't tell me you're not freezing your buns off."

Actually, the scalding embarrassment was keeping me toasty, but when headlights suddenly slashed the darkness, panic speared my stomach. Oh, shit! Tally! What was he going to think of me standing here dressed like a French hooker talking to my old boyfriend? For interminable seconds I stood motionless, squinting into the glare of lights before he cut the engine, stepped out, slammed the door and marched towards us. It was difficult to envision a more awkward scenario.

"Hey," I began, smiling sheepishly as he reached the front step, "guess who just showed up out of the blue?"

The moon, now high overhead, was bright enough to easily see Tally's expression of incredulity. Critically, he scrutinized my mode of dress before turning toward Grant. "I have no idea."

"Grant Jamerson," he said breezily with a sunny smile, extending his hand. "Investigative reporter for the *Philadelphia Inquirer*."

Tally fired me a startled look as his name registered. "Bradley Talverson," he replied, his voice devoid of warmth.

Blue eyes appraised brown ones as the two men shook hands warily. It was one of those supremely embarrassing moments where I would have been elated if the ground had opened and swallowed me. "Wait thirty seconds and then you can both come inside," I announced, slamming the door.

As fast as I could manage in the high heels on the tile floor, I sprinted across the candle-lit living room to the safe haven of my bedroom. Standing behind the closed door, I expelled a long breath. Suddenly shivering all over, I stripped off the flimsy garments while attempting to collect my wits. Replaying the inconceivable scene over and over in my mind brought tears of humiliation to my eyes. How the hell was I going to handle this thorny predicament?

Curled in her usual spot on my pillow, Marmalade woke up, yawned and stared at me curiously. I'd begun to learn that cats are amazingly intuitive creatures and can sense a change of mood in their humans. "I am in deep guano, my little friend," I murmured to her as I pulled on jeans and a sweatshirt. What had possessed Grant, whom I hadn't heard a word from in eleven months, to pull such a stunt? After our heart-wrenching breakup and my hasty exit from Philadelphia last spring, I had not expected to see or hear from him again. It was curious timing for him to show up at my doorstep now...but then maybe not. I suspected there was a connection between his sudden appearance and the note I'd written to his mother last week. Had the two of them joined forces with *my* mother to try and thwart my marriage plans? The timing was more than a little suspicious.

My hand on the doorknob, I inhaled a few deep breaths, hoping to restore a modicum of composure. The thought of having to go out and face both men sent my stomach into an uproar. More than anything I wished I could just stay in my bedroom and never come out again. Unfortunately, the reality was that I had no choice but to deal with the situation. Dragging my feet, I returned to the living room to find that Tally had turned off the music, extinguished the candles and switched on every light—a sure sign our romantic rendezvous was dead in the water. Grant stood with his back to the fireplace. Neither man looked happy. Still shaken by the unexpected events, I wasn't sure how to proceed. But we were all mature, civilized adults, right? I should be able to diffuse the situation. "So? Can I get either of you anything to drink?"

Simultaneously, Grant answered yes and Tally no. They exchanged an emotionally charged glance and I cringed inwardly at my poor attempt at diffusing.

"Actually, if it wouldn't be too inconvenient," Grant said to me, maintaining a matter-of-fact tone, "I was sort of hoping maybe I could stay here tonight."

"What makes you think that would be even a remote possibility?" Tally growled, his face as obstinate as an angry bulldog.

Grant raised a defensive hand. "No harm intended. It's not my fault you guys have only three motels in your little burg and it just so happens they're all full. Something about a big art and craft show starting tomorrow," he concluded with a small shrug. "Anyway, there won't be a room available until Monday afternoon."

"Just how long are you planning to stay?" Tally inquired, his jaw muscles hardening.

"I don't know. A couple of days, possibly a week." I could tell he was baiting Tally, who slid me a 'so what's the deal?' look. We both knew Grant was telling the truth about the shortage of motels in town and it seemed ungracious to insist that he leave now.

"We have plans this evening," Tally informed him with a tone of finality, making no attempt to hide his annoyance. I signaled him with my eyes to cool it. After all, this was a man who'd held a very important part in my life at one time and there was no cause to be boorish.

Looking victimized, Grant directed his gaze at me. "I was thinking maybe I could crash on your couch, but if it's going to create a huge problem I'll head back to Phoenix and see if I can find a place to stay."

A decisive nod from Tally. "Good plan."

Arizona was heavily into the snowbird season and he'd be downright lucky if he could find a room at this late hour, considering the fact that there was a huge convention, a car show and a national marathon in town. Mammoth fireworks would erupt if Tally knew the second reason Grant was here. Nevertheless, it seemed petty to send him packing at this hour. "That won't be necessary." Shrinking beneath Tally's flinty glare I said, "I'll be glad to make you a sandwich and you can stay here tonight, but you'll have to make other arrangements for tomorrow." I stepped beside Tally and took his hand. "We both have to get up early so—"

Grant's grateful smile was nothing short of endearing. "Thanks. I'll be on my way first thing in the morning." He rubbed his palms together. "Okay then, I'll get my bag."

The front door had no sooner clicked shut than Tally took my elbow and swiftly steered me into the kitchen. Exasperation ruled his face. "Well, you were right. This isn't a night I'll soon forget." I wouldn't either. "What's the big idea inviting him to stay?"

"Take it easy. It's just for one night. You're going to be here too—"

"You better believe it."

"Okay then, so what's the big deal?"

"I don't want him here."

I frowned at him. "What would you suggest? Should I ask him to sleep outside in his car?"

"I don't have a problem with that."

"Oh, come on, Tally, don't be silly. It's freezing."

Eyes narrowed to slits, he griped, "You think I don't know what he's up to?"

He was more intuitive than I'd given him credit for. I turned away to pull lunchmeat and bread from the refrigerator. "I can't control what's in *his* head, but there's nothing for you to worry about on my account. I'm so over him."

"Really? Well, you'd never know it judging by that little show you put on, strutting around in that skimpy outfit."

I edged him the evil eye and slapped sliced turkey onto the bread. Without much conscious thought, I added mayonnaise, lettuce and sweet relish, just the way Grant always liked it. And that stopped me cold. The feel of Tally's eyes drilling into my back alerted me to the fact that he'd also noticed the personal touch. I turned to him feeling slightly defensive. "That little show, as you put it, was for your benefit and you know it. Who else would I be expecting at this time of night?"

He considered my explanation for a couple of seconds before adding, "I don't buy the story that he's merely here to cover Riley's funeral."

Oh brother. If Ginger was here, she'd pronounce this a fine kettle of fish. My gut instincts told me I should level with him right now regarding Grant's dubious intentions *and* my decision to move forward with Ruth's request. But I knew him well enough to know the outcome of such a confession and I sure didn't want to start a rip-roaring argument in front of Grant. "Us sniping at each other won't solve anything. The situation is what it is." I sliced the sandwich with force and plopped it onto a plate before swinging back to face him again. "The last thing on my mind tonight was having a fight with you so let's just call a truce. The fact is you're the one I love, you're the one I'm going to marry and you're the one who'll be spending the night with me. Grant will be out of here in the morning." I walked over to him and planted a kiss on his unresponsive lips. "So, quit your bitchin'."

He started to respond, but clamped his mouth shut when the front door opened. I don't know why, but the sound of Grant's familiar whistle made my insides tense. Warning bells clanged in my ears as my heart remembered how deeply I'd once cared for him. In my wildest dreams I never expected to be caught in the middle of such a conundrum.

Grant appeared in the doorway announcing in a genial voice, "Can I join the party?"

When we both responded in stony silence the smile fell off his face. I pulled a soda from the refrigerator and set it plus the sandwich on the table. I pointed to the hallway. "The bathroom is the first door on the left. I'll get some bedding." I wished now I'd gotten around to cleaning out the spare bedroom, which was piled high with boxes I'd never unpacked and the bed was buried under a stack of stuff I'd planned to get around to sorting through some day—and that some day was almost upon me since I had out-of-town company coming soon.

I had to hand it to Grant. He was doing a superb job of ignoring Tally's 'I'd like to punch your lights out' expression. "You guys are really helping me out of a jam," he said, suddenly solemn, "and um…I'm sorry if I spoiled your evening." He was making a heroic effort to be cordial, but when Tally made no effort to reply, I decided it would be best to separate them as soon as possible.

"We're going to hit the hay now." I didn't miss his pointed expression as his eyes strayed to my engagement ring. Even though I'd convinced myself that my feelings for him were nonexistent, as Tally and I headed towards my bedroom, I couldn't help but feel a measure of empathy for him.   It was also disconcerting to admit that the characteristics that had drawn me to Grant in the first place—his charming personality, Nordic good looks, sunny disposition, quirky sense of humor and zest for adventure—were still strangely appealing.

8

Sleep was elusive that night. It was quite some time before Tally finally drifted off to sleep, and even as I cuddled close, listening to his even breathing, I couldn't shut off my brain as memories of my year-long romance with Grant paraded endlessly through my mind. Sensing my distress, Marmalade decided to park herself on my chest. Her steady rattling purr, reminiscent of my grandmother's old sewing machine, combined with the rhythmic kneading of her razor sharp claws contributed to my restiveness. After hours of trying to lie still so I wouldn't wake Tally or the cat, I finally eased Marmalade onto my pillow, rose and crossed the room to stand near the window. The extreme blackness of the clear winter sky accentuated the radiance of the stars. Indeed, the Big Dipper looked close enough to reach up and touch as it hung winking above the dark outlines of those magnificent piles of rock and dirt that make up Arizona's mountain ranges. There appeared to be no hint of the storm that had been predicted, but the hazy corona ringing the moon as it edged towards the western horizon heralded a weather change. The elation I'd felt earlier in the evening diminished even further as I continued to second-guess myself. What was I thinking? Even if I were successful in discovering some piece of evidence that would help track down Riley Gibbons's murderer would it really change how Ruth felt about me? Unlikely. No matter what I did would she continue to be a source of friction between Tally and me? Very likely. That grim realization had me looking back with fondness on my fun-filled involvement with Grant. None of the tensions that punctuated my relationship with Tally had existed between us and on top of that I'd truly adored his mother. I wished the evening could be a do-over so I could back out of my agreement with Ruth. But envisioning that confrontation seemed far worse than sucking it up and confessing to Tally. Backed into a corner of my own making and super annoyed with life in general, I returned to bed and slept fitfully for a couple of hours.

I awoke in the pre-dawn hours head throbbing, stomach icy and feeling worse than if I'd not slept at all. I slipped from the bed and tiptoed to the bathroom. A couple of aspirin stilled the headache and a hot shower revived me somewhat. As I pulled on slacks and an emerald green turtleneck, I heard Marmalade's plaintive mewing outside the door. I cracked it open and lifted her into my arms after she squirted inside. "Hey, baby love," I whispered, nuzzling her face against mine, "want some breakfast? I need coffee. Gallons of it."

The digital clock glowed six-thirty as I crept past Grant and slid the pocket door to the kitchen shut behind me. After feeding Marmalade I brewed coffee, poured a cup and then opened the window over the sink, welcoming the sweet smell of a newly minted day and the refreshing sensation of cold air caressing my face. The faint halo of aqua-gray glowing above Castle Rock blotted out the stars as dawn slowly siphoned the darkness from the sky. It's funny how daylight helps diminish the demons of the night. Within a half an hour I had fried up a pan of bacon and was scrambling eggs when I heard the door slide open behind me. I turned and smiled a greeting as Tally walked in, searching his eyes for signs that his black mood had improved. "Everything okay?"

Cognizant of the underlying meaning of my words, his pensive gaze was steady. "So far."

"Want some breakfast?"

His glance strayed to the wall clock as he pulled out a chair. "Sure, but I don't have much time and I'm not leaving until *he's* out of here," he announced, thumbing over his shoulder, "so you'd better wake his ass up."

Okaaaaay. He was obviously still in a snit. On the one hand his protective stance was deeply flattering but another part of me wanted to fire back, "Don't tell me what to do!" Instead, I bit my lip and set his breakfast in front of him. He'd get no more ammunition from me. "What time do you think you'll be finished with your buyers today?"

"Don't know for sure. I'll be tied up most of the day and probably a good portion of tomorrow."

"Are we still on for dinner tonight?"

He shrugged. "Depends. I'll have to call you later."

Yeah, he was still pouting big time. "Okay, well, I'll have my cell phone on. Let's plan for six o'clock at Angelina's." He nodded and I added quickly, "I hope you can make it because I need to talk with you about something."

"What?" The angst in his tone revealed his unease.

Quick to reassure him, I soothed, "Relax. It pertains to a couple of things your mother said to me last night."

"Just tell me now."

I hesitated. "It's too long and too complicated. I'd rather wait until…we won't be interrupted."

Before he could question me further I walked into the living room and roused Grant, who complained loudly about having to get up at such an ungodly hour. Tally extended the coldest of shoulders when he finally entered the kitchen. But true to his curious nature, Grant refused to be ignored and launched into a series of questions about Arizona—the weather, population growth, real estate and job opportunities—while he dug into his bacon and eggs. It didn't take long for the conversation to come around to Riley Gibbons. "Got any ideas on who might have taken the old guy out in such a dramatic fashion?" he inquired, looking straight at me while piling jelly onto his toast. "You must be all over this story."

Tally and I exchanged a pointed look. Grant would be blown away by my answer. What would he think when I told him that the eager young reporter who'd latched onto her mentor like a scorpion to its prey to hungrily absorb his techniques for top-rate investigative journalism, was not? "Umm, actually I've got someone else assigned to this story." Reacting to his quizzical stare I hurriedly added, "Just so you know, that old guy, as you call him, was Tally's uncle." Even to me the excuse sounded lame but I think Grant was perceptive enough to get my drift.

He flicked a momentary look at Tally as if to affirm his suspicions before saying, "No kidding? Well…um, sorry about that." He hesitated ever so slightly. "But, because of that, I'm sure you're in close communication with the authorities regarding the case's progress."

I knew Grant well enough to know he was on a fishing expedition and it was obvious by Tally's taciturn

93

expression that he had no interest in taking the bait, on or off the record. "Yep," was his only response. He caught my eye and tapped his watch to signal the time.

"Grant, I hate to hurry you along but we both have appointments this morning," I said, rising to pile the dishes in the sink.

"Oh, right." He popped the last bite of toast into his mouth. "I don't suppose you know of someplace close around here I could stay a couple of nights since Hotel O'Dell isn't available?"

His little joke fell flat and Tally fixed him with an arctic look that effectively closed the door on any thoughts he might have of spending a second night.

I said, "There are a couple of B&B's in town and one in Yarnell."

"Yarnell? How far is that?"

"About twenty-five miles from here."

"I'll check 'em out." Then he paused and frowned. "Say, um, I read a couple of pieces about the judge's death on your paper's website before I left Philly and one of them mentioned that he'd bought a place called Hidden Springs. Is that far from here?"

Again, I felt like a total doofus on the outside looking in. "Well, to be honest I don't know. I've...never been there."

"Really? Now that's surprising."

I didn't miss his mild sarcasm. In his eyes I was falling down on the job. The slight twitching at the corners of his mouth made it hard to resist making a face at him.

Tally grabbed his hat and coat from the rack. "Why do you want to know?"

Grant gave an innocent shrug. "Welllll…I'm here to cover the man's funeral and I'm curious to learn something about his life and maybe his death."

"We're both in a hurry," Tally said, bristling, "and neither of us has time for chitchat."

Grant's expression turned infuriatingly earnest. "Oh, sorry. Hey, I really appreciate your hospitality." I didn't miss the "thanks for nothing" inference in his voice and I'm sure Tally didn't either. The two men were staring at each other in defiance when the phone rang. Glad for any distraction I glanced at the caller ID, recognized Ginger's cell number and grabbed up the receiver.

"Well, good mornin', sunshine," she chirped in my ear.

"Hey. What's up?"

"I don't suppose you could do me a little bitty favor?"

I could tell by Tally's scowl that he was itching to go but had no intention of leaving me alone with Grant. "What do you need?"

"Dummy me, I went off an' left the moneybag with all the change we're gonna need for the show in my desk. I'd sure appreciate it if you could stop by an' pick it up before comin' over?"

"Okay, but it's going make me a little later getting to the fairgrounds. Is that going to work?"

"Well, there ain't a whole lot of choice since I'm already here gittin' ready to set up."

"Where's the moneybag?"

"In the top right hand drawer."

I glanced over at Tally standing with his hand on the doorknob twirling his hat with obvious impatience.

"Ginger, I have to go now. What's your space number again?"

"C-11." She giggled. "You won't have much trouble finding us. Just follow the heehawin'."

"The what?"

"Heehawin'. We ain't but a stone's throw from the corral where they'll be holdin' the BLM wild burro auction later on this afternoon."

I couldn't help but smile. "All right, I'll see you there." I hung up, tossed the palm-sized camera into my purse and shouldered it before following Tally and Grant out the door.

A light wind from the northwest was spreading gauzy white clouds across the normally pristine blue sky. Tally and I climbed into our respective pickups while Grant yelled, "Thanks again," as he unlocked his white compact rental car. I couldn't shake the sinking sensation that had settled in my chest. The whole weird state of affairs still had a dreamlike feel, as if everything were happening to someone else. Our three vehicles caravanned along Lost Canyon Road and at the intersection to the paved road, Tally saluted me with two fingers and turned north. Grant and I headed south. Traffic seemed unusually heavy and I attributed that to the Hanson House dedication and the craft show. I glanced in the rearview mirror and noticed that Grant was talking on his cell phone. We'd just passed through the only stoplight in town when I signaled a turn and swung onto Mariposa Lane. Grant sounded the horn and waved farewell. I waved back, glad to be disconnected from the uncomfortable situation, but intuitive enough to know that it was probably far from over.

With great difficultly, I shoved the current state of affairs to the back of my mind in an effort to concentrate on the task at hand. Both sides of the narrow street were already lined with cars, so I was forced to park several blocks away and hike back to the Hanson House, a stately turn-of-the-century Victorian, and one of six such structures of its type remaining in Castle Valley. Festivities were already underway as I strolled along the walkway beneath a colorful banner that snapped in the uneven wind. Among the populace already assembled, I spotted Thena Rodenborn, prominent town socialite and publisher of the *Sun,* standing on the spacious wrap-around porch chatting with another woman. Serving as the president of the local historical society, she looked every bit the part of a nineteenth century dowager replete in a navy-blue high-collared gown, all but a few tendrils of her white hair gathered beneath an ornate hat festooned with silk flowers—a picture of grace and panache. She was also shrewd enough to recognize a good photo op since she would be officiating the ribbon-cutting ceremony due to begin in half an hour. She caught my eye and gestured for me to join her. Poised, effervescent, and intelligent, this exceptional lady never ceased to impress me. She appeared to have taken a real liking to me, which was extraordinary considering that a tragic and unintended consequence of completing my first assignment last spring had been my involvement in the inadvertent death of her only son.

"Kendall, how lovely to see you this morning." She reached out to grasp one of my hands as I came up the final stair. "This is a truly significant event for Castle Valley. I trust you brought your camera," she inquired, a benevolent smile highlighting her refined features.

I patted my purse. "Got my new digital one thanks to your generosity."

"Oh my dear, it's hardly worth mentioning."

But her philanthropic efforts *were* worth mentioning. Besides spearheading a host of fundraising events that benefited many of the charitable organizations in town, she had stepped forward and single handedly rescued the newspaper from oblivion. The infusion of funds had paid for the major remodeling project and purchased all new state of the art computer equipment enabling us to modernize and streamline production, including notebook computers and camera phones that made life easier for all of us.

"Kendall, meet Gretchen Hutchinson. She's the new president of the Yarnell Historical Society. And this fine young woman," she said to the other woman, laying a gentle hand on my arm, "is Kendall O'Dell, our star reporter for the *Castle Valley Sun*. Gretchen is in the process of trying to save the old Ice House from the wrecking ball."

Smiling, I shook hands with the stocky, flaxen-haired woman with blunt facial features. I had a real soft spot in my heart for the tiny town of Yarnell because it was at the top of Yarnell Hill the previous April that I had first met Tally. "What's the Ice House?"

Her eyes brightened with interest. "Ohhh! It's a magnificent old building built around 1880. Over the years there have been a number of businesses housed there, a beanery, a candle making operation, a welding shop," she recited, counting on her fingers, "but the locals still refer to the place as the Ice House because in its heyday in the late 1800's and early 1900's it was used to store ice for delivery via narrow gauge railroad to many of the surrounding copper mines to be used in the smelters in places like Wagoner, Fort Misery and Congress." I could tell she was really into the subject because her cheeks glowed with color. "Records show that the basement, which was used to store the ice, has insulation at least four inches thick made from pressed animal hair and sawdust and the floor above it is at least twenty inches thick. At one time, there was an ammonia ice making machine operating down there and supposedly there are some parts of it remaining which we'd like to preserve."

"Who's trying to demolish the building?"

Her nostrils flared with a derisive sniff. "The usual suspects. As I'm sure you know, out of state developers are devouring every square inch of vacant land here in Arizona and now a syndicate of California doctors has filed an application to rezone the property for a housing development. We've been working to get historic designation for almost five years now plus working with the owner to try and keep her from selling out. But," she continued with a defeated sigh, "the lady has just gone into a nursing home, poor dear. Her relatives are clamoring for her to give them power of attorney so they can file the papers for condemnation." She made eye contact with Thelma. "It's been such a long battle and right now, it's not looking too good that we'll be successful in saving it."

Thelma placed a comforting hand on her shoulder. "Have faith, dear. There were many dark days when I could have just torn out what's left of my hair over this place, but look at the results of my efforts. I finally prevailed and now this grand old house belongs once and for all to the people of Castle Valley." She turned back to me. "Kendall, do you remember that series you did last summer? I sincerely believe that your articles greatly influenced the heirs to change their minds about selling

Hanson House. Perhaps you could do the same for Gretchen."

Reacting to her hopeful expression, I said, "I can certainly give it a shot. Give me your phone number and e-mail address and we can set something up. Next time I'm in Yarnell, I'll get some exterior shots and maybe a few interiors to accompany the piece."

Gretchen's brows dipped in uncertainty. "I don't know about photographing the inside. Right now, it's being rented on a month-to-month basis and the tenant didn't seem too keen about the idea of having us intrude. Perhaps you'll have more luck than I did."

"I'll do my best." It was almost time for the dedication ceremony so after shooting a series of photos I wandered among the balloon-toting citizens, jotting down quotes from various civic leaders, concluding with several shots of the ribbon cutting ceremony that was followed immediately by an inside tour showing off the newly refurbished rooms and antique furnishings.

I stayed longer than I should have, and it was a quarter to ten when I left the old house and joined the long line of departing cars. Since the office and fairgrounds were at opposite ends of town the wait to get onto the main street chewed up another ten minutes. Feeling the pinch of time I hurried to the office, retrieved Ginger's moneybag and then sped towards the fairgrounds taking note of the smoky-gray clouds gathering above the northern mountains. Would the impending storm hold off until the craft show ended?

Any hope I had of making up for lost time evaporated when I reached the main entrance. The choke of traffic slowed from a crawl to a complete stop. Oh man. Ginger was probably having a gigantic freckled cow by now. I plucked the phone from my purse and dialed her cell number. It rang repeatedly before going to voicemail. Oh well, I'd tried. Drumming my fingers impatiently on the steering wheel I sat watching the bustle of activity in the vendor parking lot. Crafters and artisans were still in the process of unloading racks of clothing, jewelry, paintings, pottery and woodwork items from a variety of trucks and trailers before piling their wares onto handcarts and heading towards the colorful sea of canopies ringing the rodeo stands.

Suddenly the discordant roar of Harley-Davidson motorcycles drowned out all other sounds. A flash of irritation coursed through me as ten bikes rolled past the long line of waiting cars just because they could. My patience was near an end by the time I found a parking spot. Now closing in on ten-thirty I trotted towards the front gate and entered the fairgrounds in a crush of chattering teens, slow-moving seniors and young mothers pushing toddlers in strollers. The overwhelming blend of diverse aromas—cotton candy, burgers, French fries, Mexican and Chinese food—made my stomach churn with hunger. As I passed by the multitude of tents I made a mental note of some of the crafts being displayed to feature in my article. Amid the blare of country music and shrieking kids from the carnival rides came the distinct braying of wild burros. Sure enough I spotted Ginger's canopy. She was busy depositing items into a plastic bag while her wheelchair-bound grandmother, Nona, conversed with two other elderly women. There were at least a half a dozen people gathered around her booth perusing and picking through the handmade items. I ducked beneath the tent and moved to her side. "Sorry, traffic was a bear. I tried to call but got your voicemail."

She swung around and fixed me with a look of wide-eyed relief. "Land sakes, girl, I wuz about to send the sheriff's posse out lookin' for ya!" She grabbed the moneybag, rifled through it and turned to a generously built woman holding a gigantic flower arrangement. "Okay, darlin', I can change that hundred for ya now." As the woman waddled away with her purchase Ginger rolled her eyes, sighing, "I've been busier than a cat trying to cover poop on concrete!"

Giggling at her hilarious colloquialism, I turned to Nona and bent down to kiss her withered but brightly rouged cheek. "How're you doing today?" For a woman well into her eighties she was still sharp as a tack mentally.

Dressed flamboyantly in purple, including a wide-brimmed hat clustered with lavender flowers, she smiled up at me, her faded eyes sparkling with good humor. "Well, if it ain't, Miss Candy O'Donnell? Missy, I'm fit as a fiddle and ornery as an old goat."

I marveled at the ongoing game she played, striving to come up with yet another skewed nickname for me each time we met. She hadn't repeated herself yet.

"Did you have fun at your friend Oscar's 100th birthday party last night?"

She crooked her finger for me to bend closer. "I had a ball. After everybody helped him blow out all the candles I told him if he was just a few years older I could really go for him."

I laughed at her quick wit. "Nona, you're one of a kind."

"You got that right, honey."

Ginger grabbed my elbow and pulled me aside. "Okay, let's have it. What happened last night? Did Ruth have a coronary when y'all spilled the beans?"

"Yes and no."

Ginger's eyes widened. "What's that mean?"

At that moment we were deluged with customers. "It's too long to go into now. I'll tell you later." The three of us worked nonstop for the next hour selling and bagging the handmade items for scores of enthusiastic buyers. Ginger whooped with excitement after we sold the last of Nona's hand-embossed pillows.

"The other gals at church ain't gonna believe this!" she crowed, clapping her hands in glee. "If this keeps up, we're goin' to sell out everything in one day!"

"I had no idea this was going to be such a big deal," I marveled, eyeing the noisy crush of humanity moving past the canopy.

"People come from all 'round these parts to attend this show." She paused momentarily. "Oh yeah, that reminds me. She's here!"

"Who's here?"

"The ice lady."

"Who?"

"Remember the gal I wuz tellin' you about at lunch the other day?" Responding to my blank look she added peevishly, "You know. Myra Colton. The one who does the fancy ice sculptures?"

"Oh. Right."

She tilted her head thoughtfully. "What's goin' on? You seem a tad distracted today."

"You could say that."

"It's gotta have somethin' to do with last night." Her eyes blazed with interest. "Did Ruth have an atomic hissy fit?"

"That and other…circumstances too complicated to go into now."

"Oh, I hate it when you do that! Just give me the short version."

How much to tell her? "Okay, Ruth wasn't exactly thrilled with our announcement but grudgingly gave us her blessing."

Ginger looked properly stunned. "Well, slap me silly, that's mighty unexpected, but pretty dang good news."

"Yes, and even better than that was Tally's surprise engagement present to me." I knew mention of that would derail further questions about Ruth.

"Come on, sugar, I'm waiting!"

"He presented me with my very own beautiful horse."

"A horse!" Pretending to swoon, she pressed a hand to her heart. "What a prize that man is! Did I not tell you from day one that he was the catch of the century?"

"That he is. But now I'm really under pressure to come up with something equally as great for him. And I don't have a clue. Any ideas?"

Her answer was a blank stare. "I'm gonna have to think on that one for a spell."

"Me too and I don't have a lot of time." I switched gears. "Okay, so where is this lady's booth?" I really couldn't have cared less about having an ice sculpture but didn't have the heart to disappoint her.

"As soon as Doreen and Wilma get here we can mosey over yonder an' yak at her."

"Sure."

We were unpacking boxes and piling embroidered dishtowels and silk flower arrangements on the table when she suddenly drew in a startled breath. "Mercy! Take a gander at that fearsome-looking bunch."

I looked up, following her gaze to the half-dozen or so multi-tattooed and pierced guys pushing through the crowd—probably the Harley riders I'd seen earlier. Not far behind them were several rough-looking women. It took only nanoseconds to recognize that these were not rich urban bikers out for the weekend attempting to look cool. Nope. These people appeared to be the genuine article. Clad in tight jeans and matching black leather vests or jackets, they rolled through the crowd like a dark wave of intimidation, obviously reveling in the fearful responses their presence invoked. Parents yanked children closer while other fairgoers averted their eyes and cleared a wide path for them.

"You see that moose of a guy with the paunch?" Ginger said under her breath. "The one with the ponytail and red checked bandana?"

"Yeah."

"That there's Randy Moorehouse."

"Is that so?" I studied the ex-con with interest. He was a strapping man well over six feet tall. His beefy arms looked to be as big around as my thighs and it was obvious that he'd spent a substantial amount of time working out. Dressed from head to toe in black, his expression aggressive, he looked the epitome of the outlaw biker. The group paused at the canopy directly across from us to examine T-shirts and hats while the women stopped to pick through jewelry and sunglasses at the adjacent booth.

"Don't make eye contact with any of 'em," Ginger warned, but it was too late. One smarmy-looking dude with spider web tattoos lacing his elbows zeroed in on me and veered towards our canopy. "Oh, good Lord, deliver us from evil," Ginger moaned, shrinking to the back of the tent with Nona as he and a second man arrived at the table.

I fired her a 'thanks for deserting me' glance before turning to face them.

My chest tightened with annoyance and just a touch of apprehension as the taller of the two looked at me up down and sideways while transferring a toothpick from one side of his mouth to the other, probably to make sure I saw the bolt in his tongue. I'm sure he thought it was a major turn-on and to be honest, he wasn't a bad looking guy— well-defined muscles, narrow waist and square-jawed. He was also close enough for me to notice the patches on his vest. One of them confirmed my suspicions when I read the words DESERT DEVILS. "Good afternoon, ladies." His insolent smile revealed startlingly white teeth. "Whatever you're selling, Red, I'm buying."

My face warmed. Unfortunately my fiery mane of hair attracted not only swarms of bees and hummingbirds but sometimes the unwanted attention of men as well. Unflinching, I met his gaze. "Excellent. How many dishtowels and flower baskets would you fellows be interested in?"

The second man, shorter, heavier and bearded, guffawed loudly then said with an insinuating grin, "Hey, sweet thing. Is it true what they say? That red on the head means *wiiiiilllld* in bed?"

I had to dig deep to ignore his crude remark. With no sheriff's deputies or security guards in sight I cautioned myself to remain cool. I lifted a quizzical brow. "Does that line actually work for you?"

His smile quickly dissolved while the first man appraised me with renewed interest. "Cute. Very cute." He leaned in closer. "How's about you an' me getting together later for a beer?"

Suppressing a little shiver of revulsion I replied coolly, "How's about we don't."

Apparently unaccustomed to being rejected his eyes changed from flirty to flinty. He couldn't know that in the course of performing my job during the last six months I'd come into contact with men far more sinister than he perceived himself to be. "Now then," I continued with forced sweetness, "back to business. How many dozen dishtowels were you thinking of purchasing?" I could just imagine Ginger's horrified reaction to my confrontational behavior, but I had no intention of being cowed even though I was cognizant, having done several pieces on rival outlaw biker gangs, that these people believed that rules, regulations and laws that apply to the rest of society didn't apply to them.

Locked in a concentrated eye duel I wasn't exactly sure what my next move was going to be when a male voice from across the street called out, "Hey, Bo Bo, your little Ladybug needs some cash for trinkets. Get your tight ass over here."

Bo Bo? Ladybug? Very slowly, he turned towards another biker standing beside a chunky blonde in an ultra-low-cut tank top. "Hang loose a minute, Thumper!" he shouted. Then, his cocky attitude still intact, he returned his attention to me. Smirking, he clicked his tongue. "Catch you later, Red."

Stung by his brazen behavior, I breathed a sigh of relief as he swaggered away. My relief was short-lived when the intuitive sense that I was being watched swept over me. At that precise moment, I locked eyes with Randy Moorehouse—and it was distinctly disconcerting. Behind the passive curiosity lighting his deep-set eyes burned a host of emotions I could not decipher. Whatever he was feeling at that moment, his down-turned mouth and piercing stare punctuated by thundercloud black brows seemed designed to strike fear in people's hearts. As he turned away from me striding into the crowd, people shrank away. Now I was more curious about him than ever. Was he truly just an innocent man who'd been wrongly convicted or the monster everyone believed him to be? Remembering that his new and rather incongruous vocation was delivering flowers made me wonder about the wisdom of people opening their doors to such an intimidating person. It wasn't a difficult stretch of the imagination to envision this bull of a man hacking his girlfriend to pieces or the vengeful beheading of the judge who had sent him to molder away on Death Row.

9

"Tell me somethin'. Did you like to play with matches when you wuz a kid?" came Ginger's brusque demand when the bikers were out of earshot. "For Pete's sake, have you got a death wish? What in the name of Davy Crockett are you thinkin' mixin' it up with a guy like that?"

"What should I have done? Taken him up on his offer?"

"Well, no, o' course not. But, geez Louise, what if he comes back?"

I shook my head. "Doubtful. I think that was all for show."

"Darlin', you better hope so." She glanced over my shoulder, her face mirroring relief. "Oh good, the other gals are here."

We exchanged greetings with the new arrivals and brought them up to speed on remaining stock before we left Nona dozing in the back of the canopy and joined the ocean of people jamming the aisles. "Myra's tent is on the west side of the rodeo arena," Ginger informed me. "Wait till you see her stuff."

Strolling among the animated crowd, I jotted more notes regarding the wide array of merchandise being offered for sale to use in my piece for next week's edition. Within minutes we arrived in front of a doublewide canopy marked only with a small sign reading MYRA COLTON ORIGINALS that was packed with a dazzling array of artwork. As I wandered among the items displayed my admiration mushroomed as I studied each intricately created piece. The artist's work ran the gamut from woodcarvings of galloping horses to impressive plaster busts of stern-faced Native Americans, all the pieces well beyond my price range. Her ceramic angel collection was nothing short of amazing. Each of the various sizes of figurines had been created with loving detail right down to the dimpled cheeks on the smiling cherubs. When Ginger eyed me with one of those 'what did I tell you' looks I nodded my confirmation of the woman's genius. One piece in particular caught my eye. Circling a three-foot high sculpture of a roping rider astride a rearing horse a vague concept began to percolate in the back of my mind.

"Told ya you'd like her stuff," Ginger murmured, elbowing me gently in the side.

"I do indeed and especially this one." But, when I spied the asking price of $4000 for the exquisite piece, my breath faltered. "Good grief," I muttered, "get a load of the price tag!"

"May I help you with something?"

We swung around to confront a statuesque woman with spiked, whitish-blonde hair staring back at us with intense, close-set brown eyes and a faint smile of polite inquiry. Her sallow complexion, sunken cheeks and willow-thin physique made me wonder if she was ill.

"Are you Myra Colton?" Ginger inquired breathlessly.

"Yes."

Pink spots of color appeared on the woman's cheeks as we lavished praise on the quality of her work. Smiling, she thanked us and then Ginger inquired about the possibility of her creating an ice sculpture for the engagement party. She puckered her lips in thought. "I'd love to tell you yes, but I'll be out of town several times during the next month and in addition I'm preparing to exhibit some of my work at the Prescott Fine Arts Association in a couple of weeks." Responding to Ginger's downcast expression she quickly added, "I don't have my events calendar with me at the moment, but perhaps I could get back to you ladies on Monday after I get home."

I traded an expectant glance with Ginger who eagerly jotted our phone numbers on the back of a shopping receipt. "I'm keepin' my fingers crossed that you're gonna have time to do it."

"I'll certainly do my best," she replied, accepting the paper and folding it into her pocket.

We thanked her for her time and halfway back to our canopy I stopped in mid stride when the idea germinating in the back of my mind fully blossomed. "You go ahead," I told Ginger, "I have another question I'd like to ask Myra. It'll only take me a few minutes."

"I gotta run to the pot anyway," she said, waving as she headed towards a row of blue portable toilets fittingly dubbed KAROL'S KANS. "Shoot, look at that!" She pointed to the dark clouds stacked above the ridgeline of the northern mountains. "I sure hope the rain holds off until the show closes tomorrow!"

"Me too." I wheeled around and when I arrived back at the artist's tent I found her slumped in a director's chair in the rear, a book in her lap, her forehead resting in one hand. "Are you all right?"

Her head shot up and it seemed as if the shadowy circles beneath her eyes looked more pronounced than before. "Oh...yes. I'm just a little tired today. Is there something else I can do for you?" Closing the book, she rose from her chair with a look of cordial expectance.

I pointed to the horse and rider sculpture. "How long would it take you to create something similar to that?"

Faint frown lines creased her forehead. "Well...it depends on what else I'm working on and what medium you choose. That particular piece took me about two months to complete. Why?"

It was hard to contain my growing excitement. "Can you do an exact likeness of someone's face?"

Her expression remained pleasant, but I thought I noticed a melancholy shadow pass swiftly behind her eyes before she answered. "Of course I can."

I squeezed my palms together. "This is my lucky day! And the timing couldn't be better." I walked over to the sculpture and ran my finger along the horse's smooth muzzle. "Something along these lines would make a perfect engagement gift for my fiancé, but I would need to have it in six weeks?"

She looked dubious. "That's asking a lot—"

"I know, I know, and I also have no right to ask you to come down on your usual price...but if you could create one that isn't quite as large as this one, I might be able to swing your fee." When she still appeared hesitant I charged ahead. "Here's the situation. Last night my fiancé gave me a gorgeous Appaloosa mare as an engagement gift and I've been wracking my brain trying to come up with an appropriate gift for him. In a million years, I never dreamed that there would be any chance that I could even come close to matching it...until now." I knew I was laying it on a bit thick, but what the heck.

She mulled over my proposal for another moment before a compassionate smile revitalized her drawn face. "Well, as Aristotle once said, 'Patience is bitter, but its fruit is sweet.' I'll tell you what. Because it's a special gift for such a special reason...I will do my level best to have it completed by your engagement party for a charge of...say fifteen hundred dollars? I'll need half down to begin and I'd prefer cash. Does that sound fair?"

Ouch. Fifteen hundred would still be a hard nut to crack. That settled one thing. I would not be buying the cool new car I'd been thinking about. "Fair enough. Thank you!" I felt like whooping like a kid and performing a couple of cartwheels but restrained myself.

"I'll need a photo of your fiancé and the horse as soon as possible. Actually several photos that show various angles of his face would be preferable. I'll need them enlarged to a minimum size of sixteen by twenty if possible. My eyesight isn't what it used to be," she tacked on apologetically.

I was elated. Tally was going to be absolutely blown away. "Done. By the way," I said, proffering my hand, "my name is Kendall O'Dell. I'm sorry. I should have introduced myself earlier. I'm an investigative reporter for the *Castle Valley Sun*."

Her probing gaze grew attentive. "Is that so? I wonder if I've read any of your articles."

"If you subscribe to the *Sun*, you probably have. I've uncovered a series of pretty amazing stories the past few months." She appeared mildly interested, yet her eyes looked distracted as if she were thinking of something else. "Anyway," I continued, getting back on track, "do you live here in Castle Valley?"

"No, in Yarnell."

"Oh, that's right. Ginger mentioned that to me." My mind raced ahead. It was going to take some time to find the right photo or series of photos. Since the copy shop was closed on Sunday it either meant a trip to Phoenix or wait until Monday. "I should be able to have them for you by Monday afternoon."

"I won't be back home until late that evening."

"Oh. Well, I could mail them...oh wait, I just thought of something. I'll be in Prescott on Tuesday attending a funeral. I could drop the photos off to you on my way back, probably before five o'clock. Would that work?" Right now the plan was to ride along with Tally and his family, but then how was I going to keep it a surprise? I'd have to think of a reason to go in a separate vehicle, and in any case the thought of traveling with Ruth didn't exactly thrill me. "I'll need directions to your house. Do you have a card or something?"

She patted her pockets. "I'm all out." Striding to the counter, she laid the book down, slipped on a pair of reading glasses then jotted on the back of a blank receipt. "Drive to the north end of town. The road is easy to miss because someone crashed into the street sign two weeks ago and it hasn't been replaced yet. Watch for a boarded up blue house and turn west directly afterwards. The pavement ends after a half a mile and you'll come to a fork in the road. Go right at the first fork and left at the second.

I'm kind of all by myself out there and I don't have a land line so I'm including my cell number in case you get lost, although I can't always get a signal because of the mountains. If I don't answer leave a message and I'll call you back."

I accepted the paper and grinned my appreciation. "I can't thank you enough."

She patted the book she'd set on the counter. "I've just been reading some of Robert Browning's poetry about love and I must say I think this is a very romantic gesture on your part."

I grinned. "He's worth it."

She tilted her head to one side. "I'm sorry to hear that you're going to a funeral. Losing a loved one is the hardest thing in the world. What a...what relationship...?" Her voice trailed off and she appeared chagrined. "I do apologize. I didn't mean to pry into your personal affairs."

"No problem. I never actually met...the deceased but at one time he was married to my fiancé's aunt and remained a close family friend. It's a pretty high-profile case. You may have read about it in our paper...Judge Riley Gibbons."

A slow, sympathetic nod. "Oh my. Yes, I am aware of...that very unfortunate event. What is your fiancé's name?"

"Bradley Talverson. He owns the Starfire Ranch northwest of here."

"I see." She looked at me expectantly. "So, are you investigating the judge's death?"

"That's my intention." Her troubled demeanor prompted me to ask, "Did you know him?"

"Actually, I did meet him a couple of times."

"I'd be interested in anything you can tell me about him."

"Not much, I'm afraid. I've had more personal contact with Mrs. Gibbons. We met at a social gathering last year. She admired the ice sculpture I'd done and hired me to create several pieces to display in the old hotel they're in the process of restoring." Looking grim, she added with a slight shrug, "I still haven't been paid for the last piece the judge commissioned that I delivered there a few weeks ago."

At that moment two well-dressed women walked into her canopy oohing and aahing so I backed away. "Looks like you've got some customers so I won't take up any more of your time. Thank you so much. See you Tuesday." She waved goodbye and walked towards the potential customers.

It was hard to keep from skipping as I walked back to Ginger's canopy where I found her tucking a shawl around Nona. The wind had picked up and the temperature was heading down. Predictably, Ginger was curious as to why I'd returned to Myra's booth, and when I told her she beamed with pleasure. "Ain't you happy now that I drug you over there to see her?"

"Absolutely."

"Now, we gotta decide what kind of ice...hold the phone," she said, peering over my left shoulder in wide-eyed admiration, "now *that* is one yummy-looking hunk of man! And...if I'm not mistaken he's lookin' right at you."

"What?" I swung around and my stomach fluttered nervously at the sight of Grant standing in front of the booth across from us. He lifted a hand and smiled affably at me. Stunned and speechless I turned back to Ginger, my cheeks on fire.

"What's goin' on? Your face is redder'n a baboon's butt." Her eyes searched mine for answers. "You know that guy?"

"Yes, I know that guy."

Her freckled face was a mask of pure bemusement. "Well?"

"That's Grant Jamerson."

It took a few seconds for my answer to penetrate, but when it did she clapped a hand over her mouth. "Your ex-fiancé! What's he doing here?" When I didn't respond immediately she insisted, "Come on, girl, spit it out before I drop over dead from curiosity!"

Without going into great detail, I told her how'd he shown up unannounced at the same time Tally had arrived. "And I'm guessing Tally ain't too thrilled about it."

"Your guess would be correct."

"Well, ain't you in a fine pickle. Mercy me. Don't look now but he's walkin' this way."

I turned to meet his guileless blue eyes and my heart contracted with a mélange of emotions I couldn't even begin to arrange into a cogent thought. As if my life weren't complicated enough already. A charismatic smile aimed at Ginger accompanied his "Hi, I'm Grant Jamerson." It took him all of sixty seconds to figuratively charm the pants off her, Nona and the other two ladies. I could have happily choked him.

When he finally refocused on me I asked pointedly, "What are you doing here?"

"Shopping."

"Really."

"Yep, thought I'd pick up a few souvenirs to commemorate my visit to the Grand Canyon State."

"That's nice." I deliberately kept my back to Ginger and the other women but I could feel their inquisitive eyes on me.

"Yeah, I'm heading down to Phoenix now. Got an appointment to interview one of Judge Gibbons's associates. See if I can scare up anything new on the case."

I could tell he was needling me again. Maintaining his incandescent smile, he lowered his voice. "We need to talk."

"No, we don't."

"Yes, we do."

He showed no signs of backing down. I swung around to Ginger. "Could you hold down the fort for a moment?"

"You bet your sweet bippy." Her inquiring gaze promised an inquisition for all pertinent details upon my return. "Y'all take your time now."

I fired him a look of annoyance and literally flounced from the canopy, marching towards the wild burro corral some fifty yards away. "Hey, slow down," he panted, trotting beside me. "Why do I get the feeling that you're not happy to see me?"

Almost to the corral I halted and whirled around. "Grant, what are you doing? Why did you follow me? Are you deliberately trying to ruin my life? Again?"

He appeared momentarily taken aback. "I didn't exactly follow you."

I gritted my teeth. "Really? Then how did you know I was here?"

"You probably won't buy into the notion that I'm psychic?"

"Get real."

His disarming grin seemed designed to lighten the mood. "Okay. The truth is I overheard your phone conversation this morning when you mentioned that you'd be here. Come on, Kendall. That's Investigative Reporting 101 remember? Pay close attention to everything people say? Or have you forgotten all the things I taught you?" The coy nuance in his voice and smoldering glint in his eyes betrayed his double entendre.

Choosing to ignore it, I folded my arms. "Get to the point."

Heeeee Hawwww! Heeee Haaaaaawwww! I looked over my shoulder at one particularly vocal burro that was soon joined by several others, causing a cacophonous racket.

His eyes sparkled with good humor. "This is a really classy place."

"No one's keeping you here."

He didn't respond and appeared for the first time to be ill at ease. Hands in his pockets, he rearranged a couple of pieces of gravel with his shoe before meeting my unflinching gaze again. "Can we talk about us for a few minutes?"

"No. We can talk about me," I said, pressing a thumb to my chest, "and we can talk about you, but we can't talk about *us...because* of you."

He absorbed my accusation with aplomb. "Have you been waiting a long time to get that off your chest?"

"You have no idea." We eyed each other steadily and as I stared into his mesmerizing blue eyes, an uncomfortable tremor traveled through me as the air between us became charged with emotion. Danger! Danger!

"I said I was sorry, Kendall. What can I do to make it up to you?"

"Nothing. Let's just leave it alone."

"So, we can't even be friends? We used to be good friends," he went on, apparently trying a softer approach. "Have you forgotten all the things we had in common? All the amazing times we had together before…?"

I cut him off. "Before I developed asthma and couldn't ski, couldn't dance, couldn't hike anymore? You mean before you got bored with me and started sneaking around behind my back with Elise? No, I haven't forgotten, not for a second. But you know what? I have a new life now. You see this?" I asked, brandishing my diamond in his face. "You had your chance! I'm engaged to Tally now. Whatever you and I had together is over. Period. End of story." I drew in a shuddery breath. "I really hated you for a long time, Grant, but I'm past that now. I've moved on with my life and you should do the same."

"So there isn't anything I can do, anything I can say, to talk you out of marrying this…backwoods cowboy?"

His disparaging tone got my blood boiling. Backwoods cowboy? Why did that sound familiar? I glared at him. "Wait a minute, what's going on here? Has my mother been talking to your mother? Did they put you up to this?"

His ever-so-slight shrug in conjunction with the chastened expression on his face confirmed my suspicions. Nonetheless, some of the resentment I'd held against him for so long in my heart diminished a couple of degrees. What had he been thinking? That he could swoop in here unannounced and sweep me off my feet again? Did he think I'd still be so enamored of his good looks and charm that I'd chuck my new job, new life, and my new man to go running back to Pennsylvania with him? "This isn't a romance novel, Grant," I said softly. "I'm...I'm truly flattered that you feel the way you do, but I *love* Tally, I love Arizona and I'm very happy in my new job. I'm sorry, you're on your own."

He reached out and clasped my shoulders, his eyes beseeching. "Kendall, are you sure? We had a great thing going and you know it. Are you absolutely sure this isn't just a...a rebound thing?"

"Positive." I stepped back, breaking his hold on me.

He searched my eyes for another few seconds before sighing heavily. "You can't fault me for trying." He held out a hand. "Friends?"

I hesitated a couple of seconds before tentatively extending my hand. "Okay, friends."

Heeeee Haaawwwww! We turned to see a burro with his neck craned over the pipe corral. He was shaking his head up and down, his teeth bared as if he were grinning in approval. "Apparently our buddy here concurs," Grant remarked with dry humor, still gripping my hand. "Well, I'll see you around." Then, before I could object he leaned forward and kissed me lightly on the lips. "Just a little kiss between friends," he said before turning to stride away. Bemused by his behavior, I stood still, staring after him. As he merged into the crowd my heart jolted uncomfortably when I noticed Lucinda Johns standing across the aisle staring at me with a calculating gleam in her dark eyes.

10

Accompanied by erratic gusts of wind I swung onto the narrow blacktop road that would take me to Hidden Springs. According to the Arizona roadmap my destination resided at the base of a mountain intriguingly named the Praying Nun. Within three miles, after passing a large RV park and scattered homes, the pavement abruptly ended. For the next twenty minutes I bounced and jostled along a dirt road pocketed with cavernous potholes and irregular ruts—telltale evidence of the recent heavy rains. As much as I tried to focus my attention on my clandestine mission, the disconcerting incident with Grant still bothered me. It disturbed me greatly that the sensation of his kiss lingered on my lips. Ginger had grilled me mercilessly when I'd returned to the canopy and stood in open-mouthed amazement when I recounted the mortifying events of the previous night as well as the recent encounter with Grant.

"Good Lord, girl," she'd lamented, shaking her head, "you got yourself trapped between the devil and the deep blue sea."

No kidding. My repeated calls to the Starfire had gone unanswered and the vision of Lucinda making a beeline out there to tattle her twisted account of my innocent exchange with Grant added to my guilty angst. But one thing was in my favor. She might not have any better luck than me tracking him down.

I tried Tally's number one last time and then lost the signal. I dropped the cell phone on the seat wondering if I should abort my mission to Hidden Springs and just head for the Starfire. Oh well, I'd explain everything to him later when we met for dinner. Might as well relax and enjoy the scenery.

The washboard road meandered its way among a series of boulder-strewn hills that gave way to desert vistas dotted with plentiful stands of plump saguaro, prickly pear and barrel cacti. One bonus from the recent rains was the softening effect on the normally harsh landscape created by patches of vivid green winter grass sprinkled with colorful wildflowers. The eye-catching panorama provided a vastly different setting from the dreary, gray winters I'd known in Pennsylvania. After traveling another five miles and not encountering a single dwelling or passing vehicle I began to wonder if I was on the right road. I held the map in one hand and eyed it again. Yep. I was correct. I tossed it back on the passenger seat thinking that it was curious why anyone in his right mind would open a B&B so far off the beaten path. Little wonder it was called *Hidden* Springs.

I eased to the left hand side of the road to avoid a sizeable rock and about jumped out of my skin when a gravel truck suddenly rounded one of the switchbacks. Gasping, my heart constricted with horror, I wrenched the wheel to the right as the giant vehicle clattered by only inches from me. A quick glimpse of the driver revealed a young Hispanic male seemingly oblivious to our near collision.

My thundering heart was still locked in my throat when a second gravel truck roared by followed minutes later by a third. What the hell? As soon as I rounded the bend my question was answered. Beyond a sun-bleached sign reading RITTENHOUSE EARTHWORKS, domes of colored rocks and gravel dominated the desert landscape. Not a pretty sight. The ravaged ground, scraped clean of foliage and strewn with heavy equipment, presented a real eyesore in contrast to the pristine environment. A squat concrete building, probably the office, sat well off the road flanked by two dirt-caked pickup trucks. Still feeling limp from the after effects of the adrenaline rush, I drove on. There were no signs that civilization had ventured any further with the exception of one abandoned ranch, its overgrown fields, sagging fences and peeling adobe house all crumbling to ruin.

I accelerated up a steep, gravelly embankment and when I reached the crest I drew in an appreciative breath. From behind me the subdued rays of mid-afternoon sunshine highlighted the burnished pink radiance of a granite and quartz butte standing guard over a secluded valley. Fascinating. From this perspective I could see how the formation earned its unique name, the Praying Nun. It looked amazingly like a woman kneeling, her head bent in solemn prayer. Centuries of wind and water erosion had etched a series of stair stepping pleats in the rock that formed the impression of a nun's habit gracefully draped to the ground. A prominent spire fronting it created the illusion of hands uplifted in prayer. Looming beyond the amazing pinnacle of rock, the hazy blue peaks of the Bradshaw Mountains, crowned with a soufflé of black-bellied thunderheads, created a striking panorama worthy of any calendar picture. I grabbed my digital camera and recorded several pictures before continuing down the hill. The accumulation of clouds, combined with the increasing strength of the wind, left little doubt in my mind that rain was imminent. The road dipped into the valley revealing the outline of several structures nestled beneath the clusters of cottonwood, sycamore and dark green tamarisk trees. Lush grass and mature foliage confirmed the presence of an abundant water table, creating an inviting oasis amidst the harsh landscape.

The road finally bottomed out and almost immediately a sign announcing HIDDEN SPRINGS sprang into view. Below it, a smaller sign read: VACANCY. Man. Talk about living out in the boonies. This was the middle of nowhere. Even more surprising was a massive collection of date palms that looked incredibly out of place in this desert setting. There must have been a hundred of them lining the main drive. They'd obviously been planted a long time ago, because the graceful yet gnarled trunks had arched towards each other allowing the fronds to intertwine and form a lacy canopy. Dappled sunlight filtered through as I passed by several outbuildings, a crumbling tennis court and an empty swimming pool that appeared to be in the process of renovation. The mouth of the curving drive widened to reveal two cars parked in front of a waist-high wall fashioned from smooth river rock. I braked to a halt. Directly ahead were three cottages and several hundred yards beyond them, partially obscured by desert willows, stood a two-story stone building. Judging by the architecture, I surmised it was the old hotel. A small REGISTRATION arrow pointed toward it.

I slid from the truck and stood there listening to the cheerful rhapsody of birds accompanied by the soothing rustle of palm fronds. I looked around. The shell of an abandoned stable stood off to my left, tall grass and weeds choking a narrow pasture. Odd. The place appeared deserted, no signs of life anywhere. But then it was only a little past three. Perhaps today's guests had not yet checked in. As anxious as I was to investigate the crime scene, I figured it would be wise to obtain permission from Riley's widow first. I headed towards the closest residence. The cottage sported a coat of fresh rose-colored paint and its neat flowerbeds were bursting with red, white and purple petunias. I pushed the gate open, made my way along a flagstone walk that appeared new, and rapped on the front door. No answer. I knocked again and this time the curtain on one of the open front windows moved slightly. A cranky female voice called out, "Didn't you see the registration sign? Check in is at the hotel. Follow the walkway."

Interesting. Not the sort of greeting one would expect from an establishment catering to paying guests. "Are you La Donna Gibbons?"

Hesitation, then "Who are you?"

"Kendall O'Dell. I'm a reporter for the *Castle Valley Sun*."

"What do you want?"

"To talk to you."

"Why?"

"If you'll open the door, I'll explain."

"I'm not dressed."

"I can wait."

A full five minutes passed before the door was thrown open, revealing a gaunt-looking woman dressed in jeans and an unevenly buttoned flannel shirt. Shoulder-length, blonde hair streaked with gray framed her drawn features. I could tell by the delicate bone structure of her face that she'd once been a striking woman. Today, she looked pale, tired and not particularly happy to see me. I smiled in greeting. "I'm sorry to disturb you, but I was wondering if I could ask you a few questions concerning the recent...occurrence here."

Her eyes flared with displeasure. "You know what, I'm not having a great day and to be frank, I'm sick and tired of pushy reporters snooping around, tramping all over my property and then writing lurid stories about Riley. It's disgraceful and it's ruined our business. The last thing I need right now is another gruesome article that will chase away the few interested guests we have left, especially since the authorities still haven't made any headway in identifying who might have done this...horrible thing. So, if you'll excuse me—"

She was in the process of closing the door so I decided it was time to play the connection card. "Wait! I know this has been a difficult time and I hate to bother you, but...I'm kind of indirectly involved in this case."

"What do you mean?"

"Your husband was my fiancé's uncle."

Her brows bunched together. "Oh? And who is your fiancé?"

"Bradley Talverson."

First a blank look then recognition registered in her bloodshot eyes. She nodded slowly. "Oh, yes, I remember meeting him and his sister last year. They were decent to me."

"Their mother is very distraught about the judge's...passing and asked me to look into it."

She appeared to be reconsidering her decision to expel me. "I don't know what else I can tell you that I haven't already told the sheriff and that bunch of news scavengers...but you can come in for a few minutes."

"Thank you."

She ushered me into a cozy living room filled with cheery floral-patterned Early-American-style furniture. Two cats lounging on the couch and one perched on the top of a wing back chair looked up at me with mild curiosity and yawned widely.

"Well, hi there, beautiful kitties," I said, allowing the cats to sniff my hand before petting each of them. Loud purring filled the otherwise silent room. "I just adopted a kitten a couple of weeks ago." Her expression of mild approval signaled that my innocent remark had earned me some points.

"I'm sorry. I didn't mean to be so short. I haven't slept much the past couple of weeks."

"I don't think anyone has slept very well knowing there's a madman roaming around someplace."

She massaged her fingers as if she were in pain. "Would you like a cup of tea? I was just in the process of making myself one."

"Sure, that would be great."

She shuffled around the corner and I continued schmoozing with the cats, the gentle clinking of glassware and purring the only sounds besides the keening wind outside. Glancing towards the kitchen doorway I noticed six or seven prescription drug bottles lining the windowsill above the sink. It was then I remembered that La Donna Gibbons suffered from fibromyalgia. I didn't know a lot about the debilitating disease except that some symptoms included extreme fatigue, headaches and arthritis-like pain.

I knew from talking to Tally that she was in her early forties, but her waxy complexion and lethargy made her appear much older.

Arms folded behind my back, I wandered around the room studying several paintings of local landmarks, one being a stunning oil of the Praying Nun towering over Hidden Springs. Beneath it, on the top shelf of a cherry wood bookcase sat two porcelain angel figures with smiling cherub faces. Closer inspection confirmed my hunch. The tiny initials MC identified Myra Colton as the creator. Once again filled with admiration for the woman's artistic talent, it reminded me that I needed to set aside some time either tonight or tomorrow to choose the best photo of Tally and Geronimo. On the second shelf were several framed pictures. One showed a smiling, much healthier-looking La Donna standing beside Riley. Damn, he'd been a handsome man. Another photo showed her standing next to a teenage girl in a school uniform. I turned when she re-entered the living room.

"Here we are," she announced, setting a tray on the glass-topped coffee table. "Green tea is supposed to possess a lot of medicinal properties. I hope you like it."

The plate of chocolate chip cookies interested me more, but I said, "Oh, yes. Thank you."

I sat down on the couch and selected two cookies before she handed me the cup. She settled in a chair and sipped her tea while one of the cats rose, sniffed my snack, and then apparently disappointed, jumped to the floor and sauntered from the room.

"So, Miss O'Dell, since you work for the newspaper and are connected with the Talverson family I presume you already know quite a lot about what happened." Her penetrating gaze held mine. "What makes you think that you're going to be any more successful at finding the monster who did this than the bevy of reporters and the law enforcement people currently working on this case?"

"I'm not sure that I will be, but if you'll permit me to ask some questions and take a look at the crime scene I'd like to give it a shot." She looked dubious, so I added, "My specialty is investigative reporting. I've been successful at cracking several difficult cases in the past six months."

"Indeed." She placed her cup and saucer on the coffee table and sat back, looking pensive. After a moment's silent reflection she said, "All right. When you leave here follow the walkway past the hotel entrance and take the right hand path. It will lead you to the natural springs. Riley's body was found in the largest pool next to the bathhouse we're having built. Be careful. There's construction material everywhere." Her voice sounded weary, resigned. "Now, what do you want to know?"

The fuzzy peach-colored cat that reminded me a little of Marmalade stood, stretched and decided to take up residence on my lap. I stroked the animal gently then opened my notepad. "I really don't know that much about the judge's personal life. Some background information would be helpful."

"I would think the Talversons would be more qualified than me to give you that information."

"I'm looking for more recent information. Say, the last five or six years."

She drummed her fingers on the arm of the chair. "All right. Riley and I met about seven years ago. I'm a flight attendant and he was on my Phoenix to Philadelphia turn. I'd been a widow for two years and...needless to say I was lonely and vulnerable. There was a mutual attraction and even though I sensed he was quite the ladies' man, he seemed like a nice person. I hadn't planned to get involved with him, not seriously. I knew he was seeing other women, but I couldn't resist when he finally asked me out. Anyway, we dated on and off for almost four years. I should have left it at that." Her eyes clouded with misery. "I can't believe I was so gullible. I can't believe he'd—"

A dissertation on their courtship wasn't really the information I wanted. "But you married him anyway."

She closed her eyes momentarily and when she opened them, her gaze held a sad, dreamy quality. "Did you ever meet him?"

"No."

Languidly, she pointed over her shoulder to the photo of them together. "As you can see Riley was an extraordinarily handsome man and also a very charming one. He took his work seriously and was highly respected by everyone. Life was good...or so I thought." She took another long swallow of tea. "Things started to go downhill when he found this place. What a disaster. The first time I saw it I thought he'd lost his mind. It was so terribly run down. There had been a fire in the old hotel, there was water damage and the place was riddled with termites, but he convinced me that finding a piece of property this size for the asking price was a real steal. He thought opening a B&B would be a great investment and also something we could do together after he retired. I suggested we tear that decrepit old building down and start over, but he wouldn't hear of it."

"Why not?"

Her lips curved in a wry smile. "Because he wanted it preserved and renovated. He was captivated with its one-hundred-and-twenty-five-year-old history, and he didn't want to disturb the...resident ghost."

131

11

A delicious shiver of expectation swept over me. "Really? Crumbling old places that are supposedly haunted have always intrigued me."

She narrowed her gaze, apparently trying to determine if I was joking. "Yes, well, according to local legend the hotel is inhabited by the spirit of an eight-year-old boy whose mother rode off one day to meet her lover and never came back. The child waited and waited for her and it's said that he finally died of typhoid fever. That was around 1890."

"That's a tragic story."

"Whatever. Several guests claim they've seen the apparition near the stairwell leading to the third floor or sometimes roaming the hallways. Some have even claimed to have heard a child weeping." She gave a noncommittal shrug. "I don't believe in such things myself."

Maybe she didn't, but the subject sure fired up my interest. Since childhood I'd been fascinated with the notion that some places were haunted with the spirits of some unfortunate souls destined to spend eternity stranded in some in-between world from whence they could neither live again nor embrace the final rewards of heaven. On more than one occasion I'd scared the living daylights out of myself reading ghost stories alone late at night, and then there had been the unexplained phenomenon at my Aunt Beverly's creepy old house in Ohio. "Tally told me that the judge was quite a mystery enthusiast. Owning a haunted hotel must have been right up his alley."

"It was. He had high hopes that it would help attract people who thrive on that baloney, you know, for these mystery weekend retreats, but then…everything happened. Since then we've had nothing but cancellation after cancellation." Her shoulders sagged with dejection. "Did Tally also tell you of Riley's affinity for practical jokes?"

"Yes, he did."

Her mouth compressed into a bitter smile. "He certainly had the last laugh on me. Several actually."

"How so?"

She inclined her head towards the old hotel, partially visible from the living room window. "First off, he sweet-talked me into spending the bulk of my savings to renovate that dilapidated old place and make property improvements—" she paused suddenly. Wincing softly, she pressed two fingers to her temple then let her hand drop limply in her lap.

"Are you okay?" I asked.

"My head is killing me. I'll be right back." She rose stiffly and moved to the kitchen where she downed pills from several of the prescription bottles before returning to her chair. She gathered the flannel shirt tightly around her thin frame. "I began not feeling well about a year ago," she began in a halting tone, as if talking was suddenly too much effort, "and blamed my constant exhaustion on my flight schedule and the endless amount of work here. Something had to give so I finally went on medical leave. I had every test known to man before being diagnosed with fibromyalgia. As if that weren't bad enough, about six months ago Riley came home one night sat me down and told me he wasn't happy. I know it wasn't easy for him because of my deteriorating health, but I thought we could work things out. The next thing I knew he served me with divorce papers."

Having gone through a similar experience with Grant I couldn't help but feel instant empathy with the woman. "Had you been experiencing marital problems?"

"Well...we had some disagreements over the years, what couple doesn't? There's no doubt that buying Hidden Springs put a strain on our relationship but I never dreamed..." her voice trailed off and she looked so wretched my heart went out to her.

I permitted a moment of healing silence before venturing, "I'm aware of his alleged relationship with Marissa Van Steenholm."

"I can't believe he's...was involved with a woman only a few years older than...my daughter would have been." Tears misted her eyes as she gestured towards the photo of the young girl. "Tara and my first husband were both killed by a drunk driver."

"I'm sorry to hear that."

For a minute she looked like she was going to lose it and then she inhaled a shuddery breath. "God has given me a heavy burden to shoulder. Widowed twice, losing my beautiful daughter and now my health." She laid her head back and stared at the ceiling for a time before making eye contact with me again. "And then we come to the last laugh. Riley told me that he had collected a substantial number of gold coins over the years and had them stored in a safe deposit box. I found the key several days after his body was found and since I was still legally his wife…his widow, I went to the bank. Imagine my shock to find the box empty. Considering the fact that I may not be able to return to work having a nest egg to rely on would have saved me a lot of grief."

"What do you think happened to them?"

Resentment blazed in her eyes. "For all I know he may have given *her* a key. If he did, don't you think it provides the perfect motive for a murder? Of course she denies taking them. So what am I to think? I suppose Riley could have sold them and not told me but then…what happened to the money?" She swallowed the remaining tea and set the cup down with a bang. "You want to hear the most ironic thing of all?"

I munched on the second cookie. "Sure."

"I have no choice but to rely on that little tramp to help me run this place. The volume of work is simply overwhelming. Some days I'm in too much pain to do much of anything and to make matters worse she's been sick the past couple of weeks. We make quite an odd pair."

"What about your housekeeper, Bernita Morales?"

"She's a jewel but she's got her hands full with laundry and cleaning all four residences. I can't ask her to take on the cooking, the reservations, bookkeeping and everything else involved. Not even half of the renovations are completed. I owe everybody in town and if I don't finish what Riley and I started I'll never be able to build up the clientele enough to make this place pay off or even sell it." She rose and paced the room. "It's so unfair. I'm literally marooned here because of that damn stipulation in his will. I own the property and guesthouses, but Riley deeded the hotel to Marissa and I don't have enough money to buy her out. Isn't that rich?"

"Definitely…not cool."

"To say the least." Her gaze hardened noticeably. "Don't presume that I don't know what people are thinking. Tell me, is that what *you're* thinking, Miss O'Dell?"

"I don't know what you mean."

"Come on. I wasn't born yesterday. The wronged wife would be the prime suspect in his murder, am I right?"

I'm not sure how she expected me to respond, but I kept my face expressionless because the thought had already crossed my mind. "I suppose that's one theory."

"Well, think about it," she snapped impatiently. "I barely have enough energy to get out of bed in the morning let alone—"

"Any thoughts on who may have done it?"

"Only a couple of hundred people if you count the number of criminals who stood before him in his courtroom, not to mention the extended families of all those lowlifes he sentenced to prison over the past fifteen years. I wouldn't know where to start."

"Did he ever talk about any specific threats made against him regarding past cases?"

A slight shrug. "He'd told me there'd been verbal threats, you know the usual, 'I'll get even with you' or something else unmentionable and I vaguely remember something about someone stalking him for a couple of weeks, but that was years ago. He said it came with the territory."

"But nothing current?"

"If there was, he didn't communicate it to me."

"How about his personal effects? Did you find anything that might provide a clue?"

"Detectives and forensics people have gone over every inch of this place. To be honest, I haven't had the heart or energy to go through all his belongings yet. As I said, we haven't been living together for over four months. There's still a lot of stuff remaining at the condo in Scottsdale. I don't know what Marissa has done with his things that were in the room we shared over at the hotel."

"I see. So...what about his frame of mind? In the past month or so, did he appear to be disturbed about anything? Distracted? Withdrawn?"

"How would I know? Why don't you ask *her*?"

I planned to. And I also wanted to verify the allegation that La Donna and the judge had bitterly fought the night before his disappearance. "What about someone he'd met recently, like one of the guests here?"

"Your guess is as good as mine." She moved to the window and stood there looking out in extended silence before turning back to me. "Even though I despise what Riley did to me, I wouldn't wish for anyone to die in such a horrible manner."

"Are you planning to attend his funeral?"

She rubbed her arms as if she were suddenly cold. "I don't know. It depends on how I'm feeling. I may just send flowers." She searched my face for signs of disapproval. "I know that may seem crass, but I don't want to go if Marissa is going to be there. I think it would be a very awkward and taxing situation for me."

"Is she taking care of the arrangements?"

"No, his sister Charlotte is. She still lives in Prescott. That's where his family was from originally, you know."

"Yes, I knew that. Well, I'm going to be there with the Talverson family and I'll be covering it for my paper.

My major focus right now is to concentrate on this case so if you think of anything else that might be helpful would you please call me?"

She fell silent, her eyes glinting with shrewd speculation. "I'm going to show you something." She left the room and returned carrying a white envelope, which she handed to me in silence. Puzzled, I opened the flap and pulled out two sheets of white paper. Printed in neat block lettering on the first one was: DEAREST LA DONNA, TO ERR IS HUMAN TO FORGIVE DIVINE. The second sheet read: LET YOUR HOOK ALWAYS CAST. IN THE POOL WHERE YOU LEAST EXPECT IT, WILL BE FISH. –OVID I looked up at her intrigued, my pulse quickening.

"I assume these are from Riley."

"It's his printing style."

"Any idea what these mean?"

"The first one sounds like a half-assed apology for his reprehensible behavior, the second, I haven't the foggiest. They could have come from one of the many volumes in his library."

"Where did you find these quotes?"

"They were delivered this morning." She handed me a cream-colored envelope with the firm name MILLS, DAVIS AND PAYNE on the upper left hand corner. "Richard Mills was his attorney."

I unfolded a letter explaining that he'd been given instructions to mail the enclosed message to La Donna in the event of Riley's death. I looked up, my frown meeting her expression of perplexity. "Well, this is…certainly thought-provoking. There has to be some good reason that Riley laid out such specific instructions with his attorney."

"Yes, well I won't pretend to know what he meant by sending it to me." Her eyelids drooped. "I'm sorry," she said suddenly. "I have to lie down now."

"I understand. Thank you for your time." I rose and headed towards the door.

"Please make sure you close the door securely," she called after me in a tired voice. "I don't want my cats to get outside."

"Will do." Pulling the door closed behind me, I wasn't quite sure what to think about her or the significance of the peculiar messages from beyond the grave. In addition I questioned the sincerity of her vehement denial of any involvement in Riley Gibbons's death. The ailing, victimized widow had more than enough reason to dispatch her philandering husband. And even if she didn't have the wherewithal to do it herself, it wasn't out of the question that she could have hired someone to do it for her. One could almost understand why she might shoot him in a fit of jealous rage, but I still could not fathom why she would go to the extra trouble of slicing off the man's head.

I returned to my car, dropped the notepad on the seat and reached for my windbreaker. The waning afternoon sunlight cast a pleasing buttery glow over the landscape, but provided little warmth against the incessant wind as I followed the walkway towards the old hotel. I was tempted to stop and interview the Van Steenholm woman, but there was a finite amount of daylight remaining to view the crime scene. Passing by the old hotel, I noted the piles of new boards, drywall, cans of paint and tools, but there were no signs or sounds of anyone working. The sandy path wound its way through well-tended rock gardens sprinkled with cacti, wildflowers and native succulent plants. But the further I walked the more the path narrowed and the foliage became jungle-like, creating a cloistered effect that even muted the birdcalls. Suddenly, I felt isolated. Try as I might, I could not banish the visual of someone hacking away at Judge Gibbons's neck in this secluded hideaway. I shook off a chill of unease as the oncoming clouds echoed with the distant rumble of thunder.

Listening to the muffled thud of my footsteps, I hurried along the path which finally widened into a clearing that contained a series of small pools, some no more than fifteen or twenty feet in diameter. I knelt beside the first one, dipped my fingers in the cold water and sat back on my heels surveying the amazing desert sanctuary. I rose and continued along the winding pathway until I came to a much larger body of water encircled by oleanders and massive cottonwood trees. Standing there listening to the lonesome rush of the wind through the treetops brought home how perfect this solitary place was to have committed a murder.

The temperature was dropping, so I zipped my jacket to the neck and pulled the hood over my head. I continued circling the perimeter of the pond searching for anything unusual, even though chances of finding anything significant were slim considering that the authorities had swept the area a multitude of times. But, it couldn't hurt to look. I kicked over stones and used a stout stick to rummage through bushes and tall waving grass alongside the well-worn trail that eventually led to a gate where a sign advised hikers that they would be entering a wilderness area with no facilities. The terrain looked rocky and daunting as I looked beyond the gate towards the Praying Nun.

I turned to retrace my steps and had walked only a few yards when a shrill screech from above startled me. I glanced upward to see a brightly colored parrot staring down at me. No doubt the bird had escaped from somewhere nearby and I wondered how this domesticated creature could survive in this remote area. My attention distracted, I didn't see the tree root sticking up in front of me. I caught my toe and went sprawling, the sudden impact with the ground knocking the wind out of me. My chin in the dirt, it took several seconds to catch my breath. When I pushed to my knees, the bird let out a cackle that sounded suspiciously like laughter. "Very funny," I called out, watching it flap away. Afterwards I would marvel at the fact that if I hadn't been in that exact spot looking up in the tree, I wouldn't have seen what looked like a piece of white cloth fluttering in the breeze among the brown leaves. Curious, I rose to my feet and tried to reach it, but it was just beyond my grasp. Balancing on a nearby rock, I used the stick to pull the end of the branch towards me. Carefully, I removed the white object. Hmmm. It looked like a piece of raw cotton, like the little puffs that come inside a prescription bottle. Probably nothing important, but I stuck it in my pocket and moved on past the pool. I halted in surprise at the unexpected sight of what appeared to be a dirt road flanked by dense foliage. Apparently Hidden Springs was not as hidden as I'd thought. On closer inspection, the road looked freshly carved and underbrush had been cut away to form a crude trail. Perhaps a hundred yards beyond, situated on a gentle rise, stood an unfinished structure with concrete blocks piled adjacent to it. Must be the new bathhouse La Donna had mentioned. I hiked up the hill and peeked inside. It was difficult to see clearly because of the low light, but I made out four shadowy alcoves with benches that would no doubt be changing rooms. Along the back wall were two bathroom stalls. Not a bad idea considering how far the springs were from the hotel and cottages.

I ambled back to the narrow road, knelt down, and ran my fingers along a multitude of recent tire tracks. With this back entrance a host of possibilities opened up as to who the perpetrator may have been. It was feasible the judge had been killed nearby, but it was just as likely that the body had been brought in and dumped. That actually made a lot more sense and would explain its discovery nearly two weeks after the judge's disappearance. Had the killer performed the gruesome task of removing his head before or after arriving at this idyllic spot? The lack of incriminating physical evidence present seemed to indicate the former, but if he had been killed near Flagstaff, where had the body been all this time and why would the killer go to all the trouble of hauling the corpse here?

Huge drops of rain began to spatter on my head. I looked up, shocked to see low black clouds gathered overhead. Unlike the swift-moving summer monsoons that charged in leading a powerful entourage of wind, lightning and deafening thunder, the winter storms kind of sneaked up on me. Time to go. I stood up, pulled the hood tighter and made a beeline for the path, flinching when a blinding bolt of lightning struck nearby. Then the sky opened up. Whoa! That was unexpected. According to Tally, electrical storms this time of year were rare events.

It was difficult to see even three feet in front of me. I slowed my steps, thinking that I could either make a run for my car and get thoroughly soaked or wait out the cloudburst in the unfinished bathhouse. At that instant, the downpour turned into a barrage of hail. That settled it. I sprinted up the hill and ducked inside the building. There were no exterior doors, but I felt thankful that at least the roof had been completed as I stood listening to the steady percussion of hail clattering from above. The hail vanished as quickly as it had come, but heavy rain resumed. Every now and then a flash of odd violet-colored lightning and a loud clap of thunder added to the drama. I thoroughly enjoyed the rip-roaring excitement of a good thunderstorm. Rivulets of water cascaded down the hill while the cottonwood trees pitched madly in the fickle wind, which suddenly blew the rain horizontally through the doorway, soaking my jeans and shoes.

Reluctantly, I retreated to the rear of the building, slapping the water from my clothing. I bent down to tie one sodden shoelace and froze. There was a dark mound beneath one of the closed stall doors. I stared breathless, waiting for another bolt of lightning. A brilliant, sustained blaze confirmed my suspicions as, clearly visible, was a pair of muddy, black boots.

12

In the space of a nanosecond several scenarios streaked through my mind, the uppermost being that the boots belonged to the murderer. I rose and dashed for the doorway. At the same instant the stall slammed open and I collided headfirst with someone. We both went sprawling on the wet floor. A searing pain ricocheted through my head and white pinwheels danced before my eyes. Several seconds passed until my vision cleared enough for me to make out the form of an athletic-looking young woman dressed in jeans and a tan jacket. With a groan of pain, she pushed to a sitting position, holding one ear. When I sat up, the hood of my windbreaker fell back and damp tendrils tumbled around my cheeks. I reached up and gingerly touched the lump growing on my forehead. A deafening roar of thunder shook the building and through the hazy curtain of rain slanting in the open door, the stranger and I made eye contact. I could see my own apprehension reflected in her startled gaze, apparently each of us thinking the same thing.

Patting the floor around her, a look of relief softened her face when she picked up a pair of glasses and slipped them on. She stared at me hard. A slight twitch began at the corner of her mouth and bloomed into an incredulous grin. "I don't believe it," she gasped. "Stick? Is that you?"

My mouth dropped open. I hadn't heard my childhood nickname for fifteen years, and only one person had ever called me that. We both scrambled to our feet and as I moved closer to get a better look at her, a warm glow of recognition flooded my veins. "Fitzy? Oh my God? What the...? I mean...how...? You scared the ever lovin' crap out of me!"

"Ditto!" Her greenish hazel eyes danced with humor as she pushed aside dark brown curls to massage her right ear. "I always knew you were hardheaded but did you have to knock me on my ass to prove it?"

Tears of joy stung my eyes while fond memories of our eight years as inseparable buddies marched through my head. I threw my arms around Nora Kay Fitzgerald, my best friend from third grade, and she returned the hug affectionately. Then I pulled back to study her oval face, which had changed a lot and yet seemingly not at all. "I don't know what the odds are of us both being at this particular spot at the exact same time, but they have to be astronomical. I am just blown away."

"If you hadn't been wearing that hood I would have recognized that frizzy red hair earlier," she remarked, wiping mud from the sleeve of her jacket. I noticed that the knees of her jeans were also soiled, as if she'd been crawling around in the dirt. "And you're still stick thin, damn you."

"This is amazing. I still can't believe it," I murmured, overwhelmed with a sense of wonder. "The last time I saw you we were standing in your front yard crying our eyes out while your dad and brother were loading the U-Haul for your move to Idaho."

"I know. That seems like light-years ago."

"I remember we vowed to never lose touch," I remarked softly, "but after you got married and moved to Los Angeles I didn't hear much from you. Then my Christmas cards started coming back. I called your folks and they said you'd moved to San Diego and were going through a divorce…gosh, was that seven years ago?"

The force of the rain was diminishing and the remains of thunder rolled over the ridgeline, rumbling like felled bowling pins.

A look of chagrin flickered in her eyes. "It's my fault. I just…lost touch. I kept meaning to write or phone. I don't have a good excuse except time got away from me. I was pretty depressed and life got really crazy after Larry and I split up. I went back to school, I was working two jobs, and then I met a really nice guy by the name of Eddie Bartoli. He swept me off my feet and we got married. He sells medical software and travels a lot, we moved to Houston, then he got transferred to Denver…" she hitched her shoulders. "So, what are *you* doing here in Arizona? Last I heard you were still working at your dad's newspaper there in Spring Hill and engaged to that pharmacist. Did you marry him?"

I nodded. "Major disaster. It lasted barely two years. After that I moved to Philly and worked at the *Inquirer* on the investigative team. I got engaged again and then developed severe asthma so he dumped me. My doctors suggested a warm dry climate so here I am. I work at the *Castle Valley Sun* now."

She nodded sagely. "I see. So you're here on assignment and you suspected I might be the murderer, right?"

I grinned. "Don't tell me you weren't thinking the same thing about me?"

"In spades." We both laughed.

"Now, are you going to tell me what *you're* doing out here in the boonies? Are you a guest here? I didn't see any other cars out front. Where are you parked?"

She pointed behind me towards the makeshift road. "At the bottom of the hill. I'm investigating this case too."

I stared at her blankly. "You are? Why?"

"It's part of my job." She swept her hand down indicating her muddy jeans. "I've been here all afternoon crawling around in the bushes looking for evidence that may have been missed. I got a little jittery when I saw you skulking around because it's not unusual for the suspect to return to the scene of the crime."

Bewildered, I repeated, "Return to the scene? Are you a detective?"

"No, I'm a forensic anthropologist."

I gave her a blank stare. "Bartoli? Oh my God, *you're* Dr. Nora Bartoli?"

"That's me." Her animated smile accentuated the dimple in one cheek and brought back fond memories of sleepovers where we'd laugh and talk until the wee hours of the morning.

"I don't know why I should be surprised," I remarked, still in awe. "Everyone else in biology class was close to retching, but you loved dissecting worms, frogs and those poor little bunnies. And now…you've moved on to people."

"It's definitely not for the faint of heart."

"Do you like this line of work?"

"I love it. I couldn't do it otherwise. It's got its high points and some days, really low points," she said with a solemn nod, "but all in all it's stimulating and challenging."

We both flinched when another gigantic roll of thunder shook the building and the rain started hammering the roof again in earnest. I looked out the door at clouds that seemed close enough to reach up and touch. "Doesn't look like this is going to stop anytime soon. We'd better get out of here. If the washes are already running, we may be spending the night at the hotel."

Her eyes darkened with concern. She dug her cell phone from her pocket and flipped it open. "No signal," she said with a sigh of annoyance. "Rain or no rain, I've got to be back in Phoenix by six o'clock."

"Oh. Can't you stay? Why don't you come into town and have dinner. We have a ton of catching up to do."

"Can't. As usual, Eddie's out of town and my sitter has other plans this evening."

"Your sitter!" Fists on my hips, I exclaimed with mock severity, "That's a rather important piece of information to leave out of your life's story. So, how many kids do you have?"

Grinning, she waved away my comment. "Just one. Mason will be six in March."

"Wow, we definitely have to talk and now that I know what you do, I'd like to discuss the Gibbons case with you."

Her gaze turned guarded. "Actually, I'm not at liberty to disclose much at this point in the investigation."

"How about off the record...for an old friend?"

She hesitated and seemed to be considering my request. "Depends on what you want to know."

"Anything that would help me narrow down the list of suspects. Turns out I have a personal connection with this case."

Little frown lines crinkled her forehead. "How so?"

I filled her in on the sketchy details of my relationship with Tally, his tie to Riley Gibbons, our recent engagement—which she congratulated me on—and his mother's surprising request. She nodded morosely. "Well, you do have yourself boxed into a corner."

"Tell me about it. I still haven't told Tally and when I do, it's gonna hit the fan."

"I'd like to help, but I'm still conducting tests on the tissue samples...and they're not conclusive." Her eyes softened at my obvious disappointment and she added, "I can tell you this much in confidence. The cause of death was from the gunshot wound to the chest, so you can assure...what's her name?"

"Ruth."

"You can assure Ruth that he was already dead when his head was removed."

I was silent a moment as I reordered my thoughts. "So, in your professional opinion, when do you think that happened?"

"I'm still in the process of establishing that."

"I've got to tell you, this missing head thing creeps me out, but I'm guessing you've worked on cases like this before."

"Each situation is unique, but yeah, I've seen it happen before. Perhaps the thinking is we won't be able to identify who it is, but with advances in forensic science, that's less and less the case. I don't know why but some criminals feel compelled to hang onto some of the victim's body parts. In cases like this one," she said, giving me a mischievous smile, "I call it keeping a trophy head."

"Trophy head? Whoa. That is so sick."

Her nonchalant shrug seemed to convey that this type of bizarre behavior did not surprise her.

I looked at her sharply. "What do you think? Was he killed here or someplace else?"

"The authorities conducted standard line and grid searches, lake patrol divers searched the pools and so far there's no evidence to indicate that he was killed here. No blood, no bullets, no shell casings, no identifiable footprints. So," she said, spreading her arms wide, "I don't know for sure where it happened, but I came here today to satisfy myself that we haven't missed anything."

"What kinds of things are you looking for?"

"Drag marks, hair, fabric, skin, fingernails… nothing so far. But I'm ninety-nine percent sure that his body was transported here. My guess is the suspect came in that back road, drove right up to the edge of the pool and…splash."

"I assume the body was weighted down with something?"

"Yep. Tied to a couple of the concrete blocks just like the ones piled up outside."

"Were there any identifiable tire tracks?"

"They're still working on that. Unfortunately, two weeks of rain and snow and other vehicles driving in and out have made it difficult to isolate one particular track. By the time I got here it was just a big muddy mess, but we did get a variety of soil samples that we're now analyzing."

"What about the handyman, the guy who found the body? Anything to tie him to the murder?"

"Can't say right now."

"Okay. According to the sheriff's report, besides his vehicle, a flower delivery van was here that day along with several other trucks transporting construction materials. And apparently some of the posse members drove in here the night the judge's body was discovered."

She made a wry face. "It would be nice for me if the crime scene was uncontaminated, but it doesn't always happen that way. I get called in on a lot of cold cases where someone's stumbled upon a couple of bones in the desert and that's all that's left for me to work with."

My admiration for her grew by the minute. "I've watched some of these crime scene investigation shows on TV. What do you think of them?"

Her laugh was scornful. "In some ways, they've actually made my job a little harder because criminals are mindful of the progress in forensics and they're more careful not to leave behind incriminating evidence." She shook her head. "I find it kind of funny that the job is made out to be exciting and glamorous."

"And I'm sure it's not."

"Anything but. People seem really impressed now when they find out what I do. I call it the 'cool factor,' but I wonder how those same people would react if they could have been with me a month ago while I was prying the ribs apart on a mushy torso found in a trash barrel after it had baked in 100-degree-plus temperatures for a week. Bet they wouldn't think that was too cool. Truth be told, it's tedious, exacting and smelly."

"Doesn't sound like something I'd want to do for a living. You must have an iron stomach."

"I guess. But, I'm able to deal with it because when it turns out to be relevant, it feeds something in me. There's a lot of satisfaction in solving the mystery of how someone died." Her eyes grew animated. "There's nothing quite like that moment—that *ah-ha* moment when I *know*. Then I can give people an answer as to what really happened to their loved one."

"Interesting. I feel the same way about what I do. Guess our jobs aren't all that different, except mine's not quite as messy as yours." I paused and added with a sardonic grin, "Most of the time."

"You'll have to fill me in on all the stuff you've been up to." She glanced outside into the gathering dusk. "Looks like the rain is letting up. I've got to go, but what say I drive you around to your car."

I accepted and we made our way down the slushy road to her maroon Toyota pickup. Hesitating, I stared with dismay at my dirt-streaked clothes and muddy shoes. "I hate to mess up your truck."

Her good-natured grin stretched ear to ear. "Are you kidding? You're talking to someone who has traveled some of the roughest roads in the state into wilderness conditions in weather worse than this to examine remains. Heck, I spent the better part of three months at one of the landfills in Mobile sifting through chicken bones and dirty diapers looking for some poor woman who'd been stuffed in a dumpster."

I stared at her, marveling. "You worked on that one? I take it back. My job is downright cushy compared to yours. I'd sure love to join forces with you on this case. It's weird. People kill people all the time and you almost get immune to it, but to cut the guy's head off? That bugs me. It's like…I've killed you, now I'm going kill you again." I gave her an earnest look. "I've got to know. What kind of implement was used to…you know?"

Her thoughtful expression turned skeptical as she contemplated my question. "I remember you were always up for just about anything when we were kids, but tell me, do *you* have an iron stomach?"

My mind flashed back to the horrific scene I'd witnessed a month ago at the Mexican border while investigating my blockbuster story. "Sometimes."

She tilted her head in question. "Sure you want to know?"

"I asked."

"I can't give you all the details because of who you are and because all our tests on the soft tissue and cut bone are not yet conclusive. This much I can tell you. When we did the tool mark analysis we found it to be a very clean cut. Whoever decapitated him used a reciprocating saw, you know, like a Sawzall."

13

Nora's blunt statement sent cold shockwaves rolling through my gut. As she maneuvered her pickup along the uneven road, I could not dispel the nauseating image of Riley Gibbons's handsome face being severed from his body. Considering what she'd said about the murderer often returning to the scene of the crime, I was more thankful than ever that it had been her hiding in the deserted bathhouse. Okay. Now I knew what I was dealing with. Not a madman as first suspected, but a cool, calculating individual who knew how to wield a reciprocating power saw. Choosing from the pool of local suspects pretty much narrowed it down to Randy Moorehouse or Winston Pendahl—each having a bone to pick with the judge.

Bone to pick? Yikes! My thoughts were starting to travel down the same road as Walter and Jim's. When Nora pulled into the parking area, we spent another fifteen minutes or so sitting in her truck reminiscing about our childhood. We only had time to touch briefly on current events with the exception of my upcoming engagement party.

"I'm anxious for you to meet Tally and all my friends from the paper too," I said, opening the door. A chill breeze rushed inside the warm cab. "You'll come won't you, and bring your husband and little boy? And guess what else? My folks, my brothers and some of my cousins from Ireland are flying in as well."

Her rosy complexion affirmed her delight. "I'll be there. Your dad was always such a kick to be around. Wow. It really will be like old home week."

"Super! Sure you can't join Tally and me for dinner tonight? We've got so much to catch up on." I also wanted to grill her for more information about Riley's case, but she declined, expressing her need to return home.

Suddenly, I remembered what I'd found. "Hold on a minute," I said, reaching into my pocket. "I don't know if this is anything important, but it was hanging in a tree near the pond where the judge was found." Grasping it with just my fingernails, I carefully pulled out the clump of cotton and handed it to her. "Doesn't it look like the cotton they stuff in the top of prescription drug bottles?"

"It sure does." Her eyes lit up as she reached underneath her seat and pulled out a box of plastic gloves and a paper bag. She snapped the glove on, carefully took the cotton ball from me and placed it in the bag. "I'll have it sent to the lab for immediate testing."

"How come you're using a paper bag? I thought plastic was used to collect items for analysis?"

"No. We use paper so as to not contaminate the biological evidence."

"What do you mean?"

"Plastic is moisture holding and doesn't breathe, so if you put biological evidence into a plastic bag, any moisture allows the DNA to degrade while fomenting mold like crazy, thereby contaminating your specimen. Law enforcement has moved towards using containers that have breathable paper on one side and plastic on the other so they can write on it, but I think the safest thing is to package everything in plain brown paper bags."

"Huh. I learn something new everyday. Well, anyway, assuming that the cotton did come from a prescription bottle," I ventured, remembering the row of them lined up on La Donna's windowsill, "will they be able to identify the type of medication?"

"If they weren't capsules there's a good chance there might be traces left."

"How long until you know something?"

"I'll make sure it's a top priority. Hopefully just a day or two."

"I'll call you." We exchanged phone numbers and e-mail addresses, hugged each other goodbye, and as I stood there watching her drive away, I wondered how much of what she'd told me I should share with Ruth. Would telling her that the judge had first died of a gunshot wound to the chest and *then* had his head chopped off make her feel better or worse?

I checked my watch. Best get cracking since I had no idea what the road conditions would be like following the storm. I'd just cleared the raindrops from my windshield and shifted into reverse when a sporty white SUV pulled in and parked near the low wall. A guest checking in? Curious, I paused and watched a petite, young woman wearing jeans and an oversized pea-green sweatshirt slide from the driver's side. The wind caught her short-cropped chestnut hair and blew the bangs away from her forehead. When she spotted me, she smiled and raised a hand in greeting before opening the rear hatch of her vehicle. The interior was stuffed with cardboard boxes and grocery bags which she began gathering towards her.

I grabbed a business card from the dashboard and slid my window down. "Excuse me. Are you Marissa Van Steenholm?"

She looked over her shoulder, her expression pleasantly inquiring. "Yes?"

"Kendall O'Dell, reporter for the *Castle Valley Sun*."

The welcoming shine in her eyes diminished immediately. "Yes?"

I held out the card to her. "I'm on my way out, but I was wondering if I could talk with you another time, perhaps tomorrow?"

She stepped towards me and retrieved the card. "What about?"

"Riley Gibbons."

"You know what?" she said, pursing her lips, "I'm really not in the mood to talk to any more reporters about that...awful situation."

I sighed. Time to cash in the connection card once again. "Judge Gibbons was my fiancé's uncle. Did he ever mention the Talverson family to you?"

Still wary, her shoulders relaxed slightly. "A couple of times. Why?"

"Well, naturally the family is very distraught, so any additional information you could provide might be helpful."

"I've been following the coverage in your newspaper. It appears to be pretty thorough. I don't think there's anything I can tell you that you don't already know."

I'll be the judge of that, I thought, but said aloud, "Sometimes simple things are overlooked. I'd appreciate a few minutes of your time." I issued her a friendly smile.

She paused, tucking a thatch of hair behind one ear. "Oh, all right, but I won't have any free time until after our guests check out in the morning."

"Whatever time is convenient for you."

"How about eleven-thirty?"

"That'll work."

She nodded goodbye, loaded her arms with grocery bags and toed the gate open. Her swift backward glance in my direction before she turned away made me wonder if there was more hidden here than pools of water.

I was almost to the main road when I rounded a corner and saw a white pickup and trailer stopped sideways in the middle of driveway, blocking my exit. The hood was up and a man was bent over the truck's engine, obviously tinkering with something inside. He had a generous mass of wavy salt and pepper gray hair and his beefy shoulders looked a mile wide. I searched for a place to squeeze past, but there wasn't enough room between the truck and the fence on either side. I coasted to a stop and stuck my head out the window. "Excuse me, could you please let me pass?"

Obviously startled, the man swung around, saw me, turned back to what he'd been doing and then did a classic double take, staring hard at me. He had a neatly trimmed mustache and beard and I guessed his age to be mid-forties. Wiping his hands on a smudged cloth, he ambled towards me with a look of shrewd appraisal. When he reached my truck, he showed me a mouthful of very white teeth and leaned in the window, effectively invading my comfort zone. "Well, hi there, pretty lady. Anybody ever told you that you have amazing red hair?"

"Once or twice."

"I'll bet. Say, you think you could give me a jump?"

He made no secret of checking me out and my cheeks flamed with irritation when his eyes lingered long on my boobs. Pretty brazen dude. Coolly, I answered, "I suppose so." How else was I going to get him out of my way?

"Great. Pull 'er up closer to me and pop the hood." I did as he asked while he ran to the trailer, opened the back and after a moment returned and clamped jumper cables to the respective batteries. He hopped in his truck and signaled me to start my engine. I did and after several tries, his truck roared to life. He gave me two thumbs up, jumped out and trotted back to my truck. "Hey, thanks a bundle. Say, do you live around here?"

Oh yeah, that was an original pick-up line. "Around. How about you?"

Again, the wide display of shining teeth. "Winston Pendahl at your service. I'm doing all the renovations at the hotel."

"Is that so?"

"Yep. And if you ever need anything fixed, built or serviced, anything at all, I'm your man." His meaningful wink made my skin crawl. He whipped a card from his pocket and held it out to me. "You can call me anytime."

So, this was the guy who'd spent six years in prison for beating another man to death with a hammer. A quick glance at his muscular forearms and hands confirmed that he possessed the physical wherewithal to have easily performed such a feat. Operating a power saw would be a piece of cake for him as well. "Kendall O'Dell." I pulled one of my cards from the dashboard and exchanged it with his.

"Kendall, huh?" he repeated with an expectant gleam in his dark green eyes. "Well, well. Looks like you and me got something in common."

I didn't want to have anything in common with this smarmy guy and it took supreme effort to keep my face expressionless. "Oh? And what would that be?"

"We rhyme!"

"I'm not following you."

"Kendall and Pendahl! Get it?" He laughed heartily at his lame pun. It was on the tip of my tongue to tell him to take a hike, but I wanted to reserve the opportunity to question him later.

"Yeah, I get it."

"Well, thanks again, I owe ya one." He glanced at my card and his face fell. "Oh? You're a reporter."

"Yes I am. And I'd like to hear all the details concerning your discovery of Judge Gibbons's body."

It was fleeting, and if I hadn't been looking right at him I'd have missed the wary expression that flickered behind his eyes. He stroked his beard. "I...I can't talk right now. I'm late getting this stuff to the hotel."

"Well then another time soon," I pressed, watching him closely.

His fawning disposition morphed into petulance. "I already gave my statement to the sheriff and I already talked myself blue in the face answering questions for all those other nosy reporters who were hangin' around here a couple of weeks ago, so I ain't got nuthin' new to say."

I could tell he was retreating and mustered up a genial smile. "I'd prefer to hear your firsthand account myself just in case you remember something else germane." I could tell by his vacant look that he didn't know what germane meant.

"I ain't got nuthin' to hide." A trace of belligerence underscored his words.

"I never said you did."

He appeared to be thinking it over. "Okay. How about you meet me this evening for a drink? I'll be at the Hitchin' Post around six."

Sure. Meeting this sleazeball after dark at a biker bar sounded like a really smart move.

"I'm tied up this evening," I replied, keeping my voice pleasant, modulated. "Another time would suit me better."

"Sure. Sure. Like I said, I don't got a thing to hide."

"That's good to hear. We'll talk again."

He ran back to his truck and I pulled back to allow him to drive by. Black lettering on the side of his truck read: PENDAHL'S HANDYMAN SERVICE. I glanced in my rearview mirror in time to see him staring back at me. I decided that Winston Pehdahl's dubious behavior suggested the man had plenty to hide.

Clearing the shadowy canopy of palm fronds, I turned onto the main road thinking that my membership in the Fourth Estate certainly hadn't earned me any accolades today. As Hidden Springs faded from sight my thoughts returned to Riley Gibbons's intriguing message from beyond the grave. LET YOUR HOOK ALWAYS CAST. IN THE POOL WHERE YOU LEAST EXPECT IT, WILL BE FISH. I'd read enough verse and prose of well-known philosophers like Longfellow and Ralph Waldo Emerson to know that the words could be open to more than one interpretation. But, what had the judge meant by choosing that particular phrase?

Patches of robin's egg blue sky appeared overhead as I reached the top of the hill, and I stared in delight at the wide sweep of cantaloupe-colored sky to the west where feathery lavender clouds fanned out in preparation for twilight's grand finale. The bulk of the storm had pushed southward towards Phoenix, but judging by the charcoal hue of the clouds congregating above the northern mountains, it was apparent we were going to get clobbered again.

I switched into four-wheel drive and after negotiating a series of deep water-filled potholes in the rutted road I approached the first major dip with trepidation. There was only a trickle of water running through it. I sighed in relief. When it came to crossing desert washes in bad weather I was still uneasy as a result of being stranded in the middle of one in a raging torrent last summer. The water level was running a little higher in the second wash as I splashed across. In all likelihood, it was already raining or snowing in the higher elevations. The sooner I got to a paved road the better. When I passed the gravel quarry, I exercised extra caution rounding the sharp turns. Apparently inclement weather hadn't halted deliveries, as evidenced by the cavernous tire tracks carved in the mud. It made negotiating the gummy surface challenging.

Even though I was looking forward to seeing Tally, the thought of confessing my pact with Ruth filled me with anxiety. Mindful of his hectic schedule this weekend it might be wise to confirm our dinner date. I fished out my cell phone but had to travel another mile before I got a signal. A glance at the screen indicated that I had voicemail. I dialed the number and listened to Tally's message with dismay. The rancher driving in from Colorado with his mares had broken down and was stranded at a remote place called Chambers, Arizona, on the Apache Reservation. Tally and Jake were on their way to meet him. Could we reschedule our dinner for tomorrow? Frap! Double frap! The more time that passed the more deeply enmeshed I'd be in this story.

Mild irritation washed over me, but I shook it off. Might as well take advantage of the unexpected gift of time. I scrolled to Ginger's number and her younger brother Brian answered on the second ring.

"Hey, Kendall, what's up?"

"Oh, this and that. Your sister there?"

"Yeah, hang on."

He set the phone down and I could hear the din of the TV in the background and Nona's little dog Suzie yipping up a storm.

"What's cookin', girlfriend?" Ginger said, coming on the line.

"How did the rest of the show go? Did you get rained out?"

"Talk about a gully washer! We'd no sooner buttoned 'er up, when down she came."

"No kidding. Hey, what are you up to this evening?"

"Not much. Just settin' here watching TV with Nona."

"My dinner plans with Tally fell through and—"

She cut in, "Did you tell him yet?"

"No." I repeated his message to her.

"In a way you got a lucky break. If he ain't at the ranch that means Lucy ain't had a chance to rat on ya either."

"True. Anyway, do you want to get together and go over plans for the party?"

"Is a pig's hiney made o' pork?"

I laughed. "I'm about twenty minutes from town. How about we meet at the florist and then if you're up for it we can eat dinner at Angelina's or I can get takeout."

"I think the flower shop closes early on Saturdays, but I'll give Rulinda a jingle and buzz ya right back."

As I swung onto the main road my thoughts involuntarily strayed to Grant. I wondered how his interview in Phoenix had panned out and thought how odd it was that we were working the same story, albeit unintentionally. Even though it was best that we not meet again, on a professional level I wished I could compare notes with him because he was the best in his field and would no doubt have an interesting take on the whole situation. The phone's merry tune burst into my musings.

"Hey, Rulinda's closing up in five minutes," Ginger announced, "but she's gonna do us a favor and bring a bunch of catalogs and a couple of sample arrangements back to her place. She says we can come by tomorrow afternoon after church and have a look at 'em. You want to meet me there around one o'clock or so?"

"I thought you were going to be at the fairgrounds again."

"Naw. Some of the other gals from church will be holdin' down the fort if we don't get flooded out. But I'm free tonight if you want to work on some of the other stuff. Why don't you pick up dinner? I'll take the beef enchilada combo, no green onions."

I hung up thinking that this arrangement would actually work to my advantage. A visit to Rulinda's place might give me an opportunity to learn more about her brother Randy's activities since his release from prison.

After I picked up the food, I arrived at Ginger's place and chatted with Brian regarding his progress researching Judge Gibbons's past rulings. He told me he'd already forwarded details on more than two-dozen cases to both Walter and me. I thanked him and then Ginger and I settled at her kitchen table. Following a lot of back and forth, which included a staggering list of her suggestions, I finally settled on announcements, music and the menu. And she reminded me that as soon as Myra Colton made her decision on the ice sculpture we'd choose a theme. With directions to Rulinda's house tucked in my purse, Ginger accompanied me to my car, quizzing me each step of the way for additional details about Grant. But I sidestepped her questions stating my haste to get home and begin my quest for a suitable photo. And besides, I was totally beat.

By the time I eased into the driveway and killed the engine it was closing in on eight o'clock. My energy level hovered somewhere around zero. The two fitful hours of sleep from the night before had finally caught up with me. But bedtime would have to wait awhile.

I paused at my front door to breathe in the pungent scent of wet earth and rain-soaked desert plants noting that the cloudbank I'd seen earlier had sailed in and snuffed out the usual blaze of stars. Muted silver moonlight glowed against the outer rim of the thunderheads. While I was happy to have the much-needed moisture after the long, dry summer, it didn't look too promising for the outdoor craft fair tomorrow or the second day of the antique car show.

Seated at my kitchen table, yawning periodically, I sifted through the collection of photographs I'd taken at the Starfire over the past seven months. Not wanting to be left out of the action Marmalade made a nuisance of herself playing with them, lying on top of them and finally knocking a pile onto the floor.

"Cut it out, you little stinker!" I admonished her lightly, leaning over to pick up the spilled contents of one envelope. But then, as if by magic, there it was right in front of me—the perfect picture of Tally sitting tall in the saddle astride Geronimo. Damn, he looked good on a horse. Imagining what the completed sculpture would look like and his reaction when I presented it to him triggered a smile of anticipation. Chuckling, I scratched the purring kitten's chin. "Good job, Sherlock. I owe you an apology."

The phone rang. I frowned at the screen, not recognizing the number. I hit the TALK button. "Hello?"

"Hi, Kendall, it's Tally."

"Hi there yourself. Got your message. Where are you?"

"A motel in Holbrook. We're in the middle of one hellacious snowstorm. I-40's closed up ahead. Big accident." His voice had a gravelly undertone and he sounded whipped.

"Oh no. Guess that means more rain here. Well, as long as you're safe that's all that matters. What are you going to do with the mares?"

"Check on them throughout the night. Get them out, walk them around and try to keep them out of the wind. We didn't have any other choice. Sorry about missing dinner."

"Don't worry about it. So…what time do you think you'll be back tomorrow?"

"Depends on road conditions. It's pretty icy. Could be late."

I might be off the hook until Monday at this rate. "I hate to bug you again, but it would sure be nice and a lot safer when you're going to be out in the middle of the boonies if you'd get a cell phone."

Silence, then, "Yep, I'm thinking about it."

At last! "Good."

Another stretch of silence, then, "So…you going to tell me what my mother had to say to you last night?"

My chest tightened. "It'll keep until tomorrow."

"I don't like the sound of that. Just lay it out for me now."

I hesitated. Even though I would have rather waited and told him in person, why not get the pain over with? "Okay, here's the deal. She's willing to give us her blessing to marry in exchange for…my investigative services."

"What?" The decibel level of his voice rose significantly. "What exactly does that mean?"

"That she's out of her mind with worry over Riley's death. I tried to explain to her how you felt about me taking this story, but she's frantic to know what happened to him. She's not sleeping, not eating. She's got it in her head that because of this bad luck curse of hers, that now you or Ronda might be in some kind of danger."

A short hesitation, then, "That's just nuts. And you agreed? Kendall, I meant what I said."

Again I was flattered by his protective nature, but at the same time irked. "Wait. Just hear me out. I appreciate your concern, but at some point, you're going to have to relax and let me do my job."

"I don't want you getting into the middle of this."

167

"So, what exactly are you saying? That I can't accept any assignment that you deem…risky, without having a chaperone?"

"You could have used one a couple of weeks ago."

"Funny."

"Look, I'm not talking about all stories, I'm simply asking you to leave this one alone. I think it's too dangerous."

"Tally, you know how your mother feels about me. How many other opportunities will I have to make amends for…things?"

"So, you're going back on your word."

"Not at all. Come on. Be reasonable. Besides, how much trouble could I possibly get into? I'll be working here in Castle Valley right under your nose."

"Somehow I think you'll manage."

"Walter is going to stay on this story and I'm just going to do a little low-key snooping, make a couple of calls—"

"Oh, well that puts my mind at ease," came his swift, caustic reply. "What good does it do to have my mother's blessing if you wind up someplace minus your head? She had no business involving you in this and she's getting a piece of my mind when I get back."

Crap. He was just as annoyed as I'd feared. Was he right? Was it worth getting into a battle royal merely to please his loony mother? I had to admit to myself that it was more than that. But, as much as I yearned to immerse myself in the assignment, the answer was probably no. Deflated, I covered my true feelings with a crisp, "I thought it was a good idea at the time. I thought it might be a rare chance to get on your mother's good side and bring a little peace to the household, but you know what? It's not worth upsetting you. I'll go see her myself tomorrow and tell her I can't do it. Will that make you happy?"

"Yep."

"Okay then. Done." I hoped my bravado masked my acute disappointment. I primed myself to mention Grant's appearance at the fairgrounds, but then I clamped my mouth shut. Why provoke him further?

"Tally?"

"Yep?"

"I love you. Be careful driving home."

"Love you too."

I'd no sooner hung up than the phone rang again. Recognizing my folks' number, I suspected the game of phone tag I'd been playing with my mother had ended. I drew in a long, calming breath and pressed the TALK button. "Hi, Mom. What's up?"

"Finally! I know you have an awfully busy schedule, but it shouldn't take you a week to return a phone call to your mother. Do you know how much it hurts my feelings when you ignore me?"

A flare of exasperation heated my chest. She was a master at playing the injured party while doling out copious quantities of guilt. But she'd chosen the wrong moment to lay it on me. "Speaking of hurt feelings, what about mine? Thanks a pantload for springing Grant on me with no notice. You could have given me a heads up. And what's the big idea giving him my address and phone number without consulting with me first?"

"It's not as if I haven't tried. I can't help it if you won't return my calls. But enough recriminations," she said, her severe tone turning solicitous, "I'm glad to hear that he did manage to find you. So, what do you think? Doesn't he look marvelous? He's such a sweet young man, so intelligent, on a great career path with such a bright future in Philadelphia—"

"Mom—"

"But the poor dear has lost so much weight since you broke up with him. His mother told me he's been distressed and repentant about his naughty misadventure and that he's willing to do whatever it takes to patch things up between you. By the way, Phyllis sends her love."

Naughty misadventure? "Mom, you and Phyllis can stop now."

"What do you mean?"

"I'm on to your little conspiracy. Listen to me carefully, I am not getting back together with Grant."

"What makes you think there's a conspiracy?"

"Oh, no reason, except you've made it quite clear from the beginning that you disapprove of my choice of men and that you two obviously designed Grant's surprise visit for a reason. Do the words 'backwoods cowboy' ring a bell?" She'd used the derogatory phrase a half dozen times in the past couple of months.

"Whom are we talking about, dear?"

"Come on, Mom, you know. Tally?"

"Well, honey, if you think he's a backwoods cowboy perhaps you should rethink your decision to marry him."

My head felt like a pressure cooker whistling at full steam. We had arrived at our usual impasse—two stubborn Irish women butting heads, neither willing to back down. It reminded me of how my dad used to get up and quietly leave the room at the barest hint of trouble brewing between us. I knew her well enough to know neither of us would win this verbal exchange so best to end it.

Switching gears, I modulated my voice to a more pleasant tone. "Guess who I ran into today?"

"Who?"

"Do you remember my friend Nora Fitzgerald?"

A slight hesitation. "You mean the girl who used to call you Stick?"

"One and the same."

"Really? What's she doing in Arizona? I thought she was somewhere in Idaho or Oregon."

"Turns out she's the number one forensic anthropologist at the medial examiner's office in Phoenix and we're working the same case."

"What an amazing coincidence. How is she?'

I filled her in then added, "I invited her to our engagement party. She's looking forward to seeing all of you again."

"That's nice. Speaking of the party, I'm still waiting to hear all the particulars."

"I know. I know. I'll e-mail you all the information soon. I still have a few decisions to make for final arrangements. Oh, and you'll be pleased to know that we may even have an ice sculpture created by a very prominent artist who lives in Yarnell, which is a little town not too far from Castle Valley."

"Well, how lovely. Your little desert community must have much more sophistication than I thought."

I didn't miss her dig. "Yes, Mom, and we have running water and electricity here too." Before she could respond, I said hurriedly, "Listen, I've got to hit the hay. It's been a really long day and I'm pooped. Thanks so much for calling. I'm really looking forward to seeing all of you in December. Say hi to everybody. Bye now."

I clicked off before she could say another word and went straight for the refrigerator. After devouring four scoops of vanilla ice cream smothered in hot fudge sauce topped with cashews, I was so charged up that I completed a week's worth of housework and laundry before tumbling into bed around midnight and slipping into a sugar coma so profound it felt like I was sinking through the mattress.

I awakened only once during the night to hear rain hammering on the roof. Snuggling beneath the covers, I fell back into blissful sleep until the irritating noise intruded on my slumber. *Brrrrinnnnng! Brrrrinnnngggg!* Relentless. Persistent. *Brriiinnnng*! What was that noise? It wouldn't stop. *Brrrrriiinnggg!* Was it a phone? I tried, but couldn't fit it into the entertaining dream I was having of galloping on my new horse across the open desert. There were no telephones in the desert, were there? I struggled to wake up but felt like a great weight was pressing down on me. With concentrated effort, I fought my way to consciousness and reached for the phone, croaking, "Hello?"

"Is this Kendall O'Dell?"

I squinted at the caller ID. I didn't recognize the voice or the number. "Yes."

"This is Marissa Van Steenholm."

"Uhhhh…hi." Blinking, I peered at the clock. Not quite seven. What an ungodly hour to be awakened on a stormy Sunday morning.

"I'm sorry to bother you so early, but um…well, it's about this guy who checked in last evening. He was in an accident and his car was totaled. He asked the sheriff to drive him here and—"

"Excuse me, but why are you telling me this?"

"Because he seems like he's in a lot of pain."

"A lot of pain," I repeated back to her, trying to break out of my lethargy and make sense of what she was saying.

"Yeah. I told him I think he needs to see a doctor. He gave me your number and asked me to call you."

I bolted upright, accidentally dumping Marmalade onto the floor. "Who are you talking about?"

"Well, he *claims* that he's your fiancé."

"My fiancé?" My mind reeled in confusion. Why was Tally at Hidden Springs?

"Yeah. His name is Grant Jamerson."

14

Her words were like a slap in the face. Fully awake now, I threw off the covers and sat on the edge of the bed. "Can you please put him on?"

"Sure."

Muted voices. A scrabbling sound as the phone changed hands, then a weak, "Hi."

The first thing I wanted to do was read him the riot act for misleading Marissa on the status of our relationship, but asked instead, "Grant, what's going on?"

"I totaled my car."

"I heard. Are you all right?"

"Not really. My ribs are giving me fits and my neck and right shoulder are killing me...."

"Well...if you're injured, why didn't you call for an ambulance?"

"I didn't feel that bad last night. Only a little sore. I figured I just got roughed up a bit, so I took a couple of aspirin and went to bed. But, this morning, Jesus, I could hardly crawl out of bed."

"What are you doing at Hidden Springs?"

"I took your advice."

"*My* advice?"

"Yeah, I called around yesterday on my way back from Phoenix and this place had a vacancy."

Why didn't you just stay in Phoenix? I wondered, but didn't voice the question, instinctively knowing the answer.

"I was driving over here, just taking my time, admiring the scenery when this humongous gravel truck came out of nowhere. The stupid shit ran me off the road and just kept going. Luckily another guy came by and went someplace to call the sheriff. Did you know there's no cell service in parts of this state?"

"Yes, I know that."

"Anyway, after I filed the report and the tow truck hauled off my rental car, the sheriff gave me a ride here."

"So...are they bringing you a replacement car?"

"Yeah, but they can't get it out here until sometime tomorrow afternoon or Tuesday."

"I see."

When I didn't say anything else, he responded with, "Sorry to bother you. I didn't know who else to call. Is there a hospital in this one-horse town?" His voice sounded plaintive, like a little lost boy. Rats! I sat there wrestling with my emotions, feeling trapped just like I had during the confrontation with Ruth in Joe Talverson's study. Considering Grant's abysmal treatment of me, he didn't deserve one ounce of sympathy. The opportunity to give him a taste of his own medicine was tantalizing, but then my heart caved.

"No, but there is a clinic." I sat there indecisive for long seconds. "We only have one doctor in town. Tell you what," I offered, my mind racing ahead, "I'll try and get hold of Dr. Garcia and see if he can make a house call."

Initial silence greeted my statement before he sighed, "Okay." I'm sure that wasn't the answer he was expecting. How naïve did he think I was not to guess his ulterior motive?

"Hang in there. I'll get back to you." I set the phone down and looked up the doctor's number. In Philadelphia, I could have chosen from any number of hospitals, scores of urgent care clinics or, if I'd tried my doctor, I would have reached his service. In Castle Valley Dr. Garcia answered the phone himself.

"Good morning." His voice sounded hoarse. Little doubt I'd wakened him. I explained the situation and he stated it would be preferable, since he might have to take x-rays, if someone could bring Grant and meet him at the clinic around nine. I thanked him and clicked off. Someone, of course, meant me.

With a groan of capitulation I called Marissa back and told her I'd be there in less than an hour to get him. I hoped. A glance out the window revealed a milky white sky, and the falling temperature had produced patches of ground fog. It wasn't raining at the moment, but there was no telling what the condition of the Hidden Springs road would be after an all-night soaking.

I showered, dressed and fed Marmalade in record time. With a breakfast bar stuffed in my mouth, I shrugged into my coat, called goodbye to the cat and headed out the door. Climbing into the pickup I paused to admire the awesome spectacle of Castle Rock. Shrouded in mist, the summit barely visible, the jagged monolith appeared more imposing than ever. I breathed in the brisk air feeling invigorated. At that moment, the discomfort of the merciless summer heat seemed nothing but a distant memory.

On the drive towards Hidden Springs I mentally flayed myself. Why was I allowing myself to be manipulated by Grant and become mired in yet another predicament? How much more complicated could my life possibly get? I soon found out. The first couple of miles of dirt road were decent, but the further less-traveled section soon deteriorated into a slippery river of mud. Even in four-wheel drive some spots were damn near impassable. My shoulders tensed and my hands fastened in a death grip on the steering wheel as I struggled for control, and more than once I feared I'd be the one stuck waiting for a tow truck. I was relieved when I finally jostled to the top of the hill. Across the valley, the ethereal beauty of the Praying Nun, cloaked in a swirling veil of fog as she knelt in eternal prayer, took my breath away. It was a dicey drive downhill, several times almost sliding off the road, but moments later I reached the valley floor and entered the dark palm tunnel. How different, how somber and mysterious the old hotel appeared that morning nestled darkly in the gloom of the overhanging trees.

While I stood at the door banging the brass doorknocker, rainwater dripped off the eaves and splashed into a wheelbarrow filled with at least two inches of water. The hinges of the scrolled wooden door emitted a shrill screech as Marissa swung it open.

"Come in." Unlike yesterday, she looked relieved to see me.

The first thing I noticed when I stepped inside, besides the ultra-creaky floorboards, was the musty, dank smell. I guessed it was just the odor of age that had permeated this more than one-hundred-year-old building.

And it felt damp and chilly even though a fire crackled merrily in a stone fireplace situated in the room to my right. "He's in there," she whispered, pointing.

"By the way," I advised in a low tone. "Just to set the record straight and clear up any confusion, Grant Jamerson is my *former* fiancé. I'm engaged to Bradley Talverson now."

She gave me a small, knowing smile. "I guess that wishing something is true doesn't always make it so."

"I'm afraid not."

She gestured for me to follow her. I did, but paused at the entrance to what looked like a sitting room filled with dark old-fashioned furniture to admire a bronze statue of a Native American woman holding a small child. I immediately recognized the distinctive style.

"I just met the lady who does these sculptures," I remarked to Marissa. "Her pieces are outstanding. Have you met Myra Colton?"

"Yes. She delivered this a couple of weeks ago. Seems like a nice lady."

When I walked through the doorway Marissa nodded towards the couch where Grant lay stretched out, a blanket pulled over him, his blonde hair ruffled. His eyes were closed, but I sensed he was not asleep. I tapped him gently on the shoulder. "Grant?"

He turned his head slowly and opened those amazing cornflower blue eyes while reaching for my hand. "That's my girl. Kendall to the rescue."

"We don't have a lot of time," I replied, ignoring his overt compliment while trying to douse the growing suspicion that he wasn't really hurt at all. "Dr. Garcia is waiting for us." His hand tightened around mine and he started to sit up but then groaned in pain.

"Christ, that hurts." He grabbed the back of his neck with his free hand and his complexion grew so pale I thought he might pass out.

"Just take it slowly," I urged sympathetically, now convinced that his injuries were genuine. With Marissa holding his other arm, we eased him off the couch, out the door and into my truck.

"Sorry to be such a baby," he moaned, finally settled in the passenger seat as I slid behind the wheel. "Guess I shouldn't have waited so long to see someone."

"Guess not." I turned the key and shifted into gear as rain spattered on the windshield. "Hang on. It's going to be a rough ride." I don't think he believed me until we'd cleared the gravel drive and turned onto the rough, muddy road.

"Nice pickup."

I glanced over at his apprehensive expression. "It's not mine."

"No?"

"Tally loaned it to me until I can get a new car."

"What happened to your Volvo?"

"It got kidnapped and destroyed on my last assignment."

"Sorry to hear that." He winced as I swerved to miss a deep pothole. "So...you sure you're able to handle something this size?"

"If you're worried, I'll be happy to let you drive," I answered tersely, shooting him a challenging look. I think under normal circumstances, he may have taken me up on it, but he backed down, murmuring, "No, that's okay."

I drove as carefully as possible, but there was no way to avoid the giant swales in the road that rocked the truck from side to side. By the time we reached the clinic his jaw was locked and his eyes looked glassy with pain.

Good to his word, Dr. Garcia met us at the front door and ushered him into a cubicle. Seated in the waiting room I flipped through several month-old magazines, looking up when I heard raindrops spattering against the windowpane. Talk about dark and depressing. It was an odd phenomenon to see the sky blanketed with dull gray clouds. Tally had been right again. I'd scoffed at his prediction that I would become addicted to the perpetually blue skies and brilliant Arizona sunlight. As I watched the nearby palo verde trees sway in the wind there was little doubt in my mind that the craft show would to be rained out and I wondered how things were going at the Starfire with Tally's buyers. It was a really sloppy day, but everyone would probably be inside the spacious barn. Thinking of that made me anxious to visit my new mare again.

Forty-five minutes later, a blurry-eyed Grant and Dr. Garcia re-emerged from the back of the clinic. "He's got a couple of badly bruised ribs, pulled shoulder muscles and a nasty case of whiplash. I gave him an injection for pain, but you'll probably want to get these filled as soon as the drug store opens," Dr. Garcia advised me, scribbling on a prescription pad. To Grant he warned, "You need to take it easy for a few days, young man, and I would strongly advise you not to drive while taking these medications."

I thanked Dr. Garcia for meeting us on such short notice and on a Sunday as well while Grant fumbled with his checkbook. Driving towards McCreary's Drug Store, I glanced at my watch. If all went well I'd still be able to make my appointment with Ginger at one o'clock.

I was the first customer at the prescription window and we were on our way back to Hidden Springs within twenty minutes. Now that Grant was no longer groaning in pain, I was hoping to find out if he'd learned anything of importance concerning Riley Gibbons from his exploratory visit to Phoenix yesterday, but he was zonked out for the entire trip. A light rain continued to fall, but the drive was far less harrowing than it had been earlier. He stirred and yawned as I drifted to a stop beside Marissa's SUV.

"Feeling any better?" I inquired, shutting off the engine.

"I think so," he replied sleepily, his boyish yet beguiling smile just a tad goofy. He moved his head back and forth gingerly. "Dr. Garcia dispenses some great drugs. I don't feel like there's an ice pick stuck in my neck anymore." Our eyes connected and held for several seconds causing my pulse to spike involuntarily. Mayday! Mayday! The fact that I still found this man even remotely attractive disturbed me greatly. "I hope I'm going to be able to drive by Tuesday. If I can't, that's gonna really suck."

"What do you mean?"

"My editor's going to hang me out to dry. Having me cover the judge's funeral was the sole reason he flew me out here."

"With any luck, you'll be okay by then."

"Hopefully. Hey, listen, I...um...guess I owe you one for helping me out today."

"I think that can be arranged."

"Yeah? How?"

"You could tell me what you found out about Riley Gibbons yesterday."

Eyeing me through half-opened lids, he arched a skeptical brow. "Thought you weren't covering this story."

"I am now. Sort of."

He nodded approval. "That's my girl."

An uneasy feeling came over me. How welcome his words and attentions would have been a year ago. How fantastic it would be now to work with a man who encouraged me in my career instead of inhibiting me. The fact that I'd even permitted that thought to enter my head filled me with self-reproach. I threw up a protective shield. "I'm not your girl anymore so quit inferring to people that I am."

"What people?"

"For starters, Marissa."

"Who?"

"Come on. The young woman at the hotel who called me on your behalf."

"Oh, her. Well...I was out of my mind with pain. It was an honest mistake."

"I'm not buying it."

His playful grin betrayed him and I counseled myself again not to succumb to the magnetic power of his blue eyes. "Can't blame a guy for trying, can you?"

"I'm serious. Any further communication between us has to remain on a strictly professional basis. Got it?"

He studied my face for long seconds, probably trying to determine if I was serious before venturing, "This might interest you. I spoke to a Judge Creston Towers while I was in Phoenix yesterday."

"Who's he?"

"Good friend of the deceased. He told me that Gibbons had confided to him about receiving a couple of disturbing messages a week or two before he was murdered."

"Disturbing how?"

"Apparently, the envelopes arrived a few days apart and were postmarked from several other states. Each one contained a single sheet of white paper with a quotation printed on it."

I threw him a sharp glance. "What? What kind of quotation?"

"You know, like the ones we were forced to read in English Lit class. Judge Towers pointed them out to detectives when they were going through Judge Gibbons's personal papers at his office."

"Do they believe that they're in any way connected to his murder?" If they didn't think so, I sure did.

"I talked to a Detective Lansing in Homicide and he admitted there wasn't much to go on. According to the lab analysis they could have been printed at any copy shop on any computer and there were no fingerprints."

"Do you remember what the quotes said?"

He ran a hand over his forehead. "I can't recall all of them right now. I've got them written down in my notebook. I think one of them referred to...dreaming of revenge or something like that."

An uncomfortable chill invaded my stomach. "I'd like to see the exact quotes."

"Sure."

"What cities were the letters mailed from?"

He thought for a moment. "San Luis Obispo, California, and Santa Fe, New Mexico."

"Did Judge Towers have anything else to say?"

"Just that Riley seemed worried and preoccupied during his last week at work."

This story was getting more intriguing by the minute. Just the way I liked them. "It's been my contention all along that we're dealing with someone out to even the score."

"Sounds like it. But who? That's the ten million dollar question. And who's got time to sit and go through the guy's entire caseload for the past fifteen or twenty years trying to find out?"

"Actually I've got two people researching it now, the authorities are working on it and I met up with an old friend who just happens to be the forensic anthropologist on this case. I'm hoping I'll get lucky and get some inside information not widely available to the general public."

A look of pride blazed in his admiring gaze. "I knew you were going to make a dynamite investigative reporter the minute I met you." He paused before saying softly, "We made a great team didn't we?" When I didn't answer he added hastily, "You know you're wasting your talent in this little hole in the—" He caught my withering look and swallowed the remainder of his sentence. "Know what? I need to get in a prone position right away or you're going to have to carry me inside."

His complexion had lost its rosy appearance as he slid from the truck and I was very aware of his arm coiled snugly around my waist while I assisted him to the hotel entrance. Marissa met us at the front door and we followed her up squeaky wooden steps. When we reached the landing, I immediately noticed yellow caution tape stretched across the dark mahogany newel posts at the base of a second staircase leading to the upper floor. A crudely written cardboard sign taped to the bottom step warned: VERY DANGEROUS CONDITIONS BEYOND THIS POINT! KEEP OUT!

Just ahead of where we stood, I could see a long, dim hallway crowded with furniture. A ladder, stacks of drywall, cans of paint and a myriad of power tools scattered on drop cloths were visible in the murky light seeping through tall windows. Marissa opened the door nearest to us, explaining that it was one of only three usable bedrooms on the second floor until renovation was completed.

Within seconds of helping him into an impressive four-poster bed and tucking him underneath a comforter, Grant promptly fell asleep. What I wanted more than anything was to go through his notebook, but I couldn't very well rummage through his personal belongings with Marissa watching me. Agitated, I set his medications on an antique side table before we quietly left the room.

"What's the story with that sign?" I remarked, as we passed the roped-off staircase.

"Oh. Our handyman put that up a few weeks ago because he said it's too dangerous to take a chance on having guests wandering around up there." Her gaze turned wistful. "Riley loved to hang out and read in one of the rooms he turned into a library. It's still in pretty good shape but the rest of them are a mess. The man who owned this place before Riley was either lazy or didn't have the money to make repairs."

"I understand there was also a fire."

"Yeah, that was a long time ago, but there's also been a lot of water damage over the years from the leaky roof. Winston says the floors are all rotted because of that and termites. He said he almost broke his leg when part of the floor collapsed so he's real adamant that nobody go up there until he gets things fixed. Right now, he's bustin' his hump trying to get the other rooms on this floor repaired so we can at least get them ready to rent out."

"Looks like you've got your hands full," I remarked, as we descended the stairs.

"More than you think." She was silent for a couple of seconds before inquiring, "Is Mr. Jamerson going to be all right? I hate to sound petty, but I really don't have time to play nursemaid to the guests."

I briefly explained his injuries then added, "The doctor thinks he'll be okay in a couple of days, but feel free to call me again if he seems worse."

"I will."

We reached the first floor and I paused. "Is this a good time for us to talk?"

She averted her eyes, my question appearing to put her on guard. "I guess it's as good as any." I accompanied her into the sitting room again and she motioned for me to sit on the elegant claw-footed sofa. She knelt and fussed with the fire in the hearth for a few minutes until a warm glow filled the room. Wrapping the bulky sweater around her middle, she curled into a gold brocade wing backed chair. I observed her pallid complexion as I opened my notepad.

"Mind if I take a few notes?"

She fingered the material of her long skirt. "I suppose not."

Her aloof demeanor puzzled me. "I understand you worked in Judge Gibbons's office."

"That's right."

"What was your position?"

"Clerk."

"And what were your duties?"

"Lots of things. Filing, computer work, arranging Riley's court schedule, running errands for him and other administrative staff members." A careless shrug. "Stuff."

"How long did you work for him?"

"About a year."

"When did you become...romantically involved with him?"

"Before you go any further I want to set the record straight. I'm sick of being referred to as the *other* woman," she raged, making air quotes with her fingers. "I'm not a slut or a home wrecker. Riley was a good and kind man. He took me under his wing and helped me when I was on desperation's doorstep."

"What do you mean?"

She sighed deeply. "It's kind of a long story."

"I've got time."

Her attention was diverted to the doorway and I turned to see a stocky Hispanic woman clad in blue jeans and a sweatshirt. She wore thick glasses and her dark hair, pulled tightly into a bun, was streaked with gray. "Mail from yesterday," she announced, waving a handful of envelopes. "Do you want me to put it in the kitchen for you?"

"No, I'll take it now," Marissa said, holding out her hand.

The older woman passed by me inquiring, "You feeling any better today?"

"A little," replied Marissa, languidly accepting various sized envelopes from her. Frowning, she opened one of them, saying in a distracted tone, "Bernita, this is Kendall O'Dell. She's a newspaper reporter from Castle Valley."

Smiling, I said, "Hello, Bernita, nice to meet you."

She returned the greeting and pushed her glasses to the bridge of her broad nose.

Marissa beamed an affectionate smile at the older woman and it brightened her morose expression, revealing how attractive she could be minus her perpetually sad demeanor. "Truth be told, it's Bernita who does the lion's share of work around here."

Looking humble, the older woman shrugged and murmured, "We all do our part to keep this place going."

I thought again what a weird situation it was having the judge's widow and girlfriend forced into this uneasy alliance in order to sustain the faltering business. Bernita's black eyes reflected an obvious fondness for Marissa before she turned and left the room. Might be interesting to get her take on the judge's murder.

I turned back to ask Marissa another question and was startled to see her staring at a sheet of paper in openmouthed shock.

"What is it?"

"A letter from Riley's attorney. It says that he received this one week before Riley disappeared and was instructed to mail it to me in the event of his death," she said in an awestruck tone, waving a second sheet. "But, I don't know what it means."

Curious, I rose and moved to her chair. "May I see?"

After a fraction's hesitation, she extended the paper to me. My pulse ratcheted up a notch when I recognized the same meticulous block printing as contained in La Donna's note. LOVE BUILDS BRIDGES WHERE THERE ARE NONE. -R.H. DELANY and DO NOT GO WHERE THE PATH MAY LEAD, GO INSTEAD WHERE THERE IS NO PATH AND LEAVE A TRAIL. -RALPH WALDO EMERSON. Okay! Now things were really getting interesting. The apparent pattern of the carefully selected quotations fired my imagination. What they meant, I had no clue, but the manner in which they'd been sent did much to reveal character and told me that the man had obviously possessed an impish spirit of fun and adventure.

I quickly copied the quotes into my notebook and handed the sheet back to Marissa. She reread the passages with a bewildered expression before meeting my gaze again. "That was one of the things that I admired about Riley. He always had his nose in a book. Anyway, he always had a penchant for repeating these types of philosophical sayings or quoting poetry. But, I've never heard these before." Question marks danced in her eyes. "What am I supposed to make of this?"

"I don't know," I answered honestly, debating as to whether I should mention La Donna's cryptic missive. I decided to wait and see what else developed.

She closed her eyes momentarily and when she spoke her voice sounded despondent. "This whole thing has been a nightmare. Sometimes I wish I'd never come here."

"Why do you stay?"

"That's part of the long story."

"I'm listening."

She hesitated, appearing unsure, then said, "Okay, I'll make it short. My adoptive parents are both dead and I have no relatives that I know of."

"Have you tried to find your birth mother?"

An impatient shrug. "I never wanted to. Anyway, instead of finishing my last year of college, I ended up marrying this guy I met at a party. He came on really strong and I fell for him. Big mistake."

"Why do you say that?"

She picked a few pieces of lint off her skirt. "Eric Van Steenholm was tall and blonde and really hot. He was in the service and we moved around a lot. Because of that, I never made many lasting friends. It was a pretty lonesome life and," she finished in a whisper, "a lot of times, I didn't want anyone to see me."

Uh-oh. "Why not?"

She ran her tongue across her lips, her expressive eyes revealing deep sadness. "Because he turned out to be a drunk. Booze turned him into a monster and more than once...he beat me up pretty bad."

"Sorry to hear that."

Her wistful smile held a trace of triumph. "God got even with him. He died last year of complications from liver disease. I was free from him at last, but he left me saddled with a mountain of debts to pay. I lost everything. Finally, I had no choice but to declare bankruptcy and I went to work at Riley's office. That's pretty much my life in a nutshell." She shifted in her chair. "And just for the record I didn't set out to break up his marriage. We were just good friends. One day we were talking and he confided to me that he'd made a mistake marrying La Donna...that they didn't have much in common and hadn't been happy for a long time...at least he wasn't happy."

"Apparently he forgot to mention that fact to her. I understand she was pretty upset when Riley's will was read."

Her eyes widened. "Upset? She was a raving maniac! For someone who's supposedly so sick that she can hardly lift a finger, she practically tore my hair out. She was screaming about me stealing gold coins and going on about how me and Winston had plotted to kill Riley. Crazy stuff! I would never—"

"Did you know about the coins?"

She flinched when the log snapped behind her, sending a plume of sparks spiraling up the chimney. "He mentioned them to me one time, but I never had a key to the box and I didn't even know what bank they were in. How do we know *she* doesn't have them? She could be lying just to get even with me."

Interesting theory. "I understand you overheard her and Riley having an argument the night before his hunting trip. What was that all about?"

Her gaze grew distant. "Everything. She was ranting about him squandering all her savings and ruining her life, she was complaining about all the work she'd done here and that she had no intention of leaving. Of course she had some choice things to say about me...but most important," she said, leaning forward, her eyes burning with intensity, "I overheard her say that she wished he would drop dead."

Much more interesting. "Really?"

"Really."

"Tell me, how did he seem the last couple of weeks before his disappearance? Was he upset or preoccupied?"

She chewed on a fingernail. "I don't know. Maybe. But then, he was so busy all the time and he was getting ready to go on his trip. Listen," Marissa added earnestly, "nobody was more surprised than me about this whole unbelievable mess. I mean, I had no idea he was going to leave me this...creepy old place, and because he did, La Donna hates my guts."

She seemed totally sincere, totally convincing, but then I'd run up against performances like hers from other people who turned out to be guilty as hell. "I've seen photos of Riley. He was a very attractive...older man."

A touch of color tinted her prominent cheekbones. "I knew that he was thirty-one years older than me, but you know the age difference didn't seem to matter. He was an amazing man and I adored him." Wistfully, she added, "He always called me an old soul."

"So there's no truth to the rumor that you were romantically involved with—"

"Winston?" Her eyes flashed with indignation as she shot to her feet. "That's an out and out lie! La Donna made that up! She knows damn well he's been working here on the property almost every day, but then so have a lot of other people. She's such a spiteful bitch! If I could I would leave here tomorrow."

"Why don't you?"

She crossed her arms defensively and an odd look flitted across her face as she stared at the rivulets of rain cascading down the wavy old windowpanes. "Because other than this…hotel, I've got no place to go. I don't have a dime to my name, no job nor any prospects and…" she said in a small voice, fastening melancholy eyes on me, "I'm pregnant."

15

By the time I parked next to Ginger's car in Rulinda's gravel driveway, I was engaged in a raging battle with myself, my mind awash with the myriad of interviews and perplexing data. I felt as if I'd been handed a brightly wrapped package filled with dazzling and mysterious contents that I was forbidden to open. But, what choice did I have? In order to placate Tally, I now had to yank the rug out from under myself, and it was an effort to banish the cold burn of resentment gnawing at my insides. Piled onto that loomed the unpleasant task of informing Ruth that I was backing out on my promise to her. There was really no winning on either front.

Feeling emotionally drawn and quartered, I laid my forehead against the steering wheel unable to stop thinking about Judge Gibbons's life and bizarre death. The questionable timing of his enigmatic messages to La Donna and Marissa, coupled with Grant's discovery of similar communiqués delivered to the judge in the weeks prior to his death, convinced me that I was standing on the doorstep of something extraordinary. The icing on the cake was

Marissa's surprising admission. Before I'd left Hidden Springs, she'd shared one more piece of unexpected information. According to her, and I remembered that La Donna had also alluded to it in an offhanded manner, the one thing Riley had craved in life that neither of his wives had been able to provide for him was a child. Marissa admitted that she'd considered terminating her pregnancy, but because of her own dubious birth history and out of respect for Riley's memory, she'd decided to carry the baby to term. My head felt like it was going to explode, so great was my longing to continue forward with this compelling story. To say that I was disappointed at not being able to follow it to its conclusion would be the understatement of the century.

The rain had finally stopped, but there was no break in the gloomy cloud cover, so unlike the brilliant sapphire skies I'd grown accustomed to. The temperature had edged down several more degrees and the wind held a sharp bite as I squeezed past a white van with the Posey Patch Florist logo painted in flowers emblazoned on the side. When I reached the front door, it was obvious that the tan slump-block house was badly in need of repair. The chipped concrete patio was crowded with moving boxes, an array of broken clay pots filled with dead plants, several sets of lawn tools and dusty furniture covered with plastic. I rang the bell. While I waited for someone to answer, it occurred to me that, under the present circumstances, taking time to select flowers seemed like a frivolous endeavor.

I heard footsteps approaching and the door swung open to reveal one of the homeliest women I'd ever seen in my life. Whew. Talk about an unlucky genetic draw. It was an effort not to stare at her round pumpkin-like face, complete with puffy eyelids, numerous chin moles and topped off with a bulbous red nose. Copious facial hair fluttered in the wind like cobwebs and...was that a bag clip perched in her steel-wool-gray hair?

"You the O'Dell girl?" the woman inquired gruffly, thumbing the straps of her bib overalls onto her wide shoulders with one hand while holding a beer bottle in the other.

"Yes. Rulinda?"

"In the flesh. Come in." She gestured for me to enter and I almost tripped over a mangy little dog that blended in with the brown braided rug. It yipped loudly. Oops!

"Sorry, I didn't see you, little fella." I reached down to pet it, but quickly withdrew my hand when it snapped at me.

"Kiko, be nice!" Rulinda admonished the mutt while pointing to an arched doorway. "Your friend's in the dining room."

Ginger waved at me from a long table adjacent to a picture window with tape plastered over several cracks in the pane. "Over here, sweetie!"

I crossed through the living room, trying hard not to stare at the hodgepodge of furniture, bric-a-brac and plastic bins of all shapes and sizes piled almost to the ceiling. The décor screamed second-hand store. In contrast, on the table in front of Ginger, amid vases, giant rolls of ribbon and a large pair of serrated shears, sat three unique floral arrangements. As I studied the eclectic selection, I knew it would be difficult to make a final choice for the centerpiece.

"Well, what do ya think?" Ginger asked, her infectious grin wide and expectant.

I shot an admiring glance at Rulinda who stood with arms folded, beaming over her creations. A housekeeper she was not, an artist she was. "They're all...amazing." Did I want the simple black vase holding an exquisite purple orchid accompanied by a delicate spray of baby's breath, the colorful cluster of pansies set in shimmering gold paper offset with wispy feathers or the small glass bowl half filled with water resting on a flat saucer of smoky mirrored glass? A single red rose sprinkled with gold glitter floated in the water and the bowl was surrounded by tiny flickering candles—magical in its simplicity.

"I love this last one," I remarked to Rulinda. "How do you get the glitter to stay on the petals so perfectly?"

Rulinda gave me a cagey smile. "Tricks of the trade," she said, then added quickly, "Spray paint."

I exchanged a glance with Ginger who nodded her approval. "Let's go with the roses," I said.

"Okay, then." Rulinda set her bottle of beer down and eased her substantial bulk into a chair with a grunt. She filled out the paperwork while I wrote a generous deposit check. "So, who's the lucky groom-to-be?" she asked, sliding the receipt towards me as she reached for my check.

My mind zipped back to her inflammatory statement about Riley Gibbons rotting in the darkest corner of hell and concluded that she would not be pleased when she found out. Ginger and I exchanged a wary glance before I answered, "Bradley Talverson."

The transformation in Rulinda's face was immediate. Her shaggy brows clashed together and her eyes turned frosty. "You're shittin' me!"

"Afraid not."

"So, I guess you already know that your fiancé's uncle was the rotten bastard responsible for the...the ruination of my family!" Her ample bosom heaving, she tacked on, "Personally, I'd like to hand out a prize to whoever cut the sonuvabitch's head off."

She'd delivered her tirade with all the subtlety of a snapping turtle and I was a bit taken aback. Never mind the fact that Judge Gibbons had based his decision on the available evidence presented during the trial at that time. "Well, if you don't want the job, I guess we'll be going." I held my hand out as if to ask for the check back, being half serious, half facetious, but the humor was lost on her. Appearing uncertain, she frowned as Ginger chastised lightly, "Aw, come on, Ru, it ain't Kendall's fault and it ain't the Talversons' fault that any of that stuff happened."

"Well...I suppose not."

Even though I'd be removing myself from the story in a matter of hours, I charged ahead. "Did Ginger tell you that I'm a reporter?"

"Yeah, so?"

"I'd be interested in hearing your take on the whole situation."

"You really want to hear it?"

"Yes."

She sat back in her chair, tapping the table thoughtfully. "Okay, my take is pretty simple. In my opinion, Judge Gibbons is responsible for shit-canning just about everything in our lives. Did you know that because my brother had to spend ten years in that hellhole, I ended up having to raise his kid?"

"No. I didn't know he'd been married."

"Well, he wasn't, but the whor...I mean kid's mother took off when he was six months old and we never saw her again. Pretty sad. But anyway, Donny was a handful and a half. He already had a shitload of emotional troubles, but thinking that his daddy was a murderer all those years was the capper and really screwed him up something awful. Jesus, the poor kid wet the bed 'til he was nine, suffered from migraine headaches, got into all kinds of trouble at school…" she shook her head forlornly. "You know where he is now?"

I exchanged a quick glance with Ginger. "No."

Scowling, Rulinda thrust her substantial chin out. "Dead, that's where he is."

I blinked in surprise. No one had mentioned that fact to me. "What happened?"

"He overdosed on drugs five years ago when he was only fourteen, and if you want to lay blame, I trace it all back to Judge Gibbons's wrong-assed ruling."

"I'm sorry to hear that."

"*You're* sorry?" she jeered. "I'm just getting warmed up. Randy had worked for years to build up a real successful towing business and it's all gone now. And, in order to pay the god-awful legal bills, I had to sell my dry cleaning business and mortgage this place to the hilt. My mother had to sell her house and move in here, and I haven't even begun to talk about the humiliation of having all our friends and everybody else in town thinking that Randy was this monster who'd cut his girlfriend to pieces." She leaned towards me, getting so close I could smell her sour breath. "Does that about sum it up for you?"

"Pretty much." Part of me felt sorry for her, but considering the intensity of her hatred and the fact that she was built like a tank, it occurred to me that she could have taken the judge out herself.

"Just a few more questions about your brother's whereabouts prior to the judge's body being found."

She rolled her eyes in obvious exasperation. "You know what? I'm tired of answering questions. Reporters from hell and gone have been circling around like vultures, hounding us for the past two weeks." She pushed to her feet. "If you got more questions, go ask Randy yourself. He's working on the garage. Why don't you just walk your narrow fanny through the gate in the back yard and you'll find him."

I hadn't intended to piss her off and half expected her to return my check as she escorted us to the front door, but apparently she had enough sense to separate business from her personal feelings.

Outside in the chilly wind, Ginger buttoned her coat and slipped on gloves as we walked to her car. "Heavens to Betsy! You sure as heck didn't score any points with her."

I shrugged. "So far, she's number three on my list of possible suspects with that same reaction."

She put a restraining hand on my arm. "What? You think Rulinda could've done it?"

"It's possible. She's got a strong motive, she's a big enough woman and did you see the size of those shears that were laying on the table?"

Ginger, looking understandably shocked, opened her car door and eyed me critically. "I thought you wasn't workin' on this story."

"I'm not."

"In a pig's eye." She planted her feet firmly.

I grinned at her. "You really like pig sayings, don't you?"

"I mean it. I ain't budgin' 'til you tell me what you're up to."

"Okay, here's the deal." I sketched a quick version of the circumstances and her eyes sparkled with bemused speculation. "For pity's sake! How'd you manage to get yourself into such a fix in less than forty-eight hours?"

"I had to work pretty hard at it."

She shook her head in dismay. "I don't envy you havin' to break it to Ruth that you're droppin' out."

"Me too."

"On the bright side, it's gonna make Tally a happy camper."

I gave her a wry smile as she slid behind the wheel and started the engine. "Good luck, sugar. Call me later." She slammed the door, but powered the window down, adding as she backed out, "Be careful givin' Randy Moorehouse the third degree. Just lookin' at him scares me."

I watched her drive away and then strolled around behind the house, threading my way past a muddy white pickup with a camper shell, assorted piles of junk and rusting car parts until I came to a chain-link fence intertwined with overgrown shrubbery. Through openings in the thick foliage I spotted the unfinished second floor on the top of the garage and heard the ear-piercing screech of a power saw. I paused at the gate to read a crudely lettered cardboard sign. DOG HIDING IN BUSHES. HE KNOWS YOU'RE HERE. ACT CALM.

Original. Funny. Also a bit disconcerting. Nudging the gate open, I looked around cautiously, half expecting to see a Doberman or some other type of ferocious dog bound out of the brush. Nothing. Just the sound of the wind rustling the foliage. The clouds massed above the distant mountains had darkened precipitously. Calculating that I didn't have much time before another storm hit, I proceeded through the gate into a clearing and immediately smelled the burning odor of freshly sawed lumber. The continuous whine of his DeWalt Sawzall muffled the sound of my arrival, affording me the opportunity to observe Randy Moorehouse for a few seconds, unseen. Apparently black was his favorite color as evidenced by his coal black jeans, shirt, boots and leather jacket. His pockmarked face was set in total concentration as he examined the board he'd just cut. Okay. No question that he knew how to wield a power saw.

Like his sister, Randy had been bequeathed an interesting genetic legacy. His formidable size, combined with his perpetual scowl, created a palpable aura of menace. With the red bandana tied around his forehead and the long gray ponytail, he looked like a modern-day pirate, which I'm sure is what he had in mind. The shiny black and chrome Harley-Davidson motorcycle behind him completed the image of the bad-assed biker.

I flinched violently at the sensation of something warm and wet on my cold right hand. Turning, I stared down at the strangest looking dog I'd ever seen, licking my fingers. It had a pig-like pink nose, gigantic head, wild hairy eyebrows, one brown eye and one very expressive blue one. Kinky gray and white fur covered the front half of his body while the hind end and wagging tail appeared almost hairless.

"Well, hello there," I murmured, scratching the matted, thorn-speckled fur on the dog's neck. He needed a good brushing. And a bath.

"Who the hell are you?"

I jerked my attention back to Randy, involuntarily tensing as he advanced towards me with purposeful strides, still holding the saw like a weapon. His close-set eyes, a penetrating color of pale blue and looking cold as ice, completed the intimidating picture.

"Some watchdog you are," he roared at the alien-looking creature, its tongue lolling comically from one corner of its mouth. "Get lost, Hoopchuck!" He kicked the animal in the ribs with the toe of his boot and it yelped in pain.

Hoopchuck? Tail tucked between its legs, head hung in disgrace, the dog low-crawled into the garage. Anger burned my throat. I was poised to give him a piece of my mind, to tell him that only a coward would mistreat an animal, but for once I said nothing. This was not a guy to antagonize. And if I did, it would most likely kill any hope I had of extracting information from him. I doubted that he'd appreciate my standpoint on animal cruelty anyway. Tally had said he was a mean and aggressive kid. It didn't appear that he'd changed one bit.

He fastened a withering stare at me. "Okay, lady, I'm gonna ask you again what you're doing here?"

Undeterred by his belligerence, I maintained eye contact while extending my card to him. "My name is Kendall O'Dell. I'm a reporter for the—"

"Reporter! I got nuthin' to say to you."

"*Castle Valley Sun*," I persisted. "Your sister told me you'd be here and I'd like to ask you a few questions about the Gibbons case."

"I don't give a flyin' shit where you're from," he thundered, a firestorm of fury erupting in his eyes. "All you goddamned people want to do is harass me an' my family. If I read one more lie printed by one of you so-called *journalists*, I'm gonna puke my guts out!"

Jeez. Now I really *was* starting to get a complex. I stood my ground. "Look, I don't work for a sleazy tabloid. It's not my style to sensationalize stories to sell papers, Mr. Moorehouse. I verify and report only the facts. I know you've been questioned by the authorities and I should think you'd want to take the opportunity to tell *your* side of the story to our readers."

"You're either real brave or real stupid."

"I've been accused of both."

He fished a cigarette from his breast pocket and had a little trouble lighting it in the brisk wind. When a whiff of the acrid smoke blew past my face, I was heartened to note that his glacial expression had thawed just a tad. "Why should I trust you?" he grumbled, fixing me with a callous stare. "And what difference does it make what I say? You think anyone is gonna believe me?" He wheeled around, stomped back to the sawhorse and picked up another board.

I trotted after him. "It's my understanding that you've only been back in Castle Valley for a couple of weeks. Did you know that Judge Gibbons owned Hidden Springs before you went out there to deliver flowers?"

He positioned the board on the sawhorse, his chin jutting outward. "Yeah, Ru told me."

"Considering how your family feels, I'm surprised she'd do business with him."

His guttural laugh sounded downright evil. "She was happy to charge him double what everybody else was paying."

Nice. "I understand you can account for all your time the day his body was found."

"You bet your sweet ass I can. Those shit-for-brains sheriffs' detectives have dragged me in twice already tryin' to trip me up, tryin' to get me to change my story. Don't they think I know the ropes? Don't they think I know they're gonna keep after me until they trump up a case against me just like before?" Teeth bared, his expression livid, his voice grew ragged. "You got any idea what it's like to be accused of something you never did? Lose everything you ever worked for? You got clue one as to what my life's been like the past ten years? What it's like to sit on Death Row day after day, just existing, watching your life waste away, waiting, wondering and praying that some kind of a miracle would happen? Shitfire, there was days I wished I could just die and get it over with." His eyes were dark and haunted.

I murmured, "I can imagine."

"No," he said roughly, "you can't." He switched on the power saw. As I watched the blade screech into the board, I tried not to think of those sharp teeth sawing into Riley Gibbons's neck, but my insides shrank with horror when the chunk of wood thumped to the ground. "Tell this to your readers," he advised, slapping away the sawdust, "I had ten years, ten long years to build up a full head of steaming god-awful hate for the good judge. There ain't no way I'm ever going to forget that egotistical asshole sitting up there in his black robe, spouting a bunch of stupid proverbs and lecturing me on how I was the worst kind of scum that ever walked the earth!" He brandished the saw. "If I'd wanted to I could've chopped his friggin' head off, but I didn't, even though he deserved that and worse."

Whew! For someone who supposedly had nothing to say, he was doing a pretty good job of spilling his guts.

"How many times did you deliver flowers to Hidden Springs?"

"Look, I already told the sheriff and the detectives all this stuff a hundred times in a hundred different ways."

"I'm hoping there might be a piece of information you may have omitted or forgotten about," I pressed.

"If you know what's good for you, you won't write anything that will make me look bad, Missy." He jabbed his forefinger in my face. "I'd rather kick the bucket than ever go back to that place." The tip of the cigarette glowed red as he sucked hard, dropped it and squashed the butt beneath the heel of his boot.

"Are you threatening me, Mr. Moorehouse?"

"Nawwww. Just call it a strong...suggestion."

I absorbed his veiled warning, keeping my face impassive and thinking how foolhardy I was to be interviewing this hot-tempered man alone. But it was comforting to know that I was within shouting distance of his sister's house. Determined, I repeated my question.

He scrunched his massive shoulders. "I dunno how many trips I made out there before that day."

"Do you know a guy named Winston Pendahl?"

"Sure. He's one of my drinkin' buddies."

"Is that so?"

"Yeah, that's so."

"Did you see him at Hidden Springs that particular day?"

"I don't remember. I do know we wuz both over at the Hitching Post for a couple of hours. We played some pool, drank a couple of beers. He can vouch for my whereabouts and I can vouch for his. So if you think you got something cookin', you don't."

He could have easily been lying. Was it possible they'd worked together to dispatch the judge? Each man held a major grudge, each possessed a strong motive and each had the means and opportunity. "Did you see anyone else while you were at Hidden Springs?"

He pounded another cigarette from the pack, his brow furrowed in thought. "Well, I saw Mrs. Gibbons. She told me to take the flowers to the other little gal over at the hotel."

"Marissa?"

"I guess that's her name."

"Did you see anyone else?"

His eyes fogged over for a few seconds. "Well, there wuz a couple of snot-nosed kids running around, a Mexican lady and some other tall, skinny broad in the lobby."

I'd have to check the guest register for that day. "Did you see the judge during any of your visits?"

"Nope."

His lips stretched in a wicked smile, revealing several irregular teeth. "Sorry I can't tell you what you wanna hear." He fingered the saw blade, closely watching my reaction to see if I'd cut and run. "Ex-con confesses to revenge killing, right? That's the headline everybody's waitin' to see."

A sudden blast of freezing wind whipped my hair around and a couple of snowflakes grazed my cheeks. I looked up, startled to see jet-black clouds almost overhead. Randy noticed them too. "I'm outta time," he said abruptly, tossing the unlighted cigarette and hurrying towards his Harley. "Gotta get my baby inside." He toed the kickstand and pushed the motorcycle towards the garage. Poor, dumb

Hoopchuck stood in the doorway, his tongue still hanging out, wagging his tail in welcome, all forgiven.

"Thank you for your time." I walked a few steps towards the gate then whirled around. "Just one more question. I don't suppose you and your biker buddies took a ride to the Flagstaff area any time during the past couple of weeks, did you?"

He hesitated and when he turned around, I noticed his jaw muscles working overtime. "Maybe we did. What of it?"

16

Dillydally. An old-fashioned word often uttered by my grandmother when she suspected I was guilty of procrastinating. Fully cognizant that I was doing just that after leaving Rulinda's house, I ran several errands and stopped at the grocery store before driving back to my place. Why face Ruth's wrath any sooner than I had to? And why not take advantage of the few hours I had left to track this fascinating story?

Borne by a powerful northeasterly wind, snowflakes blew horizontally at the windshield as I bounced along Lost Canyon Road. It made for tricky visibility. Again I marveled at the transformation of the dry, oven-like desert now masquerading as a Christmas card scene. I stopped and snapped a few pictures of the fluffy white makeover. Stunning! Unfortunately, by the time I reached my driveway, the snow had changed to sleet. I got good and soaked carrying the groceries inside. After dropping the bags on the countertop, I hurried to the bedroom with Marmalade trotting behind me mewing loudly, giving me the business for leaving her alone all day.

"Sorry, little one," I murmured, picking her up and stroking her soft fur, "I'll make it up to you. How about a kitty treat?"

I turned up the heat, peeled off my damp clothes and changed into dry jeans and a flannel shirt before checking to see if Tally had called. Disappointment surged through me when I found no messages waiting. Had he been forced to stop again because of the bad weather? Why hadn't he called?

I spent a little more time schmoozing with Marmalade and she purred up a storm. I wished I didn't have to go back outside and was thinking how nice a nap would be, but decided to check my e-mail instead. No question. I was definitely dillydallying. I e-mailed the party information to my mother and zapped most of the incoming messages, until I got to the one from Brian outlining some of the noteworthy cases that had come before Judge Gibbons during the past several years. As I read through them, the graphic details of the heinous crimes made my stomach turn cartwheels. Husbands murdering and dismembering wives, wives dispatching husbands with every method imaginable, including one disturbing case where a woman injected her live-in boyfriend with antifreeze. In another case that literally made my skin crawl, one sorry excuse for a human being had set his two-year-old stepdaughter on fire. There was a sad story of a couple's only daughter mowed down in a crosswalk by a drunk driver. I scrolled down further, realizing the magnitude of the job ahead of me. It seemed the judge had an endless list of potential enemies.

Another report described the sickening tale of a couple who'd plotted the death of the woman's six-year-old son. Her boyfriend had dressed up as Santa Claus, lured the unsuspecting child into the desert and then murdered him for a paltry twenty-thousand dollar life insurance policy. God! My heart shrank when I read the story of a nineteen-year-old who'd shaken her four-month-old triplets so hard they'd suffered permanent brain damage. The prosecutor's office had recommended the death penalty and it was enlightening to read that the woman's husband had been so outraged when Judge Gibbons sentenced her to only life in prison without parole that he'd rushed the bench and had to be restrained. I replied to Brian's e-mail thanking him for his time-consuming research and then asked him to dig a little further into the particulars of each case to see if he could find out any more pertinent details. Then I answered and deleted several more messages before dialing Walter's number. "Hey, it's Kendall. Sorry to bother you at home on a Sunday afternoon."

"That's okay. Hey, how about this weather? Man, we're really socked in."

I glanced out the window at the gray gloom giving birth to an early twilight. "Yeah, it looks pretty nasty."

"Guess there's more comin'. What's up?"

"I was wondering if you'd made any progress researching Judge Gibbons's past cases."

"Oh yeah. Readin' about all these whacked-out people and all the sick things that they've done is really grossing me out," he replied bluntly.

"I hear you."

"Kendall, this is going to be like finding a rusty old needle in a haystack the size of Castle Rock. I've already been through about twenty cases of convictions, mistrials, hung juries, dismissals and plea-bargained reductions of charges for some of these monsters. It leads me to believe that any one of either the victim's relatives, or relatives of those sitting on Death Row who think the convictions were faulty due to legal technicalities, or what ever else, could have had reason to go after the judge."

"Give me some specific cases."

"Let me pull a couple of 'em up on my computer." I could hear keys clacking. "Okay, how's this for starters. A woman pimped out her eleven-year old daughter, then used the money to buy drugs. One of the johns murdered the girl. Apparently the father of this girl was in another state and he raised quite a media stink when Judge Gibbons handed down a sentence of only fifteen years."

"Oh my. That doesn't sound right."

"Well, before you ahem...pass judgment on the judge, you have to read the fine print to realize all the shenanigans these defense attorneys pull to get their clients a lesser sentence. Sometimes it's as simple as a lab error, misplaced evidence or a key witness not showing up. In a lot of cases, judges have to stay within sentencing guidelines when I'm sure that personally they'd like to hang some of those creeps out to dry."

"That's got to be frustrating. What else have you got?"

"Let's see." He paused a few seconds before saying, "Try this one on for size. How about the charming couple who kept their two kids in animal cages, starved 'em to death, then wrapped the bodies in garbage bags and left them behind a restaurant in the dumpster. You want me to go on?"

"Unfortunately, yes."

Tap. Tap. Tap. "This one's pretty recent. Some lowlife murdered his girlfriend and her two kids and buried their bodies in shallow graves west of Phoenix. There's another case of some psycho stalking college coeds in

Tempe and slashing the throat of three of 'em...." Another hesitation, more key tapping, and then, "Now this one is interesting. Here's one where a guy picked up this woman named Shayla Cunningham in a west Phoenix bar and a week later they found her headless body floating in the canal."

"Really? I'd like to see the particulars on that one."

"Says here because of lack of any physical evidence, the guy was convicted purely on circumstantial evidence." Tap. Tap. He hummed to himself while scrolling down the page. "Here's the rest of it. Apparently, the victim's brother, Robert, had lobbied hard for the death penalty and was so infuriated after Judge Gibbons's sentence of life in prison without parole that he went berserk. He was ejected, stormed back into the courtroom, threatened to kill the judge and was finally arrested."

"So, where's this Robert fellow now?"

"Don't know."

"Might be interesting to find out."

"Yeah, but I got a lot more cases." His voice sounded tired.

"Anything else jump out at you?"

"Well, the one I read about the repeat sex offender the judge was forced to release because they couldn't hold him any longer, and who then ended up killing some little four-year-old girl, would curl your hair if it already wasn't. The girl's mother was in court every day during the trial and because, again, this sicko's lawyer found that a piece of vital evidence had apparently been lost, the judge had to dismiss the charges against the guy. He walked. Says here the lowlife threw a kiss to the grieving mother on the way out of the courtroom. The poor woman lost it, lunged for the judge and finally had to be restrained...Kendall, they just go on and on. I tell ya, the criminal justice system in this country is broken. These damn defense attorneys have turned common sense on its head. Everything is upside down. Wrong is right, right is wrong, the criminals have become the victims, the victims get mired in this system and get no justice a lot of the time...I can understand if it was a member of my family caught up in this madness, I'd be wanting someone's head too...so to speak."

"Thanks, Walter. I know it's pretty depressing to read all this stuff—"

"No shit," he cut in, sounding glum. "Depressing, maddening, revolting—"

"I got you. Sorry about this."

"No sweat. Hey, it's part of the job. I'm okay. Just gotta take a break and get my second wind, that's all."

"Ginger's brother, Brian, is also going back over old court records and scouring the Internet for related articles. I'll be able to give you some help in a couple of days after I cover the judge's funeral on Tuesday."

"I heard it's gonna be a pretty big media affair with the governor attending and a bunch of local dignitaries including a couple of congressmen and a senator."

"Guess I'd better wear something nice."

We said our goodbyes and after hanging up, I continued to drag my feet for another half hour before I finally bit the bullet and left for the Starfire. Time to get it over with.

I bumped along the muddy road leading to the ranch in the remaining moments of the grayish-blue dusk, unable to shake my growing apprehension. What would Ruth's reaction be to my announcement? Would she have a tantrum? Faint? Have a stroke? Order me out of the house? And even if I wasn't personally spearheading this story, could I, at this stage of the game, completely extricate myself?

I hated to admit it, but a disquieting thought had been loitering at the outer edges of my subconscious, and when it finally burst to the forefront, accompanying it was a rush of resentment. Grant would never have discouraged me from tackling a story packed with this much intrigue, this much excitement. No. He'd have encouraged me to go for it, and for a fleeting moment I wondered what it would be like to return to Philadelphia and experience the heady stimulation of chasing down leads with him by my side. That had been my dream. But, even entertaining such a notion generated searing guilt. How could such a consideration even enter my mind? I'd made a vow to change my impetuous ways, clean up my act, buckle down and concentrate on my relationship with Tally, and follow the wise choice to honor my promise to him.

But as the miles fell away behind me, I could not stop thinking about the captivating aspects of the case. Okay, okay. What was the harm in just *thinking* about it? Going on what little I had to work with, it appeared that there were at least four possible suspects. The scorned wife, La Donna Gibbons, possessed a powerful motive for dispatching her husband, and hatred had obviously been festering in Rulinda's heart for a long time. Her brother, Randy, whose incriminating admission that he and Winston Pendahl had been in the Flagstaff area around the same time as Riley Gibbons certainly seemed suspicious. While it seemed highly unlikely that either La Donna or Marissa could have performed such a deed, it was possible that in the muscle department, either could have enlisted the aid of Winston Pendahl. But the most fascinating development of all was the arrival of the cryptic letters from Riley Gibbons.

The lines of the quotations danced in my head, but still, I could find no connective significance among them. If this was an example of his propensity for pranks, it was the definitive practical joke. But, in my gut, I sensed something far more significant at the heart of his motivation.

It was fully dark when I pulled up to the ranch house and parked. The soft light spilling from the windows onto the light blanket of snow made the distinctive structure look cozy and inviting. But, when I didn't see Tally's truck, disappointment settled in. Sure could have used a little moral support. I reached for the door handle when the jaunty Latin tune resonated from the depths of my purse. I fished out my cell phone and glanced at the screen. Another unrecognizable number.

"Hello?"

"Hey, it's me."

I hadn't realized how tense I was until that moment. "Tally! Where are you now?"

"Winslow."

"You didn't get very far."

"I'm surprised we made it at all. We're in the middle of one hellacious snowstorm. Been in Arizona my whole life and I've never seen anything like it."

"I wondered why I hadn't heard from you."

"There was a reason. Where are you?"

"Sitting outside of your house."

"Sorry to stand you up for dinner again. I should have called sooner but we've had some...difficulties."

"What do you mean?"

"We got rear-ended by a truck, slid into a ditch and the trailer damn near turned over. It's been a real mess."

"Good Lord! Is everyone all right?"

"Jake and I are okay, but Gabe Horton got kicked trying to get one of the mares out of the trailer."

"Uh-oh. Is he badly hurt?"

"Yeah. His leg's broken."

"Good grief. Where is he?"

"We took him to the local hospital. Then I got in touch with a friend of mine who has a spread outside Winslow. Jake and I are at the Bar 9 Ranch now and the mares are safe in his barn. But we can't get the mares back home until we get the axle on the trailer fixed. I'm hoping we can get out to do that first thing tomorrow."

"I assume Mr. Horton is not going to be up to traveling for a day or two."

His audible sigh of frustration hissed in my ear. "Afraid not. As soon as this storm lets up, his brother-in-law's planning to drive over here in his motor home to take him back home. I spoke with Ronda earlier and at least she's got things under control there as far as my buyers go. The way things look right now, it could be sometime Tuesday before we get back."

"Tuesday? So...you're not going to make it to Riley's funeral?"

"At this point, I wouldn't bank on it."

"Oh. Well, I'm sorry you've had such a rotten day."

"Me too. Um...are you still going to talk to my mother?"

"That's the plan."

"Okay. See you soon."

"I hope so...and Tally?"

"Yeah?"

"I love you. Please be careful driving back."

"I will. Love you too."

216

I snapped the phone shut, thinking how fate has a way of working things out. As badly as I felt about Tally's situation, the dilemma of how to get the photos to Myra Colton without him knowing had just magically been solved. I was now free to travel alone to her place in Yarnell after the services, which dovetailed nicely into a ready justification for going solo. Hadn't Thena Rodenborn asked me to do a piece on preserving the historic Ice House? This way I could kill two birds with one stone. Ronda could drive Ruth to the funeral, sparing me the ordeal of spending the entire day in the dour woman's company. Anyway, there was a good chance she wouldn't even be speaking to me after I dropped the bomb on her.

I slid from the truck and was halfway to the house when I veered off towards the barn. Yep. I admit it. Dillydallying again. But then, shouldn't I take a few short minutes to bond with my new mare? The pungent smell of hay, straw and manure greeted me as several horses whinnied a cheery welcome. A warm feeling of serenity washed over me. No wonder Ronda spent most of her time here. I met up with her in the small office and we discussed Tally's circumstances before I explained the new travel arrangements for Tuesday. Being her usual taciturn self, she shrugged her agreement and went back to her paperwork. I strolled to the tack room, snagged a currycomb plus a handful of sugar cubes and managed to burn up another half hour brushing Starlight Sky. She kept nudging me and seemed to thoroughly enjoy the treat. What an awesome animal!

I returned the currycomb to the tack room and then stopped to visit with Geronimo, who stamped one forefoot and snorted as I approached his stall. "Hey there, big fella, how're you doing today?" I slipped him the remaining sugar cubes and stroked his neck. Again, I hoped Myra Colton's sculpture of Tally turned out the way I envisioned it and that he'd be as delighted with his gift as I was with mine. A little thrill of urgency reminded me that I needed to be at the copy shop first thing in the morning to have the enlargements made and I also had to stop at the bank and get the down payment for Myra.

The sound of the barn door opening caught my attention and a spark of irritation jolted me at the sight of Lucinda stepping inside and shaking out her long dark hair as she unzipped her jacket. Clad in jeans so tight they looked like they'd been sprayed on, she looked around expectantly, no doubt hoping to see Tally, and tugged her long-sleeved T-shirt down to make sure ample cleavage showed. Cow. She tapped on the office window, smiled and waved to Ronda before sauntering over to one of the stalls.

"Hello, Daisy Baisy," she cooed to her Appaloosa mare, "how's my pretty baby doing today?"

I couldn't think of anyone I'd rather see less and while her back was turned, I made a beeline for the door. I made it past the office door when I heard her call out, "Well, if it isn't Kendall O'Dell. Did you enjoy yourself at the craft show yesterday?" Her voice was underscored with animosity.

Shit. I knew she was going to be trouble. "Yeah, it was fun," I answered over my shoulder in a clipped tone.

"I bet it was," she continued, her voice ultra-sugary. "It must be a real ego trip to be such a popular person…with strange men anyway."

My face scalding, I swung around in time to see Ronda appear in the doorway. Her inquisitive gaze bounced between Lucinda and me. "What's going on, Lucy?"

Her dark eyes shining with malice, Lucinda announced, "Why don't you ask her?"

Ronda arched a brow at me. "What's she talking about?"

I felt like a thousand caterpillars were crawling around my insides. "I have no idea." Armed with the knowledge that Lucinda would like nothing better than to drive a wedge between Tally and me, the last thing I wanted was to divulge any details of my private life.

"Oh, I think you do, " Lucinda went on, her smile annoyingly smug. "I saw Kendall at the fairgrounds yesterday making out with some really hot-looking guy. He planted one hell of a lip lock on her." She folded her arms. "Kind of inappropriate behavior for a woman who just got engaged, wouldn't you say?"

Ronda pinned me with a startled gaze. "Is this true?"

One hell of a lip lock? At that moment, nothing would have given me more pleasure than to knock the ever-living crap out of Lucinda, but Ronda's questioning stare necessitated some sort of explanation. Impulsively, I decided that a simple white lie would have to do until I could explain the situation to Tally, something I should have already done, I admitted regretfully.

Struggling to maintain my temper, I said matter-of-factly to Lucinda, "That was just an old friend of mine and I've already discussed it with Tally. He's cool with it, so there's no need for you to concern yourself." It was supremely satisfying to see her face crumple with disappointment. I turned my attention to Ronda. "I have to go now, your mother is expecting me, but we'll talk more about this later." My final remark was designed to let Lucinda know that she would not be included in any further clarification and I left them both standing there with puzzled expressions as I hurried outside, feeling as though I'd dodged a bullet. For now. But I'd better get my ass in gear and update Tally before Lucinda had a chance to give him her version.

I took my good old time ambling towards the ranch house. The low cloud cover combined with the reflected light from the snow, made the ranch property look like a winter wonderland. Enjoying the frosty air, I marveled at the squeaky scrunching sound of snow beneath my boots. With the fog of my own breath illuminated in the amber light of the porch lamp, it struck me that it wouldn't be too long before my guest status would change to that of permanent resident—wife, sister-in-law and most certainly unwelcome daughter-in-law. The whole scenario still seemed unreal and generated a multitude of conflicting emotions considering the unpleasant task awaiting me now.

"Okay, O'Dell," I muttered aloud. "Let's get this over with."

I knocked on the kitchen door. When it swung open, I was surprised to see the Talversons' cook standing in the doorway. "Well, hi, Gloria. I wasn't expecting you until next week."

"My seester, she is much better now, so I come back early." She motioned for me to enter the cozy kitchen infused with the mouth-watering aroma of sautéing onions and peppers. I hung my jacket on the hook and rubbed my cold hands together while Gloria hurried back to the stove and stirred the sizzling contents of the frying pan with a wooden spoon. Tonight, I wouldn't mind staying for dinner.

"Where's Ruth?"

She tossed her head to one side. "In Meester Joe's study."

I stayed in the kitchen for a few minutes, chatting with Gloria and petting the dogs, until I ran out of ways to put off the inevitable. Reluctantly, I made my way along the paneled hallway towards the closed door. Pausing for a measured breath, not yet sure exactly how to frame what I was going to say, I rapped softly.

"Who is it?" came the muffled reply.

"It's Kendall."

Swift footfalls and the door jerked opened. "You've got some news?" Ruth stared at me, her eyes piercing, expectant. "Come in. Come in," she urged, waving me inside the dimly lit room where I sank into the leather chair. Skipping any niceties, she got right to it. "Well, let's have it."

I shared with her everything I'd learned, saving for last Nora's unsettling description of the judge's death. When I finished, her complexion was drained of color. "So which one of these...persons do you think is responsible?" she asked, firing up a cigarette.

I coughed and shifted away from the cloud of smoke. "Without proof, I can't say for certain that any of them are. I've got a couple of other people researching the judge's past cases trying to establish if there's a link between any of the ex-convicts, their relatives or any of the victims' relations who may have harbored a vendetta."

I couldn't decipher the odd expression that flitted across her face, but assumed it was because I had not delivered the news she'd been waiting for. I was preparing to mention the strange letters when she surprised me with, "I'm pleased with what you've done so far. Keep after it."

It was time. My stomach was bucking and rolling like a wild horse as the words poured out. "Ruth, I can't work on this story any more."

Goggle-eyed, she inhaled sharply. "Why not?"

"Because it's causing too much friction between me and Tally. Don't get me wrong. Given the freedom to do so, I'd like nothing better than to pursue it and I hate to disappoint you but...I just can't."

"But, what about *me*? I told you I will never have a moment's peace until you find out who killed Riley!" she shrieked. "Tally doesn't understand how...why this is so important. You don't understand—"

"No, I don't. Why don't you enlighten me?"

"Weren't you listening when I told you about all the terrible things that have happened because of—"

"I know, I know, your bad luck curse," I filled in, unable to curb my sarcasm.

"Yes, that's it. The curse," she murmured, her voice trailing off.

The furtive look in her eyes combined with her extended hesitation roused my suspicions. "Ruth, what is it you're not telling me?"

Her response was dead silence. "I should never have trusted you. I was right. You're just like—"

"Don't even finish that sentence," I interjected, my own temper flaring. "The last thing I want is to have more dissension between us. But, you're going to have to take this issue up with Tally. It's his wish that I not—"

"But...the situation is too critical for you to back out now!"

If she thought she was going to manipulate me like her children she was sorely mistaken. "I'm sorry." I rose abruptly and headed towards the door. What a total drama queen.

"Wait!"

The undertone of sheer panic in her voice stopped me. I turned back to her. "What?"

Her imploring gaze signaled such profound anguish, my heart faltered. I'd thought she was just yanking my chain, but there was obviously something else going on. "This isn't about some old curse, is it?"

"Not completely."

I had the beginnings of a tension headache. "Look, Ruth, if you've got some kind of pertinent information regarding Riley's murder it's your duty to alert the authorities right away."

She turned her head away. "I can't."

"Why not?"

"It's...complicated."

She had my full attention. "I can't help if you don't level with me."

I expected her to blow me off but instead her shoulders sagged in defeat. Slowly, she turned back to meet my inquiring gaze. "I always told myself that this would go to my grave with me," she said hoarsely.

I broke out in a cold sweat. This didn't sound good. "I'm listening."

"Can you keep a confidence?"

Her question riled me even further. "Of course I can."

Still hesitant, she ran her tongue at a snail's pace along her lower lip. "Then, this has to be...how do you say it in reporter's jargon...off the record?"

"Ruth, get to the point."

"I mean it! I must have your solemn vow that what I'm about to tell you will not leave this room. No one else can ever know."

I weighed her ultimatum against Tally's and, after several seconds of wrenching indecision, decided that my commitment to him outweighed hers. "I'm not giving in on this one, Ruth. I'm sorry."

She tilted her head slowly to one side. "Well then, if something happens to Tally it will be on your conscience."

"What are you talking about?"

"Do I have your promise?"

I stood there, eyes locked with hers and held out for another thirty seconds before curiosity got the best of me. "Okay, you have my word."

She took a drag off her cigarette so long and so deep she must have sucked the smoke right down to her toenails. Itching with suspense, I watched her expel a long stream of smoke. "Riley Gibbons was Tally's real father."

17

She might as well have told me that the moon had switched places with the sun. For several seconds, shock held me immobile and I felt like all the air had been punched from my lungs. Incredulous, I asked, "Are you sure about this?"

Her disdainful scowl implied that my question ranked several rungs below inane. "Of course I'm sure."

Well, no wonder she'd been acting so weird. Since she was already predisposed to mental issues, massive loads of guilt could only add to her psychosis. On one hand, I felt sorry for her, but I'm ashamed to say that another part of me gloated as I thought that this woman, this insufferable woman, who never missed an opportunity to criticize and stand in holier-than-thou judgment of others, had had a tawdry affair with her dying sister's husband. After all was said and done she was simply a fallible human being after all.

Involuntarily my eyes strayed to the old photograph on the wall and I studied the earnest faces of the two dark-haired young cowboys. Now that I knew the truth, the resemblance between Tally and Riley jumped out at me. Holy crap! As the magnitude of her admission slowly sank in, the ramifications were staggering. I thought about how often Tally spoke with loving reverence of Joe Talverson, how much he idolized his memory and cherished the rich family history and traditions that spanned three generations of ranching families. This land was in his blood, in his soul and I couldn't even fathom what his reaction would be if he learned the truth. My heart ached for him. I could only imagine how I'd feel if someone came to me today and told me that the man who'd lovingly raised me, the man I adored and respected so profoundly, wasn't my father. I'd be devastated. Completely devastated. His world would be turned upside down and inside out. How could I keep something this earth-shattering from him? And should I?

"Well, this is certainly...unexpected news." Major, major understatement! She couldn't hold my gaze. "Ruth, you have to tell him. He deserves to know the truth."

A strange light burned behind her eyes. "I can't."

"Why not?"

"I can't face the humiliation of him...of everyone else knowing what I've done."

"What *you've* done? It takes two to tango," I commented dryly, amazed to see her cheeks redden.

"Please don't judge him too harshly. Riley was...an extraordinary person, and even though I knew I wasn't the only other woman he...was with while he and Ginny were married, from the first moment I laid eyes on him he was the only man I ever truly loved...and still love." Tears brightened her eyes.

Still in the process of absorbing her bombastic confession, I had to ask, "What about Ronda? Is she...?"

"No. No," she answered hastily, a tear spilling down one cheek, "she's Joe's child."

So...that meant Ronda was in fact Tally's half-sister. Knowing how close they were, I wondered how this would affect each of them. I was unsure of what to say next. After a brief silence, where she noisily blew her nose, I suggested, "Ruth, this isn't nineteen hundred. These things sometimes happen—"

Her eyes glazed with long-ago memories. "It didn't just happen. I initiated our...relationship...to get even with my sister."

I drew back, surprised. "Why?"

She squirmed in her chair. "You have to understand how it was. She was the beautiful one, the smart one—the one people always gravitated to while no one ever paid me the slightest bit of attention." Her mouth twisted bitterly. "She knew how much I loved Riley and she deliberately took him away from me."

Did she actually believe her statement or was she clinging to it because it justified her actions? "So...why did you marry Joe Talverson?"

She shrugged. "I guess I was flattered that someone actually paid attention to me and it wasn't like I had a lot of prospects. He was nice enough and...I didn't want to be alone the rest of my life. I thought I could learn to love him. I really did try, but Riley was always here in front of me. You can't imagine the torture of having to constantly see him and Ginny together when it should have been me."

I flashed back to Grant's deception. "Actually," I said ruefully, "I can."

Her doubtful look conveyed that I couldn't possibly identify with her anguish. "At the same time, I hated myself for hating my sister," she lamented, dabbing at her eyes. "The greatest irony of all was that Ginny wanted desperately to have children, but she couldn't." Her bemused expression turned wistfully triumphant. "While I, on the other hand, was able to give Riley a healthy, beautiful son. Unfortunately, I couldn't tell him."

I glanced back at the photograph. "So...Joe never suspected?"

"No. Lucky for me they both had dark hair and Tally got my brown eyes. Joe had such a violent temper. If he'd found out he'd have killed Riley, and me too, probably."

"Ruth, you've got to tell Tally. I'm sure if he knew the whole story he'd forgive you."

"How can he do that when I can't forgive myself?" More tears trickled down her cheeks and she clutched her stomach, rocking back and forth. "Lord knows I've had to live with the shame all these years. I'm a terrible, awful...disgusting person! I betrayed my husband's trust! I betrayed my sister's trust...I'm sure to go to hell for what I've done—and I deserve it." She buried her face in her hands and bawled loudly.

As she wept uncontrollably, I couldn't help thinking how much it had to have cost her to admit all of this to me, a person she barely tolerated. The serious issues from her past would need to be addressed, but at this point I was more worried about the present. "I still don't understand why you think Tally's true relationship to Riley would put him in any kind of danger."

She pulled in a couple of shuddery breaths and looked up at me. "Riley came to visit me about a week before he disappeared."

"And?"

"He seemed worried."

"About what?"

"Several people he'd been involved with in the past had died recently under what he called…very odd circumstances."

I sat up straighter. "Involved with? That's rather ambiguous. Was he referring to court cases or personal connections?"

"I don't know." She paused, her eyes narrowed with recollection, then added, "But he did say he might have made a terrible mistake in judgment and feared that it had finally come back to haunt him."

"Anything else?"

"Well, he also mentioned that he'd received some strange correspondence."

I leaned forward eagerly. "Go on."

"Someone mailed him quotations."

"Did he tell you anything about them?"

She shook her head in frustration. "I can't remember the exact words."

"Just give me a general overview."

She paused, thinking, and then said slowly, "Something about a final vengeance for evil people who lie and that others close to that person would share the same fate."

She tamped out her cigarette while simultaneously lighting another. Inhaling deeply, she blew twin streams of smoke through her nostrils. "Now do you understand why I've been out of my mind with worry these past few weeks?"

I stared at her, goose bumps raising the hair on my arms. I'd been on the right track all along. No question in my mind that the judge's carefully premeditated murder was payback, plain and simple. And while I couldn't discount associations in his personal life, logic dictated that the crime more likely was linked to someone's perception of an erroneous ruling handed down in one of his past cases. But, which one? On the surface, the Talverson family's connection to the judge was tenuous at best and Ruth's fears sounded a bit overblown, but there was one thing that might validate her theory. "Ruth, did you ever tell Riley the truth about Tally?"

She averted her eyes. "Yes."

"When?"

"A few months after Joe died."

"Did he tell anyone else?"

"I don't know."

That could be a problem. Riley might have told La Donna or more recently, Marissa. But what reason would either of them have to harm anyone in the Talverson family?

"What was his reaction to your confession?"

Her face clouded with regret. "At first he was angry and then he just seemed in awe of the whole situation."

Yeah, that's kind of how I felt, sitting there trying to analyze exactly what I should do. The sick feeling in my gut confirmed that no matter which direction I chose to take, it would be wrong. But, considering the circumstances, how could I afford *not* to forge ahead in my investigation?

"Ruth, Tally has to be told."

Like a person possessed, her whole demeanor changed. She charged out of her chair and lunged at me with teeth bared like one of the wild burros. "You lying bitch! Your word isn't worth shit! I knew I couldn't trust you!" I recoiled in amazement. Either she was the most selfish woman on the face of the earth or she was prone to truly insane mood swings. "My reputation will be ruined! I know what you're up to," she screeched, narrowing her eyes to tiny slits. "You've had a plan from the beginning, haven't you? You want him to hate me so he'll send me away and you can have him all to yourself!"

How was I to reason with a person this unstable? "Ruth, worrying about your pride is the least important issue at stake here. So you made a mistake! I think Tally's safety trumps your injured sensibilities."

"No! You gave me your promise," she wailed, wringing her hands. "You gave me your promise you wouldn't tell him!" She burst into another torrent of tears and wailed like a banshee. "I'll have to kill myself! I'll kill myself!"

Good grief. She really was nuts. Could I take a chance that she might be serious? "Ruth! Ruth!" I shouted over her howling, "if you'll calm down I think we can settle this problem!"

Like shutting off a faucet, her sobbing ceased. "How?"

"I'll honor my promise to continue my investigation on the condition that you tell Tally the truth immediately."

"What?"

"You heard me. This is way too important to sit on any longer."

She turned her back to me and mulled over my proposal for what seemed like an hour before wearily conceding, "All right, I'll tell him. Now get out of here before I change my mind."

She dismissed me with a curt wave of her hand and I walked outside feeling confounded and apprehensive. How had Tally managed to deal with someone so unhinged his whole life and stay sane? And how the hell was I going to? Should I have forced her hand? Would the opportunity to cleanse her soul help heal her wounds or make her manic condition even worse?

All during the drive home, I stewed about it. Her reason for wanting Riley's killer apprehended was much clearer now. Having obsessed over the judge her entire life, I could understand why his horrifying death would send her into an emotional tailspin. But, the real dilemma was what to do about Tally. He deserved to know the truth for a host of reasons. But was it my right to deliver such intimate news? Not really. The responsibility for that lay with his mother. But could I trust her to follow through? What was that old saying? *To be forewarned is to be forearmed.* If Riley's killer was determined to harm anyone close to the judge, the threat of possible danger was frighteningly credible. I slowed down to allow two rabbits to hop across the road in front of me and, when I swung onto the main highway, another sobering thought surfaced. Ruth and Riley's ignoble conduct really could have far-reaching consequences. How on earth was Tally, a fiercely proud, principled, no-nonsense, intensely private guy going to react to the fact that Ronda was his half-sister and the baby Marissa was carrying would be his new brother or sister? I couldn't even imagine how he'd react to that news. Could things possibly get any more complex?

I exhaled an exasperated breath. Okay. Next hurdle. How to tactfully explain to Tally why it was vital that I go forward with my investigation? Overcome by the urgent need to just hear his voice, I pulled out my cell phone and scrolled to the number he'd called from earlier. Imagine my consternation when a recording announced that it was out of service. Great. I tossed the phone aside and switched on the radio. The powerful winter storm in northern Arizona was the lead story on the news. In some places, three feet of snow had already fallen, there were drifts as high as eight and another storm was on the way. Dozens of people were stranded along highways, power was out in large areas, phone lines were down, and there were reports of massive livestock losses in the remote sections of the Navajo and Hopi Indian Reservations. There was speculation that the governor would call out the National Guard. I snapped the radio off, feeling as if I were carrying a thousand-pound dumbbell on my shoulders.

The weight got even heavier when I got home and checked my voicemail. Nonplussed, I stood there listening to a call from Grant's mother, Phyllis, asking me to phone her back as soon as possible tonight, even if it was late. Now what? I hadn't spoken to her in almost a year. She and my mother were definitely up to something. On emotional overload, I collapsed onto the couch and stared blankly into space until Marmalade jumped on my lap. "Can you believe this?" I asked my furry companion, stroking her back softly. "Are the stars out of alignment or something? So what do you think? It's after eleven o'clock in Pennsylvania. Should I call her back now?" She just sat there purring and looking at me lovingly with those huge turquoise eyes.

"Well, you're no help," I grumbled. Reluctantly, I picked up the phone and dialed Phyllis's number, struggling with the strange sense that my life was spiraling out of control and I couldn't seem to do a damn thing about it. "Phyllis? It's Kendall."

"Oh, my dear girl!" she gushed. "It's so good to hear from you! Thank you for returning my call so promptly."

233

Wary, I replied, "No problem."

"Your mother was kind enough to give me your number."

No surprise there. I sensed the noose was about to be tightened. "Okay. Well, how are you doing? I understand you're recovering from hip surgery."

"Yes, yes. It's been quite an ordeal." She paused, and when she spoke again, her voice quavered slightly. "It really is nice to chat with you after such a long time. I've missed you."

The genuine affection in her voice brought back a host of fond memories and my throat clogged with emotion. "I've missed you too, Phyllis. Sorry I haven't called. I thought it might be...awkward."

"Oh, not at all. I just wish things had turned out differently between you and Grant. You two were so good together."

Yeah, until he'd screwed it up. "So...what's up? Is everything all right?"

She cleared her throat delicately. "Actually, I'm calling to ask you a big favor."

Was it an illusion, or were the walls really closing in on me? I sat down. "What can I do for you?"

Nervous laughter. "You know me, go, go, go all the time and if I wasn't still undergoing physical therapy, I'd hop on a plane and come out there myself—"

My stomach muscles tensed. "Why would you be coming here, Phyllis?"

She sighed deeply. "Grant called me this evening and the poor boy is so distraught."

"About what?"

"He told me about being hurt in the car accident and how helpful you've been."

"Uh-huh. And your point is…?"

"He told me that he's in a lot of pain and that the doctor you took him to prescribed so much medication that now it will be difficult for him to drive." I swallowed back sudden irritation. How had this become *my* fault? "He's really worried because his editor is counting on him to cover a funeral on Tuesday somewhere up in the mountains. Prescott, is it? Anyway, I know Grant. He'll be bound and determined to pursue that story regardless of doctor's orders and I'm frightened to death he's going to get behind the wheel. He's liable to end up killing himself or someone else! If I could I'd be there to help him, but since I can't well…" she paused for a breath and I knew what she was going to say next. "I was wondering, if it wouldn't be too much of an imposition…could you possibly drive him to this event?"

My inner antennae vibrated. Perhaps it was all in my head, but I could not suppress the nagging sense of skepticism. Perhaps Phyllis and my mother were not the only co-conspirators. "Did Grant put you up to this?"

"Good heavens, no! In fact, he'd be very upset with me if he knew I'd called you."

The noose settled firmly around my neck. "Phyllis, you know I'd do just about anything for you, but…I can't do this."

"Why not?" There was a note of anxious incredulity in her voice.

"Didn't you read the note I sent you?"

"Yes."

"Well, then you know that I'm engaged to someone else now."

"So? You're all mature adults. I'm sure your fiancé will understand the importance of—"

235

"Are you kidding? The two of us showing up together at the funeral—even if it is on a professional basis—could create unbelievable problems for me. This is a small town. People talk—"

"Oh, piffle! You're making a mountain out of a molehill. It would be nothing more than one friend doing a favor for another. It's not like I'm asking you to give Grant another chance, even if it would make me the happiest woman on earth if you two did patch things up, but it would just be for a few hours. It would mean so much to him and it would mean so very much to me. Please, Kendall, you know I wouldn't be asking you to do this if I didn't feel it was of paramount importance."

"But—"

"Please! You know how much I care for Grant and you. If something happened to him because of—" her voice cracked and I felt like my heart was sinking into my shoes. Choking. I was choking.

"Okay, Phyllis, I'll pick him up and drive him to the funeral."

"You are an absolute peach!" she cried in my ear. "I can't thank you enough. Your mother is very lucky to have such a fine daughter. I'll call Grant right now. What time should I tell him to expect you?"

"Tell him to be ready by noon."

I set the phone down and considered two possibilities. One, eat the second pint of ice cream beckoning to me from the freezer, or two, pour myself a huge glass of wine. Before I could do either, Marmalade's sides began to convulse and she made a couple of gurgling retches before hacking up a gigantic fur ball at my feet. I stared down at the gooey mess and remarked tiredly, "My sentiments exactly."

236

18

Monday didn't start out much better. I arrived at the copy shop at eight o'clock sharp with the photographs in hand and was apologetically told that the equipment used to make enlargements was out of order. A technician would arrive sometime on Tuesday and my order would be processed by Wednesday. I stood there for a moment, jingling my keys and debating as to whether I had time to drive to Phoenix. Nope. With Jim on vacation for the week and Tally stranded in the snow, we'd be too understaffed for me to take off, considering I'd be gone most of the following day.

Lamenting my continued run of bad luck, I left the photos and drove to the office. On the way, I dialed Myra Colton's number and got her voicemail. I left a message explaining the situation, told her that I would stop by the following afternoon regardless to give her the deposit, and then I would make a second trip to bring her the posters on Thursday or Friday at the latest.

The only cheerful note was the weather improvement. The heavy cloud cover finally broke up enough for intermittent sunshine to brighten the landscape, although according to the weather report, it was to be a brief respite pending the arrival of the next Pacific storm. I tried unsuccessfully a half dozen times to reach Tally and wondered if he'd been successful in getting the horse trailer repaired. It made me uncomfortable to think that he was snowbound on some out-of-the-way ranch without the means to communicate or perhaps even travel. I decided right then and there that if he didn't get himself a cell phone when he returned, I would buy one for him.

I managed to get through the hectic day, and by the time Tuesday morning rolled around I was up early mulling over what would be appropriate to wear to a high-profile funeral. I finally chose a black pantsuit, cream-colored turtleneck shirt and black suede boots. Calculating that I could get a couple of hours of work done at the office before picking up Grant, I filled Marmalade's food bowl, left the kitchen light on and dug my knee-length wool coat from the guestroom closet. I hadn't thought it would ever be cold enough to wear it again but I was glad I had it on when I stepped outside into the freezing wind.

"Well now, don't you look like you oughta be on the cover of a fashion magazine," Ginger chirped, giving me the once over as I entered the lobby. "You goin' to a party or somethin'?"

I grimaced. "No, Ginger, I'm covering Judge Gibbons's funeral, remember?"

"Oh, mercy!" she gasped, looking embarrassed, "I plumb forgot that was today."

It seemed as though I'd barely dug into the pile of papers on my desk when I looked up and realized it was almost eleven o'clock. Hurriedly, I put my desk in order, then waved goodbye to Tugg, who was parked in front of his computer with the phone jammed against his ear. I stopped by Walter's desk to chat for a few minutes and asked if he could do a computer search to look for any ancillary cases or past newspaper articles that may have come to light regarding anything unusual connected personally or professionally to Judge Gibbons. Dashing past Ginger's desk, I called out that I wouldn't return until the following morning and headed down the road towards Hidden Springs. Buffeted by strong gusts of wind, I traveled beneath a dome of sapphire sky so clear and sunshine so intense it was hard to imagine that it had been spitting snow this time yesterday. A quick check of the weather on the all-news station confirmed that while the roads north were currently clear, Arizonans should brace for a new storm due to blow in sometime this afternoon. I hoped the worst of it would wait until we got safely home.

I was in a strange state of mind as I followed the winding ribbon of road into the secluded valley and my agitation heightened as I severely berated myself for getting stuck in this quagmire. What I needed in the future was duct tape. Lots of duct tape. A wheelbarrow full to place over my big mouth the next time I was tempted to make snap promises to anyone. If I'd done that, I would have been unable to give my hasty pledge to Tally or foolishly become ensnared in Ruth's tangled web of deceit. And now, I'd gotten myself backed into another sharp corner because I'd lacked the guts to say no to Phyllis Jamerson. "Another fabulous mess you've gotten yourself into, O'Dell," I grumbled aloud, thinking that it might be wise to rehearse what I planned to say to Grant. I had no intention of parsing words. He must understand that I was going out of my way today as a favor to his mother, pure and simple, and if he attempted to read anything more into it, he was sadly mistaken. Period. End of discussion.

I pulled into the parking area and stepped outside, buttoning my coat against the icy, yet exhilarating wind. A second white compact car that I assumed was Grant's replacement rental car sat near the wall. Pausing to decompress before confronting Grant, I closed my eyes and listened to the soothing swish of palm fronds while inhaling the aroma of damp grass and leaves. Yes, very calming. Okay. I was good to go. As I pushed through the gate, I wondered if La Donna had changed her mind and decided to attend the funeral after all. Passing by her cottage, I was surprised to see the front door standing open and two of her cats roaming about in the garden. A third sat on the doorstep looking out. That was curious. Hadn't she made a big fuss of making sure they not go outside? I'd only advanced a few steps further when I heard what sounded like glass breaking from within the little house. Wheeling around, I ran towards the door. The cats saw me coming, froze in place, then with their backs and tails puffed up, they bolted into the house. Pausing at the doorway, I called out, "Hello? Is everything okay in here?" It was then I heard the ragged sobs coming from the direction of the kitchen. I hurried inside and froze at the sight of La Donna standing near the refrigerator in her bathrobe, hair disheveled, tears streaming down her blotched cheeks. At her feet were shards of broken glass and a clear liquid splattered across the tile floor. A swift glance at the soaked label on the remains of the bottle identified the contents as vodka. Good grief! It must be something pretty serious for her to have been so careless with her cats and be totally blitzed before noon.

"What's going on?" I asked, gingerly picking my way towards her, glass crunching beneath my shoes. A half-filled tumbler sat on the countertop next to an open prescription bottle lying on its side. I cocked my head slightly and was able to make out the name of the drug. Vicodin. So, she was mixing painkillers with booze. Not a good combination.

She focused her bleary gaze on me. "What are you doing here?" Her words were slurred.

"I'm here to drive...someone to the judge's funeral." There was no point in going into my relationship with Grant.

My innocent remark ignited a look of rage. "That *someone* wouldn't happen to be Marissa, would it? Yes," she continued, before I could correct her, "why don't you take her with you so she can flaunt herself in front of all Riley's colleagues and the TV cameras! Why not complete my total humiliation!"

"You're mistaken. I'm not here to—"

With an abrupt swipe of her hand, she cut me off. "I can hear the whispering behind my back, the snickering, their sanc...tim...on...sanctimonynus tongues wagging, especially now."

"Why especially now?" I asked cautiously.

"Because I was over at the hotel this morning doing some paperwork and I overheard that...that...that—"

"Slow down. You overheard what?"

She pressed fingers to her eyes. "I heard Marissa talking on the phone to her doctor."

Uh-oh.

"It all makes sense now, why she's been so sick these past few weeks. That little whore is pregnant with Riley's bastard!" she wailed, pointing an accusing finger at me as if I'd somehow played a part in it. She picked up the glass and took a gulp. "That lousy son-of-a-bitch! He's fixed it so I'm the one who'll look like the bad guy, turning a mother and child out into the cold. How easy is it going to be now for me to contest his will?"

I didn't have a ready response to her question, or tirade, to be more accurate. Considering her inebriated, confrontational behavior, I decided this was a bad time to try and reason with her. "I understand your feelings—"

"No you don't!" she screeched. "Nobody does!"

"Okay," I said softly, hoping to placate her. "Why don't we try and get you out of here and into bed so you can..." I was tempted to say sober up, but said instead, "rest."

"I don't want your help. I want Bernita! Go get Bernita!"

"Okay, okay. Stay right where you're at and I'll send her over."

I hotfooted it to the hotel and felt a rush of relief when the elderly Mexican woman answered the door. I explained the situation and she nodded gravely. "Mrs. Gibbons was very mad this morning. She learned about the baby and called Miss Marissa many bad words," she announced, ushering me into the foyer.

"I heard a few of them. Is Marissa here?

"She's lying down in her room. She complains of having pain here," she said, pressing on her abdomen, "but insists she will go to Mr. Gibbons's funeral anyway."

"Really? Is she driving by herself?"

"I think maybe yes."

I made an instant decision. Having Marissa along would reduce the awkwardness of having to travel alone with Grant. "I'd be glad to take her with me."

Bernita shrugged and pointed towards the hallway. "You can ask her. She is in the first room on the right."

"Thanks." I glanced around the corner into the little sitting room. No sign of Grant. "By the way, do you know where Mr. Jamerson is?"

"I have not seen him yet today."

That didn't sound too promising.

"I will go now and take care of Mrs. Gibbons." It was hard to miss the undertone of resignation in her voice. La Donna appeared to be profoundly unstable, not as bad as Ruth, but the woman definitely had serious issues to deal with. Bernita acknowledged my sympathetic smile with an insightful nod as she reached for the doorknob. After she left, I crossed the foyer and knocked on the bedroom door.

"Marissa? It's Kendall O'Dell."

"Door's open."

I walked in and drew in a breath of appreciation at the room's stunning décor—high scrolled ceiling, delicately flowered wallpaper, an extensive array of antique mahogany furniture, and scattered about the spacious room were several exquisite Persian rugs. Curled beneath a comforter in the center of a massive four poster bed lay Marissa.

"Are you all right?" I asked, noting how ashen her complexion appeared in contrast to her dark hair.

"I hope so." Her voice sounded faint. "I'm having some cramping and I'm not sure what it is."

"Bernita says you're planning to attend the funeral. I'm here to pick up Mr. Jamerson and you're more than welcome to ride with us. Considering your condition and the fact that there's another storm coming, do you think it's a good idea to travel alone?"

"That's really kind of you." She threw off the comforter and sat up, smoothing the skirt of her ankle-length black dress. "I guess I could go with you as long as you can bring me back by four-thirty for my doctor's appointment."

"Oh. That won't work. I have to make a couple of stops in Yarnell on the way back and I'm not sure how long it's going to take."

"Well, thanks anyway. Winston was planning to drive to Prescott today to pick up new windows and he offered to bring me along, so I guess I'll take him up on it. See you there."

I forced a smile, hoping she wouldn't notice how much her remark bothered me. "Yeah. See you."

I left the room and headed for the stairs. I liked Marissa and was deeply troubled by the implication that she would be comfortable driving alone with Winston Pendahl to Prescott or anywhere else for that matter. Did that give credence to La Donna's damning assertion that the two of them were lovers? Did it breathe life into her supposition that Marissa had prior knowledge of the gold coins that had supposedly been in the judge's safe deposit box and that she and Winston had conspired to murder him in order to get their hands on them? Yet Marissa had vehemently denied the accusation and La Donna admitted that she had never actually seen the gold. So...had the judge been telling the truth? If the answer was yes, what happened to the quarter of a million dollars worth of gold? Perhaps the two of them were sitting on it until the investigation grew cold. Or...had La Donna made the whole thing up to divert suspicion away from herself? She certainly had ample justification for killing her two-timing husband.

Another scenario could be that Marissa had innocently mentioned the gold to Winston Pendahl who'd then shared the information with his pal Randy Moorehouse. Then the men had kidnapped the judge, taken him to the bank and forced him to empty the safe deposit box before driving him to a remote spot where they'd shot him and then sawed his head off. Yeah. I liked that theory a lot better. Now all I had to do was prove it, I thought, tapping on Grant's door. "It's Kendall! You ready to go?" No answer. I rapped harder, waited, and when I heard no response, tried the knob. It turned easily, so I pushed the door open. "Grant? You in here?" The blinds were closed, but there was just enough light to confirm that he was still in bed.

"Kendall?" he mumbled, turning over and blinking at me in surprise.

Suppressing a flare of irritation, I stomped over to the window and yanked the blinds, allowing brilliant sunlight to flood the room. "Come on, lazybones, it's almost noon. Time to get your butt out of the sack."

He grimaced. "I wasn't expecting you so soon."

"Why not? Didn't your mommy give you my message?"

"Your displeasure is duly recorded." He struggled to a sitting position and swung his legs over the edge of the bed, groaning, "I'm sorry. These pills make me feel really goofy."

I folded my arms and maintained my disapproving expression. I knew it was childish, but considering how many miserable nights I'd spent crying my eyes out after being dumped by him, it felt rather good to have the upper hand.

He focused on my face, looking bemused. "What? Can't you wait until I grab a shower and get dressed, or would you rather I'd go like this?" He threw off the covers to reveal black silk boxer shorts. He actually looked pretty darn cute sitting there, bare-chested, his blonde hair all tousled. An uncomfortable heat engulfed me as memories of our past intimacy paraded before my eyes and mixed signals from my heart filled me with guilty confusion.

"If you want a lift," I said, keeping my tone crisp, businesslike, "you've got twenty minutes. If you're not ready, I'm leaving without you."

"Give a guy a break, will you?"

Unsmiling, I narrowed my gaze at him. "Consider yourself fortunate that I'm here at all. And don't think for a second that I'm not onto your little scheme."

His eyes twinkled with innocence. "I don't know what you're getting at."

"Twenty minutes." Feeling uncertain and off-balance, I backed out the door, relieved to put some distance between us. What was the matter with me? Being around him again resurrected remnants of affection I thought were long gone. Okay, Kendall, get a grip. Concentrate on other matters. I peered down the dim hallway. Might as well use the time to explore this fascinating old place.

With dusty shafts of sunlight peeking in here and there through smudged windowpanes, I picked my way around the clutter of power tools and building materials, glancing into empty bedrooms and bathrooms, all in various stages of repair, until I reached the last door at the end of the hallway. When I tried the knob, it didn't budge. Assuming it was locked, I turned away only to spin around when I heard what sounded like the latch quietly releasing.

To my amazement, the door slowly opened a crack as if pushed by an unseen hand. My scalp prickled. I'm not sure what I expected, but then I felt the breeze. Oh. I'd probably jarred the lock loose and then a draft from above had blown the door open. Of course, that was the logical explanation. I felt strangely disappointed. Had I been expecting a visit from the hotel's alleged ghost?

Pushing aside that capricious thought, I pulled on the doorknob and was amazed to find not a room but a hidden staircase. How cool was this? Remembering Marissa's warning about the dangerous conditions above, I tentatively placed my weight on the first step. It creaked a little, but appeared sturdy. I looked around for a light and pulled on the chain snaking down the wall from a bare bulb high above me. It wasn't a very bright light, but better than none at all. With care, I ascended the steep, spiral steps unable to contain my excitement. The antiquated building reminded me of descriptions I'd read of brooding, haunted mansions in countless spine-tingling murder mysteries from childhood. I could identify with how enamored Riley Gibbons must have been with this place, since he'd shared the same propensity for whodunits. Sure enough, when I reached the top, I was confronted by yet another closed door. I turned the crystal doorknob and the hinges squealed in protest when I tugged it open to reveal a small kitchen with ancient-looking appliances and a rusty sink. The steady drip of water from the faucet echoed in the silence like a ticking clock. No doubt I'd entered the third floor via the servants' entrance.

Moving on, I stepped through the next doorway into a spacious sunlit room, marveling at the height of the ceiling, probably twenty feet at least, and the ornate crown molding trim. It was easy to see where the draft was coming from. In several areas, clumps of plaster hung down and I could see evidence of daylight from above. Dark splotches staining the walls told of recent water damage, but even devoid of furniture, the massive size and lofty windows gave the room an elegant cathedral-like appearance. Since it was obviously too large to be a bedroom, I presumed that it must have served as a drawing room in bygone days. It was easy to imagine the room filled with genteel ladies attired in starched lace blouses and long skirts sipping tea to the accompaniment of soft harp music, or groups of men arguing the politics of the day as they puffed on cigars and drank from snifters filled with fine brandy. *My, my, O'Dell, aren't we fanciful today.* Forcing my mind back to reality, I moved past the wide entrance to the staircase, also strung with yellow caution tape, and stopped in front of a magnificent white marble fireplace. For some reason, large sections of the wall on either side of the hearth had been bashed in. How odd. Curiosity drew me to the gaping cavities, but my fear of spiders necessitated finding a scrap of wood to thrash around inside the hole before I gingerly eased my head inside for a look. Other than catching a whiff of musty timbers, it was too dark to make out anything in detail.

At that moment a strange shushing sound reached my ears. Startled, I jerked my head out and spun around. Relief poured through me when I finally identified the source of the noise. A bird. It soared around the room several more times and then vanished through an opening in the ceiling. I wondered how many other critters had set up residency in the abandoned rooms.

Wandering into the hallway, I had to watch my step because of the yawning cracks where rotted planks had apparently been removed. I continued, peeking into the empty rooms, noting with interest that holes had been cut in various locations in the walls and again, some sections of wood flooring had been removed. I ran my hand over the smooth wall surface. How strange. Except for those specific areas, however, the thick plaster walls and floorboards appeared to be in stable condition. So, why had Winston Pendahl declared the third floor a danger zone?

At the end of the hallway, I stopped in front of a closed mahogany door complete with a crystal doorknob and what looked like a new lock. Interesting. This was the only room where the door had not been standing open. I tried the knob and to my surprise, the door opened easily. I stepped inside and drew in a breath of delight. The room was furnished. And nicely at that, although half-filled moving boxes scattered throughout the room suggested that someone was in the process of packing up the contents. I peeked inside some of the boxes, noting assorted vases, lamps and bric-a-brac wrapped securely in bubble wrap, and nearby, several more filled with books. Adjacent to a small fireplace stood several partially filled bookshelves. I crossed the room to study some of the remaining titles, not surprised to see scores of mystery novels by Edgar Allen Poe, Sir Arthur Conan Doyle, Agatha Christie, Raymond Chandler and many more. There were also volumes of philosophy, prose and poetry. So this must have been Riley Gibbons's library, the place he retreated to for solace from his hectic professional and, most certainly, personal life.

When I turned towards the arched window, I was afforded a breathtaking view of the Praying Nun. From this angle the two shadowy wind-carved crevices on either side of what looked like the lady's nose gave the impression of eyes set in the unique rock formation.

Perhaps it was my overwrought imagination, but it seemed as if the inquisitive eyes were staring directly in the window. On a nearby pedestal stood a bronze statue of a dreamy-faced young girl. Her eyes were cast skyward and her arms outstretched towards two golden butterflies suspended above the palm of each hand on delicate strands of almost invisible wire. The piece was eye-catching and extraordinary in its detail. Again, I recognized another of Myra Colton's unique creations. Was this the piece she'd not yet been paid for? On the way out, I stopped and looked again at the new lock. Had it been installed to preserve this room's integrity? Ah, but then, why had several of the floorboards adjacent to the fireplace been removed? Puzzled, I pulled the door shut behind me, and continued walking towards a stained glass window at the very end of the hall. As I approached it, I could see that one corner of the windowpane was broken. The wind blowing through the hole sounded eerie and lonesome, like a far off train whistle.

It's hard to explain in words what happened next, but all at once, a chill invaded my body and an irrational but crushing sense of melancholy consumed me. Every hair on the back of my neck quivered. At first, I attributed the bizarre sensation to the draft, but then I began to tremble violently from a cold so profound, so intense, it was as if my bones had frozen solid. Even more disturbing was the innate knowledge that I was no longer alone. Rooted to the spot, I gasped aloud, feeling as though an icy presence had actually passed through one side of me and out the other. Spellbound, I stared at what appeared to be a swirl of dust motes kicked up by the fickle breeze. But within seconds, the hazy cloud vanished, as if magically pulled through the wall.

19

I don't know how long I stood rooted to the spot, mesmerized and unable to come up with a logical explanation for the phenomenon. Given the ethereal ambiance of the place, it would have been easy to dismiss the incident as pure fantasy, but my intuition convinced me that I had just experienced something not of this world. While intriguing, the encounter, if that's truly what it had been, unsettled me so much I lost the desire to stick around any longer. With haste, I retraced my steps and beat a path down the angled staircase. Twice as traumatic as the haunting episode, was colliding in the semi-dark stairwell with Winston Pendahl. We both gasped aloud, our faces only inches apart before I leaped back up a step and he stepped down several.

Breathing heavily, he bellowed, "Sweet Jesus! What the hell were you doing up there?"

"Just...having a look around." I hoped my voice sounded matter-of-fact. It wouldn't be good for him to know that I'd come close to wetting my pants.

"No one is supposed to be on the third floor. Can't you read?" he demanded with a menacing scowl as he swung one muscular arm behind him towards the open door below. "The sign says to stay out! It's too dangerous for people not familiar with the...with the ongoing renovations to be snooping around."

Snooping around? His belligerent attitude infuriated me. "Hey, back off, buddy. There's no need to shout." In addition to the blaze of fury in his eyes, I'm pretty sure I saw a trace of alarm. Was my supposed welfare the only reason for his apparent distress? When he realized that I wasn't cowed by his threatening behavior, he retreated from his hard line stance and squeezed out a cheesy smile that *really* creeped me out.

"Sorry. It's just that we can't take a chance on any of our guests getting injured."

His proprietary attitude irked me even more. *We? Our guests?* "I didn't realize you were one of the owners of this establishment."

"Well...I'm not," he backpedaled, his smile collapsing. "What I mean is, I'm just thinking of Mar...I mean, Miss Van Steenholm's welfare. If someone accidentally got hurt, it could be...bad, ya know? She could get sued."

Why was he trying to pretend he didn't know her very well? "You needn't worry. I was very careful. Now, if you don't mind moving out of my way, I'm on a tight schedule."

"Sure, sure. Me too." He turned and trotted ahead of me down the remaining steps into the hallway, stopping to pick up a power saw and plug it into an outlet. I breezed past him and when I reached Grant's door, the sudden screech of the saw sent a little shock of horror running through me. I flicked a glance over my shoulder only to find him glaring back at me, his hooded eyes furtive and speculative. I turned away and knocked on the door while several disturbing thoughts crossed my mind. Now that I really thought about it, there appeared to be some deliberate reason behind the systematic pattern of holes that had been created in the floor and walls. But for what purpose? His uneasiness concerning my so-called snooping around on the third floor now seemed highly suspicious to me. This guy definitely bore watching.

Emotionally pummeled by the number and magnitude of events that had occurred within a twenty-four-hour period, it was hard to concentrate on the barrage of questions Grant fired at me while I negotiated a series of tricky hairpin switchbacks on the one-way divided highway that climbed steeply up Yarnell Hill four miles to the summit of Table Top Mountain. Why was the funeral being held in Prescott instead of Phoenix? Did I know which dignitaries would be in attendance? How long would it take to drive there from Castle Valley? Was there more snow forecast and was I sure I could actually handle this big 4x4 pickup on these narrow roads? It wasn't until he fell silent that I finally glanced over to find him staring out the window, apparently transfixed by what I considered one of the most spectacular views in Arizona—a stunning panorama of the sprawling valley below encircled by a palisade of mountains and topped off with a boundless expanse of clear cerulean blue sky. As we sped by the scenic overlook, vivid memories of meeting Tally there for the first time passed before my eyes. It was mind-boggling to realize how much my life had changed since that April day and I felt a twinge of wistful regret when I thought ahead to the sky-high hurdles awaiting both of us—especially after Ruth broke the news to him about Riley.

The lack of chatter from Grant prompted me to glance at him. He was staring a hole right through me, the expression in his bright blue eyes provocative. "What?"

"You seem…preoccupied. Something bothering you?"

He had no idea. "A little of this and that."

"Anything you want to talk about?"

"No."

"Oh, I get it. Even though I'm trying my best to be sociable, you've decided to stay pissed off at me."

"Everything isn't all about you, Grant."

Apparently choosing to ignore my remark, he responded in a cheery tone, "Maybe I can help. Want to talk about it?"

"No, I don't."

"Yes, yes, you do."

I directed him a look of mild irritation, not surprised to see his face set with a look of smug satisfaction. He knew me too well, but then, I knew him too. He had his reporter's cap on now and, like a small dog with teeth firmly embedded in someone's pant leg, there was no way he was going to let go until he found out what was troubling me. We'd always shared that particular mulish trait. "Okay. I've been kicking around various aspects of the Gibbons case."

"Ah, so Kendall O'Dell, investigative reporter extraordinaire, is back in the saddle. Just thought I'd throw in some western lingo." His impish grin indicated he was pleased with his little joke.

"Temporarily, anyway," I murmured, watching a cluster of white waffle-like clouds push over the ridge, no doubt the forerunner to the impending weather change. As we crested the summit of boulder-capped Table Top Mountain and followed the meandering road through the village of Yarnell, picturesquely sandwiched between the towering ridges of the Weaver Mountains, Grant sat quietly studying the scattering of antique stores, cozy cafes and small businesses that included several offering crafts from Native American tribes and Mexican imports catering to the tourist trade. I'd told Grant earlier that I had to make a stop on our way back and as we approached the north end of town I began to search for the boarded-up house Myra Colton had told me to look for. It was nearly hidden in a grove of overgrown trees and as I cruised by, I spotted the side road snaking away to the west just as she'd described.

We left Yarnell behind and entered a lush basin filled with deep gorges rimmed with mammoth clusters of granite rocks and rolling pasturelands dotted with cottonwood and black walnut trees—home to the peaceful ranching community of Peeple's Valley. I glanced ahead, taking note of the frothy storm clouds beginning to pile up to the north. The windshield was beginning to fog up so I reached to switch on the defroster as we rolled past a mishmash of cottages and small businesses, which included names like the Muleshoe Animal Clinic and Saddletramp Saloon. After traveling past miles and miles of white pipe fencing it was a joy to see the scores of beautiful horses frolicking or grazing in the wide fields at a thoroughbred horse ranch. Then we left the grassy meadows behind and cruised into a tawny patchwork of chaparral, mesquite and scrub oak—high desert land known as Up Country to the Arizonans living in the valley below.

"I liked all the big trees back there, kinda reminds me of home," Grant remarked, turning to look back before he slapped a hand across the back of his neck and yelped in pain.

Flinching, I asked, "What's wrong?"

"Damn, I shouldn't have done that. Now my neck is killing me again."

"Didn't you take your pills?"

"I took one early this morning," he answered, massaging the nape of his neck, "but I didn't want to take any more until after the funeral services. They put me in la-la land."

"Gotcha."

He laid his head back against the seat rest and was silent for several moments before saying quietly, "Kendall, you seem...different."

I glanced over to find him staring despondently at my engagement ring then quickly refocused my attention to the road. "How so?"

"Lots of things. I keep remembering you as a city girl who loved museums and the theater, eating out at nice restaurants, skiing, dancing, hiking, and now here you are living in the middle of nowhere all tanned and buff-looking, driving a pickup and looking like a...cowgirl."

"That's meant to be a compliment, I hope."

"Oh, yeah. And if you tell me that in your spare time you're out riding the range herding cattle, then I'll know there's no way that you're coming back to Philly...even though I'm hoping the thought has at least crossed your mind once or twice."

It had in the beginning when I wasn't sure I'd be able to adapt to the snail-paced lifestyle, starkly different landscape and scalding heat, but I replied, "Not really," as I swerved around a squished lump in the road that looked like a dead coyote.

He sat in silence again for thirty seconds, before blurting out, "Don't you go nuts with boredom? I mean, are you sure you want to stay out here in this wild country for the rest of your life?"

"Don't let the wide open spaces fool you. This place is not as tranquil as it looks. In fact, I've broken several unbelievable stories since I arrived here. Surviving the summers will always be a challenge, but all things considered, yes. I love Arizona...for many reasons."

"The scenery is great, but I don't know if I could live with just cactus and rock and dirt forever. Be honest, compared to Pennsylvania, don't you think it's kind of...barren-looking, for lack of a better word?"

I shrugged. "To each his own."

"Come on," he cajoled, "are you saying there isn't anything back home that you miss?"

I caught the subtle inference in his tone and slid him a warning look as he inched closer and nonchalantly slid his arm along the back of the seat. "Where are you going with this, Grant?"

"What do you mean?"

"I'm onto your little game and you're wasting your time."

"Geez, you're so suspicious."

"It's part of my nature, remember?"

"Yes," he said softly. "That's what makes you such a damn fine reporter."

"Thanks."

"So, you're telling me you don't even miss your family?" he persevered, his fingertips now only inches from my shoulder.

"Of course I do."

"My mother misses you a lot."

"And I miss her." Boy, did I ever. For the umpteenth time, I wished that Phyllis were going to be my mother-in-law instead of Ruth. But the familiar pang of guilt reminded me that, unfortunately, Tally's eccentric mother came with the territory. "I'd be lying if I told you I didn't sometimes miss the change of seasons, flowers and green trees," I went on, trying to keep the subject matter on neutral ground, "but if for no other reason, I have this little asthma thing, remember? This barren place as you call it, has made it a whole lot better and unless the earth has shifted on its axis since I left, and Pennsylvania has moved closer to the equator, the weather there will continue to be damp and cold the majority of the time."

"You call this warm?" As if to validate his statement, he nodded towards the craggy snow-dusted mountains looming above the small town of Wilhoit.

I made a face at him. "All right, I'll give you that one. But, it's unusual. According to the locals this has been one of the coldest winters on record and there hasn't been this much snow for forty years. You should feel right at home in Prescott because by the look of those clouds, we're going to get some more. Soon."

"Well, who knows, I might just learn to like it here after all."

He met my sharp glance. "And what exactly does that mean?"

"That I've been doing a lot of thinking. Lying around there in that quiet room at Hidden Springs has given me time to assess what's important in my life and a change of pace might be good for me."

"What are you saying?"

"That maybe I'll relocate to Phoenix."

My heart fluttered and a heavy sensation, like the time I ate one too many buckwheat pancakes at my grandmother's house, settled in my belly. "Get serious."

"I am serious, Kendall." The silky, persuasive quality in his voice rattled me, plunging my emotions into treacherous territory. Taking everything into consideration, it made no logical sense that anything he said or did should affect me one way or the other. But, since when does the heart take notice of logic? Was it possible that I had unresolved feelings towards him? No. Having him in Arizona long-term would not be a good thing.

"Don't delude yourself, Grant. I thought I made myself clear on Saturday. You and I are history." A sidelong glance at his hangdog expression confirmed that my dig had hit home.

He threw his hands into the air. "All right. I'm just going to say it. Why are you rushing into marriage with this guy?"

"I'm not rushing."

"Your mother thinks so."

My temper blazed. "The three of you have been conspiring behind my back, haven't you?"

A nonchalant shrug. "I'll admit that we've had a few discussions about it. She thinks you're doing it to get even with me. Are you? If you would just stop being so stubborn and find it in your heart to give me another chance, I swear I'll do whatever it takes to make it work for us this time." He edged closer. My heart curled into a protective ball and I placed my right palm firmly against his chest and pushed.

"It's too late for that. Move back on your side, Grant."

"Oh, come on baby, you know how good we are together."

"Hey! You agreed that we'd be just friends, remember? If you want to bounce around some ideas concerning the Gibbons case with me, fine. Otherwise, you'll be walking the rest of the way to Prescott."

Undeterred, he beamed me an irresistible smile. "You don't really mean that."

I jammed on the brakes and skidded to a stop on the narrow shoulder. My pulse pounding furiously, I turned to glare at him. "Try me."

There was a measure of disbelief beneath his incredulous expression as we locked eyes and then he reluctantly slid back towards the passenger door and folded his arms. Staring straight ahead, he growled, "Okay, have it your way. Bounce away."

Instant relief slowed my fast-beating heart. Feeling confident that I'd regained control of the situation, I pulled onto the final stretch of upward winding road where squat piñon pines, junipers and scrub oaks began to give way to tall ponderosa pines. Here and there small clumps of snow appeared. In Grant's favor was the fact that he really knew his stuff and might offer some new insight. It chewed up the better part of the next half hour as I maneuvered around endless switchbacks up the mountain, but when I finished filling him in on everything I was at liberty to say, he wore a concentrated frown.

"Whoa, Nelly. Sounds to me as if each one of these suspects possesses a strong motive." He pensively tapped one finger against the end of his nose and began speaking in an English accent worthy of a stuffy detective straight from Scotland Yard. "So then, let me see if I've got this all straight. First, we have the judge's vindictive widow who has in her employ a swarthy ex-convict who possesses intimate knowledge of power tools, saws especially. Veddy, veddy incriminating. Then we have a second ex-con, allegedly innocent, incarcerated for ten years, who harbors a seething hatred for the judge and has recently been sprung from Death Row. Yes," he added with an evil laugh, rubbing his palms together, "then we stir into the murderous brew his spiteful sister, adroitly skilled in the use of sharp cutting shears, add seasoning in the form of the judge's penniless paramour, who just happens to be preggers with his spawn and serve hot with a cache of missing gold coins. Oh, this is just too good!"

I couldn't help but smile at the entertaining delivery of his analogy. "I thought you'd be intrigued."

"Of course, as you know so well," he said, continuing in his Sherlock Holmes persona, "besides motivation, the question always comes down to means and opportunity. I'm sure you've considered the idea that it's also none of the above."

"Of course I have. There's always the possibility there's just some madman running around out there chopping off heads."

"But, you don't think so?"

"Not really. I'm thinking textbook premeditation by someone who knew the judge's schedule, knew he was going hunting near Flagstaff and either followed or lured him to that remote forest service road which is where the authorities believe he was fatally shot."

"Where is Flagstaff in relation to Castle Valley?"

"About three hours northeast in the mountains. Elevation is approximately seven thousand feet and they've had a ton of snow, which explains why posse members didn't spot his white truck during the initial air search."

"Is the truck still impounded?"

"As far as I know."

"So...the four glaring questions are, how much time elapsed between the moment he was killed and his body was discovered in the pool, what was the significance of transporting it all the way back to Hidden Springs, where is the murder weapon and, most importantly, what was the point of beheading him and where is...said head?"

"All valid questions," I remarked thoughtfully, taking note of the thickening cloud cover and increasing wind. "I still think the answer is buried among the myriad of details in the court transcripts or in past newspaper articles we're currently researching." I also filled him in on the wisp of cotton I'd found at the crime scene, my meeting with Nora Bartoli and her tip that a Sawzall had been the decapitation weapon.

"Hmmm. And that would implicate both of our ex-cons who each happen to own a reciprocating power saw. That's almost too convenient. And what's the reason again that you think our hunky handyman is single-handedly dismantling the third floor?"

"Call me paranoid, but I think he's using the renovation as an excuse to tear the place up and search for the missing gold coins."

"Hmmm. Getting his hands on them would have created a strong motive, but what makes him think the judge hid them on the third floor?"

"I'm not sure, except that's supposedly where Riley hung out a lot reading and probably trying to escape the wrath of La Donna."

Grant raised one well-shaped brow. "And do we suspect that he's working alone, in tandem with Mr.

Moorehouse and his sister, or is he in cahoots with the widow or the new girlfriend?"

"I don't know."

He fell silent for a few seconds before asking, "I noticed the warning tape stretched across the stairwell. Why did you go up there anyway?"

I thought back to the bizarre episode of the locked door suddenly opening and hesitated. Should I tell him about my ghostly invitation? "I was just looking around and...sort of got there by accident."

When I didn't follow up he urged, "Don't stop there."

I hadn't meant to tell anyone, but the yearning to share my story burst out. His eyes glittered with speculative amusement when I concluded. "So, what are you saying—that you had a physical visitation by the wandering spirit of the young boy who'd been abandoned by his mother?"

"Honest to God, I don't know what it was, but I've never experienced anything like that before in my life. I mean...for a period of time I actually felt like someone...something else was inhabiting my body."

He began to clap his hands slowly and I turned to see his lips curled in laughter.

"What's so funny?"

"Nothing. It's just that...well, you always seemed so practical and this sounds—"

"Fanciful, I know. Okay, don't believe me. Maybe it was just the wind, but stranger things have happened. Remember the story I told you about my Great Aunt Beverly's house in Ohio?"

He frowned puzzlement and then his eyes widened in remembrance. "Oh, you mean the one where you and

263

your two brothers stayed at her haunted mansion for a couple of weeks?"

"You can mock, but I saw it with my own eyes. No one ever had a logical explanation for how that silhouette of a man in a top hat always appeared on the wall in her bedroom in the same spot. She told us the previous owners of the house had painted over it three times, wallpapered and finally installed paneling, but the silhouette always reappeared in that exact place. It scared the living daylights out of us." My phone played its cheery jingle and after digging it from my purse, I glanced at the caller ID, not recognizing the number. "Hello?"

"Hi, Stick, it's Nora."

"Fritzy! I was just talking with someone…about you," I said, mouthing her name to Grant. "You must be telepathic."

"Believe me, it would make my job a lot easier if I was," she replied with a chuckle. "Anyway, you got a minute?"

"Absolutely."

"Cool. I've got some news for you on that fragment of cotton you found at the crime scene."

My expectations surged. "Shoot."

"A friend from the lab just called. They were able to pick up a trace of a substance that is found in a drug commonly used for pain called Vicodin."

Her disclosure shattered my concentration for a few seconds. Hadn't I just seen a bottle of the very same drug in La Donna's kitchen less than two hours ago? "That's very interesting." I remarked, cautioning myself not to jump to conclusions. "Anything else?"

"This is not for public consumption yet, so keep this under your hat, okay?"

"Okay."

"It's taken the pathologist a little longer to finish his examination of the slides of Gibbons's tissue, but he did confirm my suspicion based on the bone analysis that something didn't seem quite normal."

"What do you mean?"

"Considering the estimated time that had elapsed since his death, there was something strange about the consistency of the samples. The tissue was amazingly well preserved and the cut was clean, suggesting that the tissue was firm and solid, not slippery, so I can now confirm a couple of things. One, prior to the body being found in the pool it had been frozen solid and two, the decapitation happened sometime before the body thawed out."

I didn't even want to form a mental picture. "So...what are you saying? That he was shot and then what? Someone buried him in a snow drift for a few days, came back, dug him out, sawed off his head and then transported him to Hidden Springs all without a soul hearing or seeing what happened?"

"That sounds about right."

"But the search team was all over that area where the truck was discovered. If his body was even within a five mile radius, it would have been found, don't you think?"

"Well, obviously not. I can't really tell you where the body was frozen, just that it had been prior to its discovery."

"And the reason for decapitation while frozen?"

"A whole lot less messy."

"I see. Hey, thanks for the heads-up, Fitzy."

"Don't know if that'll help you or not, but it's all I've got right now. Catch you later."

I snapped the phone shut and shared the new information with Grant. "Moorehouse admitted that both he and Pendahl were among a group of bikers riding in that general area around the same time the judge was there, and while he didn't specify that particular weekend, it's a good guess that the authorities are in the process of confirming just that. And speaking of the authorities, you were supposed to give me the exact wording of those quotes that were in those threatening letters the judge received."

"Oh yeah." He reached into his jacket pocket and his face went blank. He searched in the other pocket, pulled out a notebook and then burst out, "Crap! I left my cell phone on the charger in my room!"

"Don't sweat it, I've got mine. Read the quotes."

"Okay." He flipped through the pages and my apprehension resurfaced as he began to read aloud. "LIFE BEING WHAT IT IS, ONE DREAMS OF REVENGE and REVENGE IS A KIND OF WILD JUSTICE." He paused as he turned the page over. "And here's the kicker, "FALSE WORDS ARE NOT ONLY EVIL IN THEMSELVES, THEY INFECT THE SOUL WITH EVIL. BEWARE THOSE WHO FEAST AT THE TABLE WITH THE EVILDOER." He flipped the notebook shut. "Yep. That last one sounds like a real threat. This person's definitely got an agenda."

My stomach did a swan dive envisioning the horrific fate that could await the next victim on the killer's list. And what if Ruth was right? What if it was Tally? I set my jaw with firm conviction. No matter what risks lie ahead, it was imperative that the murderer be found soon— before it was too late.

20

I'd only been to Prescott three times before that day, but each visit increased my appreciation for the mile-high community situated in a pleasant valley on the northern boundary of the Bradshaw Mountains. Tally had mentioned that the population of the area had tripled during the past ten years, but, even with the explosion of growth, thus far, the thriving city had been able to retain its small town appeal and unique charm, most notably the elm-shaded courthouse located in the center of downtown, which was bordered on three sides by Gurley, Cortez and Goodwin streets, each boasting a succession of stately buildings which housed quaint stores and small businesses. The fourth side of the square, Montezuma Street, known to the locals as Whiskey Row, had once been home to dozens of saloons, houses of ill repute, and frequent rip-roaring gunfights. Now the shop-lined street boasted only three saloons, which mostly catered to out-of-state tourists and groups of Harley riders.

Driving through a quiet residential neighborhood, Grant peered out the window at three once-elegant

Victorian houses, each in the process of being refurbished. "I like this place. It has a real nice Midwestern feel to it."

By the time we reached the Arizona Pioneer Home Cemetery on Iron Springs Road, the sky was turning the color of dirty dishwater, accentuating the gloom of the already solemn event. There was a long line of cars stopped ahead of us and I could see local police officers directing traffic to a shopping complex a block away from the wrought iron entrance to the cemetery. However, several stretch limos with dark tinted windows—most likely part of the governor's motorcade along with other local dignitaries—were singled out and directed through the gate and up the winding road, which was bordered by dry brown grass and sparsely dotted with piñon pines and scraggly leafless trees.

"Guess we don't rate a prime parking spot," Grant grumbled.

When we finally reached the crowded parking lot and began a quest for a vacant spot, a little flicker of surprise went through me when I noticed the white Posey Patch Florist van. I could just make out the shadowy outline of someone seated behind the steering wheel while Rulinda, dressed in black slacks, coat and stocking cap, stood by the open rear doors next to a longhaired young man I'd not seen before. She pointed to the top of the hill, then handed him two colorful funeral wreaths. Taking into consideration her deep loathing for the judge, it seemed the height of hypocrisy for her to be at his burial, but then it occurred to me that many Castle Valley citizens would have ordered flowers for the occasion, including the Talversons. And as I now knew, Rulinda wasn't one to pass up a buck and had probably overcharged everyone to make it worth her while.

We finally located an empty parking spot beside a white van with television call letters from Prescott while two other vans, displaying Phoenix television stations' call letters, stood nearby. La Donna had been right. Riley's funeral was going to be a big media event.

Unfortunately, the weather had decided not to cooperate. When I stepped from the truck, tiny snowflakes stung my cheeks like icy needles. Bundled up in heavy coats, hats and gloves, Grant and I had to hoof it several blocks fighting the ever-increasing wind. Just prior to reaching the gates to the cemetery, I noticed Winston Pendahl's white pickup waiting at the stoplight, a morose-looking Marissa sitting beside him in the passenger seat. Grant's steps faltered as he stared at the line of people trooping up the steep slope. "Damn. You didn't tell me we were going to have to scale Mt. Everest to get there."

"I think the more important you are, the higher your final resting place," I replied dryly before tilting my head at him questioningly. "Since when has a little hill been an impediment to you, Mr. Downhill Racer, Mr. Cross Country Biker, Mr. Hiker of Many Mountain Peaks?"

"Sweet. Hey, I'm not exactly feeling myself today."

"So, what do you want me to do? Carry you?"

He made a face at me. "Funny."

With a sigh of resignation, he pulled the collar of his coat higher and we began our climb up the paved road, which was becoming slicker with each passing minute. Judging by the look of wonder on his face, I knew what he was thinking. This lonesome windswept cemetery bore little resemblance to the ones in Pennsylvania we'd visited where the dearly departed rested in eternal sleep beneath carefully tended headstones surrounded by lush, emerald green grass and shaded by groves of thickly leafed trees.

269

This stark hillside offered only scattered crumbling headstones and flat grave markers, some looking sadly neglected with overgrown weeds, while a special few were well-tended and decorated with faded plastic flowers.

We trudged past the sleek hearse and joined the assembly of somber-faced mourners filing towards rows of chairs ringing one of the few gravesites graced with a small cluster of pines, which whipped back and forth in the capricious wind. Protected beneath a flapping white canopy, the flower-festooned coffin stood poised above a dark rectangular cavity rimmed with mounds of freshly dug earth. Although I tried, I couldn't banish the mental picture of his headless corpse lying inside and it gave me one of those sickening little gut jabs.

With difficulty, I shook off the macabre image and glanced at my watch. Services were scheduled to begin in less than ten minutes. I gave the crowd a quick overview, searching in vain for Tally, hoping against hope that he'd been able to brave the storm and make it after all. I checked my cell phone for messages and with a pang of disappointment, finally accepted the fact that he wasn't coming. Was he still stranded in northeastern Arizona with no phone service or was he en route to the ranch? My heart felt as overcast as the leaden skies at the thought of him driving in this wind pulling a horse trailer.

I spotted Ronda and Ruth huddled together in the front row of chairs as I approached the gravesite. Ronda raised a hand in greeting and when I waved back, I didn't miss her speculative glance at Grant. How could she even know who he was since she'd never met him? Oh. Of course. Lucinda had given her a head to toe description of him after she'd finished tattling about me. I was all set to step forward and introduce him when my attention strayed to Ruth. Clad completely in black, she stared straight ahead at the coffin, her grief-stricken profile as pale as the snow settling on her headscarf. She must have sensed me watching her because she turned her head slightly. For a brief interlude our eyes connected. In those few seconds, we shared an intimate, uneasy bond. Out of all the people present that day to pay their final respects, including her daughter, I was the only one who shared her dark secret and understood the true magnitude of her torment.

Her gaze slid back to the coffin and as the wind rose to a whistle, I noticed two coal black ravens perched on the swaying limb of a nearby pine tree. The irony of the moment was not lost on me. From what I now knew about Riley Gibbons's penchant for the mysterious, I think he would have been pleased by the foreboding ambiance nature had provided for his final farewell. And then in another odd quirk of fate, Winston Pendahl appeared, dusted the snow off a chair directly behind Ruth and offered it to Marissa. Wow. There they were—two women from different generations unaware of each other's significance—one having produced the desired offspring Riley had always yearned for yet could not acknowledge, while the other carried a child he would have cherished but would now never know.

"Guess I'll go do my thing," Grant said, plucking his digital camera from his pocket. "I'll see if I can harvest a couple of interviews to please my boss."

"Wait a minute—" Before I could stop him, he turned and melted into the crowd. Just as well. His absence granted me a reprieve from explaining to Ronda why we were together. I kicked around the thought of joining the two of them for the services and then just as quickly dismissed the idea, opting to give myself the freedom to roam about and gather material for my own piece. As I strolled among the milling throng, I estimated that there were about two hundred people present. Impressive.

The full brunt of the storm arrived, and the snow came down hard and fast, snuffing out the silhouettes of Thumb Butte and Granite Mountain to the west. I wondered how anyone was going to hear the pastor, who had just arrived and was shaking hands with various people gathered near the casket, including a tall, refined-looking woman with short cropped white hair who appeared to be in her early sixties. Because she bore such a striking resemblance to Riley Gibbons, I deduced she must be his sister, Charlotte. I snapped several pictures of the governor giving her a comforting hug. Also paying respects was a host of state senators, representatives, uniformed members of law enforcement and two U.S. Senators—certainly demonstrative proof that Judge Riley C. Gibbons had been held in high esteem by his peers.

By the time the services ended, at least an inch of fresh snow had fallen and near whiteout conditions stripped the color from the surroundings, reducing everything to varying shades of gray. One by one mourners approached the casket. Many bowed their heads and mouthed prayers while others touched, kissed, or laid flowers on the polished lid. Marissa, her chin touching her chest, tissues pressed to her nose, wept audibly. Winston appeared to be supporting her full weight as she placed a bouquet of yellow daisies on the casket and then, with no warning, she collapsed to the ground. I rushed forward as the crowd surged around, murmuring concern. Winston dropped to his knees, cradled her head under his arm and tried to shield her from the blowing snow. Grant appeared from somewhere and we both knelt by her side. "What's happening?" he asked with obvious concern.

"She fainted. I think maybe I better take her back home," Winston said, attempting to lift her inert body.

"Hold it," I cautioned, staring with growing unease at her bloodless lips, "considering her condition, I think you'd better call an ambulance."

"What condition?" he asked, his forehead puckered in puzzlement.

"She's pregnant," I said, keeping my voice low.

Judging by his stunned expression, it was obvious she hadn't revealed her secret to him. "Pregnant?" he yelped loudly enough for those around us to hear clearly. "Are you sure? She never said nuthin' to me about that."

"Yes, I'm sure." I rose to my feet shouting, "Is there a doctor here?"

"Coming through," came a call from somewhere in the crowd as a middle-aged man pushed to the front. After that everything moved swiftly. Someone fetched a blanket from somewhere, cell phones were whipped out and within ten minutes paramedics arrived on the scene, lights flashing, sirens blaring. While everyone's attention was focused on Marissa being loaded into the ambulance, I realized I'd lost track of Ruth and Ronda. I looked around for them and happened to glance back towards the gravesite, which was now almost completely obscured in fog, just in time to notice an indistinct silhouette appear from behind the small grove of trees and swiftly approach the coffin. Because of the poor visibility, I could not tell whether the person was male or female. The wraith-like figure, shrouded in black, tossed something onto the coffin lid and then as if I'd imagined the entire thing, vanished into the mist.

"You ready to go?" Grant asked, massaging his neck and shoulder, his face contorted with pain. "I gotta take a couple of my magic pills pretty quick or I'm going to have to crawl into that ambulance with Marissa."

"Yeah, sure," I answered in a distracted tone, digging in my coat pocket for the keys. "Take these. I'll be along in a minute." I trotted back down the hill to the canopy and ducked beneath it, listening to the steady patter of snow granules falling on the canvas as my eyes adjusted to the gloom. At first I didn't notice anything out of the ordinary, however my pulse spiked when I spotted something unusual nestled among the flower arrangements. I blinked the snow from my eyelashes and looked closer. Was that a *black rose*? Mystified, I reached out a gloved hand and plucked it from the coffin. Curious. Of course, the first name that came to mind was Rulinda, who possessed the materials and expertise to have created such an item. But, how did I know that Randy hadn't been the driver? There was also the possibility that it could have been Winston. I'd not seen him since the ambulance left. Had he followed Marissa to the hospital or doubled back here?

As I twirled the flower slowly in my hand, I noticed that a small piece of paper, painted the same color as the stem, had been wound tightly around it. I hesitated for a few seconds, wondering what to do. Did I have any right to read this private message specifically meant to be buried with the deceased for eternity? Well, if I didn't, it would be lost forever. Carefully, I peeled the paper away from the stem and rolled it open. As I read the inscription, icy shivers skated along the back of my neck. HATE HAS TURNED MY DAYS AND NIGHTS INTO HELLISH TURMOIL.

21

I looked up, searching the fog, firmly convinced that I'd just caught a glimpse of Riley's murderer. Above all the quotes I'd read thus far, this one exemplified the heated depths of this individual's rage and infinite anguish over some actual or perceived wrongdoing. Cognizant of the fact that I might have a vital clue, it was imperative that it be preserved for forensic examination, since there might very well be fingerprints or other identifying material on the flower or delicate onionskin paper. I rewrapped the paper around the stem, tucked the rose beneath my coat and hurried to the truck, wondering whether it would be better to contact Sheriff Turnbull and Duane Potts, or perhaps Detective Lansing in Phoenix. Either way the rose would have to be sent to the crime lab for analysis. Could I expedite things faster if I delivered it personally to Fritzy tomorrow?

There were only a few cars still parked along the steep road as I tromped downward, slipping several times on the icy surface, fighting the bitter wind. When I finally made it to the parking lot, I grew more suspicious when I noticed that the Posey Patch Florist van was nowhere to be seen.

Grant had the engine running and the heater blasting by the time I climbed into the truck cab. His eyes widened in amazement as I showed him my find and shared my suspicions as to which person on our list of suspects it might have been.

Grant pondered the information before stating, "That was a pretty gutsy, in-your-face action, if you ask me. Apparently, our killer has graduated from sending anonymous messages to making a personal appearance. Kind of a 'catch me if you can,' kind of thing."

I nodded thoughtfully. "Right. We've both talked to enough homicide detectives to know that the criminal's ego is usually their downfall. The fact that they either can't keep their mouths shut, or for whatever reason find it necessary to begin dropping clues to prove just how clever they are."

I put the truck in gear, and as I waited for traffic to clear, Grant pointed across the street. "Hey, you mind if we stop by that convenience store over there?" He extended his palm to reveal two white pills. "I'm supposed to take these with food, so I gotta get some munchies and I could use a hot drink."

"Sounds good. I'll pick up a bag to secure the rose." Moments later, armed with our provisions, the flower secured in a brown paper bag, I backtracked through the snow-covered streets, headed out of town and retraced our path down the steep mountain pass. As we descended in elevation, the snow dissolved into sleet and I estimated that if we didn't run into any road problems, we should make it to Myra's place by four.

I savored the warmth of the hot chocolate while Grant downed the pain pills along with a sandwich and coffee. The medicine must have been potent because he was sound asleep by the time we reached Yarnell, his head lolling gently with the sway of the truck. I smiled wryly to myself. Phyllis had been right. It would have been a grave mistake for him to drive while taking those pills.

I glanced in the rearview mirror at the charcoal clouds closing in behind us. We'd outrun the storm temporarily, but if the temperature dropped much further, the sleet would soon turn to snow. Again, I wondered what Tally was doing. Not knowing where he was or if he was safe re-ignited a feeling of hollow anxiety. If he'd made it back to the ranch, why hadn't he called me? I fished my cell phone out and sighed in annoyance at the NO SIGNAL announcement flashing at me. Well, that answered that. It was disheartening to notice the low battery warning also. Great. I could have kicked myself for not recharging it before I'd left.

I turned the phone off to preserve power and tossed it back into my purse, deciding to skip my planned visit to research the Ice House until my next visit. Best get started back to town before the weather got much worse. Downtown Peeple's Valley was mostly devoid of traffic, but that made it easy to spot the Posey Patch Florist van parked in front of the Saddletramp Saloon as I coasted by. Rulinda must have stopped for a hot toddy and who could blame her?

I turned onto the poorly maintained road and drove west towards the boulder-covered mountains dodging gigantic potholes brimming with rainwater. Sure enough after a half a mile or so, the pavement ended and I maneuvered along a secluded dirt road listening to the rhythmic swish of the windshield wipers. When I came to the first fork, I angled right and perhaps a half a mile later, steered to the left. Positive that I'd already traveled two miles, I was beginning to think I'd taken a wrong turn when out of the mist loomed a two-story building of blackened brick. I gawked at the unexpected sight of finding such an odd-looking structure sitting out in the middle of basically nowhere. Barely visible, perhaps a mile further to the west, a smokestack from what had probably been an old smelter, jutted into the swirling gray mist.

I bumped along an uneven weed infested driveway and rolled to a stop in front of scratched double doors. Uncertain, I stared up at three rows of high domed windows, some bricked shut. Just above the rooftop, dark storm clouds loomed, creating an atmosphere that was downright creepy. I reached over and tapped Grant on the shoulder. "We're here." When he didn't respond, I poked him again and he finally stirred and cracked his eyes open. Totally spaced out, he squinted in stupefaction at the building. Rain poured like a waterfall off one side of the roof where it looked like the gutter had long ago corroded. Judging by the architecture, it appeared to have been built somewhere around the turn of the last century. Doubt jabbed me. Why would anyone, especially a woman, choose to live in such an out of the way spot in what looked like a deserted old factory?

Mirroring my thoughts, Grant remarked, "What a weird looking place. Where the hell are we?"

"We're supposed to be at Myra Colton's house."

"Hmmm. There seem to be an abundance of these ramshackle places here in Arizona," he remarked with a wide yawn.

He was right. The building did look as though it had been built around the same time as the hotel at Hidden Springs, but I turned to him with an amused frown. "Ramshackle? Who even knows what that word means anymore?"

He chuckled. "Okay, how about dilapidated? And why are we here again?"

"She's an artist I met recently who's going to create something for me." He didn't need to know the details of my engagement gift.

"Looks like a set for a horror movie," he quipped. "Think it's haunted too?"

I arched a brow at him. "*Now* who's being fanciful?" I shut the engine off and glanced down at the directions. "According to what's written here, this has got to be it, but I guess there's only one way to find out." We made a dash through the pelting rain and the metal door echoed like a kettledrum as I pounded on it. After a minute or so, it swung inward to reveal Myra Colton clutching a shawl around her thin shoulders, her complexion so pale it looked almost bluish. "Oh, hi," I said with a relieved smile. "I wasn't sure this was the right place."

"Come in, come in," she urged, standing aside to allow us entry.

Grant and I stepped into the foyer. As we stood there on the cloth rug dripping like two wet dogs, I caught her slanting him an odd look while he brushed raindrops from his jacket.

"Miss O'Dell, if you'd like to step into my studio, we can talk." Addressing Grant, she suggested, "I've got a fire going in the kitchen, hot water for tea is on the stove and there's a bottle of brandy on the table if you're interested."

"Thanks." He favored her with one of his charismatic grins and the slightest touch of color tinted her high cheekbones. Oh brother. It appeared that no female on earth, regardless of age, was immune to his charms. He flicked me a smug look that indicated that he was aware of his affect on women and I wrinkled my nose at him as he headed towards the crackling fire. I turned my attention to Myra.

"Please call me Kendall."

"And you must call me Myra." She beckoned me to follow her along a narrow, drafty hallway dimly lit by ancient wrought iron light fixtures. I reached out my hand and touched the cold exposed brick walls.

"If you don't mind my asking," I asked, moving to her side, "why are you living in a…in this—"

"Rundown old building?" she finished, sliding me a discerning look. "The short answer is that it was available, private, the rent is very reasonable and even though it's a bit damp and cold, it's ideal for my purposes." Underscoring her words, she ushered me through a door into an enormous room with a high vaulted ceiling where at least a dozen globe lamps hung suspended on long black chains. Gracefully arched windows spanning two walls offered a spectacular view of the Weaver Mountains looming in the distance, but the fast-approaching storm clouds would soon obscure the irregular peaks. On a normal day, sunlight would blaze through the expanse of glass, brightening the gloomy interior considerably.

Outside, backed up to a second set of high double doors, sat a white panel truck. Beyond it, tucked beneath a dark canopy of trees, a garage fashioned from the same aged brick as the building sheltered an older model silver

Honda and a white trailer inscribed with faded lettering that read: CREATIVE ICE SCULPTURES.

"I see what you mean about this place being perfect for the type of work you do." I paused to admire several of her exquisite creations while other pieces, apparently not ready for viewing, stood draped beneath bolts of material.

"Do you attend a lot of festivals like the one last weekend in Castle Valley?" I asked her.

"Oh, yes. For quite a few years now, I've traveled to shows all over the southwest and a few on the East Coast."

"How do you pack and unpack all this paraphernalia by yourself?"

"I don't. There's a very nice gentleman in town who helps me load the truck and then I have to hire someone at the other end to help me unload and set up my canopy."

"Doesn't it bother you living out here in the sticks by yourself?"

Smiling reflectively, she slanted her head towards the lifelike depictions of Native Americans, rugged cowboys and young girls frolicking in various poses with bunnies, kittens and puppies. "I'm not really alone."

I smiled. "I meant, don't you have any family around?"

Similar to the first time we'd met, a flicker of sorrow passed behind her serene gaze. "Not anymore. They're all gone now."

My cheeks burned. *Open big mouth, insert size nine shoes.* "I'm sorry. Force of habit. I shouldn't have—"

"Don't concern yourself," she said benignly. "It was a long time ago. What's that old axiom, 'waste not fresh tears on old griefs' or something to that effect? Life goes on." With that she quickly switched the subject to her work.

We conversed for about fifteen minutes about what kind of pose I had in mind for Tally's sculpture and when we finished I looked around the cavernous room again murmuring, "What was this building originally, do you know?"

"I understand it was used to store ice for the mines."

My mouth fell open. "No way! *This* is the Ice House?" My mind zoomed back to the conversation I'd had with Gretchen Hutchinson on Saturday. "Talk about dumb luck. I can accomplish two things at the same time."

"What do you mean?"

I told her about my meeting with Gretchen from the Yarnell Historical Society and that my publisher had leaned on me heavily to do a story on her efforts to save the building from being razed by developers. I gave her a discerning grin. "You must be the uncooperative tenant she was talking about."

She moved to a small table, eased into a chair and motioned for me to sit opposite her. "I can sympathize with her desire to save this place," she said, flicking something from her dark brown slacks, "and I'm sorry she's unhappy with me, but I don't feel comfortable having strangers troop through here taking pictures and possibly getting injured." She gestured to the adjacent workbench piled with cardboard egg cartons, assorted paintbrushes, boxes and a substantial array of bottles. "I work with some pretty strong chemicals." She explained that she worked with wax heated to eleven hundred degrees, which she used in the 'lost wax' process, as well as ferric nitrate to achieve the gold bronze patina on her sculptures and cupric nitrate to create her greens and blues. "I also utilize turpentine and lighter fluid to melt the clay, not to mention that I have dental and other sharp carving tools lying around. It's really not safe. But they can come in and do whatever they want after I'm gone."

The undertone of finality in her voice prompted me to ask, "Are you moving?"

"I've been looking at smaller studios in Jerome and Sedona. I appreciate the roominess of this place but I can't get the relatives of the woman I signed my lease with to make any repairs. The roof leaks, the furnace doesn't work very efficiently, the lock on the back door is broken and the wiring is ancient—" As if to confirm her statement, the lights dimmed and flickered momentarily before brightening again. "See what I mean? That's why I keep a supply of candles and kerosene lamps on hand," she said, pointing to a crowded shelf above the table containing both items. She must have noticed my look of concern because she added hastily, "Don't worry, if the heirs don't kick me out of here beforehand I plan to stay here until the end of the year. I should have your piece finished well before then."

"Listen, if it wouldn't be too intrusive, it would sure help me out to have a tour of the place, if you have time. Gretchen told me that there are parts of an old ammonia ice-making machine in the basement and I'd love to have a couple of pictures for my article." I flashed her a persuasive smile. "I promise I'll be careful and not destroy anything."

She pulled in her lower lip, appearing thoughtful. "I'll tell you what. Take all the exterior pictures you want, but it's much too dangerous to go into the cellar. The stairs are all rotted and there's standing water from seepage, not to mention the rats. I would feel terrible if you got hurt."

She gathered the shawl closer. "It's dark and damp. I never go down there."

I masked my disappointment with a slight shrug. "I'll take whatever I can get. By the way," I said, reaching into my pocket, "here's your down payment."

Nodding, she accepted the money, her expression turning quizzical. She inclined her head towards the kitchen, whispering, "I thought you wanted this to be a surprise for your fiancé?"

"I do."

"Well then...why did you bring him along?"

I blinked my confusion. "Oh, that's not Tally. That's...Grant Jamerson. He's... an old friend of mine."

A raised brow. "Oh? I just assumed—"

"I'm sorry, I should have introduced him when we came in."

"That's quite all right. Well then, I'll start on your piece as soon as you bring the posters."

"Thank you. You have no idea how much this means to me."

"And have you decided on a theme for your ice sculpture?"

"Not yet, but I think I'll leave that to your imagination since it appears to be much more fruitful than mine."

"How kind of you." With a puzzled frown, she searched around on the table for something, moving piles of catalogues and papers before rising from her chair. "I must have left my receipt book in my purse. I'll be right back."

"Oh, that's not necessary," I began, but she waved away my objection. "Because it's cash, I'd feel better about it."

"Whatever." After she left the room, I wandered around admiring more of her amazing sculptures: an eagle, a mountain lion and a peacock, looking startlingly lifelike with its blue, gold and black tail feathers fanned out. The escalating whistle of the wind blowing through an inch-wide space between the second set of double doors opening to the rear of the building alerted me to the fact the storm was gaining momentum. Wet footprints and a pair of muddy boots sitting on the concrete floor nearby indicated that Myra had also been out in the rain recently. I continued my 'art walk' and peeked through an open doorway towards the far corner of the room. In a narrow alcove, dimly lit in the glow of one bare bulb, I noticed a long countertop overflowing with at least a hundred of her signature cherub-faced angel figurines. It was amazing to note that the face on each looked identical and yet they did not appear to be mass-produced.

I returned to the table, sat down and picked up a pamphlet entitled *Southwestern Show Guide*. The booklet listed hundreds of upcoming arts and crafts festivals for cities in most of the states west of the Mississippi. As I leafed through it I wondered what it would be like to constantly travel around the country like Myra did, exhibiting her sculptures, dealing with the weather, meeting thousands of people, eating out and sleeping in different motels. I assumed it was profitable or she wouldn't do it. Hearing the light tap of her footsteps, I rose and met her in the hallway. She handed me the receipt and we walked together towards the kitchen. "Would you like a cup of tea?" she inquired politely.

"Thank you, but I think we should get going before we get slammed by this storm. It'll be dark soon and it was snowing like crazy when we left Prescott."

We entered the small kitchen, which had to be twenty degrees warmer than her studio, and spotted Grant, cup in hand, sitting with his shoes off, his stocking feet propped up on the hearth in front of the fire. "Oh, yes," she murmured, "I'd forgotten today was the judge's funeral. Such a tragedy. Was there a large turnout?"

"Huge," Grant volunteered in a loud voice, turning to face us, "and we were treated to a bit more drama than your average funeral."

I eyed the open brandy bottle critically. Like La Donna, I wondered how wise it was for him to mix pain medication with alcohol.

"Grant, meet Myra Colton."

He rose unsteadily to his feet and said with a lopsided grin, "The pleasure is all mine. Great tea." He swayed and sat down hard, almost missing the chair.

Myra exchanged a quizzical glance with me before moving to the counter and picking up the teakettle. "What kind of drama?"

Before I could speak, Grant blurted out, "Marissa, the judge's little girlfriend, was so overcome with emotion she fainted dead away in the snow right in front of the casket. Then Kendall informs us that the poor girl's knocked up and she's whisked away in an ambulance," Grant stated, brushing his hand though the air with great flourish.

"Well, I guess that is kind of dramatic," Myra remarked, looking mildly interested as she poured hot water into a cup.

"You betcha." He squinted longingly into his empty cup. "But the best part was later on when Kendall spied a ghostlike figure skulking around the coffin and then whoosh, vanishing into thin air."

Myra's lips twitched with amusement. "How intriguing."

Grant reached for the brandy bottle, which I quickly moved from his grasp. "If it was the murderer," he went on, blinking as he tried to focus on my face, "whoever it was better watch his ass because ace reporter Kendall O'Dell is on the job. Yep. She's the best in the business." Looking pleased with himself he tacked on, "And you can bet your bottom dollar if anybody can catch this person, it's gonna be her." He gave me a silly grin and I rolled my eyes.

"Grant, get your shoes on. We've got to go."

Myra dunked a teabag into her cup several times. "Are you referring to the young woman who lives at the Hidden Springs Hotel?" she asked softly. "I think I met her when I delivered that last piece to Mrs. Gibbons a month or so ago."

"That's right," I replied, watching Grant struggling to tie his shoelaces.

"My goodness, what a tangled legacy the man left behind." She reached into her pocket, tossed a couple of pills into her mouth and washed them down with a gulp of tea.

I hauled Grant to his feet. "Come on, let's get you home." Giving Myra a sheepish grin, I said, "I'll see you on Thursday."

She leveled me a observant look as I hooked my hand through his elbow. "I have several appointments that day so Friday afternoon would really work better for me."

"Friday it is."

There was very little daylight remaining when she showed us outside. Snow was just beginning to come down in earnest. "Be careful going down the hill," Myra called after us from the doorway, "it can get really icy in spots."

"We will. Bye now." We retraced our path along the dirt road and through the sleepy downtown area without incident, but after we'd traveled about halfway down Yarnell Hill, I knew we were in trouble. The freezing rain had created treacherous black ice conditions and made for slow going as strong wind gusts pummeled the truck. I switched into four-wheel drive and felt marginally confident following the taillights of the vehicle in front of us, but then they suddenly disappeared from view as I fought to keep from sliding on a particularly dicey hairpin turn. I grabbed the wheel tighter, straining to see the road as snow began to blow hard against the windshield. Perhaps a half-mile behind me, dim headlights glowed intermittently through the fog. "I hope you're not depending on me, buddy," I muttered under my breath. Should I pull over to the side of the road and stop or would that create an even greater danger? I had visions of a chain reaction accident that decision could cause. It would have been nice to have a second pair of eyes to help navigate, but Grant was slumped against the passenger door, his barbiturate and alcohol cocktail having apparently rendered him comatose.

Things swiftly went from bad to worse. Within minutes, near blizzard conditions had reduced visibility to mere feet. I could no longer make out the centerline and anxiously tried to gauge where I was with no highway markings to guide me away from the sheer drop off situated somewhere to my left. I chastised myself severely. Why hadn't I followed Rulinda's lead and waited out the storm in a cozy café?

I slowed to a crawl and then became sickeningly aware that the hazy headlights were bearing down on me from behind. Someone was coming at us fast—way too fast. I fumbled for the emergency flashers, shouting, "Grant! Wake up!" As the lights grew brighter, I pictured one of those huge gravel trucks careening out of control and instinct kicked in. The safest course of action would be to pull over to the right and bail out before we were rear-ended. Hollering, "Grant!" at the top of my lungs, I frantically tried to maintain control as I reached over to shake him. "Come on! We've got to get out of here! Now!"

He stirred and blinked at me stupefied, his face a surreal mask of light and shadow. He mumbled, "What's going on?" just as the vehicle slammed us from behind.

"Slow down, you idiot!" I screamed, trying to keep the wheel steady. Fear turned to bone-chilling horror when we were violently bumped a second time. Suddenly, the offending vehicle swerved, accelerated, and began to pass us on the right. It bounced along the narrow shoulder, swerving closer and closer. "Are you insane?" I shrieked. "What the hell are you doing?" Through the blinding snow, I was fairly certain I saw a flash of white just before the vehicle rammed us. My heart raced as we did a one-eighty in the middle of the road, spinning out of control like some nightmarish carnival ride and then, almost as if it were happening to someone else, I watched in helpless disbelief as the blinding headlights came at us, knocking the truck against the guardrail hard enough to deploy the airbags with a loud bang. With sickening alarm, I felt the protection of the guardrail give way and the truck began to slide backwards. Grant's panicked shouts mingled with my choked screams as we plunged over the edge of the cliff.

22

Powerless, petrified, rational thought suspended, all I could do was hang on to the steering wheel for dear life as we hurtled backwards downhill into the snowy darkness. The pickup hit something solid, lurched sideways and then we started to roll. Totally disoriented, unable to see, not knowing up from down or right from left, my fear was so all consuming, that all I could do was say a last prayer. Time seemed to stop as we performed I don't know how many revolutions and then incredibly, we landed upright with a mighty bounce, slid across the level, icy surface of the lower road before continuing downward again, jostling over rocks, crashing through brush and trees, everything a tangled whirling blur until we came to a metal-crunching stop that knocked the breath out of me. For long seconds there was no sound except the roar of the wind accompanied by our tortured breathing. I had no idea how far we'd fallen, but guessed by the way the truck was slanted that we were facing uphill at about a forty-five-degree angle. The deflated airbag left behind a powdery haze that burned my eyes and made me cough. Limp from the adrenaline rush, I gingerly moved my neck, arms and legs—whew! Everything was working. It took awhile for my eyes to fully adjust to the gloom and I could just barely make out Grant practicing the same maneuver, flexing his arms and legs.

I reached out and touched his shoulder. "Are you all right?"

"I think so," came his dazed response, pushing the airbag away. "Nothing appears to be broken. You okay?"

"Yeah, I think so." It was miraculous that we were unhurt and I sent up a thankful prayer that we were both still alive.

Then he startled me by exclaiming, "Amazing. That was like a super chiropractic adjustment. My neck doesn't hurt anymore. Whoo-hoo! Hell of a ride! Better than Disneyland!"

"I'm glad you enjoyed it," I responded dryly. "If you were weren't so zonked on pain killers and brandy, I doubt you'd find this amusing."

"Just trying to lighten things up. And for your information, I drank just enough to get a nice buzz." When I didn't respond, he added softly, "What happened anyway? I thought you said you knew how to handle this truck."

"I do!"

"Really? Could've fooled me."

"This wasn't my fault! Someone deliberately ran us off the road!"

"Are you shitting me?"

"No, whoever was driving the other vehicle managed to ram us accidentally four times."

"So, you're not subscribing to the notion that the driver may have just lost control on the ice?"

I hesitated, suddenly unsure. "It happened awfully fast. I suppose it's possible."

"Did you get a look at the vehicle?"

"Not clearly, but I saw a flash of white and based on the height of the headlights I'm betting it was some kind of truck or van."

"And do any of our suspects drive a white van?"

With growing unease, I pondered his question. "Huh! That's interesting."

"What?"

"It didn't dawn on me until you mentioned it, but they all do. Both Randy and Winston drive white pickups, and Rulinda drives a white van. And someone else was in the driver's seat when I saw her today at the funeral."

"You think it was big brother Randy driving?"

"I don't know. I didn't get a good look at the driver."

Grant fell silent for an extended period. "So, is it your theory that one of them just made an attempt to permanently remove you from the Gibbons story?"

"Looks pretty suspicious, doesn't it?"

"Yep." A powerful burst of wind shook the truck. "Well, we're in a hell of a mess. How far off the road do you think we are?"

It seemed as if we'd slid and rolled downhill for miles, but most likely it was only a couple hundred yards. "I have no idea, but we've got to get help soon or we're going to freeze to death."

"Try the engine," Grant suggested through chattering teeth. "At least maybe we can run the heat for awhile."

I tensed and turned the key. The instrument panel lit up, the fan and lights came on, but the engine wouldn't start. I tried several times to no avail. "Shit."

"One of the rocks we hit on the way down probably bent the oil pan bad enough so the crankshaft won't turn," Grant said with a sigh of resignation.

At least the horn worked. I ran the wipers to clear the snow from the windshield and honked the horn until Grant shouted, "Maybe we shouldn't run the battery down."

Numb with anxiety, I unhooked my seat belt and peered out the window. Nothing but blackness. I shoved hard on the door, but it wouldn't budge. "Can you get yours open?"

He pushed his door repeatedly and it finally opened, allowing the icy wind to rush inside. My heart leaped with expectation only to plummet in disappointment when he grunted, "Damn, it'll only open a couple of inches. We must be wedged in between some rocks." He pulled it shut. "Maybe we can climb out the windows."

I lowered them about half way. The driving snow pelted my face and I shivered all over when the tiny flakes blew down my collar. I reached outside and my fingertips immediately touched a cold, irregular surface. "Can't get out on this side," I said dejectedly, closing my window. "What about yours?"

"Nope."

The knowledge that we were trapped inside the truck set my heart hammering with unreasonable panic, threatening to generate both an asthma and claustrophobic attack. It took every bit of willpower I could summon to maintain calm. I must not become hysterical in front of Grant.

We closed the windows and brushed the snow from our clothes. "Let's think about this for a minute," he said. "Even if we could somehow pry my door open, is that something we want to do? Maybe we shouldn't be doing anything that might dislodge this baby. How do you know the back end of this truck isn't dangling off the side of this mountain?"

I didn't. The horrifying vision of nothing but a thousand foot drop below us shoved me to the brink of panic again. *Calm down!* I forced myself to take long, steadying breaths. Until the snowstorm abated there was no way to assess our situation. "Good point."

In spite of the fact that I was shivering with cold, my palms were sweaty as I frantically searched the floor for my purse. I finally located it beneath my seat, but all the contents had spilled and it seemed to take an eternity to find my cell phone. *Please let there be a signal!* It powered on, but then my spirits hit bottom when the low battery message flashed at me. There were also four voice messages, two from Tally and one each from Brian and Walter. I dared not waste what was left of the battery returning their calls.

I punched 911 and waited with bated breath for the number to connect. Dead air. I glanced at the screen. *Call Failed* pulsed back at me. "Damn it." I hit redial and when I heard a woman's clipped, "911 Emergency," relief turned my bones to jelly. I filled the operator in as quickly as possible and gave her the general vicinity of our location, well aware of the gravity of our situation. Due to the severity of the weather, it was doubtful rescue efforts could begin until daylight.

Impulsively, I dialed the Starfire Ranch. The sound of Tally's pleasant voice warmed me. "Tally! It's Kendall!"

"Hey, where are you? Ronda and my mother just now walked in. I've been trying to call you for—"

"Listen to me! My cell phone is about to die and I don't have much time. I got forced off the road coming down Yarnell Hill. It's colder than hell and we can't get out of...Tally? Tally?" I looked at the screen and sure enough it had gone black. In a temper, I threw the phone against the windshield. "Worthless things!"

"Take it easy," Grant said in a soothing tone. "It worked long enough to get help. I wished to hell I hadn't been so careless and forgotten mine."

"Me too."

"Let's look on the bright side. At least you had enough juice left to alert the authorities, so all we have to do is wait it out until they find us. We've got a couple of bottles of water and some snacks, so we won't starve."

Starving wasn't my biggest fear. As I listened to the incessant wail of the wind, I could not stop thinking about Riley Gibbons lying dead and buried in a snowdrift undiscovered by rescue teams. Would the same thing happen to us? Weeks from now would Tally be the one among the rescue party to find our frozen bodies? I would never have the opportunity to explain to him why my last hours on earth were spent with Grant. Lucinda would happily blabber her version of the fairground incident and that would be his final remembrance of me. Ruth would be off the hook, she'd never have to tell him the truth, Lucinda would be there to comfort him, they would get married and have several children while I lay forgotten in some weed-choked cemetery where Ginger would bring fresh flowers every so often to decorate my grave. And what about my darling Marmalade? Who would take care of her? Tortured by my fertile imagination, hot tears spilled onto my cheeks at the same instant Grant scooted to my side and gathered me into his arms.

"What are you doing?" I demanded, trying to shove him away, unable to see his face clearly in the low light.

"Don't be stupid, Kendall. You know as well as I do that frostbite is a very real danger. We've got to keep each other warm and we've got to stay awake." Hesitating, I kept him at arms length until he insisted, "Come on, you know I'm right."

I relaxed, acutely aware of the irony of the moment as he wrapped his arms around me and forcibly tucked my cold hands underneath his coat. The feel of his lean body was at once comforting and distressing. How many times during those long, lonely months following our breakup had I dreamed of being cocooned in his embrace again? As he pulled me closer, his warm breath caressed my neck and unbidden, from beneath the layers of built up resentment, traces of familiar emotions stirred inside me creating an odd emotional contradiction. Does love really die forever or does it lie dormant, waiting for a word, a look or a simple touch to resurrect it? *How fickle the human heart.* Guilty and confused, I wondered why I felt insecure about my commitment to Tally. I took a mental step backwards, allowing cool logic to allay my fears. It was more likely that my sudden confusion was due to a simple transference of emotions based on the dire circumstances; the same way strangers come together in a crisis. Yes, that was a more likely explanation. But, if we did somehow survive this ordeal how was I going to explain to Tally how I'd wound up in this predicament with Grant?

23

"There, that's better," Grant said with a contented sigh, rubbing my arms and back briskly, "but the big problem is going to be keeping our feet warm."

"How do you propose we do that?" I asked, trembling as much from anxiety as the intense cold.

"Well, we're going to have to put them someplace on each other's body to heat them up."

I drew back. "And where would that be?"

"It's going to be really uncomfortable for a few minutes, but I read a story about these two hunters who got stranded in snow for a week and they took turns warming their feet and boots under each other's armpits."

"That's gross."

"You got a better idea?"

"No."

"Okay, I'll let you go first."

"Oh, thank you."

Much to my surprise, after the awkwardness of removing my boots and lying back against the window to stretch out my legs, it really did work and my aching toes were actually warmer when I slipped my boots back on. I did the same for Grant and we alternated back and forth, chitchatting about anything and everything to stay lucid. We drank the water sparingly and munched on granola bars. It was a poor substitute for the barbeque beef dinner I'd planned to enjoy with Tally, but far better than nothing. Outside the storm intensified, the howling wind buffeting the truck while snow drummed against the windows like icy fingertips. From somewhere in the distance came the sound of muffled thunder.

"What was that?" Grant asked sharply, tilting his head to one side.

"Thundersnow."

"What's that?"

"It's a rare meteorological phenomenon that sometimes happens during a heavy snowstorm when a warm draft of air causes favorable conditions for lightning and thunder."

"Interesting. How did you know that?"

"It was a sidebar to a story I did on our monsoons last summer."

The storm raged on and on. Intermittently, I used the wipers to clear the windshield so we wouldn't be completely buried. Hopefully, we'd be able to get our bearings when daylight finally came. I also honked the horn and flashed the lights on the slim chance that someone driving along the road above would see or hear us. It occurred to me that we might have to break the windshield in order to get out. And just how would we do that with the tools locked in the bed of the truck? Not good. Not good at all.

The blizzard finally abated around four in the morning and the ensuing silence was deafening. When I cleared the windshield we were treated to patches of starlit sky visible now and then between fast-moving clouds and within minutes cold blue moonlight illuminated the landscape enough for us to make out the dark outlines of the boulders that imprisoned us, but at the same time, had prevented us from plunging any further down the steep slope. Again, the odd paradox of being in this specific spot struck me. My heart shattered by Grant's betrayal, my health ravaged by asthma, I'd fled to Arizona to start a new life, and probably less than a mile from where we now sat stranded, Tally had arrived at the scenic overlook and rescued me from a herd of jaw-snapping javelinas. Of course, I'd learned since that they were basically harmless creatures, but hadn't known that at the time.

Shivering uncontrollably, I sat clasped in the arms of my ex-lover, thinking that I would never again complain about the summer heat. At that moment, the furnace-like winds, scalding pavement and countless incidents of burning my fingers on the door handle of my car would have been a welcome blessing. I also couldn't help but marvel at the total irony of Phyllis's plea that I drive Grant to prevent him from having an accident. What would his mother think of me now? Time dragged on interminably until I finally groaned, "I have to move. My left foot is asleep." In an awkward attempt to disengage myself several strands of hair got tangled in his coat button. "Ouch."

"Hold still," he murmured, fumbling to free me, his face inches from mine. Suddenly his movements stilled and before I knew what was happening his lips came down hard on mine. My senses in turmoil, I tried desperately to decipher my true feelings for this man I had once cared for so completely. No question about it. In the kissing department, Grant was in a class all by himself. But even though it was a familiar, pleasurable sensation, deep inside I couldn't help feeling a measure of triumphant vindication when my heart rebelled.

I snapped my head back tearing the hairs out by the roots. "Stop it!"

"Oh, Kendall, " he moaned breathlessly, "I was such a damn fool to let you go! It was such a stupid, stupid mistake. Won't you give me one more chance? I swear I'll never give you reason to doubt me ever again."

Keeping him at arms length I said firmly, "Grant, listen to me. I meant what I said before. This isn't going to happen. Don't get me wrong. I'll always cherish the memory of what we had together and I think you're really a decent guy to finally admit you were wrong, but understand something and understand it well. I am in love with Bradley Talverson now, plain and simple." Just saying the words aloud banished my misgivings and sent a joyous tingle coursing through my veins. "If you want my friendship, you've got it. Can you be satisfied with that?" It was a decidedly awkward moment considering we needed to keep our bodies fastened firmly against one another in order to survive.

He cleared his throat a couple of times before sighing, "Jesus, you're breaking my heart."

I could have said, 'Now you know how it feels,' but instead murmured, "I'm sorry."

"Well, I guess friendship is better than nothing."

"Of course it is," I said, relieved to have diffused what could have been an explosively hurtful scene for both of us. Having no choice but to place my trust in him, I laid my head against his shoulder and we huddled together again. We chatted about world events, our jobs and then he rambled on with stories of his childhood, but after awhile my mind grew foggy and his words made no sense. Sleepy. I felt very sleepy. And comfortable. I struggled to concentrate, listening to his voice drone on and on, sounding further and further away. Maybe I'd just close my eyes for a minute. So sleepy.

"Kendall! Kendall! Damn it! Wake up!" A stinging slap on my cheek. I fought to open my eyes. "Come on, Sleeping Beauty, talk to me," came Grant's terse demand. It seemed like his hands were all over me, rubbing forcefully. "Kendall!" Another stinging slap.

"Cut it out!" I whined, grabbing his hand. "That hurts!"

"You cannot sleep! Keep talking!" he cried, his voice underscored with fright as he vigorously massaged my arms and legs.

"I'm sorry. I…guess I nodded off."

"No kidding. This cold is insidious." He forced me to drink water then commanded, "Come on, pick a subject."

With extreme effort, I shook the icy cobwebs from my head and tried to organize my thoughts. "Okay. Let's review the Gibbons case."

"I was going to opt for something trivial like sports or movies, but all right. That ought to tax our intellect and keep us awake for the next fifty years."

"I thought that was the idea."

And so we talked and talked, warming each other's feet and fighting to stay coherent while recapping everything with the exception of Ruth's secret. It helped a lot to distract me from the numbing cold, but even with both of us attacking the story from different directions we wound up back at square one. "Christ, my head hurts," Grant complained, "but I'm going with the assumption that the charming Moorehouse siblings cashed out the judge's chips. One or both of them followed him to Flagstaff the day he left for his hunting trip, shot him and then...you know, did the deed."

"But...why cut off his head?"

"I don't know. Just because Moorehouse was released from Death Row on a technicality doesn't mean he wasn't guilty as sin of chopping up his girlfriend, right?"

"Right."

"So, maybe it's one of those situations where you get away with something once, so you try it again. He certainly had enough time to plan it."

"Could be, and considering how much he and Rulinda hated the judge it would seem a perfect final vengeance, but so far there's no physical evidence to prove it and we can't discount the fact that Winston may have had a double motive, revenge plus greed. Oh no wait, maybe there's a third reason. He gets Marissa in the bargain too."

"Excellent hypothesis," he agreed. "How do we know the baby isn't his?"

"We don't."

"But, we also must not forget that La Donna may have hired him to exact revenge on her wayward husband. You know, the hell hath no fury theory. One thing's still puzzling me though," he mused, drawing in a shuddery breath. "What's the significance of those quotations the judge prepared for the two special ladies in his life? Do they have anything to do with his murder or do we handle them separately? Let's go over them again."

"I can't remember each of them verbatim without looking at my notes, but the first one to La Donna said something like, *let your hook be cast and in a pool where you least expect it there might be...no, will be fish.*"

"Interesting quote. Okay, so if we take that apart, *hook be cast*...you think that means be prepared for something?"

"Sounds logical."

"Or...how about be attentive? And *where you least expect it, there will be fish* might mean...be observant and you'll find something in an unexpected place."

I stiffened, repeating, "An unexpected place? Wait a minute! I just remembered a conversation I had with Tally and his sister. Riley Gibbons was a mystery aficionado. He devoured whodunits and frequently attended these mystery weekends that are sometimes held in old houses or hotels. Are you familiar with this concept?"

"Yeah, I've heard of 'em. Each person gets a series of clues to follow and the winner gets some sort of prize at the end for solving the mystery."

"Right. In fact, La Donna told me they had plans to host one of these weekends at Hidden Springs." My mind worked feverishly. "What if...what if the judge designed these messages to function as clues?"

"Clues to what?"

That stumped me. "I don't know."

He sat in silence for a little while then said, "Let's suppose your assumption is correct. What were the quotations in Marissa's letter?"

Apparently my brain cells had frozen solid because I really had to tax my usually reliable memory. "I think it started out with *love builds bridges where none exist and then...something about not walking where the path leads, but going instead where there isn't one and leaving a trail* or something to that effect."

"Man, that's an ambiguous statement. Makes no sense to me," Grant remarked thoughtfully. "We've got to assume that the wily judge chose those particular phrases for a specific reason, but what the significance is I don't know."

"Let's try to imagine his mindset," I said slowly, going over them again in my mind. "Separately these proverbs don't mean anything, but what if he designed them to be linked together?"

"Ahhhh! Excellent point." Again we sat in silence a long time before Grant finally spoke. *"Love builds bridges, love builds bridges.* Okay, so for some strange reason known only to the judge, he devised this little mystery game so these two women who despise each other would be forced to communicate with each other. Why?"

"Beats me, although if you think about it, deeding the hotel over to Marissa already binds them together, but the letters take it a step further. Building onto what you just said, we could postulate that if they compared notes and worked together, they would find *something unexpected if they take a path where none exists now.* How does that sound?"

Grant let out a groan of frustration. "Plausible, but I still wouldn't have any idea where to start."

"Yeah. I agree."

Silence fell between us again, but then he asked in a mystified voice, "So…what's the prize?"

Good question. If the quotations had actually been designed along the same lines as the mystery weekends then… "Holy guacamole!" I whispered in sudden awe, as my thoughts lined up like birds on a phone wire.

"What?"

"That's it!"

"What's it?"

"The coins. It's got to have something to do with the missing gold coins!"

"Son-of-a-bitch," he replied, his voice rising with contagious excitement, "that's a provocative theory, but, why would he risk that much money for the sake of a game?"

"Who knows? But from what little I know about him, planning a stunt like this would certainly epitomize his mischievous sense of humor and his lifelong habit of playing practical jokes."

"That's one heck of a final joke, if you ask me. Why would he take such a risk? Think about it. If the two of us can't decipher what this stuff means, and I think we're reasonably intelligent, what made him think either Marissa or La Donna would be able to figure it out?"

"Since there's no way we can know for sure what he was thinking, all we can do is hypothesize."

"Hypothesize away."

"Okay. Let's assume that after Riley received those threatening quotations, he feared for his life." I could not reveal to him that I already knew this to be true. "But because he'd made such a mess of his personal life and anticipated that La Donna was poised to take him to the cleaners, he arranged to hide part of his assets. Now, according to what Tally told me, Riley Gibbons was also quite the romantic and had a reputation as a ladies' man." *Boy, was he ever.* "So, what if he felt really guilty about hurting La Donna and came up with an ingenious way to force both women in his life to come together to find the treasure? Doesn't that sound like a wonderfully mysterious way to be remembered?"

"Sounds like a Hardy Boys adventure to me."

"Yeah, and I'll bet he read every one of them. Or, how about this one? What if Riley suspected that Marissa and Winston were fooling around and that she'd told him about the existence of the gold coins? Winston dispatches the judge, hotfoots it for the safe deposit box only to find that Riley had beaten him to it. Wouldn't that explain why he's been using the renovation as an excuse to tear up the third floor of the hotel because he suspects they're hidden there?"

"Good theory, but what if La Donna cleaned out the box and then staged that whole scene at the reading of the will to divert attention from herself and thereby assign blame to Winston and Marissa?"

I mulled that over for a minute. "But if that were the case, why would Riley bother to compose those letters? It makes more sense to believe that they were designed to act as brainteasers or clues to the missing gold, don't you think? But then, we have to remember that he was also an attorney and it doesn't make sense that he would leave something like finding thousands of dollars worth of gold coins to chance. He must have created an alternate plan."

"Hell, I don't know," he grumbled, a shade of frustration evident in his voice as he shifted to a more comfortable position, "this whole thing is officially driving me crazy. If Riley did devise those proverbs to serve as clues, why didn't he provide more information? There's not enough to go on. There's something else missing—"

Suddenly I stopped listening to him when a remark he'd made earlier struck me. *The two special ladies in his life*...but there had actually been *three* women counting Ruth. *Something missing*...my mind reeled backwards to an incident that had seemed insignificant at the time. The evening Tally and I had made our surprise entrance to announce our engagement Ruth had shoved a piece of white paper into the photo album. Whoa, mama! It made perfect sense that Ruth had also received one of the judge's cryptic letters and if I was on the right track, it might contain a vital clue. A faint thumping in the distance diverted my attention. I sat up straight. "What's that?"

Rigid with anticipation, I held my breath as the sound grew progressively louder and then all at once a dazzling blue light shattered the darkness and illuminated the snowy windshield. "The rescue helicopter!" I shouted, seeing my own joyful relief reflected in the radiant flash grazing Grant's face. As I scrambled to turn the ignition key, Grant clapped, whooped and hollered, bouncing up and down in his seat like a little kid. As the chopper moved away we were returned to our dark cave. The battery must have been on its last legs because nothing happened. "Come on!" I screamed, pounding on the windshield. Sluggishly the fan motor groaned to life. The wipers scraped against the icy glass brushing enough snow aside so that we could see the vivid shaft of light sweeping the hillside. I'd done a piece on the Yavapai County Sheriff's Search and Rescue Team and remembered that deputies would be equipped with night vision glasses. I flashed the headlights and honked the horn repeatedly. The chopper moved away, circled back, angled away again, returned, hovered low and fastened its blinding beam directly on the truck. A booming voice from a loudspeaker asked if we were all right, so I honked the horn and Grant shouted out the window. We were told that rescue operations would commence at first light and then the deafening roar of the chopper faded away. High above us, just barely visible on the highway, we could make out the flashing lights of emergency vehicles. Thank God rescue was close at hand.

Grant sang out, "Praise the Lord!" Breaking into gales of laughter, we hugged each other. The last hour until daybreak seemed more like a week and as we sat there waiting and waiting, blowing on our hands and moving as much as we could to keep up our circulation, I couldn't help but think of the ancient proverb Myra Colton had recited last Saturday, *Patience is bitter, but its fruit is sweet.* Truer words were never spoken.

Darkness finally relinquished its grasp on the night sky and gave way to the soft gray light of dawn. Within minutes the swirl of clouds above us glowed bright crimson—a harbinger of more bad weather to come, but we were finally able to see why we'd been unable to open the doors. Miraculously, the truck had become wedged between two massive rock outcroppings. We could also clearly see each other for the first time since the ordeal began and it wasn't a pretty sight. Grant looked disheveled, pale and haggard and I couldn't resist a peek at my reflection in the rearview mirror. I didn't look much better, but knowing that rescue was at hand gave me a burst of energy and I quickly gathered the spilled contents of my purse and made sure I had the bag with the black rose in my possession.

When the first rays of fiery sunlight broke over the horizon around seven-thirty, it transformed the surroundings into a glittering wonderland that I would have appreciated a lot more if I hadn't been so cold, hungry and exhausted. All at once, the clattering chopper appeared and we watched the welcome sight of our rescuer being lowered from the sheriff's helicopter. The dark-bearded young man unhooked himself from the harness and trudged towards us through knee high drifts, shouting, "Does anyone need immediate medical assistance?"

The battery finally gave out so we couldn't lower the windows. Grant called out, "No, I think we're okay, but we're trapped inside!"

The rugged-looking man quickly signaled for backup and after that everything seemed to move in fast-forward. In addition to the sheriff's helicopter, two other choppers from television stations in Phoenix hovered overhead, creating an ear-shattering racket as a second team member came swinging downward. They tried, but could not move the truck far enough from the rocks to open the doors. There was no choice but to break out the back window. My throat constricted with emotion, I waited impatiently for them to clear away the broken safety glass and when we climbed out, it was a gut-wringing shock to see how close we'd come to certain death, having stopped not twenty feet from the edge of a sheer precipice. And when I got a good look at the mangled truck body I said hoarsely, "Is there going to be any way to salvage this?"

"Doubtful," remarked the second man, shaking his head. "Most likely we'll have to call a back country recovery service to have it cut up and hauled out of here."

Within minutes, the first man on the scene hooked me securely into a harness and I waved goodbye to Grant as we sprang upward into the frigid morning air. Dangling from the end of a rope several hundred feet above the mountainside was a stomach swooping sensation comprised of fright and exhilaration. Overcome with the urge to laugh wildly with relief and weep with joy, I was fiercely aware of the brilliance of the spinning blue sky and the luscious warmth of the sun's golden rays touching my cold cheeks. What a super-amazing adrenaline rush! It was not my first near-death experience and I suspected not the last, but just like each of my previous scrapes I took away a new perspective, which reinforced my love of life and appreciation for everything genuinely important. Fleetingly, it occurred to me that if it had not been for the accident, I would never have been in that exact place at that exact moment and would never have been afforded such a dizzying, yet spectacular panoramic view of the wide valley below that I called home. It was a natural high like no other I'd ever experienced and as we descended over the swarm of people and flashing emergency vehicles squeezed onto the narrow highway, the irony of the situation hit me at the sight of several media vans. Instead of reporting the news, Grant and I had now become the news.

Deposited once again on solid ground, paramedics settled me on a gurney, wrapped me in warm blankets and gave me some juice to drink. They were busily taking my vital signs when Sheriff Turnbull ambled up to me, his ruddy features fixed with concern. "Well, Kendall, you sure got everybody's attention," he said, gesturing to the news helicopters hovering overhead. "How you doing?"

"I've been better."

"Want to tell me what happened?"

The creases on his forehead deepened as I gave him all the particulars of the accident. "Road conditions were pretty bad last night. There were a half a dozen other accidents reported, but yours was the most spectacular."

"Apparently."

He tilted his head. "You sure the other driver didn't just lose control of his vehicle?"

Confronted with the possibility in the clear light of day, I wavered. It had all happened so fast, was it possible I'd imagined malice where none existed? "Well, I can't prove it, but let's just say it seemed awfully suspicious."

"Your passenger see anything out of the ordinary?"

"No."

The dubious look in his eyes sent a wave of embarrassment zinging through me. "Look, Marshall, I don't know if there's any connection but I've got something here that may hold some significance in the Gibbons case," I said, reaching under my coat to hand him the bag containing the black rose. He listened intently, rubbing one forefinger back and forth across his snowy handlebar mustache.

"Are you familiar with the anonymous letters that the judge received a few weeks prior to his death?"

He nodded and told me that he'd been contacted by Phoenix detectives. "So it's your contention that this person feared that you may have seen him or her, followed you and forced you off the road?"

"That's one theory."

"Okay, well, I'll have somebody get this to the lab right away."

"Thanks."

"I'm going to have one of my deputies get all the particulars from you. Take it easy, Kendall." He turned to leave and then swung back. "Oh, and try to stay out of trouble for a few hours."

"You're wasting your breath, Marshall," came a familiar resonant voice. I looked around to see Tally strolling towards me, his lips set in a straight line, his complexion appearing drawn and pale. "It's not in her nature." After exchanging a meaningful glance with the sheriff, who flashed him a wry smile in return, he moved to my side and my pulse rate escalated when he grasped me in a firm embrace. "God damn it, Kendall," he whispered, his warm breath in my ear, "what am I going to do with you?"

Funny how adversity can make a murky issue seem crystal clear. I rejoiced at the feel of his muscular arms closing around me and the last vestiges of doubt about my profound love for this man vanished forever. I vowed that I would make a renewed effort to be less self-centered, less impetuous and return our relationship to solid footing, even if it meant swallowing my pride and learning to live in peace and harmony in the same house with Ruth. If that's what it took to make this man happy then that's the way it would be. "I'm sorry I worried you."

He pulled away and tipped his hat back, staring at me thoughtfully as he removed his gloves. "I'm just happy to see that you're alive," he said gruffly, wrapping his hands around my cold fingers.

I couldn't believe it. I'd managed to hold it together throughout the entire arduous ordeal, but his welcome presence brought instant tears to my eyes. There was so much I needed to tell him, so much I couldn't tell him. I edged him a self-conscious smile. "You have no idea how glad I am to see you."

"That must have been pretty scary for you. You okay?" His gaze was intent, probing, solicitous.

"Much better now. Thank you for being here." My voice quavered on the last word and he squeezed my hand.

"Of course I'd be here," he said softly. "By the way, don't worry about Marmalade. I drove over to your place early this morning and fed her."

"Thank you," I said, beaming him a grateful smile as I squeezed his hand back. "Tally, I am so sorry about your truck. I'm afraid it's totaled."

A sideways grin. "That's two vehicles in a month's time. Hope you're not planning to make a habit of it."

His black humor made me smile, but then his hand slipped from my grasp as I was lifted into the ambulance. "Wait! Where are you taking me?"

"To the Yavapai County Medical Center in Prescott," the husky female paramedic informed me.

"Wait! I don't want to go to the hospital. Really. I feel fine. I'm just hungry and tired."

Her shrug was noncommittal. "You can decline treatment, but considering how long you've been exposed to the elements we'd recommend you be evaluated."

"I'll take her to our local doctor, " Tally chimed in, reaching into his pocket and handing me a granola bar. I thanked him and devoured it in short order, thinking I'd never tasted anything quite so good in my life.

At that moment, the steady roar of the helicopter focused everyone's attention on Grant being lowered to the ground. "Man oh man, what a welcome sight!" he whooped, his face glowing as he passed out high fives to those close to him. "Kudos to you all for a job well done!"

The Search and Rescue volunteers reacted to his effusive praise with wide smiles and when the paramedics descended on Grant he offered no objection to being loaded into the waiting ambulance. Seconds before the doors shut he locked eyes with me, his questioning gaze brimming with a multitude of emotions only I could understand. Unfortunately, Tally witnessed the exchange too. Uh-oh. A feeling of uneasiness rolled over me as I watched his expression hardened to the consistency of granite. Shit. He hadn't known that I had not been alone all night. The wounded disappointment in his eyes broke my heart, but before I could offer an explanation, he turned away from me without a word.

24

I could hardly keep my thoughts straight while the young deputy grilled me for details and it took more than an hour to complete the accident statement and answer pointed questions from reporters. I got an eye-opening taste of what it was like to be on the receiving end of my job and it was after ten o'clock by the time Tally assisted me into his truck and we started down Yarnell Hill. I knew we were both thinking the same thing. I could tell by his stone-faced expression that he was spoiling for a fight so I broke the uncomfortable silence first. "I know I have a lot of explaining to do, but let me begin by saying this whole thing isn't what it looks like."

His jaw muscles twitched. "Well then, that would differ from the fascinating accounts of your cozy get-togethers with Grant that I've heard from both Lucy and Ronda."

"Crap, I was afraid of that."

"I guess you would be."

I groaned inwardly, not feeling mentally or physically capable of defending myself as the adrenaline seeped from my body, leaving me weak with fatigue and hunger. All I really wanted to do was soak in a hot bath, have a hearty meal and fall into bed.

"Tally," I said wearily, "hear me out before you jump to conclusions."

"Am I supposed to blow off the fact that you and Mr. Pretty Boy Reporter have been spotted all over town since I've been gone?"

"All over town? That's slightly exaggerated."

"That's not what I heard."

"Exactly what did you hear?"

"That you two were caught kissing and groping each other in public at the fairgrounds."

My cheeks flamed with rage. "Groping?" I spluttered. "Tally, that's not—"

"Do you deny that you and he were thick as thieves at my uncle's funeral, which by the way you were supposed to attend with *my* family? I have no idea what went on between the two of you last night, I'm not even sure I want to know, but I'm sure as hell not blind. I didn't miss the look you shared back there."

I folded my arms and stared straight ahead as we rounded the last hairpin turn and the road bottomed out into the flat desert basin. "Are you finished?"

"No, I'm just getting started," he said, firing a withering glare that challenged me to remain silent. "What am I supposed to think, Kendall? I thought a relationship, a marriage, was supposed to be based on trust. First you break your promise and take on Riley's story behind my back, using my poor mother as an excuse, then you agree to back off but then you don't. And now just what I feared would happen, did. Your sleuthing has pissed off this madman. Does this sound familiar? 'Oh, Tally, how much trouble could I possibly get into?'" he mocked, falling into a rather bad imitation of my voice. "'I'll be here working right under your nose.'"

Unable to contain myself any longer, I blurted out "You don't know all the facts! If you'll just chill for a minute, I'll give you the details. Look, I'm really sorry I upset you, but there's a very good reason why I've continued on with this story."

"What reason?"

Oops! Should've kept my mouth sealed. It was painfully obvious Ruth had not yet told him the truth and I seriously debated as to whether I should go ahead and break it to him myself. But I held my tongue. How could I deliver news of such a devastatingly intimate nature to him? It would let me off the hook in the immediate sense, but would no doubt seal my fate for any future relationship with his mother forever. And considering his argumentative mood, would he even believe me? "I wish I could tell you, but I can't."

"You mean you won't."

"I mean I can't."

His sidelong glance sizzled with irritation. "Why not?"

"Because, it's far more complicated than you might imagine."

"Well, why don't you enlighten me?"

"I...can't. Not yet. Let me say this much. I've actually stayed on this story for your sake."

His eyebrows shot up. "My sake?"

"That's right. Someone out there has got a vendetta against anybody connected to Riley Gibbons and because of...um...certain circumstances, you may actually be in far greater danger than I am."

"Me? That doesn't make any sense."

"It will. You need to speak with your mother."

"Oh, no. Don't tell me we're back to her stupid bad luck curse? Admit it, you're using that as an excuse to get your own way, as usual."

"Wait just a minute," I cut in, the downside of the adrenaline rush spawning a raging headache. "If I recall correctly, along with your initial request, you also said you wouldn't try to stop me from doing my job."

He absorbed my statement in silence, braking to a slower speed as we approached the outskirts of town. The rare sight of the usually dull brown landscape blanketed in white sidetracked me for a moment and I marveled at the stark beauty of sunbathing saguaro cacti backdropped by the grandeur of Castle Rock capped with snow. "So, is it your contention that Lucy is lying?" Tally pressed.

"Oh, Lord have mercy," I moaned, rubbing my sandpapery eyes. "Okay, here's the deal. Grant did kiss me at the fairgrounds, but I didn't kiss him back. I let him know in no uncertain terms that I have no intention of re-kindling our relationship."

"Then why was he with you at the funeral?"

"His mother asked me for a favor." I gave him the background on Grant's car wreck, Marissa's phone call, our trip to see Dr. Garcia, and then Phyllis's tearful plea. Of course, I couldn't reveal that my visit to Myra Colton was the main reason I couldn't travel with his family. "I'm not kidding you when I say that shit has been raining down on me from all sides. I'm trying to do the right thing and please everybody and I've ended up pleasing no one. Yeah, most of it's my fault, but you've got to believe me when I tell you that there's nothing going on between Grant and me other than we're both working the same story." He never needed to know about Grant's conduct last night.

He pulled into the medical clinic's parking lot, shut off the engine and sat there drumming his fingers before saying somberly, "Kendall, I see the way he looks at you and it bothers the hell out of me. It's pretty obvious to me that he's still in love with you."

"Relax, cowboy, whatever he's feeling, it's all on his end."

His eyes searched mine. "Level with me. If you're feeling any doubts about us, any doubts at all, please tell me now."

I slid to his side and looped my arms around his neck. "Hey, big guy, are you forgetting that I asked *you* to marry *me*?"

His arms tightened around me. "I was getting there, but you, being the impetuous, hot-headed woman that you are, beat me to it by a couple of seconds."

"Whatever," I murmured, pressing my mouth to his sensuous lips. We kissed until we were both breathless. When I pulled back, I looked him straight in the eye. "I'm really flattered that you're jealous of Grant, but you needn't worry."

"Positive?"

"Positive. Actually, you owe him a debt of thanks."

His expression bordered on incredulity. "For what?"

"Number one, because of his quick thinking and perseverance I didn't freeze to death last night; two, it gave me a new perspective on a lot of things I might not have gotten any other way; and three, it laid to rest all the old ghosts that have been haunting me since I left Philadelphia. So, that's a good thing for us."

"So you're going to be happy with the living arrangements after we're married?"

"You already know I'm not crazy about moving into the same house with your mother, but I have to say that over the past few days, I've learned a lot more about what makes her tick and well, I'm hoping for the best."

"I wouldn't worry too much about that if I were you. Sometimes things have a way of working themselves out."

The incisive glint in his eyes prompted me to ask, "What are you talking about?"

"You'll find out soon enough."

25

I spent the remainder of Wednesday afternoon sleeping so soundly I didn't even dream, and felt slightly disoriented when I was awakened around five that evening by Marmalade happily kneading my chest, purring and drooling. "Hi, baby," I murmured, still feeling groggy. She'd been all over me when I'd gotten home and had stayed on my lap while I consumed two cans of hot soup and a turkey and cheese sandwich that Tally said would have choked one of his horses. The slew of phone messages waiting, calls I needed to make to the office and posters that needed to be picked up at the copy shop weighed on me, but I'd been too exhausted to do anything but fall into bed. As I lay there savoring my warm sheets and scratching Marmalade's soft chin, my thoughts slipped back to the events of the last forty-eight hours. The horror of our plunge down Yarnell Hill, followed by the long night spent in the freezing, claustrophobic confines of the truck cab now seemed like a nightmare. No matter how many times I went over the accident in my mind, the exact events prior to and during the accident were a tangled blur, and where I'd felt positive before that it had been deliberate, I now began to question myself. Was it possible that the other driver had simply lost control on the icy road? Sheriff Turnbull and the deputy taking the accident report had both worn dubious expressions when I'd voiced my accusation. But if it had actually been an accident, why had the driver not contacted the authorities after we went over the edge? I wondered how Grant was fairing. Had he been treated and released? If so, how had he gotten back to Hidden Springs? I also wondered about Marissa's condition.

I yawned, stretched, threw off the covers and padded into the bathroom with Marmalade following in my footsteps. She sat on the rug washing her face as the tub filled. While brushing my teeth, I glanced out the window into the fading light of the persimmon-colored dusk, noting with interest that, with the exception of a few deep drifts nestled into crevices on the mountains, most of the snow had melted.

With a satisfied sigh I sank into the scalding water perfumed with a mountain of jasmine-scented bubble bath. Considering the circumstances, I felt pretty darn good. Following Dr. Garcia's examination, he'd pronounced me to be in surprisingly good condition. The tingling sensation on the end of my nose, he explained, was slight frostbite and he recommended plenty of fluids and bed rest.

Earlier, on the drive to my place, Tally had filled me in on his own adventures during the snowstorm, detailing the long list of problems he'd encountered while being stranded for hours along I-40—his friend's injury, the damaged horse trailer and his own harrowing trip back to the ranch yesterday with the mares in tow. He made no bones about the fact that he'd seen enough snow to last him for a lifetime and I was in total agreement. Treasuring the feel of the warm sunlight streaming in the window of the cab, I'd only had time to share about half of everything I'd discovered during my investigation by the time we pulled into my driveway. He expressed reluctant admiration at the amount of progress I'd made in such a short time, but was still firm in his belief that my involvement was too risky. "I don't want to lose you," he remarked solemnly, laying his hand over mine.

I squeezed back. "I don't want to lose me either."

"What am I going to do with you?" he asked with a frustrated sigh. "When I met you, I suspected that you were a type A personality, but I was wrong—you're a quadruple type A personality when it comes to your job."

"I know, and sometimes I wonder why you put up with me."

He grinned at me. "No question about it, you can be a total pain in the ass."

I smiled back. "Thanks. Listen, if it will put your mind at ease you're welcome to tag along with me next time I'm on assignment."

"I may take you up on that." He stayed long enough to tuck me into bed, unplug the bedroom phone and promise to return later. "I think I can scrounge up another vehicle for you to drive until we go car shopping this weekend."

"You sure you trust me with another one?"

"It's my father's old truck," he said with a wistful smile. "He beat the hell out of it so I don't think there's too much damage you can do to it at this point." My stomach dipped at the words, 'my father's' and I wondered again what his reaction would be when Ruth told him the truth.

Thinking that my bed had never felt so soft and so warm, I smiled up at him. "Sounds like a plan."

"Yeah. Maybe you should consider buying an armor-plated tank."

"Thanks for the vote of confidence."

"Call me when you wake up," he'd chuckled, planting a tender kiss on my lips, "and I'll come get you."

"Okay," I'd replied sleepily, cuddling under the covers, barely able to keep my eyes open as he headed out the door. "And tell everybody at the office I'm fine and to expect me in the morning." I think I'd been asleep before he reached the front door.

The steady trill of the telephone in the living room interrupted my thoughts. Damn, I should have brought the cordless into the bathroom. I looked at my pink, pruned skin and decided that I'd probably had enough anyway. The phone jingled again as I toweled off. "Hold your horses," I shouted, shrugging into my robe. I sprinted to the living room and snatched up the cordless phone.

"Hey, Kendall, it's Walter. You get my messages?"

"Not yet."

"Uh-oh. Hope I didn't wake you."

"Nope, but I'm still getting myself together." Marmalade had followed me and was mewing for her dinner.

"That's good. Well, how're you doin'?"

"Still feeling kind of muddled, but all in all not bad."

"You gave us all one hell of a scare."

"Sorry. That would be total irony, wouldn't it? I go to cover a funeral and end up being at my own."

"Not funny."

"No, it really wasn't."

"Saw you on the five o'clock news," he announced. "Pretty dramatic rescue."

"Tell me about it. How'd I look?"

"Like hell."

"Wonderful. Well, what's up?"

"Got something you might find intriguing. You were right, Ginger's brother is a whiz at finding stuff on the Internet. Anyway he came across a bizarre unsolved homicide case that occurred during the time frame you gave me that may or may not hold any significance."

That jerked me out of my stupor. "I'm listening."

"Let me preface by saying that because this homicide took place out of state, I don't know if there is any connection to the Gibbons case, but thought I ought to pass it along to you anyway because at one time this person had ties to Arizona."

"Shoot."

Tapping on the keyboard, Walter hummed off key to himself for a couple of seconds before saying, "Okay here we go. Three years ago the body of fifty-eight-year-old Harrison Reese was discovered in the backyard of his plush hillside home in Monterey, California. He'd been shot once through the heart at close range. At one time Reese had been a prominent defense attorney in Phoenix. He'd only resided in California for nine months when the murder occurred. There was no apparent motive and nothing inside the home had been disturbed. Because there wasn't much to go on at the crime scene, the case went cold."

"I hate to say that a shooting sounds routine, but nowadays that's sadly true. Why did you say it was bizarre?"

"The guy's tongue had been cut out."

With a twinge of alarm I remembered Riley's words to Ruth on his last visit. Several people he'd been involved with in the past had recently died under what he'd described as very odd circumstances. Could this person be one of them? If so, it narrowed down our search considerably. "Good work. This could be the link we're looking for," I told Walter, unable to suppress the eagerness in my voice. "Keep digging. Have Brian check out every case that Reese argued before Judge Gibbons."

"Just the felony cases?"

"Primarily, but have him also look for anything else that strikes him as out of the ordinary. Oh, and I'd also be interested to know who represented both Moorehouse and Pendahl during their trials."

"Will do."

I called Tally to let him know I'd be ready to go in an hour and then hunger pangs drove me to the kitchen again. Marmalade and I shared dinner, a gigantic tuna salad and potato chips. While I munched on cookies, I dropped my newly charged cell phone into my purse before reviewing the barrage of messages on my home phone. Good grief! It seemed like half the town had called to check on my welfare. It was nice to know so many people cared. Living in a small town, where everyone knew what everybody else was doing, really was like having an extended family.

I returned Tugg's call, told him I'd be in early to file my story on the Gibbons funeral, brought him up to date on the particulars of the case, and he urged me to take as much time as I needed to recover.

"Hey, if you don't have any wheels, don't break your neck trying to get in here at the crack of dawn," he'd advised. "I got everything covered. In fact, if you feel like it, take the rest of the week off."

I thanked him for his concern, explained that Tally was arranging to loan me another pickup, then said goodbye. I hit the speed dial for Ginger, who sounded at first relieved to hear from me, but then took the opportunity to bawl me out. "Girl, I can't let you out of my sight for a second," she complained with mock severity. "You scared the ever-lovin' pee out of everybody!"

"Sorry, but at least I accomplished one thing you'll be pleased about. Myra Colton agreed to create the ice sculpture for the party."

That made her happy, but she wanted to hear every single detail of the funeral, my accident, the night spent alone with Grant, and it was a good twenty minutes before I finally got her off the line. And that was only after I promised to have lunch with her the following day. Then I dialed Grant's cell number. It rang four times and I was poised to hit the OFF button when I heard him croak, "Hi, there."

"Oh, crap. Did I wake you?"

"Yeah, but that's okay. I've been sleeping for hours."

"Are you all right? Are you still in the hospital?"

"I'm fine and back in my lonesome little bed at Hidden Springs."

I let his comment slide by. "How'd you get back from Prescott?"

"I hitched a ride with Winston and Marissa. He was waiting to pick her up and she was kind enough to offer me a lift."

"How's she doing?"

"Apparently she's anemic. The doctor prescribed iron pills and she's supposed to stay in bed for a couple of days."

An awkward silence developed between us, which he finally broke. "So how's everything with you? I couldn't help but notice the expression on Tally's face when he saw me this morning. I figured you might be in the doghouse."

"No, quite the contrary. Everything is great."

Then he surprised me by saying, "Kendall, I'm heading home tonight."

"Tonight? I thought you weren't leaving until tomorrow."

"I booked an earlier flight. Not much point in hanging around any longer."

After an extended hesitation he said, "I was kind of hoping to see you again and say goodbye in person but...maybe it's best if we just leave things the way they are and..." he cleared his throat a couple of times, "I sure wish things had turned out differently for us, but they didn't...and that's cool," he finished with forced optimism. "Anyway, again, I'm sorry about screwing everything up between us. I hope you and Tally will be very happy together and I hope he knows what a lucky bastard he is."

In a way, I'd be sorry to see him go, because it was unlikely our paths would ever cross again. His visit had accomplished a couple of things though. It allowed me to let go of the bitterness I'd been hanging onto, and helped me realize just how much I really did love Tally. Grant had surprised me. It had taken a lot of courage for him to come here and make an effort to put things right, an attribute I'd never credited him with before. Maybe he really had changed. "I hope you'll be happy too, Grant. If it's any consolation, I'll always be grateful that you were with me last night. And, thanks for slapping the crap out of me."

His small laugh was touched with despondency. "Well, at least I got half of what I came here for, plus a little more excitement than I originally planned on."

I told him of Walter's recent phone call and he whistled his appreciation. "You're getting close to breaking this story. I can feel it in my gut. Wish I could hang around to be in on it when you do, but I gotta get back to the grind."

"Grant, thanks for your insightful comments. It really was great working with you one last time."

A lot of throat clearing. "Yep. Like I said, we always did make a hell of a team."

"Take care of yourself and give your mother my best."

"I will. Bye, Kendall. If you ever need me for anything…well, you know where I'll be."

"Same here. Have a safe trip."

I shook off the momentary sadness I felt at saying that final good-bye and rushed to get dressed. I had just finished trying to tame my frizzy curls when I heard the familiar rumble of Tally's truck. I grabbed my coat, dashed outside into the cold night air and was met by Attila's deep-throated bark from the truck bed. I stopped to pet his glossy black coat for a minute, and by six-thirty we were on the road driving towards the Starfire. While I was anxious to have a vehicle again, the more important part of my agenda was to corner Ruth to find out if my hunch was correct. The first thing I told him as we bumped along the gravel road under the star-studded sky was the news that Grant would be flying back to Philadelphia within hours. His reaction was immediate: the impact of my announcement generated a long, contented sigh accompanied by the noticeable release of tension from his stiff shoulders. "Can't say as I'm sorry to hear that," he remarked quietly.

Not wanting to dwell on Grant, I quickly switched subjects and filled him in on the remaining details of the Gibbons case, including the ghostly visitation I'd experienced at Hidden Springs, to which he eyed me with extreme skepticism. "So, I'm supposed to believe that you were temporarily possessed by the spirit of a dead boy? Come on, Kendall, you're usually more logical than that."

There was no way to apply logic to what I'd experienced, so I swiftly moved on to the quotations Marissa and La Donna had received. "So, what do you think?" I asked. "Is *that* a logical supposition on my part?" The only thing I omitted was my suspicion that Ruth might be in possession of the third clue.

He flashed me a peculiar look. "Not only does that sound exactly like something Riley would do, I wonder if he included me in this little game."

"What do you mean?"

"Buried under the pile of mail I had waiting for me this afternoon was a package from Riley's law firm."

I inhaled sharply. "What? Don't tell me you got one of the quotations too?"

"Nope. A book."

"What kind of book?"

"The complete works of Edgar Allen Poe."

I'm sure my mouth hung open as I blinked at him in complete bewilderment. "That's it? Just a book? Nothing else?"

"There was a short explanatory letter from his lawyer stating that they'd been instructed to mail it to me in the event of his death. I didn't attach any significance to what Riley had written on the inside cover until now."

"What did he write?"

"A quote from Sir Arthur Conan Doyle."

I pictured the mystery books lining the shelves in Riley's crowded little sanctuary on the hotel's third floor. I was beyond curious. "What does it say?"

"I can't remember offhand. I'll show it to you when we get to the house, but don't get too excited. I could be wrong. The book is old, published in 1899, and is probably a collector's item. For all I know it might be nothing more than a posthumous gift."

I suspected it held greater significance than that. As soon as he braked, Attila and I made a beeline for the kitchen door. When I rushed inside, Gloria, who was busy loading the dishwasher, inquired about my health and flashed me a welcome smile, which I immediately returned. Judging by the pungent aroma of garlic, onions and chili peppers still lingering in the air, I regretted that I'd missed one of her succulent Mexican dinners. The other dogs barked and begged for attention while I hung my coat and purse on the wall hook. The second Tally walked in behind me I pounced. "Well, where is it?"

Unsnapping his coat, he walked to the kitchen table and picked up a hefty volume. "Right here."

Reverently, I ran my hand over the worn leather cover of the book and then opened it to read the inscription. WHEN YOU HAVE ELIMINATED THE IMPOSSIBLE, WHATEVER REMAINS, HOWEVER IMPROBABLE, MUST BE THE TRUTH. -SIR ARTHUR CONAN DOYLE

I swiftly ran through the other quotes in my head, hoping that this one would shed some light, but I was more puzzled then ever.

"So, what do you make of it?" Tally asked, leaning over my shoulder.

"I'm positive he meant to convey something to you, although I don't know exactly what. One thing interesting, the ink doesn't appear to be faded so it's a good bet it was written fairly recently."

"Oh, something else," Tally said, picking up a small slip of paper from the table. "This fell out of the book when I was leafing through it."

I eagerly read the note. PEOPLE ONLY SEE WHAT THEY ARE PREPARED TO SEE. -RALPH WALDO EMERSON. I met Tally's quizzical frown. "This could be really important. I don't suppose you have any idea what page this marked, do you?"

"No."

"Damn." I fanned through the pages, hoping there might be a second note, something scribbled in the margins, any other hint as to why, considering all the other titles I'd viewed in his vast collection, Riley would choose this particular book to bequeath to Tally, but could find nothing notable on my cursory examination. "Would you mind if I hang on to this for a little while? I'd like to study it again when I have time to go through each page more carefully."

"Sure. If nothing else you'll enjoy the stories, if you haven't already read them."

"Meees O'Dell," Gloria sang out, rocking a plate from side to side, an enticing grin plastered on her round face. "There is one piece of flan left if you would like it."

"How can I refuse?" I replied, accepting the golden square of custard smothered with her special honey caramel sauce and a generous dollop of whipped cream.

Tally re-snapped his jacket. "Jake and I are finishing up on a couple of repairs needed on the truck. He's putting in a new battery now, so it should be ready for you to test drive in an hour or so."

I planted a heartfelt kiss on his lips that would have lasted longer if Gloria hadn't been watching us. "You're the best, big guy," I purred warmly. "Got any plans for later on?"

His brown eyes twinkled with affection. "I do now." He headed out the door and I dug into the flavorful dessert with gusto. His absence presented me with an opportunity to go through the book and also talk to Ruth alone before his return. With avid expectation, I opened the old volume and ran my index finger along the story titles on the contents page. THE FALL OF THE HOUSE OF USHER (1839), THE MURDERS IN THE RUE MORGUE (1841), THE PIT AND THE PENDULUM (1842), THE TELL-TALE HEART (1843), THE GOLD BUG (1843), THE BLACK CAT (1843), THE CASK OF AMONTILLADO (1846). It had been a long time since I read the macabre tales and I wracked my brain trying to fathom what significance they might have. I re-read the inscription again, but nothing jumped out at me. With a sigh of disappointment, I closed the cover, scooped up the last spoonful of caramel sauce, gave Gloria a hug of thanks and when I stepped into the hallway, almost collided head-on with Ronda.

"Whoa!" she said, holding me at arm's length. "Sorry, I didn't see you coming. Hey, I'm glad to see that you're okay."

"Thanks. And just to put your mind at ease, there was a good reason I was with Grant in Prescott yesterday."

"Yeah, Tally told me. I'm sorry if I jumped to the wrong conclusion about you two being together yesterday. Lucy told me what happened at the fairgrounds, and well I just—" Her voice trailed off and at least she had the grace to look contrite.

It was probably an honest mistake on her part, unlike Lucinda whose motivations were calculated and malicious. But, it was over and done with so I decided to let it go. "I need to speak with your mother. Is she around?"

She thumbed over her shoulder. "She's in her bedroom watching TV, but I have to warn you that she's been really depressed since yesterday. She's in one of her weird moods and won't communicate with anybody."

While I didn't doubt she was truly distraught, I had a sneaking suspicion Ruth was using the emotional aftermath of the funeral as an excuse to delay her confession to Tally. I badly wanted to say *you mean she's acting weirder than usual?* but managed to restrain myself, substituting, "I'll take my chances."

"Knock yourself out," she said, matter-of-factly, moving past me towards the kitchen.

I could hear the TV blaring when I rapped on her door. No answer. I knocked again. "It's Kendall. I need to talk to you." No answer. Oh no. Not this stupid game again. I knocked with authority. Quiet footsteps alerted me to the fact that she was on the other side of the door. "Come on, Ruth, I know you're there. This is important. Did Riley give you anything the last time he was here? A letter containing a poem, a proverb or something to that effect?" No response for a few seconds and then the door whipped open. It was hard not to gasp. She looked like

333

absolute hell—her face gaunt and gray, her eyes dark with remorse. And I knew why. She hadn't yet followed through on her part of our agreement.

"How could you possibly know that?" she demanded crossly, the ever-present cigarette smoldering between yellowed fingers.

"We need to discuss a couple of things." Funny. She'd looked fairly decent for the funeral yesterday, but had now returned to her rag-lady persona—stringy, matted hair, a threadbare old bathrobe and she didn't smell particularly good. I could tell by her tight-lipped demeanor that she'd rather not talk to me, but I wasn't going away and she knew it. She cast an apprehensive look over my shoulder and waved me inside a spacious bedroom where smoke hung in the air like a thin blue curtain. Instant tears sprang to my eyes and I sneezed hard three times. My throat hurt. Oh my God, how was I going to stand living in the same house with this woman?

"Tally told me what happened yesterday and I just saw you on the news. I'm...I'm glad you weren't hurt." I wondered if she was being sincere. My death would have spared her the discomfort of ever having to tell Tally the truth. "Let's sit over here," she said, gesturing for me to follow her to a loveseat and chair positioned near a bay window. I asked her if I could open it a crack and then got right to the point, sharing everything that I'd learned. When I told her about the figure at the graveside leaving the black rose, her eyes widened with fear. "You have to stop this person before it happens again."

"I'm working on it, but I need your help. Show me what Riley gave to you."

She folded her arms, her lips pinched together tightly. "No. It's...personal."

Obstinate, annoying old lady. "Maybe, maybe not. La Donna received a letter containing some old proverbs, Marissa did too, and he sent Tally a book with an odd inscription included. I have my suspicions that he chose each one for a particular reason. I haven't figured out the nuances of each quotation yet, but it appears to be some kind of game, like connect the dots."

Her wide-eyed expression of surprise held a shadow of doubt. "No, you must be wrong. He meant this one for my eyes only."

I dug deep in my shallow well of patience. Keeping my tone soothing, I urged, "Ruth, you asked me to help find Riley's killer and that's what I'm trying to do. I need your cooperation. Because of his special connection to you, yours may hold the key."

She appeared to be thinking it over and then abruptly rose, crossed the room and extracted two pieces of paper from a jewelry box. She stood there with her back to me for a long time before returning and wordlessly placing them in my outstretched hand. My hopes rising, I unfolded the first sheet. DEAREST RUTH, IF WE DENY LOVE THAT IS GIVEN TO US, IF WE REFUSE TO GIVE LOVE BECAUSE WE FEAR PAIN OR LOSS, THEN OUR LIVES WILL BE EMPTY, OUR GREATER LOSS.

I edged a quick look at Ruth. Riley had been a very perceptive man and these wise words, which I'm sure he meant expressly for her, were certainly good advice for any of us to follow. I quickly unfolded the second sheet. PURE OF SOUL, SHE RESTS IN SOLITUDE, HER LONE COMPANION THE ETERNAL SILENCE OF UNTOUCHED BEAUTY and further down the page, THE TREASURE OF THE YEARNING HEART IS REVEALED THROUGH REVERENT EYES.

Man oh man. What did they mean? As I read and re-read the baffling quotations, my euphoria slowly evaporated. I'd been banking on the fact that one word or phrase would provide an obvious piece in this intriguing puzzle, but that did not appear to be the case. If anything, I was more confused than ever. "Did he say anything when he gave these to you?" I asked, looking up to meet Ruth's expectant gaze.

"No. Except, he did request that I not read them until after he'd left that day."

"Would you mind if I keep these for a while?"

"I guess not, but please be careful with them."

At the door, I turned back. "I'm still waiting for you to keep your part of the bargain."

She hunched her shoulders and avoided my steady gaze. "I'm going to tell him. I was just waiting for the right time."

Doubt that she'd ever follow through on her promise gnawed at me as I left the room clutching the papers. When I stepped through the kitchen door, the muffled tune from my cell phone caught my ear.

"I was coming to find you if it rings again," Gloria announced, pulling off her apron.

"How many times has it rung?"

"Three."

I hurried to retrieve the phone from my purse and tapped the button to see who had called. Three calls from Tugg. I glanced at the kitchen clock. Ten minutes until eight. Something must be going on for him to call this late. I hit the redial and waited.

"Hey, Tugg, it's Kendall."

"Ah, there you are. Sorry to wake you."

"You didn't. I've been visiting with Tally's mother. What's up?"

"Didn't know you were at Tally's place. Well, guess where I am?"

"Where?"

"Hidden Springs."

My heart did a jerky little jig. "What are you doing there?"

"If I'd known you were up and about, I'd have called you in to cover this."

"Cover what?"

"La Donna Gibbons and Winston Pendahl have just been taken into custody for the murder of Riley Gibbons."

26

By ten o'clock Thursday morning the shocking news had spread through Castle Valley faster than a dust devil on a hot August day, completely eclipsing the story of my accident as the number one topic of discussion. The collective sigh of relief from the citizenry was palpable, bringing smiles back to people's faces and seeming to lighten the air around us. Beneath the infinite azure sky dotted with puffy fast-moving clouds, the warm winter sunshine was busy melting the final remains of the rare and decorative snowfall nature had bestowed upon us. An atmosphere of gaiety and liberation filled every corner of the town, from the people standing in line at the post office and feed store to the boisterous customers at the Iron Skillet. Everyone could relax again and cease furtive glances over shoulders wondering who might be the madman's next victim.

Behind my desk once more, I'd conferred with Tugg on details of the arrest. During the time I'd been zonked out the previous afternoon, Duane Potts had received an anonymous phone tip pinpointing the whereabouts of Riley's missing hunting rifle and the saw blade used to decapitate the judge. It was not known how the tipster obtained such intimate knowledge and in spite of the fact that the call had been traced to a pay phone in Surprise, Arizona, a search warrant had been signed within the hour. The rifle in question had been found in La Donna's laundry room stashed behind the washer and dryer. Ballistic tests still had to be run on the weapon and DNA tests would have to be performed on the bloodstained blade discovered at the bottom of a toolbox located in Winston Pendahl's utility trailer. It occurred to me that the informant might very well be Bernita. Who else knew more about the skeletons in the closet at Hidden Springs than the housekeeper?

Even though I didn't know her that well, I nevertheless felt a twinge of relief that Marissa had not been implicated and wondered if the fragment of cotton I'd given to Fritzy would pound another nail of guilt into La Donna's coffin, so to speak.

Yes, all the pieces appeared to have fallen into place, returning an aura of tranquility to Castle Valley. While I shared the town's point of view that, following weeks of anxiety and fear, things should now normalize, I could not suppress a crushing sense of disappointment. I'd been robbed, damn it. I'd worked my butt off to break this story and practically been killed in the process only to see it evaporate before my eyes like a mirage on sizzling blacktop.

"Mrs. Gibbons and Winston Pendahl are being held without bond at the Yavapai County jail in Prescott," Tugg announced, rising from his chair. "I can send Walter, but since this is really your baby. Do you want to take the rest of the day off and run up there this afternoon and see if you can nail down an interview with either of them, or are you too tired?"

I did feel drained, physically and mentally. I wasn't sure whether it stemmed from my ordeal in the snow, the fact that I'd had a lousy night's sleep, or the letdown from having the slats knocked out from under me. "I'm still tired, but I'll perk myself up with some caffeine and go."

"Atta girl. Call me later." After he left the room it occurred to me that driving to Prescott today and then turning around to deliver the posters to Myra tomorrow afternoon would be redundant. Perhaps I could accomplish both tasks in one trip. Even if she couldn't be there, perhaps I could leave them someplace for her. I dug out her card and dialed the cell number, which immediately rolled into voicemail.

"Hi, Myra. It's Kendall O'Dell. It's about eleven o'clock. I have to make an unscheduled drive to Prescott this afternoon and I know we settled on Friday, but I was hoping I could drop those posters of Tally by your place on the way there. You'll have them a day sooner and it will save me some time." I gave her a couple of numbers, including my cell, and hung up. I filed my piece about the Gibbons funeral, fielded a half a dozen phone calls from correspondents in some of the small outlying ranching communities and then sifted through stacks of possible story submissions for Saturday's edition. Suddenly, everything I read seemed incredibly boring, incredibly mundane. I'd tried to convince myself these past few weeks that I didn't need to be out on assignment, following one of these life-threatening stories in order to be happy; that I wasn't, as Tally claimed, an adrenaline junkie. But the Gibbons case was something I'd really been able to sink my teeth into. It got my brain cells humming, my psyche fired up.   The only piece remaining was the unsolved matter of the mysterious quotations. I looked up glumly when Walter tapped on the doorframe of my office. "Hell's bells, that was a huge surprise, huh?"

I shrugged. "Sort of. Well, not really. They were both on our list of possible suspects."

"Guess there's no need to continue busting my hump to research any more old case files now?"

"I guess not."

He must have heard the despondent note in my voice because he gave me an understanding smile. "Yeah, I know how you feel. I had my heart set on breaking this story too. Well, onward and upward. There'll always be another one to take its place."

Of course there would, I grumbled to myself after he'd left.   But what were the chances there would be another story of this magnitude in Castle Valley in my lifetime?   As I gathered the stacks of papers together on my desk, I picked up my notebook and leafed to the list of proverbs.

The first page listed the threatening letters sent to Riley Gibbons. I frowned as I read them again. FALSE WORDS ARE NOT ONLY EVIL IN THEMSELVES, THEY INFECT THE SOUL WITH EVIL and BEWARE THOSE WHO FEAST AT THE TABLE WITH THE EVILDOER. It seemed so obvious now. La Donna had full access to Riley's extensive library and they certainly had a lot more meaning when one thought of them in the context of Riley's infidelity. I turned the page to the last group, which was particularly intriguing. I kind of wished Grant was still here so I could bounce my thoughts off him. I was pretty sure we were on the right track, surmising that it was Riley's intent to bring these four people together for some reason. The quotes given to Ruth puzzled me the most. Which of the three women was he referring to when he wrote, PURE OF SOUL, SHE RESTS IN SOLITUDE, HER LONE COMPANION THE ETERNAL SILENCE OF UNTOUCHED BEAUTY? Were any of them pure of soul? I was sure the key word in the phrase, THE TREASURE OF THE YEARNING HEART IS REVEALED THROUGH REVERENT EYES was *treasure* but the reverent eyes part was baffling. It almost had a religious overtone. Again and again I read WHEN YOU HAVE ELIMINATED THE IMPOSSIBLE, WHATEVER REMAINS HOWEVER IMPROBABLE, MUST BE THE TRUTH. Okay, so all I had to do was start eliminating what seemed impossible. A lot easier said than done, I thought, stuffing the notes in my purse.

In the lobby, I stopped to chat with Tugg's daughter, Louise, and then asked Ginger if she could take a rain check for lunch figuring I'd best hit the road early. I could tell she wasn't very happy about it, but I waved goodbye and hurried outside to the parking lot before she could protest further.

While it was still sunny, weather forecasters had issued a high wind advisory and predicted falling temperatures preceding the arrival of yet another storm. Driving Joe Talverson's red and white 1978 Ford truck turned out to be a kick. Even though it didn't have all the modern amenities and the suspension wasn't the greatest, the engine had a solid growl. Tally had mentioned that it could sometimes be tricky to start and warned me not to pump the gas pedal too much or I might flood the carburetor and have to wait to restart it. Thank goodness, I only had to drive it until I picked out my new car on Saturday. Quite a few admiring glances from some of the seasoned citizens came my way as I cruised through town towards the copy shop. The owner apologized again for the delay, but I was so happy with the results I couldn't complain. Myra would be pleased too, I was sure.

Just to be on the safe side, I took time to stop by my house to pick up extra water bottles, snacks, a spare cell battery, flashlight, gloves, boots, a blanket and my heavy winter coat. I set out an additional bowl of cat food for Marmalade, kissed her goodbye, turned on lights and was on my way by one o'clock, the escalating wind whipping up an impressive rooster tail of dust behind me as I sped along Lost Canyon Road. While I still had a good cell signal, I tried Myra's number a second time but again got her voicemail.

Sipping a caffeine-charged soft drink, I sailed along the highway, tapping my fingers to a lively rock song. I'd just passed through the tiny community of Congress and was smiling at the quirky green-painted rock known locally as the 'Congress Frog' when I heard my cell phone play its energetic melody. I glanced at the caller ID, surprised to see it was Ginger's brother, Brian.

"Hi, Kendall, how's it going?"

"Doing okay. How about you?"

"Hanging in there."

"I'm sure you've heard the news by now, right?"

"You mean about those two people being arrested?"

"Yeah. Hey, I really appreciate all the effort you put into researching those cases for me. I'll get a check in the mail to compensate you right away. Sorry it was such a waste of time."

A slight hesitation then, "I'm not so sure it was."

His provocative tone of voice made my pulse hike up a notch or two. "What do you mean?"

"I came across something you might want to hear about anyway."

"Fire away."

"Did Walter tell you about the Harrison Reese homicide that was never solved?"

"The defense attorney from Phoenix."

"Right. Well, when I began pulling up all the cases where he'd appeared before Judge Gibbons, I came across one I think you'll find pretty interesting."

"Go on."

"About ten years ago there was a high profile hit and run case in Phoenix involving an ASU college sophomore named Sarah Scarborough. She and a girlfriend were walking home late from a movie when she got run down in a crosswalk around one-thirty in the morning. The guy behind the wheel was a young attorney fresh out of law school by the name of Anthony Lazar. He'd been bar hopping all evening with two friends and was traveling about sixty miles an hour when it happened."

I vaguely remembered reading about the case in his previous e-mail, but didn't remember specific details. "I assume she was killed on the spot."

"Yep. He slammed into her so hard she was nearly decapitated."

A feeling of distinct unease came over me. "Good Lord."

"He barely missed the victim's friend and she was pretty freaked out but gave police a good description of the car and the last three numbers of the license plate. She claimed the guy stopped, got out, looked at her friend and then jumped back in his car and took off. He hid the car at a friend's house and waited three days to turn himself in."

"Clever lawyer," I said, nodding in disgust. "He knew he would have flunked a field sobriety test so he delayed long enough so there'd be no possible trace of alcohol in his system."

"You got it. During the trial, Lazar's defense attorney, Harrison Reese, alleged that Sarah had not been in the legal crosswalk and that his client had no knowledge that he'd hit a person. Said he thought he'd struck an animal. The eyewitness refuted his version, but when Reese put Lazar's two passengers on the stand neither could recall him hitting anything. They did, however, admit that they'd also been drinking."

"Where are you going with this?" I asked, accelerating up Yarnell Hill again, wondering in the back of my mind if I'd be able to see the mangled remains of Tally's truck visible among the numerous snowdrifts still clinging to the side of the mountain.

"Hang on, I'm getting there," Brian muttered. He didn't say anything for a while and I could hear him tapping on the keyboard as powerful wind gusts pounded the truck. I grabbed the wheel tighter and wound my way higher up the serpentine road, feeling a slight twinge of anxiety when I passed the orange traffic cones that marked the damaged section of guardrail that was in the process of being repaired.

"Okay, here we go," he finally said. "The prosecutor's office was going for vehicular manslaughter with a maximum 25 years in prison, but it was brought to Judge Gibbons's attention that the prosecution had failed to turn over exculpatory evidence to the defense, something about the witness's prior statement to police being inconsistent with her testimony and the judge was forced to declare a mistrial."

"Justice deferred is justice denied," I commented dryly.

"No kidding. Now, here's where the second part of the story starts. According to newspaper accounts the dead girl's parents were in court every single day of the trial and when the mistrial was declared the father of the victim...let's see...yeah, the guy's name was Roger Scarborough...it says here he was the range master at a Scottsdale gun club...anyway, the article says he went absolutely ape shit and punched out Harrison Reese while the girl's mother, Jean, lunged at the judge screaming that justice had not been served and threatened to kill him. They both had to be restrained by court security. Because the key witness in the case disappeared shortly thereafter, the prosecution was unable to move ahead with the case. Fast forward nine months and I find a small story detailing Roger Scarborough's apparent suicide. A couple of months later his widow, Jean, was arrested for stalking Judge Gibbons. She stood trial and was convicted, but apparently she suffered some sort of psychotic episode while in custody and was subsequently institutionalized—"

"This is all fascinating stuff," I cut in, "but I'm still not getting—"

"Hang on. Five years ago the body of the defendant Anthony Lazar was found at a campground near Santa Fe, New Mexico. He'd been shot in the chest, it didn't appear that any of his possessions had been taken and here's the weird part. Both of his hands had been cut off."

27

Brian's startling news rattled me so much I had trouble concentrating on the road and had to force myself to calm down. The fact that three major players in this one case had died mysteriously by gunshot wound and each had particular body parts removed struck me as mighty questionable in the coincidence department. My thoughts jumped back to my first meeting with La Donna Gibbons. Hadn't she mentioned that her daughter and husband had both been killed as a result of a drunk driving accident? The thought also occurred to me that because of her status as a flight attendant, she could move about the country with ease, which meant she had the opportunity to have committed the homicides in neighboring states and within hours be thousands of miles away from the crime scene. She was also familiar with her husband's penchant for proverbs and could have been responsible for sending him the threatening quotes. Her motive for murdering Riley seemed pretty obvious, but I was stumped as to how that would apply in the other two cases. "What happened to

Jean Scarborough? Is she still institutionalized or was she released?"

"I found a related article on that too. She escaped from the Arizona State Hospital three months after she was locked up, was recaptured only to escape again, and of course there's been an outstanding warrant out on her for almost seven years, but nobody's seen her since. That's not totally surprising though, 'cause if you go to the FBI website, you'll see that there are over a million fugitives nationwide and 30,000 in Maricopa County alone. They just don't have enough law enforcement people to serve all the outstanding warrants and she's probably dropped to the bottom of the list by now."

"Anything else of interest?"

"Well...I could e-mail you a picture of the victim right now. She was real pretty."

I couldn't imagine how that would serve any purpose but he'd roused my curiosity. "Okay. I'm not going to have very consistent cell coverage in another couple of minutes, but send it along to me and I'll check messages later."

"Sure thing."

"Thanks, Brian, you've certainly given me something to think about."

"I thought so."

There were very few people stirring as I drove through the quiet streets of Yarnell. Dirty snowdrifts lined the streets while the nearby hills still sported wide patches of snow. I turned onto the narrow road leading to Myra's place, my mind straining to apply what I'd just learned from Brian to the known facts of the Gibbons case, but for the life of me I could not come up with a logical explanation to connect the three events.

I drove on along the deserted dirt road, my eyes straying now and then to the dark line of thunderheads draping shadowy capes across the distant mountain peaks. Combining their fast approach with the ferocity of the wind foretold the arrival of more unsettled weather. Oh man. Was I going to have to tackle yet another snowstorm? Relief filtered through me when the crooked smokestack popped into view and moments later I parked the truck in front of the ancient brick building. All around me, the foliage thrashed in the stiff wind as I hurried across the muddy parking area. As I stood knocking on the wide metal entrance doors, my hair whipped into a tangled mass around my face. There was no answer, so I moved to peer in the kitchen window. No movement, no sign of anyone, only the melodic drone of the rising wind.

Now what? If I left the posters propped outside the door they'd blow into the next county. Feeling foolish that I hadn't been patient enough to wait one more day, I looked around for somewhere to safely leave them, but could find no place suitable. Trotting back to the truck I suddenly recalled Myra's complaint that the lock on the back door had not been repaired. Surely, she wouldn't mind if I slipped the posters inside.

As I drove towards the rear of the building, it occurred to me that I might as well make use of the time and take some exterior shots of the old Ice House for my proposed article. Camera in hand, I stepped outside and looked up at the blackened bricks and blank windows. Yep. The place definitely had character. Even on a sunny day it possessed a brooding quality. I snapped about thirty pictures from several different angles. Thank goodness for digital cameras. I had to delete a dozen or so images because my hair kept blowing in front of the lens.

I trotted back to the truck, parked on the south side of the building and when I slid to the ground holding the posters, the insistent wind threatened to tear them from my grasp. Passing by the garage, I noticed that Myra's silver sedan still sat nestled beside the trailer. If she was here why hadn't she heard me knocking? But I answered my own question as I approached the door. The panel truck was gone.

Just to be courteous, I rapped again and hollered, "Myra! Are you in there? It's Kendall O'Dell!" When no response came I entered the cavernous room. It was a struggle to push the heavy door shut behind me. Grateful to be out of the wind, I stood in the silence for several seconds watching disturbed dust motes swirl in the narrow columns of sunlight streaming in the windows, then weaved my way around two big yellow handcarts and a stack of packing boxes. It appeared that Myra was serious about relocating to new quarters. As I moved past scores of Myra's lifelike creations towards the little table, it was disconcerting to imagine their inquisitive eyes following my every step. I shook off my sudden unease, thinking that these old places really did get my imagination juices flowing.

I set the posters down and was writing an explanatory note to Myra when the short beep on my cell phone broke the deep silence, alerting me that a text message was waiting. Ah, the photo from Brian. I dug the phone out of my purse and tapped the VIEW button. As I studied the smiling image of the striking young brunette's oval face and wide brown eyes, an odd premonition stirred inside me. This girl had been dead for ten years, so why did she look vaguely familiar to me? I stared out the window, mentally sorting through my memory files, struggling to pin down where I'd seen her before, but every time I just about had it the thought slipped away. At a loss, I snapped the phone shut, finished writing and then placed the folded note on top of the posters.

At that moment, a cloud obscured the sunlight, plunging the room into semi-darkness. I checked my watch. Probably ought to get going before the storm closed in. But then as long as I was here, why not get a few interior shots of the old building while Myra was away? It was doubtful I'd get another opportunity any time soon. I'd be careful not to disturb anything of hers, so what harm could there be? And anyway, she'd already said she didn't plan to stay much longer, so why would she care?

I wandered along the hallway and entered the kitchen, which didn't seem as warm and cheerful without the fire. Except for the whistling wind rattling the windowpanes and the steady tick of the wall clock, the building seemed wrapped in funereal silence. Yep, this was a great place for an introverted artist like Myra, but a little too isolated for my blood.

I aimed the camera, framing a nice shot of the baker's rack and ancient gas stove. The copper teakettle added a nice touch. An empty cup sat on the kitchen table next to several hardbound books and adjacent to them what looked to be a journal or diary lying open. I cocked my head sideways to read the titles and recognized the name of the famous poet Robert Frost. The second volume featured poems by Henry Wadsworth Longfellow. My mother would have approved of her choices. I decided that the exposed brick wall would make a nice background for a photo. I moved the books, cup, borrowed a candle from the baker's rack and arranged them into an interesting shot. Nice.

While replacing the books, my gaze involuntarily fell on the open page of the journal. What was this? The words THE SPAWN OF EVIL MUST PERISH written in bold dark print tweaked my curiosity. Strange. I was tempted to look further but my conscience tugged at me. I had no right to intrude in Myra's personal thoughts.

Moving on, I snapped several shots of the antique wall fixtures on the way back to the studio and as I headed towards the back door, a stunning sculpture depicting a Native American dancer in a ceremonial feather dress caught my eye. Mesmerized by the outstanding detail of the piece, not paying attention to where I was walking, I suddenly found myself face down on the floor, breath slammed from my lungs. When I regained my wits, I pushed to my knees, thankful that I hadn't injured myself, and, more importantly, that my clumsiness hadn't damaged one of Myra's sculptures.

I looked around to see what I'd tripped over and only then noticed the orange extension cord snaking across the floorboards. Uh-oh. Apparently my fall had dislodged it from the electrical socket. I reached under the table and when I plugged it in, an immediate humming sound reached my ears. Puzzled, I rose and followed the winding cord into the shadowy alcove, underneath the table where Myra's collection of cherubic angels sat staring back at me, and continued several more feet before disappearing beneath a partially open door. I leaned in close, listening intently to what sounded like the far-off drone of a refrigerator compressor. Wait a minute. Wasn't this the entrance to the basement? How odd. Hadn't Myra told me that it was too dangerous to enter because of water seepage? If that were the case, how safe could it be to run any sort of electrical appliance in standing water? I pushed the door open a little further. The hinges gave out a raspy squeal and I wrinkled my nose at the dank smell wafting up from below. I fumbled around on the wall for a light switch. Click. Click. Nothing happened. In the dim light from behind, I could see the outline of a stairway leading down into the darkness. I knelt down and ran my fingers along the first two steps. They felt solid and dry. So why had Myra told me they were rotted and unsafe? Something wasn't right.

I pondered the situation for a minute before retracing my steps and pulling one of the kerosene lamps from the shelf. It took another minute or so to locate matches and several more to figure out how to light the lantern. My grandmother had always lamented that from the time I was a toddler, I'd exhibited a true redhead's personality, headstrong and stubborn to the max. My first reaction to being told I shouldn't do something was to challenge the reasoning and then try my best to figure out how to get my way. Apparently I hadn't changed much.

My senses on high alert, I walked back to the cellar door and in the wavering lamplight, slowly descended the staircase, more worried about encountering a spider than a rat the size of a garbage truck. The stairs creaked a little, but appeared to be in pretty good shape. I wished there'd been enough light to see better, because I was pretty sure the giant rusted apparatus in front of me was the ammonia ice-making machine Gretchen had mentioned. Even with the flash on my camera, I doubted the picture would come out very good, but what the heck. Trying to hold the lamp steady, I took several shots and then moved on, passing several rooms filled with old furniture, piles of boxes and miscellaneous aging junk, following the orange cord until I found the source of the humming. A freezer. It stood alone in a tiny room illuminated by faint light from a grimy window high above it. There was nothing at all sinister about it, but for some unexplained reason, as I stood there in the thick silence, an ominous foreboding settled around me like low-lying ground fog. Taking Myra's occupation into consideration, it should not seem odd to find a freezer in her basement. But it did. Especially since she'd been so adamant about the dangerous conditions. There was no water seepage, no rotting timber and so far, not a single rat.

As I approached, my already tense stomach muscles constricted. Perhaps it was because I was already in an anxious state of mind, but when I reached for the latch, I hesitated. What was I expecting to find? Was Tally right? Was I always looking for excitement where there was none? Obviously, my imagination was working overtime again and I was going to feel like a total idiot when I opened it to discover a pile of frozen food.

I held the lamp high and lifted the right hand lid, my breath stalled in my throat. Yep, I was an idiot. With the exception of a small selection of low fat dinners piled in one corner, the space was filled with nothing but giant blocks of ice. I blew out a long relieved breath, lowered the lid and turned to leave when something, I don't know what, compelled me to turn back and open the other side. I released the latch, lifted the lid and a dim appliance bulb flashed on. A cursory glance revealed more blocks of ice, but one appeared to have a dark shadow in the center of it. As I moved the lamp closer, I thought at first my eyes were playing tricks on me. But they weren't. Sickening horror rocketed through me and my knees turned to liquid when I realized what I was looking at. His handsome features frozen in a look of perpetual disbelief, the startled blue eyes of Judge Riley C. Gibbons stared back at me.

28

Paralyzed with revulsion, my heart kicking painfully against my ribs, I didn't know whether to retch or scream. I did some of both before I dropped the lamp and sprinted away from the horrid little chamber, still shrieking, jolts of sheer terror radiating through me. Stumbling and falling, every nerve ending on fire, I groped along the rough, cold walls, lost in the inky maze of rooms. Violent shudders wracking my body, my ragged breath echoing in my ears, I fought off waves of hysteria that threatened to rob me of all intellect. *Get your shit together*! My jacket snagged on something and as I felt around the sharp edges I realized it was the old icemaker. Within seconds, and much to my relief, I finally spotted the faint rectangle of light from the doorway above. I scrambled up the stairs, my mind still grappling to comprehend what I'd just seen. When I reached the landing, I bolted ahead blindly and upended the table containing Myra's collection of cherub-cheeked angels.

The crash of breaking glass was horrendous as we all went down. Sprawled on the floor among the shattered debris of the porcelain figurines, fighting spasms of nausea, I desperately tried to gather my frazzled wits as I stared at the pile of wings, arms and angelic faces, most broken beyond repair. How could this be possible? How could someone as kind, refined and educated as Myra Colton, a woman endowed with the talent to create such haunting beauty, possibly be capable of cold-blooded murder? And what was the meaning of that horror in the basement? What had Fritzy called it? A trophy head?

I struggled to my knees. Blood from gashes on my arms and hands dripped onto several of the angels and then, as the realization slowly dawned on me, needles of renewed alarm prickled the nape of my neck. Stunned, I stared hard at the assortment of little faces looking back at me. *They were all the same face.* "All the same face," I whispered aloud, surveying my mute porcelain audience. And a familiar face at that.

With trembling hands I fished my phone out and punched the VIEW button on the text message Brian had sent me. When the picture appeared, it rocked my senses. "Jesus H. Christ!" The answer to the puzzle was spread out all around me. *All the figurines shared the identical facial features of the long-dead Sarah Scarborough.* I had to inhale a couple of super-deep breaths to stave off the new shockwaves and resist succumbing to panic. Okay. Okay. Breathe. Relax. Breathe. Relax. So there it was. Myra Colton was actually Jean Scarborough. The memory of the specter in the mist at the funeral popped into my mind along with the words HATE HAS TURNED MY DAYS AND NIGHTS INTO HELLISH TURMOIL.

Her soul *must* be steeped in hellish turmoil to have committed such a heinous act. How fascinating that she'd employed the judge's favorite genre, his veneration of the written word to turn the tables on him and what ghoulish irony that she would choose decapitation as fitting punishment for his crime of allowing her daughter's murderer, in her mind at least, to walk free. The seeds of hatred had germinated into a lifelong obsession for vengeance. In a strange way, I could understand her twisted logic. The justice system had failed her miserably. Her life had been torn apart and there had been no real consequences for those involved, so she'd invented her own unique method of punishment. One by one she'd exacted revenge upon the people she believed were either directly or indirectly responsible for her daughter's death. What had she called it in one of the letters she'd mailed to the judge? REVENGE IS A KIND OF WILD JUSTICE? And she'd taken her sweet time about it. Her axiom *Patience is bitter, but its fruit is sweet,* obviously held a very special meaning for her. Would I ever be able to erase the vision of the judge's dead eyes looking back at me? But then another ghastly thought occurred to me. Were the body parts of the other two victims also in the freezer?

No wonder Riley Gibbons had feared for his life. After he'd heard about the deaths of the other two men, he must have had some inkling that she might be the person responsible and if so, that she'd eventually get around to him. How clever she was to have insinuated herself into his life, befriended his wife and finagled her way into his home. What a perfect setup to weave her evil web around him. Her web. My blood ran cold. What was it she'd warned in her last letter to him? BEWARE THOSE WHO FEAST AT THE TABLE WITH THE EVILDOER. No wonder Ruth had been worried about Tally or anyone else close to the judge. *Anyone else close to the judge.* What had I just seen written in her journal? THE SPAWN OF

EVIL MUST PERISH. "Oh my God! Marissa!" It made sense to assume that because of her vindictive obsession, there was no way in hell she was going to permit the child of Riley Gibbons to be born!

Galvanized into action, I shot to my feet, crunched over the broken faces and raced outside, feeling enormous relief to leave the vile scene behind and breathe in the invigorating wind. On the run, I dialed 911, but of course the No Service message blinked back at me. "Stupid friggin' phone!" I jumped into the truck and turned the key. Nothing. "Come on!" Frantically, I pumped the gas and attempted again, remembering too late what Tally had said about flooding the carburetor. "Shit! Double shit!"

Groaning, I laid my head back against the seat, agonizing that in this day and age with every modern convenience of the 21st century at my disposal, I was stuck here with no working phone and no transportation. It might as well be the 19th century.

I waited two minutes before trying once more. Still nothing. My mouth dry as cotton, I thought, what if Myra showed up right now? What would I do? What would she do? And then another thought occurred to me. What if she returned, removed or destroyed the evidence of her crime and disappeared again? What would happen to La Donna and Winston? Horrified, I knew what I needed to do. No! Anything but that. I tried to talk myself out of it but realized that I had to return to the basement and get some proof.

Before I could change my mind, I picked up the camera and returned to the old building. My hands trembled as I lit another lamp. It was an effort not to hyperventilate. "O'Dell, you are truly insane," I murmured, once again descending into the dark confines of the basement. I stopped a couple of times to make withdrawals from my courage bank and then, heart hammering hard in my throat, I proceeded to the freezer and lifted the lid. Swallowing back spasms of nausea, I clicked a series of pictures. While the experience was equally as hair-raising as before, for some reason a strange calm settled over me. What was there to be afraid of really?

As I stood there studying the skin on the judge's face, it was interesting to note how well-preserved it appeared to be—ruddy cheeks, eyes still startlingly clear, perhaps just a bit of whitish freezer burn on his nose and ears as one would expect with any other kind of fleshy thing such as chicken or fish. All at once, dissecting a frog in biology class fell to the level of insignificance and my admiration for Fritzy swelled a hundredfold. Day in and day out in the course of her job she dealt with situations like this and probably far worse. Not something I could ever do. But, I did feel rather proud of myself for overcoming my numbing fear as I took the stairs two at a time. For added insurance, I stooped to pick up one of the little cherubs then grabbed the photos of Tally from the table along with the note and scurried back to the truck. This time the engine roared to life.

"All right!" I drove like someone possessed towards Yarnell, alternately checking my phone for a signal, knowing instinctively that time was of the essence. What a conniving, calculating mind Myra possessed. She'd apparently thought of everything. It seemed inconceivable, but I now suspected that it had been she who had run us off the side of the road after Grant had spilled the beans regarding Marissa's pregnancy and voiced his casual remark that if anyone could catch the murderer, I could. With all she had invested, she was not about to take a chance on my foiling the final installment of her Machiavellian plan. Feeling confident that we'd perished in the crash, she'd planted the incriminating evidence and then placed the anonymous phone call to the sheriff, which achieved the desired results—removing La Donna and Winston from the property and thereby leaving Marissa alone. She knew she had a finite amount of time to tie up one last loose end. Hadn't I recently seen a story on the Internet detailing how a woman had killed her neighbor, slit the woman's stomach open and removed the baby? Sick. Sick. Sick.

I finally picked up cell service when I reached the main road, swiftly dialed the sheriff's office and gave Marshall a rapid-fire synopsis of my gruesome discovery. "You've got to get out to Hidden Springs right away! Marissa could be in immediate danger!" I said, an urgent sense of anxiety sending my pulse sky high.

"On my way," came his terse reply.

The 411 Operator connected me to Hidden Springs, but after a dozen rings and no answer, my spirits tanked. Oh, my God! Was I too late? I punched the speed dial for Tally and maddeningly got his answering machine. I left a message, then said aloud, "Okay, old boy, let's see what you can do." A NASCAR driver would have envied the way I hurtled around the hairpin turns on Yarnell Hill. Traveling through town was a complete blur and the drive along the gravel road to Hidden Springs seemed to take forever. Behind me in the rearview mirror, voluminous charcoal clouds bore down from the northwest and obscured the waning rays of afternoon sunlight. I wasn't crazy about the idea of having to deal with yet another downpour, but at least the strong tailwind aided in pushing me up to the crest of the hill. When I reached the top and got my first look at the secluded valley, I got one of those painful heart jolts. A plume of black smoke rising from the exact location of Hidden Springs formed a dark shroud over the Praying Nun. "Oh, no!" I breathed, jamming my foot on the gas. Traveling so fast I almost missed the entrance, I wrenched the wheel and the back end of the truck fishtailed, nicking one of the date palm trunks on my frenzied turn. I blasted along the gravel driveway and skidded to a stop inches from the low stone wall in the parking area, my worst fears confirmed as I stared at the conflagration of orange flames devouring the old hotel. Holy crap! I grabbed the camera and did a quick inventory of the other vehicles as I leaped from the truck—Marissa's white SUV, two patrol cars and Myra's white panel truck with the front grill crushed in. I'd been right. Sadly right. Turning, I dashed towards the burning building, smoke stinging my eyes, my chest tight.

"Kendall!" a voice shouted. "Over here!"

I jerked around, both surprised and relieved to see Sheriff Turnbull kneeling on the ground holding a limp, apparently unconscious Marissa in his arms. Duane Potts, his uniform scorched and torn, came trotting from La Donna's house, coughing loudly and carrying blankets.

"What happened?" I asked, rushing to Marshall's side.

"You were right," he said grimly. "We found her bound and lying on her bed when we got here."

Duane cut in, "Probably overcome with smoke. The doors were all barred, so we had to break the glass to get in." He gestured towards Marissa's shattered bedroom window. "That crazy woman is still in there somewhere. I tried to find her, but she wouldn't respond. I finally had to get the hell out."

I stared at Marissa's pale soot-blackened face. "Is she all right?"

"Don't know yet," Marshall growled. "Ambulance and fire equipment are on their way."

All three of us flinched and looked up when a loud crash emanated from within the old structure, sending a shower of sparks shooting out one of the windows on the third floor. Even though I could hear the wail of sirens in the distance, it appeared that Myra's and the old hotel's fate was sealed. My reporter's instincts kicked in and I jumped up and sprinted around the rear of the structure, snapping pictures along the way. I stopped and lined up the shot I wanted, capturing the drama of the moment—the flames pouring from the windows, burning embers and ash falling around me, the smoke-hazed outline of the Praying Nun in the background. I swung the camera around for another shot and gasped in horror at the image in the LCD screen. Myra stood at one of the windows on the third floor. I was pretty sure by its proximity that she was standing in the room Riley had used for his library.

I lowered the camera, shouting, "Myra! Jump before it's too late!" It probably wasn't more than twenty or twenty-five feet to the ground and if she landed in the thick cluster of bushes it might break her fall enough so that she wouldn't be that badly hurt. It was certainly worth a try, but she just stood there immobile, like one of her remarkable statues, a serene smile pasted on her lips as the flames behind her loomed brighter. There was nothing I could do but stand there helplessly as huge drops of rain spattered on my head. I watched the inferno consume this tragic woman, knowing deep in my gut that she had planned right from the outset to destroy herself along with the last vestiges of anything that Riley may have cherished, therefore fulfilling her final destiny of avenging her daughter.

The heavens opened up and buckets of water poured from the sky causing the fire to hiss and send out billows of steam. Call it the haze of smoke in my tear-filled eyes, call it my overwrought imagination, whatever, but it looked to me as if the smiling figure of a small boy appeared beside her in the window and took her hand just before the roof collapsed.

29

My explosive front-page article, complete with a dramatic color shot of the flaming hotel, stunned everyone and by Saturday, Castle Valley was once again besieged by reporters from the national news media, print and television. It seemed that everywhere I went that weekend people wanted to buttonhole me for a firsthand account of my grisly discovery and grill me about the traumatic scene I'd witnessed at Hidden Springs. The only part I'd left out was seeing the ghost of the little boy. I had mentioned it to Tally, who'd arrived on the scene not long after the firefighters, but being the pragmatic guy he was, he had scoffed at the idea, believing that it was most likely an optical illusion caused by the thick smoke. Because I'd been in such a state of shock it was possible my eyes had deceived me, but thinking about it later I wasn't so sure. It actually helped ease the heartache of that awful moment to convince myself that Myra had not been alone when she died, that the lonesome spirit of the child who'd wandered the halls of the old building for over a hundred years waiting for his mother's return finally had some company. I felt certain it was a scene Riley would have appreciated.

It seemed as if that's where the story should have ended, but more surprises unfolded the following week. I'd only been at my desk an hour or so Monday morning when Ginger appeared at the door, chomping on gum and waving an envelope. "Don't wet your drawers or nuthin'," she announced breezily, her tawny eyes shining with excitement, "but a letter from the Great Beyond just got delivered."

I gawked at her. "What are you talking about?"

"This," she said, advancing into the room. "It's from Myra Colton."

My heart plunged uncomfortably. "What?"

She handed the envelope to me, pointing. "Looks like she transposed the zip code so that's probably why it didn't show up until this morning."

I stared at the neat block printing in disbelief.

"Well," she demanded, folding her arms. "Ain't ya gonna open it?"

Frowning, I slit it open and a little zing of surprise shot through me when I pulled out the contents. Seven hundred and fifty dollars—the deposit for Tally's sculpture. I checked the postmark. My God! It had been mailed the day she died. Ginger was agog when I explained what it meant. "Good gravy, so she already knew she was gonna check herself out of this life when she mailed it." She turned towards the door, shaking her head. "Now I really have heard everything."

Not five minutes later, I received a congratulatory call from Grant. He'd read an excerpt of my story posted on an Internet news site. "Hot damn, I knew you were right on the cusp of breaking this thing wide open," he crowed. "Wish I'd been there with you."

"No you don't," I informed him dryly. "With your squeamish stomach, you'd have fainted for sure and I'd have had to carry you out of the place."

"Thanks for the vote of confidence."

"Hey, it's true and you know it."

He laughed and then his voice turned serious. "That must have been scary as hell."

"It was definitely...sobering."

"All right, let's have it. I know you're good at what you do, but how did you find out so much incriminating information about Myra Colton considering she's not around to confess?"

"Fortunately for me and the authorities, she left a meticulous account of her thoughts and activities in her journal."

"How lucky is that?"

"Very." It had all been written down, every gory description, every heartrending emotion that ran the gamut from anguish to gleeful satisfaction, how she'd faked insanity while awaiting sentencing, then planned and executed her escape from the mental hospital. She'd moved to Maine and laid low for two years until things died down. All the while white-hot hatred festered in her heart, skewering her thought process and probably hastening the growth of her cancer. Her journal detailed how she'd gone about choosing a new identity and then begun stalking her first victim. The fact that she had the freedom to travel from state to state participating in various arts and crafts shows gave her the opportunity to mail the threatening letters postmarked from other cities. She'd been able to take her time tracking the victims, murdering and mutilating them before disappearing across state lines like dust in a high wind. And leaving a space of three years between each slaying made it difficult for law enforcement officials to make a connection. "Did I mention that she was a crack shot?" I asked, rising to pour myself a fresh cup of coffee.

"No."

"She and her husband met while they were both in the Army serving overseas. After they were discharged, he became a firearms instructor at a Scottsdale gun club. After the mistrial, he fell into a deep depression and finally took his own life."

"So, she didn't have any other family to turn to?"

"No close living relatives. According to her journal, she'd had a lot of trouble conceiving and was thirty-eight when her daughter was finally born. That's when she was informed that internal complications would prevent her from having any more children, so Sarah became the light of her life. She worshipped the girl and was devastated by her loss. She found some measure of comfort by fashioning her daughter's face in most of her creations.

"Humph. In an odd way, I can sort of understand her thinking process, but what was the point of cutting off her victims' body parts and keeping them on ice?"

"To preserve them so she could visit them every now and then and gloat, but you have to realize she'd slipped a cog."

"No shit."

"I spoke with my friend Nora Bartoli about it."

He cut in, "The forensic anthropologist?"

"Right. She said sometimes people keep various body parts around to serve as souvenirs or reminders of their crime."

Grant let out a low whistle. "Weird. So…besides the judge's head, did they find the missing parts of the other two guys in the freezer?"

"Uh-huh." I went on to explain that Myra had begun plotting the judge's murder when she overheard him making plans for a hunting trip on the day she'd delivered the piece of artwork he'd commissioned, and that reminded me of the statement made by Randy Moorehouse that he'd seen a 'tall, skinny broad in the lobby' the day he was there. She'd followed him to Flagstaff, hid her truck on a closed forest service road, walked back and flagged him down, explaining that she'd broken down. He offered her a ride, and after he'd driven her back, she confronted him and shot him in the chest with his own rifle. She wrapped him in plastic and cleaned up the area making sure there were no remaining traces of blood or tissue by scooping up the dirt around him. Fortunately for her it snowed right afterwards and the crime scene simply vanished.

"Jesus. So…she sawed his head off right there in the woods?"

"No. That didn't happen until later. First she froze him."

"What for?"

"Because it was easier and less messy to remove his head."

"That's useful information to know."

"I thought you'd appreciate that. Anyway, her expertise in ice sculpting made her proficient at using a reciprocating saw."

"But...how the hell did she get him out of there?" Grant asked.

"Her truck was equipped with a hydraulic lift so she simply rolled him onto it and then kept the body on ice inside the truck for a couple of weeks until she decided what to do with it."

"Okay, but I still don't get *why* she removed his head."

"It's pretty convoluted thinking, but from what we can gather from her journal, she kept the tongue of what she labeled the 'glib defense attorney,' the hands belonged to the young lawyer who was at the wheel of the car and Riley's head was severed to avenge the decapitation of her daughter."

"But, why'd she go to all the trouble to transport the...the torso to Hidden Springs? And how'd she accomplish it by herself? She looked kinda puny the day I met her."

"She was. I noticed the first time I met her that she didn't look well. She was dying of ovarian cancer."

"No kidding."

"No kidding. She only had a few months to live. She thought Riley was her final victim until she found out about Marissa's connection to him last week. Anyway, to answer your question, she felt pretty confident in her ability to get away with murder a third time and decided to have a little fun with the authorities. She knew there was a lot of construction going on there and with delivery trucks coming and going she calculated that with all the rain, there'd be little chance the authorities would be able to identify her tire marks. Like I said before, she was very patient, very thorough and thought everything out down to the last detail. There was a notation in her journal describing how she'd designed the incident to cast suspicion on La Donna."

"Why? She didn't have anything to do with her daughter's death."

"You have to understand her mindset. She was on a mission to destroy anything and anyone the judge cared for. Eye for an eye, tooth for a tooth, tit for tat."

Seconds passed before he said, "So, the cotton fragment you found in the tree belonged to Myra."

"Yes. It was purely coincidental that she and La Donna were taking the same pain medication. I think she knew that La Donna and Winston would eventually be exonerated, but it was all part of the game she was playing with the authorities."

"Clever lady, but there's one thing she didn't bank on."

"What?"

"You."

"Yeah, well luck definitely played a part. The timing was critical, that's for sure. I mean, if I hadn't fallen over that extension cord and Brian hadn't sent me that picture, the outcome may have been very different for Marissa."

"Speaking of that, what about all those quotes we were trying to interpret?"

I filled him in on the ones Riley had given Ruth and the book he'd sent to Tally. "I've gone over them a hundred times and I know there's a message, but so far I've come up blank. I faxed copies of all of them to La Donna and Marissa, but I haven't had a chance to share our theories with them about it yet."

"I'm sure you'll eventually figure it out."

"I'm not so sure about that."

"What happened with Marissa anyway? I liked her."

"She's still in the hospital recovering from her ordeal and the baby's okay. In fact, she called me yesterday to thank me for saving her life."

"What's she going to do now that her inheritance has gone up in smoke?" he asked.

I leaned back in my chair and twirled the blinds open, inviting the warm sunshine inside. "She told me that as soon as the insurance company pays up she wants to begin restoration on the hotel."

"Well, you certainly outdid yourself on this one. I'd bet my last dollar you'll get nominated for a prize."

"I wouldn't turn it down." Poised to hang up, I toyed with the idea of telling him about the supernatural experience, but decided against it. The actual verifiable facts of the Gibbons case were strange enough. "Thanks for your call. I've got to get back to work now."

"Yeah, yeah, me too. And if you ever change your mind—"

I cut in with a firm but kind, "Give it up, Grant."

"Right." A pause, then, "Bye, Kendall. Have yourself a happy life."

I smiled to myself, relieved to have the poisonous resentment I'd felt for almost a year purged from my heart, and felt confident the door to that part of my life was now closed. "You too, Grant. Goodbye."

30

Ruth finally got around to keeping her part of the bargain and the results were every bit as devastating as I'd feared. Tally's initial reaction of disbelief turned to anger and finally smoldering resentment. Ruth had predicted that he would withdraw from her and she'd been right. Sadly, they were both pissed at me for forcing the issue and I couldn't persuade him to talk about it with me. But, that was part of his personality. His pride was injured and he wasn't one to bear his emotions whereas I always felt better talking about my problems with someone.

Ronda reacted much the same as Tally. With understandable dismay, she hid herself away in the barn with her horses, becoming more introverted than ever. Apparently they each had that part of genetics going for them from Ruth's side of the family and I wondered how or even if they were all going to be able to get it together by the engagement party, which was only weeks away. I approached Tally several times, trying find the right words to comfort him and urged him to lighten up and hear his mother out, but he rebuffed my attempts with a sarcastic, "What? Are you her shrink now?"

So I decided it might be best to withdraw from the tense family drama for a couple of days and let things cool off. In retrospect, I wondered if I'd made a huge mistake. Perhaps this sensitive information should have gone to Ruth's grave with her.

I should have been on top of the world having scooped yet another sensational story, but instead I fell into the bluest of funks. How was I going to get back into the family's good graces now? Words from my wise Irish grandmother kept echoing in my ears. "Don't shit in your own nest." Apparently I had. It was therapeutic to bury myself in work and hope Tally would come to terms with reality and find it in his heart to someday forgive his mother for her transgression.

On Friday morning, Marissa, now home from the hospital, finally returned my call and granted me an exclusive interview. With all the national media still swarming around town like white flies, I felt an urgency to stay ahead of the pack and hurriedly wrapped up my work. I stopped by Tugg's office to let him know I'd probably be out the remainder of the day on assignment and by two o'clock I set out for Hidden Springs. I'd been surprised when Marissa had told me that La Donna had apparently experienced a change of heart and invited her to stay in one of the cottages. Perhaps the older woman's resentment towards Marissa was beginning to mellow. One would have to be incredibly cold-hearted to turn away a homeless, pregnant woman, or, maybe it was just the practical realization that they were still financially bound together. Hopefully, I'd get an interview with her as well. As I bumped along the washboard dirt road in the squeaky old pickup, I decided that come hell or high water, I was going car shopping soon, with or without Tally.

The truck must have been burning oil because it belched blue smoke all the way up the steep incline. Cresting the ridge, I slowed down once again to savor the magnificence of the Praying Nun kneeling alone on the desert floor surrounded by her flowing robes of golden granite as she guarded her secluded enclave. I thought it amazing how much more richly textured the Arizona landscape became with the addition of just a few clouds, the way their shadows created subtle contrasts in the wind-sculpted rock that weren't visible in the intense glare of the white-hot summer sun. The late autumn lighting made it easier to visualize the two dark crevices as being the nun's eyes reflecting an expression of reverent longing...I inhaled a sharp breath and whispered aloud, "Good God! I know what he meant!"

I gunned the truck down the hill, the words of Riley's provocative proverb ringing in my ears. PURE OF SOUL, SHE RESTS IN SOLITUDE, HER LONE COMPANION THE ETERNAL SILENCE OF UNTOUCHED BEAUTY. Of course! It had to be the Praying Nun! But what about her? What was the rest of the saying? THE TREASURE OF THE YEARNING HEART IS REVEALED THROUGH REVERENT EYES. Through *her* eyes. What was I to make of the revelation? My short-lived burst of elation at having solved the mystery at that exact moment ebbed when I caught sight of the charred skeleton of the old hotel. I relived again the sorrow of that day, Marissa's near death, the horror of Myra's final moments and the loss of an irreplaceable local landmark.

Bernita answered my knock and gestured to Marissa resting on the sofa in the small, but tastefully furnished living room in the cottage adjacent to the remains of the old hotel. Silvery tears glinted on Marissa's cheeks as she filled me in on how Myra had called her that day to explain that she had one final piece of artwork to deliver. But after she'd arrived and confirmed that Marissa was alone since it was Bernita's day off, she'd tied her up, started the fire and left her for dead. "Your call to the sheriff saved me," she said, taking one of my hands, her eyes moist, her voice filled with wonder. "I can't ever thank you enough."

I accepted her gratitude with the caveat that unfortunately Grant's inadvertent disclosure to Myra about her condition had actually initiated the incident, but she'd waved it away, saying that after she'd read my account in the newspaper she realized that because of Myra's mad obsession she would have eventually been targeted anyway. She told me that La Donna's attitude towards her had mellowed significantly after she'd read the quotes from Riley that I'd sent her. "She's been a whole lot nicer to me," she marveled. "I guess she accepted your theory about love building bridges." She tilted her head, pinning me with a perceptive frown. "It's pretty amazing that you're so tuned in to what Riley wanted when you didn't even know him."

"If you think about it from his perspective you each gain something you lost."

"What do you mean?"

I smiled at her. "She gains a daughter and grandchild, you gain a surrogate mother."

She stared at me dumbfounded, murmuring, "Wow, I never thought of it that way."

"Now if I could only figure out the rest of this puzzle." I told her about my latest assumption, but she seemed at a loss to grasp the meaning either.

"Who knows," she said with a poignant smile. "We'll probably never understand everything he meant."

We talked more about her plans to rebuild the old hotel and her hopes to revive Riley's vision for the place. "I feel like I owe it to his memory to do this," she said dreamily. "He wanted this to be my home...our home," she said, absently rubbing her blossoming abdomen, "and Winston thinks he can do it if we get enough insurance money. Thank God he moved most of the things from the third floor before the fire. We were able to save the furniture, most of his books and even that statue of the little girl chasing the gold bugs."

I wished her luck, thanked her for her time and was halfway to La Donna's house when the significance of her closing words sunk in. I stopped dead, my pulse thumping in my temples. *The little girl chasing the gold bugs?* My mind flipped back to that day in Riley's library. The statue of the little bronze girl chasing the gold butterflies stood facing the window, the reverent eyes of the Praying Nun fixed right on her. THE TREASURE OF THE YEARNING HEART... If I put that together with the Edgar Allen Poe story, THE GOLD BUG and combined it with the quote the judge had penned in the front of Tally's book, WHEN YOU HAVE ELIMINATED THE IMPOSSIBLE, WHATEVER REMAINS HOWEVER IMPROBABLE, MUST BE THE TRUTH, everything fell into place. The desire to laugh wildly came over me. What a rush!

In thirty seconds flat, I was back at Marissa's cottage pounding on the door. When I explained why, her jaw dropped and she quickly led me to the storage area behind the cottage where the bronze statue stood barely visible among the piles of boxes and furniture at the far end of the room. With eager anticipation pulsing through me, I weaved my way through the clutter and gently turned the sculpture on its side. Showtime. Yep. There it was, an envelope with the words BRAVO! taped to the pedestal. "Yes!" With shaking hands I peeled it off as Marissa reached my side.

"What is it?" she asked breathlessly.

"Don't know yet." I pulled the flap, fully expecting to find another clue, but the only thing inside the envelope was a business card with the name of Riley's law firm: MILLS, DAVIS and PAYNE. The office number was circled. I flipped the card over and read the message aloud. *"Tis the most tender part of love, each other to forgive. Farewell. I have loved you all dearly. Riley."*

Tears glazed Marissa's eyes as we traded a puzzled glance. "What do you suppose it means?" she sniffled, pulling a tissue from her pocket.

Finding a business card seemed an anticlimactic legacy given all the effort Riley had obviously invested in his little game of Clue and I could not suppress a pang of disappointment. "My guess is you're supposed to call this number to find the answer."

The disenchantment in her eyes mirrored mine. "So...that's it? There's nothing else to be found?"

I shrugged and leaned over to examine the statue closer. It didn't seem right that after receiving and deciphering the proverbs Riley had so painstakingly assembled that this would be the end of the trail. I stuck my forefinger into the opening in the statue's base, but felt nothing. On a hunch, I picked it up and shook it. To my utter astonishment, a shower of gold coins poured from the cavity and thudded onto the floor, some rolling away into the semi-darkness of the cluttered storage room.

Marissa let out a little squeal. "Oh, my God! The missing gold coins!" She immediately knelt and began to gather them into a pile. I watched her, chewing my lower lip. Something didn't seem right. Considering their size, they should have made a tremendous clatter when they'd hit the concrete floor. I stooped to pick one up. It sure looked like a gold coin, but...it didn't feel heavy like I imagined it should. I turned it over in my hand and with a thrill of shock realized what it was. Unbelievable. I couldn't help it. Laughter bubbled up in my throat and I let out a shout of glee. Marissa, still down on her knees, edged me a startled look. "What's so funny?"

"Riley really did have a puckish sense of humor."

Her dark brows collided. "What do you mean?"

"This isn't gold," I announced, picking at the coin with one fingernail. "It's candy."

31

I'd left a shell-shocked Marissa standing in the doorway of her cottage, phone in hand, and rushed back to the truck, anxious to share the unexpected turn of events with Tally. It seemed to take forever to negotiate the endless switchbacks before I picked up a cell signal and NEW VOICEMAIL appeared on my screen. Now that was a strange coincidence. I listened to the message from Tally. Could I get to the Starfire as soon as possible? He had important news for me.

The radiant winter sun had begun its final descent towards the western peaks by the time I screeched to a halt in front of the two-story ranch house, anxious to see Tally after our three-day separation. I rapped at the kitchen door and, amidst the cacophonous barking of the Talversons' cavorting, tail-wagging dogs, let myself in. Gloria, in her usual place at the stove, looked over her shoulder and gestured with her chin. "Hi. There is an envelope for you on the table."

"Where's Tally?"

She shrugged ignorance but I could tell by the mischievous glint in her eyes that something was going on. I picked up the small white envelope, ripped it open and read GO TO THE BARN. Frowning, I glanced up at Gloria. "What's going on?"

"I don't know." The corners of her lips twitched slightly and she quickly returned her attention to the saucepan on the stove.

Bewildered, I crossed to the barn and pushed the side door open to find Jake lounging against a bale of hay. "Afternoon, Miz O'Dell," he said, touching the brim of his ragged Stetson, his eyes twinkling in much the same way Gloria's had. Now I was really suspicious.

"Hey, Jake. Is Tally around?"

"Sort of." He reached into his vest pocket and pulled out an envelope. "He asked me to give this to ya."

I'm sure a look of confusion dominated my face as he laid it in my outstretched palm. He ambled away, stopped when he reached the door to the corral and swung around to face me. "I'll meet you out here in a minute."

"Okay." I tore open the envelope and stared at the cryptic message. GRAB YOUR HAT AND BOOTS AND MEET ME ON SIDEWINDER HILL. LOVE, TALLY. I blinked in confusion. Sidewinder Hill, about a mile northeast of the ranch house, was our favorite place to picnic. The gentle cactus-covered knoll with its pristine outcroppings of white quartz afforded a stunning view of the hills and valleys that comprised the Starfire Ranch.

Burning with curiosity, I strode across the straw-littered floor, and when I stepped outside I gasped. My new mare, Starlight Sky, was all saddled up and ready to go. She looked around, saw me and whinnied a greeting as she tossed her head. Standing next to her was Jake, holding a pair of my boots in one hand and a wide-brimmed hat in the other.

"You gonna tell me what's going on?" I demanded.

"Can't."

"Okaaay." I peered at the long shadows creeping across the desert floor and calculated that if I left soon, I'd get there right about sunset. Having no clue as to what was going on, I tucked my jeans into the boots, planted the hat on my head and let Jake give me a leg up.

"Walk 'er around the corral a couple of times, so you can get a feel for handling her before you go," he instructed, opening the gate. I walked, trotted and finally urged her into a gentle lope, thrilled by the Appaloosa's smooth gait and instant response to my every command.

"Tally's waitin' on ya," Jake commented, his leathery face scrunched in a playful grin. "You'd best git a goin'."

"Guess you're not going to give me even a hint as to what you two are up to this time, huh?"

His grin widened. "Nope."

I took off across the open desert towards the rise, delighting in the feel of the cold fresh wind blowing in my face as Mother Nature busily painted the western sky a lustrous sheen of violet, rose and magenta streaked with an array of dazzling pink-rimmed clouds. I can't remember ever having such an exhilarating ride. Sure of foot, Starlight Sky deftly maneuvered the rocky terrain, sidestepped the saffron fields of cholla and delivered me to my destination in ten minutes flat. I spotted Tally about halfway up the hill perched on a jagged outcropping, his horse Geronimo grazing nearby. Dressed in jeans and a Levi's jacket, hat tipped back, his square-jawed face turned towards the setting sun, he looked as much a part of the rough landscape as the statuesque saguaros and endless blue sky—the epitome of the Arizona cowboy.

He turned when he heard Starlight Sky whinny and waved me up the hill. As I rode up and dismounted, a smile brushed the corners of his mouth. "How do you like her?"

"I love her. Thank you again, she's fabulous." I crossed to where Geronimo was happily grazing on lush green winter grass, tethered Starlight Sky next to him, and then walked back towards Tally, lamenting the fact that I would not have his gift ready by the engagement party. I'd already decided to find another sculptor to complete the project and the cell phone I'd ordered for him online was on the way.

"It's good to see you."

The intimate gleam in his eyes made me feel flushed. I smiled at him tenderly. "I've missed you."

"I've missed you too," he said huskily, reaching out to pull me onto his lap. Then in a move that melted my heart, he held my face in his hands and looked deeply into my eyes for a few seconds before bringing my lips down to his. His forceful kiss reaffirmed the irrefutable love I felt for this kind, responsible, rock-solid man who would soon be my husband.

Breathless, I pulled back and studied his face. "Are you going to be all right?" I had a pretty good idea how much he'd been suffering these past few days, trying to reconcile his feelings of resentment for Ruth and struggling to regain his lost identity, his shattered sense of self.

"It's been a tough couple of days trying to digest far more information than I ever needed to know."

I ran my fingers through his wavy blue-black hair. "I know, and I'm sorry I couldn't tell you sooner, but it was something that had to come from your mother. Have you talked to her yet?"

"Some."

"Well, I hope for your sake and hers that you'll be able to find it in your heart to one day forgive her." I could only imagine what a bitter pill this whole sordid affair must be to a man as highly ethical as Tally.

"I've had to do quite a bit of soul searching, but I'm working on it."

I fished the envelopes from my pocket. "What's with the mysterious notes?"

He thumbed behind him to a small ice chest. "I thought you'd enjoy having a romantic twilight dinner up here with me." I could tell by the gleam of subterfuge behind his brown eyes that there was more to it than that.

"I would. So, what's the important news you have for me? I've got some for you too." After I shared my recent discovery with him, he shook his head in amazement and dug two sheets of paper from his breast pocket.

"Riley's law firm sent me a couple of interesting letters today, and also this." He reached into his pocket again, pulled out a key and laid it in my hand.

"What's this?"

"A key to a safe deposit box."

I stared at it in silence for a couple of seconds and then leaped to my feet. "The gold! He left you the gold coins!"

"Yep, and besides all the legal jargon placing me in charge of their distribution, there's also a personal note to me. Want to read it?"

"You bet."

He extended the paper and as I began to read, chills ran up and down my arms.

Dear Tally, it is with extreme pride that I acknowledge you as my son, my flesh and blood. I have only recently known this and wish your mother had told me a long time ago. But, even if she had, out of great respect, I would have never said anything while Joe was alive. He was a good father to both you and Ronda. Don't ever forget that and don't allow this revelation to tarnish his memory. Because I have known you all your life, I know you are a man of strong character and feel confident that I can trust you to carry out my last wishes should anything happen to me. I ask your forgiveness for my misconduct and pray that you will be able to forgive your mother too. We were young and foolish and never meant to hurt anyone. I'm sorry. Your father, Riley C. Gibbons. I met Tally's thoughtful gaze. "What were his final wishes?"

"To make sure that my new brother or sister is taken care of."

I inhaled sharply. "So, you know about Marissa."

Tally nodded slowly. "It's in the letter from his attorney."

The phrase Riley had written, LOVE BUILDS BRIDGES WHERE THERE ARE NONE, flashed through my mind. More than ever, I wish I'd had the chance to know him. But then as I stared at Tally, I realized that I did. Instead of Joe Talverson's legendary temper, Tally had inherited some of Riley's altruistic qualities. As if to illustrate that, Tally rose, reached around behind the rock ledge, pulled out a spade with a giant pink bow attached to the handle and handed it to me. He gestured towards the horizon, now a flaming tapestry of cherry, orange and purple intermingled with smoky wisps of clouds. "You'd best get to digging. We're losing the light."

Dumbfounded, I stared at him. "What's going on?"

He beamed me his familiar crooked grin. "Dig."

"Where?"

"Right over there," he said, pointing to several stones laid to look like a big X.

Totally perplexed, I pushed the stones aside and began to dig in the soft dirt. Barely a minute passed before the point of the spade clanged into something hard. I knelt and uncovered a long metal tube. I fixed him with a bemused look. "What is this? Buried treasure?"

Still smiling, he hitched his shoulders, feigning innocence as I brushed the dirt off and pulled one of the end caps off. A sheaf of papers rolled into a cylinder dropped out. A light breeze rushed up from the valley below and fluffed my hair as I unrolled the papers with shaking fingers. Stunned, I looked down at a set of blueprints and then back at him. "What's this?"

"Blueprints for our new house. I thought this would make a pretty nice spot for just the two of us. What do you think?" The compassionate light in his steady gaze filled my heart with a fierce joy. Tears stinging my eyes, I jumped up and threw my arms around his neck.

"I think that you're the most wonderful, generous man I've ever known and it will be an honor to be Mrs. Bradley James Talverson."

He arched a brow in surprise. "You sure? I thought you wanted to keep O'Dell?"

"Well, maybe just for my byline, but for the rest of the time, for me and for our children, it's going to be plain old Talverson, if you don't mind."

His lips grazed mine as he whispered, "Not one little bit."